PRAISE FOR
SELENE OF ALEXANDRIA

"Readers will be captivated. Fans of Gillian Bradshaw's classic *The Beacon at Alexandria* may especially enjoy *Selene* and find a promising new historical novelist who shares the same gift for wonderfully researched, vividly evoked, good old-fashioned storytelling."

—Historical Novel Society

"*Selene of Alexandria* is pure fiction magic...I couldn't put this book down... [It] made me laugh and cry, hope and despair."

—Story Circle Book Reviews

"This book is outstanding, not just for a first novel, but for any novel. Once you've read it, I'm sure you'll join me in waiting impatiently to read Justice's next project!"   *—Lacuna: Journal of Historical Fiction*

PRAISE FOR
SWORD OF THE GLADIATRIX

"By the exciting close of the novel, readers will care very much about both these women – fans of Roman historical fiction should not miss this title."
—Historical Novel Society

"An amazing and totally original and unique novel. Such a strong range of female characters are depicted, courageous, brave, cunning, deadly, deceitful; a complete gambit of credible and totally believable women."
—Inked Rainbow Reads

"I was gripped by Faith's great writing style–and hardly put it down until I reached the end. The two heroines are memorable and original. Highly recommended."   *—Writing Desk*

BOOKS BY FAITH L. JUSTICE

Novels

Selene of Alexandria
Sword of the Gladiatrix (Gladiatrix #1)
Twilight Empress (Theodosian Women #1)
Dawn Empress (Theodosian Women #2)

Short Story Collections

The Reluctant Groom and Other Historical Stories
Time Again and Other Fantastic Stories
Slow Death and Other Dark Tales

Children's Fiction

Tokoyo, the Samurai's Daughter (Adventurous Girls #1)

Non-fiction

Hypatia, Her Life and Times

TWILIGHT EMPRESS

FAITH L. JUSTICE

RAGGEDY MOON BOOKS

Twilight Empress

2017
Raggedy Moon Books
raggedymoonbooks.com

Cover design by Jennifer Quinlan
historicaleditorial.com

Paperback ISBN: 978-0692460511
Hardback ISBN: 978-0917053221
Epub ISBN: 978-1370214716
Library of Congress Control Number: 2016931966

This is a work of fiction. Names, characters, places, and incidents are either the product of the author's imagination or are used fictitiously.

To Gordon Rothman,
without whom I couldn't write about love.

"The decline of Rome was the natural and inevitable effect of immoderate greatness."

Edward Gibbon
The Decline and Fall of the Roman Empire

CONTENTS

Theodosian Genealogy

Emperors shown in SMALL CAPS.

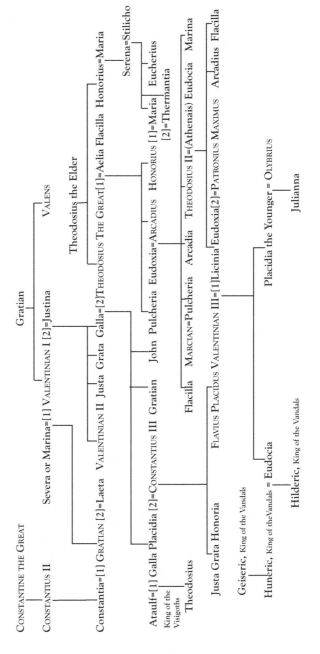

NOTE ON IMPERIAL TITLES AND PLACE NAMES

IMPERIAL ROMAN TITLES EVOLVED OVER TIME. The title AUGUSTUS (Latin for "majestic," "the increaser," or "venerable") is the equivalent of the modern "Emperor," and was conferred on the first emperor, Octavian (great-nephew and adopted son of Julius Caesar), by the senate in 27 BC. Every emperor after held the title of Augustus, which always followed the family name. The first emperor conferred the title AUGUSTA on his wife, Livia, in his will. Other imperial wives (but not all) earned this supreme title. By the fifth century, sisters and daughters also could be elevated to this status, but only by a sitting Augustus. I use Emperor/Empress and Augustus/Augusta interchangeably throughout the text.

Octavian took his adoptive father's name, Gaius Julius Caesar, but later dropped the Gaius Julius. CAESAR became the imperial family name and was passed on by adoption. When the Julio-Claudian line died out, subsequent emperors took the name as a sign of status on their accession, adoption, or nomination as heir apparent. By the fifth century, it was the title given to any official heir to the Augustus (it's also the root of the modern titles Kaiser and Czar).

Children of imperial families were usually given the title NOBILISSIMUS/NOBILISSIMA ("Most Noble" boy/girl). This is the closest equivalent to the modern Prince/Princess, though not an exact match. The title was usually conferred some years after birth, in anticipation that the child would take on higher office (Caesar or Augustus for a boy, Augusta for a girl). I generally use the modern title Princess instead of Nobilissima throughout the text.

There is no direct Roman equivalent for the title Regent—someone who legally rules during the absence, incapacity, or minority of a country's monarch. In Imperial Rome, only males could wield magisterial power. An underage Augustus was still ruler in his own name. He must sign all laws and declarations for them to be legal. In reality, adults stepped into the role and administered the empire for minors. Placidia Augusta filled that role for her son Valentinian Augustus III (*Twilight Empress*). Anthemius did that for Theodosius II in *Dawn Empress*. The legal Roman term for that person is *tutela* meaning "guardian" or "tutor" for an adult (usually a man) who handled the affairs of someone (usually women and children) who would ordinarily be under the legal protection and control of the *pater familias* (male head of the family), but who were legally emancipated. I chose to use the more familiar term Regent throughout this book.

With one exception (Constantinople for modern Istanbul), I chose to use the modern names of cities and the anglicized rather than Latin names of provinces.

CHARACTERS

In order of appearance,
alternate spellings in parentheses, fictional in *italics*.

Galla Placidia Augusta—half-sister to Honorius Augustus and aunt to
Theodosius Augustus
Paulus—maimed Vandal soldier who served in Placidia's household
Ataulf (Athaulf, Adolphus)—Brother-in-law and successor to King
Alaric of the Goths
Alaric—King of the Goths
Gaatha—Alaric's wife and Ataulf's sister
Valia (Vallia, Wallia)—Gothic noble
Machaon—Greek physician
Flavius Constantius—General, advisor to Emperor Honorius
Flavius Honorius Augustus—Western Roman Emperor and Plaicidia's
half-brother
Lucilla—Placidia's personal servant
Priscus Attalus—Prefect of Rome, Gothic choice for emperor
Bishop Sigesar—personal Arian bishop to Alaric and Ataulf
Sergeric (Singeric, Sigeric)—Goth chieftain, Sarus' brother
Vada—Ataulf's oldest daughter
Lilla—Ataulf's middle daughter
Maltha—Ataulf's youngest daughter
Ediulf—Ataulf's fourth child and son
Dardanus—Praetorian Prefect of Gaul
Sarus—former Gothic General who defected to the Romans
Sigisvult—Gothic warrior in Placidia's service, Roman General
Thecla—midwife and Machaon's sister
Nikarete—midwife and Thecla's daughter

Justa Grata Honoria Augusta—daughter to Placidia and Constantius

Flavius Placidus Valentinian III Augustus—son to Placidia and Constantius

Castinus—Roman General, advisor to Honorius

Felix—Roman General in the West, Patrician

Padusa (Spadusa)—Felix's wife

Theodoric I (Theoderic)—King of the Goths

Flavius Theodosius Augustus II—Emperor in the East, nephew to Placidia

Aelia Pulcheria Augusta—Theodosius' older sister and chief advisor, niece to Placidia

Aelia Eudocia Augusta called **Athenais**—Theodosius' wife

Licinia Eudoxia Augusta—Theodosius' and Athenais' daughter

Leontius—curator, Placidia's business and legal advisor

Angelus—shepherd and "Angel of the Marshes"

John (Johannes)—primicerius notariorum and usurper

Flavius Aetius—Roman General in the West, Patrician

Ardaburius—General (of infantry) in the East, Alan by birth

Aspar—General (of cavalry) in the East, Ardaburius' son

Helion—Master of Offices in the East

Boniface—Roman General, Count of Africa

Pelagia—Boniface's wife, an Arian Gothic noble woman

Maximinus—Arian Bishop to Sigisvult's army

Ruga (Regila)—King of the Huns

Bleda—Ruga's nephew and co-heir with Attila

Attila—succeeded Ruga as King of the Huns

Gaiseric (Genseric, Gizericus)—King of the Vandals

Huneric—Gaiseric's son

Amaltha—Huneric's Gothic wife and daughter of King Theodoric

Eugenius—Honoria's chamberlain

Bassus Herculanus—Roman Senator and Honoria's fiancé

TWILIGHT EMPRESS

PART I

PRINCESS

AUGUST 410 - SEPTEMBER 413

CHAPTER 1

Rome, August 410

*G*OD'S BLOOD, I'M TIRED.

Placidia put the parchment down, closed her eyes, and rubbed her temples in a futile attempt to ease her headache. She had had little sleep the night before, and less to eat, as she worked with the city elders to avert this most recent crisis. With the Visigoths at the gates of Rome for the third time in three years, the city was exhausted—little food, few defenders, and no hope of rescue from the Imperial Court, which was safe behind the protecting marshes of Ravenna. At twenty-two, she should have been safely married, raising children; not picking up the pieces of an empire dropped from the careless hands of her half-brother, the Emperor Honorius.

"Treason and betrayal, Mistress!"

The urgency in Paulus' gruff voice drove all tiredness from her body. Nothing chilled her blood as much as the cry of 'treason.' The word summoned unwanted images of her adopted sister Serena, struggling against the executioner's garrote, and Serena's husband Stilicho's head on a pike. The unwarranted death of the two people who raised her had precipitated her flight from the Ravenna court and her estrangement from her brother.

Placidia took a deep breath and steadied her hands.

"What treason?" She managed a calm voice despite her racing heart.

"Someone opened the Salarian Gate. The barbarians are in the streets. We must flee to safety."

1

Placidia chewed her lower lip, rapidly forming and discarding options to save her household. There were rules to sacking a city, and Placidia hoped King Alaric would abide by them. One of those rules provided sanctuary in Christian churches. The Gothic King was purportedly a devout Christian, if of the Arian heresy.

"What are your orders, Mistress?" The light of battle gleamed in Paulus' eyes. A Vandal soldier wounded in Stilicho's service, he had been with her since she was a child.

"Deploy my personal guards at the bottom of the hill. Take the rest of the servants to the Basilica of St. Peter immediately and claim sanctuary. I'll come with the guards as soon as I destroy these documents."

Placidia grabbed the nearest of several piles of parchment—letters of support; reports on food and supplies throughout the Empire—and laid them in an unlit bronze brazier. She would give the enemy no helpful information. Her hands trembled as she poured oil on the papers and lit them from her lamp. Smoke curled from the parchment, irritating her eyes.

"I'll send the servants away, Princess, but do not ask me to leave you alone. I've seen my share of sacked cities."

"I want you to go with the servants, Paulus."

His face set in a familiar stubborn cast.

"I don't have time to argue. What can a crippled old man do here?"

The stubborn look gave way to one of hurt pride.

Placidia softened her tone. "I have lost all whom I love in the past two years. The man and woman who were more to me than father and mother, my cousins, my…betrothed." Her voice caught. "I have no wish to lose the one person left from my past. I care for you, my friend, and want to see you safe."

"Do you think I care less for you?" Paulus' eyes glittered with unshed tears. "You are the last of my lord's household. I am bound to you by oath and blood."

Screams echoed down the colonnade, accompanied by splintering wood and crashing crockery. Placidia froze like a rabbit before a snake. *My people are lost. The raiders must have ridden hard and fast to get to the palace so soon.*

Paulus grabbed the small knife Placidia used to break the wax seals on her letters, and rushed toward the door. "Come, Princess, we will go to the oratory. Perhaps they will honor sanctuary there."

Placidia shook her head. "If King Alaric wants me dead, the chapel won't shelter me. If he wants me alive, perhaps I can extend that privilege to my household by being bold rather than timid."

A scream, choked off in the middle, sent Paulus through the door at a limping run. Placidia piled the rest of the papers onto the blaze and dashed out after him.

She faltered at the scene. Normally, the central garden with its splashing *nymphaeum* was a soothing refuge from the heat of the August sun. Now a cadre of at least fifty Gothic warriors systematically herded the palace servants into the leafy refuge, releasing the scent of lavender and rosemary as their leather-clad feet trampled herbs and flowers. They used the flats of their swords, sometimes striking a lagging slave, to push them into a tight knot of gibbering humanity.

Unlike the wildly varying dress and armor of most barbarian warriors, these wore more or less matching knee-length green tunics trimmed with scarlet at the neck and hem. Most also sported mail shirts and Roman-style helmets—rare, these days, even among Roman troops.

At least King Alaric sent an elite corps to take me.

One warrior spied her under the colonnade and rushed forward, grinning.

Paulus jumped in front of the man, threatening him with the letter knife. "Don't touch her! She's the…"

The barbarian brushed the knife aside with a sweep of his arm and struck Paulus with the silvered hilt of his sword.

The old man sank to the ground, senseless or dead, a large gash bleeding profusely on his forehead.

Placidia stalked into the garden, back rigid, face pale.

"Stop at once!" Her voice pierced the scene, turning it momentarily into a tableau.

The advancing warrior bared his teeth and said, in execrable Latin, "Roman woman not a mouse—more my liking."

"I am Princess Galla Placidia, sister of Emperor Honorius, daughter of Emperor Theodosius the Great, Granddaughter of Emperor Valentinian. On pain of death, I demand you leave us in peace."

The barbarian hesitated, confusion clouding his eyes.

Placidia suppressed an inappropriate smile. Her impressive list of relationships didn't square with her ink-stained fingers, plain blue linen gown, and unadorned curly brown hair.

"Leave her, Berig." A commanding voice rose from among the warriors.

A red-haired barbarian muscled his way through the pack. She had not seen him because he stood half a head shorter than most of his companions. He looked her over speculatively.

"You have the bearing of a royal, if not the accouterments." He motioned to the slaves nearest them. "Is this your mistress?"

To their credit, they all looked to Placidia before answering. She nodded permission.

Watching the by-play, the warrior said, "I commend you on your servants, Princess. They are most loyal." He smiled, showing white, even teeth in a tanned face framed by a red beard. Lines gathered at the corners of his green eyes. "I am Ataulf, General and Master of King Alaric's cavalry."

The Gothic King honors me by sending his heir and second-in-command. "General." Placidia drew her slender form into a commanding pose. "Have these…men…vacate my residence at once."

"We will leave shortly, Princess. King Alaric sent me to escort you to our camp. You are to be the guest of the King and the Gothic people."

"Do not pretty the package, sir. I am a hostage. For what other reason would you force me from my home?" She waved her right arm in a sweeping arc. "You strip Rome and seek to squeeze additional treasure from my brother."

"King Alaric recognizes your…value."

His hesitation hinted at deeper motives for her detainment. Perhaps Alaric wished more than gold from her estranged brother. *And little will he get—gold or otherwise—from that lack-wit.*

Ataulf donned his helmet. "Come, Princess." He took her arm.

Placidia sniffed. He reeked of horses, smoke, and sweat. In many ways comforting scents, evoking her martial father and, later, her guardian Stilicho. But she shook off his hand. "Not until we have medical care for Paulus." She indicated her fallen chamberlain.

Berig brandished his sword. "Bugger that. Let me finish him."

"No!" Placidia strode forward, blocking Berig with her body. "He is mine! You will not harm him."

Berig looked at Ataulf, who shook his head. The twice-disappointed warrior shrugged and backed down.

Ataulf touched her shoulder.

She flinched.

"Your man will be tended at our camp."

"And the rest of my people?" She indicated the crowd of servants, some weeping, some stiff with anger or fear, others standing in slack-jawed bewilderment. "I cannot travel without servants."

The skin tightened around Ataulf's mouth. His eyes narrowed. "The contents of this city are ours. Any slave from our tribes will be freed. We claim the rest as booty."

"But…"

Ataulf raised a hand. "You may take three personal maids and a cook."

"And Paulus. He is a free man and has pledged his service to me."

"I doubt he would bring much on the slave market." The hint of a smile played about his lips. "You may keep him."

Choosing her attendants was not the first hard decision Placidia had to make, and it wouldn't be her last, but that knowledge brought little comfort. She chose three of the youngest girls, hoping to shelter them from the horrors she imagined the rest would face, and a matronly cook to look after them.

Ataulf chose ten of his men to provide escort, and dismissed the rest to loot the palace. "Berig, you carry the old one."

Berig slung Paulus over his shoulder like a sack of cabbages.

Placidia's heart lightened when she heard Paulus moan. She turned to her four servants. "Stay close to our escort. Don't try to escape. We have the word of General Ataulf we will not be harmed, but he cannot speak for the rest of the army if you are captured by someone else."

The cook nodded and gathered the girls together in a tight knot. "You heard the Mistress, now. Stay close and you'll be safe. Don't go running off like stupid donkeys."

They walked down the north face of the Palatine Hill, their escort grumbling about time wasted when they could be pillaging.

"You'll share with the others," Ataulf assured them.

At the bottom of the hill, several more warriors guarded a picket line of horses. Shields, spears, and a few bows hung from the four high horns at the corners of the saddles.

Placidia drew a sharp breath. *Does he plan to parade me through Rome before his horse, like a conquering general in a triumph?*

At the picket line, Ataulf swung up onto a skittish bay. One of the warriors brought a mounting block for Placidia.

Ataulf held out his hand. "I'm afraid we have no litter for you, Princess. You will have to ride with me."

Knowing the royal litter or chariot would be a rallying point for resistance—if any—Placidia suspected Ataulf of duplicity.

"Can I not have a mount of my own? I am a capable rider." The idea of dashing through the streets of Rome in the arms of the barbarian chief was almost as repugnant as the thought of pacing before his horse as a prisoner.

"No. Especially if you are a capable rider." He held out his hand again. "Come."

She swung up, settling with a knee around one of the horns for balance. The general's mail pressed her back; his breath stirred her hair. She leaned slightly forward and grasped the horse's mane.

"Perhaps I should ride pillion." She turned to peer at Ataulf from the corner of her eye.

"And have you slide off and disappear down an alley? No. You stay where I can see you."

The bay stepped nervously to the side. Placidia felt the muscles in his arms tighten as Ataulf pulled sharply on the reins. His mount snorted to a stop, trembling. *I know how you feel.* She patted the animal's sweating neck. *I'm about to jump out of my own skin.*

"You!" Ataulf pointed to a warrior, not in his troop, leading a donkey and cart half filled with bolts of cloth. "I need that cart." The man looked startled but, recognizing Ataulf, meekly turned over the loot.

Berig tied Paulus' limp body over the donkey's back and installed the substantial form of Cook among the treasure. Her other servants rode pillion with three warriors.

The cavalcade started north on the Via Imperialia, through the monumental heart of Rome. Normally, Placidia never tired of gazing at the majestic buildings and memorials. Now she held back tears as the empty spaces echoed the clopping horses' hooves. No colorful crowds cheered their passing. No self-important clerks strolled under the stoa. No vendors hawked their wares in voices gone harsh with use. Placidia had never seen such desolation. It matched the growing emptiness in her soul.

They hurried through the various fora, past Titus' arch celebrating his triumph over the Jews, Caesar's temple to Venus and Rome, Trajan's markets—shuttered and silent. As they passed Marcus Aurelius' triumphal column, showing his victories over the barbarian tribes of the north, the warriors laughed and spat.

They left the silence of the fora behind and slipped into the chaos of a dying city. Now the tears came, blurring her vision, stuffing her nose. But they could not mask the smell of roasted human flesh, or wash away the sound of howling men freed from any civilizing impulse. Rats and flies infested the bodies—animal and human—strewn about the streets. Placidia swallowed convulsively to keep down her bile.

Barbarians ran past, heaped with portable booty—jewelry, costly tunics, decorative armor. Many pushed or pulled two-wheeled carts piled high with larger pieces—statues, furniture, carpets, gold and silver feasting services. What they couldn't carry or didn't value, the invaders despoiled. Bonfires frequented the open spaces. The barbarians laughed as they tossed on books, paintings, clothes, and broken furniture. Smoke gathered over the city; blood streamed in the gutters.

Honorius, my brother, you should see what you have wrought. This didn't have to happen.

Her father and Stilicho had told Placidia of the horrors of the battlefield, but that did not prepare her for the sight of the torn bodies of shopkeepers, seamstresses, children—none who should know war—littering the streets like so much refuse. Only the will not to disgrace herself kept Placidia upright. She wanted to bury her face in the horse's mane—not look, not smell, not hear, not feel—but she couldn't turn her face away. Placidia needed to brand these images in her mind and on her soul. She needed to remember.

"I would not have you see this, Princess, but my people hate the Romans for slaughtering their comrades, wives, and children—some in the churches where they fled for sanctuary."

"Don't make excuses. What my brother ordered was despicable, but is this any better?" She pointed to the bloody body of a woman clutching a dead infant. "You rightly chide us, but what of your Christianity?"

"It is our nature to return insult for insult, blood for blood. You cannot turn a wolf into a lap dog by dipping it in a basin and mumbling some words over it."

Raucous laughter burst from a small square to their left. A group of soldiers called advice and crude comments to a comrade raping a girl, urging him to hurry so they could have their turn. The girl lay naked and whimpering, bruises and dried blood on the battered left side of her face forming a grotesque mirror to the untouched right side. Blood from shallow cuts on her hands and breasts smudged her body.

The need to do something spurred Placidia. She gripped the general's arm. "Stop them! She's just a child."

"And the one in the next street, or the next?"

"I ask only for her life, if it's in your power to grant it."

"It is." He watched the soldiers for a moment, frowning. "Berig, guard the Princess."

Ataulf slid her to the ground. With a bellow, he rode through the knot of men, knocking them aside with his spear until he came on the one rutting with pleasure—a good-looking youth, only a few years older than the girl he raped. Ataulf leaped from his horse and yanked the boy off his whimpering victim. "King Alaric forbade rape. Don't you obey orders, boy?"

The lad's eyes widened in recognition. "B-b-but she's just a prostitute, Sir!"

Ataulf pointed at the battered girl, now curled up, knees and head pressed close to her chest, trembling. "That's no excuse."

The young soldier grew sullen. "'Tis our right. We took this city."

Ataulf struck the boy with his fist, splitting his lip and bloodying his nose. "No army can function without discipline. Your king gave you a direct order." He glared at every face in the square. "All of you understand? No rape. No burning churches. Sanctuary will be honored. Is that clear?" he roared.

"Yes, Lord," several, but not all, called out.

"You!" He pointed to one of the attackers draped in an elaborate silk cape. "Cover her. Filimer," he addressed one of his own guards. "Pick up the girl. She's coming with us."

Filimer, a broad-shouldered barbarian, wrapped the girl in the silk cloak. She cried out when he picked her up, out of pain or fear.

Placidia accompanied the girl to the cart. "You'll be safe with us." The girl turned vacant eyes on her and whimpered. "Cook, look after her. When we reach camp, make sure she gets help."

The matronly woman clucked at the girl, making nonsense sounds between assurances of safety. The servant girls clung to their protectors, fearful eyes darting to the despoiling soldiers.

Ataulf mounted his horse, and reached for Placidia.

The darkness creeping into her soul felt some small measure lighter. Taking his callused palm, she looked up and said, "Thank you, General."

"I hold no illusions, and neither should you, Princess. As soon as we are out of sight, they will find another. This scene is played out all over the city, with thousands of women."

Placidia glanced back at the battered girl. "At least we saved one child from an ugly death."

His shoulders slumped slightly and concern shadowed his eyes—concern for her, or for the girl?

"Will she thank you for a life filled with the memory of this day?"

Placidia shook her head. "I don't know."

CHAPTER 2

PLACIDIA WAS EXHAUSTED. They had left the ineffectual walls of Rome over an hour ago, and the horror she felt had turned to numbness. Just as she feared she might fall off Ataulf's horse, he announced they were near the camp. She looked up to see a vast wooden-walled city. Herds of cattle and horses grazed in fenced meadows. Women and children gathered a late summer harvest of cabbage, beans, olives, apples, and grapes.

As they drew closer, Placidia realized the walls were actually a circle of wagons, with portable wooden fences filling the gaps under and between. Armed Goths guarded gates spaced at regular intervals. Inside, a second circle of wagons sported leather tents attached to the sides for shelter. Communal fire pits and portable ovens for baking bread dotted the interior. Her agents had told her Alaric mustered over thirty thousand men under arms. With what was left of their families after the massacre, the camp probably held over a hundred thousand souls.

Ataulf escorted her to the hub of the camp, a sumptuous country villa—its owners fled or perished. They entered the atrium, its walls decorated with realistic paintings of peacocks, grapes and pears; then continued through to the roofed colonnade that surrounded the inner garden and provided access to all its rooms. Men with a military bearing ducked in and out of a door on the left.

The General motioned his men to remain outside, and went to the door. He talked briefly with a guard, then returned to escort Placidia into the military headquarters of the Gothic King.

"The Princess Galla Placidia, Sister to the Emperor Honorius," the guard announced as she entered.

The room—formerly the dining and entertaining area known as the *triclinium*—exuded controlled chaos. Several leather-bound trunks stood against a wall decorated in rural hunting scenes. Cloaks, mail shirts, and helmets littered the trunks and floor. Maps and lists covered a massive table inlaid with ivory, its legs carved into lion's paws. Seven men stood around the table. They looked up as one when Placidia entered.

She suddenly remembered her less-than-noble appearance—dusty clothes, disheveled hair—her sole adornment her signet ring. She twisted it around her index finger. As the cold eyes raked her from head to foot, she stilled her hands and raised her chin, returning the men's looks glare for glare.

A man with golden hair and darker close-cropped beard and mustache approached. He bowed briefly. The beard failed to hide the scar that ran from a notch in the top of his left ear across his cheek to his mouth, drawing the corner up into a slight half smile. He wore a well-made scarlet tunic, bordered with yellow. Dark blue and yellow wrappings crisscrossed over tight-fitting trousers to make a colorful fishbone pattern up to his knees.

"Welcome, Princess Placidia." He spoke in heavily accented Latin. "I am Alaric, King of the Gothic People. I hope you find your stay comfortable. I've arranged for you to guest with my wife and her ladies."

"Guests have the choice of staying or leaving."

Color rose in his cheeks and sweat donned his brow, but Alaric's blue eyes sparkled. "For now, Princess, you are under our protection. Of course, we wish to return you to your brother as soon as possible."

"There is no need to involve the Emperor. I have property and income of my own. My father was quite generous. Perhaps we can reach some agreement?"

"Do you think this is about ransom?" His voice was steely. "This is about honor and recognition. We are fellow citizens of your great empire. I fought for your father at Frigidus and lost two out of every three of my men. We shed our blood time and again to keep this empire safe."

"And you were well rewarded." Placidia gazed steadily back. "Yet instead of protecting what my father gave you in Thrace, you turned your armies against the cities. You devastated that land until General Stilicho stopped you, and stopped you again when you invaded Italy."

"When Stilicho was alive, we were able to negotiate, but the anti-barbarian faction is now too strong in the Roman court. Your brother is a weak-minded fool, under the influence of whoever has his ear." The Gothic King spread his arms wide. "If we had had more time, Stilicho's plans might have forestalled all this."

Placidia felt the blood drain from her face. "What plans?"

"Stilicho knew he could never become Emperor, but he was married to royalty, your cousin and adopted sister. By marrying his daughter to Honorius and his son to you, Stilicho ensured his grandchild would rule. And he would rule the grandchild. Who could guarantee your brother's health after an heir was born?"

"No," she whispered. "Stilicho would never have betrayed my brother. He swore service to my father, and served the Empire faithfully for over twenty years."

"Loyal to your father and the Empire, yes. But Honorius?" Alaric gave an expressive shrug. "You know your brother. Is he fit to rule?"

"You slander a good man!"

"Your brother?"

"Stilicho." Placidia's stomach clenched. "You have no proof. After he had Uncle executed, Honorius interrogated—tortured—all those associated with him. They found nothing. Stilicho was innocent of treason."

"Perhaps. But Stilicho was a shrewd man. His actions spoke louder than words, and his enemies listened. Now the Emperor's councilors are in a predicament. Honorius has no wife and no heir. That leaves the honor of providing for the future to you."

"So you plan to force me into a marriage...of your choosing?" Placidia struggled to control the quaver in her voice. She had fled Ravenna and the Imperial court partly to remove herself as a tempting marriage target for ambitious nobles.

The unaffected side of the King's mouth pulled into a suggestive grin. "We will talk later." He flicked a hand at Ataulf. "Take her to my wife and report back."

Placidia, dazed and furious, followed Ataulf from the *triclinium*-turned-headquarters to a part of the central garden shaded by trees. Leafy branches gave relief from the afternoon sun. A fountain provided a tinkling accompaniment to the low chatter of women. Ataulf led her to a woman with the same red hair and piercing green eyes as his own, working at an upright loom. Several other women sat nearby, spinning wool on drop spindles or embroidering. All talk stopped at the approach of Placidia and her escort.

"Princess Galla Placidia, may I present Alaric's wife and my sister, Queen Gaatha?"

Gaatha held out her hand to Placidia. "Come. Sit. My Latin not good." She turned to Ataulf and said, in Gothic, "Brother, tell her we mean her no harm; that we hope her stay will be pleasant and short."

"I suspect Princess Placidia understands you perfectly. She was raised in a household speaking many languages."

"Is this true?" Gaatha's face brightened as she turned to Placidia. "It would be much easier if you chose to speak Gothic, even if it is a barbarian tongue. You have a reputation for being a practical, as well as learned, lady. Did you learn in Stilicho's house?"

"Yes. I speak two Germanic languages as well as Latin and Greek."

A small army of children ran screaming through the garden, chasing a dog. Seeing the general, several broke off and swarmed to him, crying, "Father, what did you bring me from Rome?"

Ataulf laughed and hefted the youngest, a golden-haired toddler, into his arms for a kiss on the cheek. "Later, children." He put the boy down and swatted him on the rear. "Off you go." They screeched in disappointment, until a stern word from Gaatha sent them scurrying.

"Forgive them, Princess." Ataulf smiled after them. "Their mother died but a year ago, and I have had the raising of them. I'm afraid I let them have their way too often."

The thought of sitting here, making small talk about children while Rome burned, made Placidia's head pound. She swayed, hand to brow. Her vision grayed. Voices became unintelligible…

"Try this." A firm hand supported her back. Another held a cup to her lips.

She sipped and choked on the strong, unwatered wine. Her eyes focused on Ataulf's concerned face as he held the cup.

"Th-Thank you. I feel better now. It's just the shock…" She felt heat rise to her cheeks and silently cursed the pale skin that betrayed her emotions.

Ataulf turned to his sister. "Perhaps the princess should lie down. She's had a difficult day and the weather is oppressive."

Gaatha nodded toward a dark room. Ataulf gathered Placidia into his arms. "Paulus and the girl…" she protested.

"I will see they are cared for."

She relaxed when she saw Gaatha rise to follow. It was cooler in the dimness, but stuffy. Ataulf deposited her on a low couch covered with yellow silks and pillows.

Drained by the heat and the day's tensions, Placidia yawned; then clapped a hand over her mouth. The wine must have gone straight to her head.

"I'll leave you in Gaatha's care." Ataulf smiled, rose, and kissed his sister on the forehead. He said something else in a low voice that Placidia couldn't catch.

She fell into a fitful sleep, filled with dreams of fire and blood.

ATAULF STRODE BACK TO THE TRICLINIUM. Acquiring the princess had been easier than he thought. Her personal guard had scattered at the first sight of his men. He snorted. Such dogs deserved to be spitted. No one pledged to his service would show such cowardice.

Placidia surprised him. He had met her half-brother, the Emperor Honorius, at the last negotiations; a thoroughly unprepossessing person with thin hair and wispy beard, his mud-colored eyes heavy lidded as if he were perpetually sleepy. The princess, on the other hand, was vibrant. Not a classic beauty—her form was too thin and face too sharp. Most men liked a more voluptuous figure, a soft oval face with bow-like lips. Yet something about her doe-soft eyes and the way she stood up to him and his king appealed to him. She had spirit—or typical Roman arrogance. He had yet to decide which.

Ataulf entered the *triclinium* to find his brother-in-law attended by only one servant, and flushed with victory, wine, and fever. Some illness had dogged his king since they first laid their siege.

"Rome, brother, Rome! That great whore of the West has opened her legs to me." The King clapped him hard on the back. "Come. Drink." A slave handed Ataulf a large gold goblet, crusted with red gems. "Only the first of our spoils. How goes the sack?"

"You should be there, my brother."

His king wiped the sweat off his brow. "As soon as I recover my strength, I'll parade through the city in triumph."

"The men are doing a thorough job. For the most part, your commands about not burning or violating church sanctuary are being carried out." Ataulf gulped the rough red wine. "Loot and slaves are being gathered outside the city walls and brought here as wagons and carts come available."

"Excellent. And our tame Senators?"

"Valia has two ready to ride to Ravenna to negotiate for the return of the princess."

"Bring them in."

Ataulf went to the door to talk to a messenger.

Within minutes a large warrior, with gray-shot beard and a broken nose, herded two men into the room. Their dust-streaked tunics stank of fear and smoke. They prostrated themselves before Alaric, as if before the Roman Emperor, shrieking, "Be merciful, O Great One! Take pity on our poor souls!"

"Stop that caterwauling." The king kicked the pudgy one closest to him. "I have a commission for you."

They both looked up, a ray of hope lighting their faces.

"I want you to take a message to Emperor Honorius. Tell him what you have seen of Rome's pain and our mighty forces. I no longer want the paltry province and tiny measure of grain he offered last time. If he wants his sister, he must guarantee our safe passage to Noricum, provide sufficient grain for my army for a year, and make me supreme commander of his armies. Only then will I return Princess Placidia."

Hope vanished from their faces, replaced by horror. The pudgy one spoke. "You want us to make demands on your behalf to the Emperor? He'll strike off our heads!"

"If you don't undertake my mission, *I* will strike off your heads. Not only yours, but your wives' and children's." The barbarian king took a sharp knife from his belt and began trimming the nails on his left hand. "Will you take this commission?"

"Of course, Great One." They prostrated themselves again.

The king tossed them a sealed packet. "Give these papers to the Emperor and bring back an answer. If you are successful in that, I will free you and your families."

Ataulf motioned over his shoulder with his thumb. Valia hauled the two Senators from the floor.

"Come with me. I'll get you outfitted. You can use post horses and be in Ravenna in less than two days."

"Do you think Honorius will comply?" Ataulf asked as the three left.

"We've tried everything else." His brother-in-law's face suddenly looked older than his thirty-odd years. "Honorius is as inconstant as the weather; first sunny and obliging, then dark and threatening. If only that traitorous snake Sarus hadn't cocked up the last negotiations."

His king threw his goblet at the wall, bathing the hunting scene with blood-red wine.

As evening shadows crept up the walls, Placidia awoke. As soon as she sat up, a young girl scuttled out the door. Within moments, Gaatha and two of her ladies returned.

"Sleep well?" Gaatha asked.

"No. And my head hurts." Placidia clapped her hands to her head to still the pounding.

"I will send for our physician, Machaon. He is a Greek and most effective." She nodded to one of her ladies, who immediately left the room. Gaatha settled on a chair and fanned herself with her hands. "Why do the Romans build houses with such small bedrooms and no windows?"

Placidia, taken aback by the question, thought for a moment. "Most of us spend very little time in our bedrooms. We prefer to spend our waking hours in the garden, library, or audience room." She looked around. "What has become of my people?"

"They are well cared for. Your man servant has recovered his senses and is resting. I'm afraid the girl you rescued is doing poorly. Machaon reports she has lost much blood, but he fears more for her mind than her body. She refuses to speak or take food or drink. She is asleep now. Maybe when she wakes you might encourage her."

"You sent for me, Lady?" A short man with a bald pate and graying beard entered the room and bowed.

"Machaon, this is Princess Placidia. She has a head pain. Do provide her one of your excellent elixirs."

The physician approached Placidia, eyeing with disapproval her slender frame. "When was the last time the Princess took a meal?"

Placidia shook her head. When had she eaten last? "I had some dates yesterday, but little else."

"Have you moved your bowels today? Are your courses due?" Machaon asked brusquely.

Placidia stiffened.

The little man smiled, revealing strong teeth. "I mean no offense, Princess. Many things can upset the humors of the body. If I can eliminate some of those possibilities, I can better treat you."

Head throbbing worse every second, Placidia said, "I moved my bowels yesterday, and finished my courses last week."

"Good." Machaon turned to Gaatha. "Feed the princess, give her as much watered wine or juice as she will drink, and get her out of this stifling room into fresh air. If she does not feel better within an hour of a meal, send a servant and I will provide a powder."

"Thank you, Machaon." Gaatha nodded to one of her attendants, who followed the physician out.

Placidia closed her eyes and lay back until the scuffing of feet on tile announced the arrival of food. She opened her eyes on a feast of fruit, bread, and cheese. A servant poured her juice—unfermented grape—the heavy syrup cut with cool water. She drained the beaker, and the servant filled it again. Her headache subsided to a dull throb.

"Please eat your fill." Gaatha indicated the spread with a wave of her hand. "Then join me and my ladies under the trees."

"Thank you." Placidia looked at the food. Her stomach churned, but her practical side won out. She could not think with the anvil ringing in her head, and she desperately needed to think—and to plan.

CHAPTER 3

Ravenna, 410

CONSTANTIUS, GENERAL IN THE ROMAN ARMY and advisor to Emperor
Honorius, strode down the colonnade shaking with anger and fear—
anger at Honorius for bollixing the last agreement Constantius had
negotiated with the Goths, and fear for Placidia. Most of the Roman women
Constantius knew were simpering fools, good for idle chatter and little else.
Placidia was different. He would marry her even if she were a milkmaid. That
she was the Emperor's sister was a complication.

Constantius opened a low gate and stepped into a dusty courtyard. His
entrance set off a flurry of offended squawks as chickens of several fancy breeds
scurried from his presence.

If only those bloody Goths would do the same.

The Emperor, in the opposite corner, spread chicken feed with a sweep of
his hand. At nearly twenty-six, Honorius had ruled for seventeen years, but
still had the aspect of an unformed boy, with a weak chin and dull eyes. Yet
Honorius was Emperor, and therefore commanded Constantius' respect and
obedience, as had his more worthy father before him. The General only wished
the young man paid as much attention to his Empire as to his flock of fowl.

Constantius stalked across the poultry yard and found a spot free of chicken
dung in which to kneel. "Most Mighty Emperor, I bring grave news. Rome is taken."

"That's impossible." Honorius paled, looking frantically around the poultry yard. "He ate from my hand only moments ago." Honorius shot away and picked up a noisy rooster, easily the largest in the pen. "See? Here he is, safe, as I said."

Constantius rose, took a deep breath, and instantly regretted it when the dust and grain chaff sent him into a paroxysm of coughs. He motioned to a slave for a drink. The man immediately brought a cup of chilled wine. After quelling the dusty tickle, he tried again. "Not the rooster, My Emperor, the city of Rome is taken by Alaric. Your agents sped here with the news."

"Rome—not you, my pet…" Honorius smoothed the glossy black feathers of his rooster "…got what it deserved. Deposing me and setting up their own Emperor! Those traitorous Senators bent over and bared their backsides for that filthy Goth."

Only in self-defense. Constantius held his tongue with long practice.

Every time negotiations broke down with the Emperor, safe behind the impregnable marshes of Ravenna, Alaric besieged Rome. The city endured starvation, plague, and crushing payments of gold and silver, until last year, when the Senate acquiesced to Alaric's demands and raised one of their own to the purple. Only the timely arrival of troops from Constantinople saved Honorius from the ignominy of abdicating. With this third siege in three years, Alaric had evidently asked for nothing and gave no quarter.

"The Romans are a stiff-necked bunch," *and it is too late for them.* "But do you forget the Princess Placidia? She might be in danger."

Honorius' face hardened. "Placidia fled to Rome. She could have returned to safety any time during the last four years, but refused. When she comes to me, I will forgive her, but I will not beg her to return."

Constantius was determined to bring Placidia safe to Ravenna, but he knew the Emperor's moods. Now was not the time to press the subject. "Sire, shouldn't we repair to the audience chamber? The court will need your reassurances."

Honorius looked at his beloved pets with regret. "This is the only respite I have from ceremony and duty." He sighed. "But these are perilous times, and I should make myself available to my ministers."

Constantius linked arms with the Emperor and escorted him through the gate, where a contingent of guards awaited. As they entered a marble passage, a servant ran into them, sending the Emperor reeling. The man, a twitchy Greek slave with a bad complexion, threw himself onto the floor, babbling apologies, as four guards menaced him with spears.

"Get up, man!" Honorius grumbled, ostentatiously dusting himself off. "I should send you to the mines. Why careen around the corner in such a fashion?"

"An important delegation seeks your immediate attention, Your Most Forgiving Highness. They await you in your audience chamber."

"And who are these worthy gentlemen?"

"Senators from Rome, Most Charitable One." The slave threw himself on the floor again. "Please forgive your humble and obedient slave for any unintended injury to your August Person, Highness."

"Yes, yes. Get out of my way."

The slave, like many of his fellows, had perfected the art of disappearing quickly, and did so.

Before they reached the audience chamber, a horde of eunuchs, led by the Provost of the Sacred Cubicle—the eunuch in charge of the imperial household, and the emperor's most intimate servant—whisked Honorius away to be dressed for his appearance. Constantius didn't envy the emperor's obligation to ceremony and protocol. No wonder the poor man liked to escape to his chicken pen! If he were emperor…Constantius shoved that treasonous thought away. He had no ambition to be a slave to imperial eunuchs. He much preferred his current role as the power behind the throne. Constantius entered the purple marble-clad audience chamber, which was filled nearly to bursting with courtiers, and moved to the side to better observe the coming drama.

After several minutes, a trumpet blasted. The crowd quieted and went to their knees. The court announcer declaimed, "All bow before the Most Excellent and Invincible…" Constantius winced at the inappropriate honorific. "…Flavius Honorius Augustus, son of the Great and Divine Flavius Theodosius Augustus, nine-times Consul of Rome and Father of His People." The sonorous voice went on for several minutes, listing the rest of the emperor's honors and all the military victories that occurred during his reign—another irony, since the emperor, unlike his martial father, had never led troops.

With a final trumpet flourish, Honorius entered the room, enveloped in his gold thread and pearl encrusted *paludamentum*—his purple imperial cloak—fastened with a gold *fibula* in the shape of a multi-pointed star set with a brilliant ruby. Rubies also embellished the gold diadem that sat on the newly oiled and coifed curls. He carried a gold-headed staff of office. Honorius moved sedately to the center of the dais and took his seat on a gilded ivory chair, well-padded with purple silk cushions. Guards flanked him. Scribes waited to record his every word. The Emperor waved his hand in a dismissive gesture. The announcer gave the much awaited order, "All may rise."

The courtiers came to their feet with only a few suppressed groans and the occasional helping hand for the more elderly or corpulent. Constantius rose easily, but noted a new twinge in his left knee.

The announcer introduced the delegation from Rome. The two men approached the dais. They had not even changed their dusty clothes. Constantius' nose twitched at their stench. Both were pale from exhaustion; the fat one walked with a limp.

Honorius maintained a serious expression. "What news do you have for me about Rome?"

Both men threw themselves face down at the Emperor's feet, with loud cries and acclamations. Honorius let the show go on a few moments before giving the men permission to rise and asking again for news.

"Betrayal, Most August One. During negotiations, that dog Alaric gave several comely youths as gifts to high officials…"

And the greedy empty-headed asses accepted those "gifts," no doubt. Constantius could already see the outcome of their story. Alaric had more of the fox about him than the dog.

"…the young men were most compliant and professed loyalty to their new masters, yet, in the darkest moment before the dawn, they seized weapons and attacked the guards at the Salarian gate, overcoming them and letting their perfidious comrades into our fair city."

A collective gasp rose from the court.

"The barbarians stripped our city, killing those men they found in the street or any woman who resisted them. The churches overflowed, and any who could not reach sanctuary were taken for ransom or enslaved. Our guards are dead, our slaves gone, our goods forfeit. Rome lies bleeding and broken."

Tears streaked both men's cheeks.

Honorius turned visibly pale and asked for wine.

Constantius' heart raced. "What news of the Emperor's sister? Did she leave Rome for the countryside? Is she safe?"

"She is taken, My Lord," the skinny one said in a squeak he could barely force past his bobbing Adam's apple.

Constantius clenched his hands as if around the throat of the barbarian king. He had led men in battle and faced death uncounted times, but never feared for himself as much as he did for Placidia at that moment.

"What?" Honorius roared, rising. "That upstart barbarian dared put his hands on an Imperial Princess?"

The Senators again threw themselves on their faces. "She is treated as a guest, not a prisoner. Alaric asks for some small concessions and he will send Princess Placidia to you, unharmed."

"What concessions?" Honorius retook his seat, glowering at the messengers.

The Senators looked at each other, the fat one with rolling eyes and sweat pouring off his brow. The other sighed and spoke. "Most Glorious and Wise Emperor, Alaric asks that you give his people the province of Noricum in which to settle, grain for a year, and the title of Master General."

"I refuse to give the title of *magister militum* to anyone of that race!"

"Your Most Noble Majesty." The Master of Offices stepped forward with a brief bow. He held a powerful post, controlling the civil service, access to the Emperor, and, more importantly, the messenger and intelligence gathering corps known as *agentes in rebus*. Court intrigue was such that three men had held the post in three years.

"Take counsel from those older and more experienced than you in this matter. Alaric's demands are quite reasonable for what he will return—not only your sister, but much-needed troops in our battles against the other barbarians."

"I have heeded the counsel of older and wiser men, and look where it's brought my Empire! The legions of Britain rebel and invade Gaul. The Burgundians, Vandals, and Sueves flood across the Rhine and ravage both Gaul and Spain. That Gothic barbarian styles himself a king, invades Italy, and makes demands of me. Soon I will be Emperor of nothing but the pestilential swamps that surround this city!" Honorius scowled at the minister. "I will not be dictated to, by Alaric or by you. Get out of my sight! All of you! Go!"

Constantius hurried to catch up with the Master of Offices. The man was a toad and a tool of a powerful faction at court, but Constantius would make common cause with him—to free Placidia.

THE SACK OF ROME ENDED AFTER THREE DAYS.

On the fourth, Placidia tended the battered girl. Her bruises had turned alarming shades of green and yellow, a most unnatural color for flesh. The girl would bear the scars of many cuts on her face and body, as well as those unseen scars on her mind. She cried out at night, but would not speak when awake.

Placidia contemplated the mute girl as she spooned porridge into her mouth. "We should give you a name. I cannot continue to call you 'girl'."

She looked at Placidia with dull eyes.

"How about Lucilla? That's a pretty name."

No reaction.

"I will call you Lucilla, until such time as you tell me different."

Lucilla rolled over on her pallet, showing her back to Placidia.

"I will be back again tomorrow." She stroked the girl's shoulder; felt her shudder at the touch. "Cook will be in later with more food."

Placidia left Lucilla in the darkness of her small room, and returned to her own more luxurious quarters, followed by the hulking guards who accompanied her everywhere. So far, she had been treated as an honored guest, given a room of her own, and her servants returned unharmed. But the perpetual presence of these strange men gave the lie to any feelings of freedom.

"What will you wear to the banquet tonight?" Gaatha picked through Placidia's clothes with dissatisfaction. Only a few of her clothes and jewels—the most modest pieces—found their way to her storage chests from the looted palace.

The Gothic King was throwing a victory celebration for his nobles and their ladies that night. He had commanded Placidia to attend.

"I thought the blue *stola* with the cream *tunica interior*."

Gaatha picked up the blue linen gown: fine cloth in a rectangle shape with sleeves cut from the same piece as the body, rich embroidery picked out in gold and silver thread at throat, sleeves, and hem. She frowned. "We cannot have the Imperial Princess appearing at such an important occasion in this." Gaatha shook the offending garment like a terrier destroying a rat. "I will have a selection brought to you."

"Thank you, Lady." Placidia hoped the selection would not be from Gaatha's personal clothes chest. The Gothic queen towered over her by nearly a head. Placidia would look like a little girl trying on her mother's clothes. The image brought a smile to her face, one of the few she had had since Rome fell.

Within the hour, Gaatha returned with a servant staggering under an enormous pile of garments of rainbow hue. "I regret I could find nothing ready-made in royal purple, Princess. We have several bolts of silk from the warehouses, but it is too late to have one made up with the appropriate decoration."

"I do not favor purple. It makes me look sallow." Placidia looked over the selection. "I believe the rose silk will be appropriate." The delicate shade would bring color to her cheeks and complement her brown hair and eyes. She held it against her body, noting its appropriate length for her stature.

Gaatha nodded approvingly. "I will send a hairdresser to you shortly. Do you require jewelry? You may borrow some of mine."

"I believe I have enough for this fine dress. Thank you for the loan."

"It is a gift. The rest of the garments are yours as well. My husband is generous, and I and my ladies will dress well for many years."

Placidia's skin prickled. *God forgive me. I fervently pray the former owner of this dress escaped to sanctuary.*

She quickly put the garment back on the pile.

PLACIDIA ACCOMPANIED GAATHA and her ladies to the outdoor banqueting area. The Gothic Queen looked regal in a green silk gown, covered with flowers and leaves embroidered in gold thread. She displayed her husband's wealth and status with an abundance of gold jewelry. Pearl-encrusted combs held her red hair in a complicated mass of braids and curls. Emerald earrings and a matching necklace set off Gaatha's green eyes. Placidia recognized the jewels as having belonged to a middle-aged senator's wife, but firmly put away her qualms. There was nothing she could do.

In the manner of the Goths, all the ladies made a great show of their wealth. Placidia felt almost dowdy in her conservative rose silk with a girdle of gold and pearls and a few gold bracelets. An elaborate net of fine gold mesh held her dark hair at the back of her head. Her only signs of Imperial rank were the simple pearl diadem across her forehead, and her signet ring.

They left the villa and progressed to an enormous canopy set among the apple orchards. Placidia was pleased to see smoky torches stuck in the ground. Perhaps that would keep some of the biting insects, prevalent in the warm August air, from plaguing the guests. A slave lit a chandelier of oil lamps hanging from the middle of the tent pole, lighting the scene underneath. Trestles, holding planks covered with bolts of white linen, made three sides of a large rectangle. A wide assortment of chairs stood around the improvised banquet table. The king sat in the largest, a gilded throne-like affair covered in blue silk cushions. He rose from his chair and approached the ladies.

"My Queen! You are by far the loveliest woman here." He pulled Gaatha into his arms, bending her backwards in a lusty kiss. Placidia saw from his heightened color that the king had already sampled the wine.

Gaatha laughed deep in her throat, but took his hand and arm from her backside and linked it with her own. "You flatter me, Husband. After four children, my body is not that of young maid."

"Who wants a timid maid in his bed? Not I!" he roared, to loud acclamation from the other men.

In a low tone, Gaatha hissed, "Husband, the Princess."

The Gothic King seemed to notice Placidia for the first time, and gave her a slight bow. "Forgive my crude barbarian ways, Princess. I hope I have not offended you." He swung his arm in an arc, indicating the tables and chairs. "I realize this banquet is not in the Roman tradition, but I cannot abide reclining on those overstuffed couches during a meal. They are good for sleeping, but not eating."

"Thank you for your concern, Sir. As a guest, your ways are my ways."

He chuckled briefly and, linking his free arm in Placidia's, ushered both women toward the tables. "I have a surprise for you, Princess. An old friend of yours is traveling with us, and requested the honor of your company this evening."

Placidia scanned the tables. Most of the seats were filled, leaving those next to the gilded chair empty. She saw Ataulf approach from the left, accompanied by a short dark man dressed in a traditional Roman tunic and white toga with the wide purple stripe of a senator. The Roman passed a flickering torch, and Placidia saw his face.

Her heart leapt. The smile on his dark face banished the loneliness and fear of the past few days.

"Attalus! I thought you were dead!" Placidia threw herself into his arms.

CHAPTER 4

MY LITTLE FAWN, I'M SO PLEASED TO SEE YOU SAFE," Attalus whispered in her ear. He set her down at arm's length. "I had not expected so enthusiastic a greeting. Our last meeting was a bit…estranged, you might say?"

"My brother may be a fool, but he is the Emperor, and I cannot and will not support another interest against his." Priscus Attalus, former Prefect of the City of Rome, had been a regular and welcome visitor during Placidia's first year in the city. They had parted ways when the senate deposed her brother, during the second Gothic siege, and acclaimed Attalus in his place, leaving Placidia in an ambiguous position.

"You know I had little choice in the matter, my dear."

"I do." Placidia tucked his arm in hers.

Attalus had played a dangerous game, treating with the Goths, but at least Rome did not bleed and burn under his leadership. He seemed little the worse for his adventures—only a little gray streaking his dark hair, and a few lines crinkled at the corners of his black eyes.

Ataulf touched her shoulder. "Princess, I am pleased you are happy with our surprise. The Prefect frequently mentions your friendship. I thought you might appreciate his company."

"Oh, yes!" Placidia smiled up at Ataulf. "Thank you so very much."

"Come. You are to share my place of honor at Alaric's left hand." Ataulf put a hand to her back and guided her to a seat between him and Attalus. The rest of the royal company sat at the tables, Gaatha, in the other place of precedence,

26

at Alaric's right.

"How did you survive?" Placidia asked Attalus in a low voice. "When the Gothic King stripped you of the Imperial regalia and approached my brother again, I thought one of the conditions would be your head."

"Alaric says he still needs me to advise him on the negotiations. To tell the truth, I think it amuses him to keep an Emperor—if only a former one—in his service." Attalus chuckled. "Besides, he might need a puppet Emperor again. Who better to fill the role than one with experience?"

"Welcome all!" King Alaric called in a booming voice. "Tonight we celebrate a great feat for the Gothic people—the fall of Rome! Let us enjoy the fruits of our victory." A sustained roar rose from the gathered nobles. When it quieted, Alaric called on Bishop Sigesar to say the blessing. The Arian bishop launched into a prayer, asking "in the name of God the Father and the Son created by the Father" for wisdom and good health for all assembled, pardon for their sins, and mercy for the souls of the departed.

Created. Such an innocent word, Placidia thought, as the Bishop droned on. Such was the abstraction that split the Catholic and Arian Christian churches over the relation between the Father and the Son. Was Jesus God Himself incarnate or was He 'created' by God—lesser in some ineffable way? The Arians steadfastly believed the latter, the Catholics the former.

In her own mind, Placidia believed the truth unknowable, but religion remained a dangerous quagmire for the rulers of the empire. She understood the Great Constantine's plan for 'one Emperor, one religion, one empire,' but it led to conundrums such as faced them now. The Goths had converted during the reign of an Arian Emperor, and now an entire people were judged heretic because her brother favored the Catholic Church.

The Bishop drew to a close before his listeners grew too restive. At his "Amen," a babble of voices arose, and a small army of servants took the field to deliver wine and food to the eager revelers. Bowls of olives and baskets of bread already graced the tables. Competing with the clatter of plates, musicians played lyres and flutes. A pack of dogs growled over a joint that fell off a platter.

Placidia took a silver goblet from the hands of a servant and sipped the wine—unwatered, in the barbarian fashion. Though an excellent vintage from Sicily, it was too strong for her taste. She handed the goblet back to the slave. "Water my wine." The man scurried off to a mixing bowl set in one corner of the tent.

"The wine is not to your liking, Princess?" Ataulf took a large gulp of his own.

"The wine is fine. I do not wish to wake with a sore head in the morning."

Ataulf laughed. "All expect to wake with a sore head in the morning. This is a victory celebration."

"Then you understand why I do not wish to celebrate, especially in such a way as to make me ill." She turned back to Attalus' company, deliberately giving the general her shoulder, and immediately regretted her sharp words and actions. He had been nothing but solicitous of her feelings and gentlemanly in conduct. Although Ataulf was an enemy, it was unworthy of her to act in such a churlish manner.

Before she could make amends, the slaves arrived with huge platters piled high with barely roasted meat. The slightest tilt sent rivulets of bloody juice sluicing down the slaves' arms onto their garments, so they looked more like butchers than servants. The Gothic King roared for them to be more careful. Dogs wove in and out of the servant's legs, causing more chaos. The slaves offered beef, pork, goat, and whole fowls of various sizes, from tiny thrushes to roasted geese; all served on the fanciest silver platters, burnished to a bright shine, as befitted a good host.

"I would not partake of the red meat, if I were you." Attalus was a well-known gourmand. "If your body is not used to fresh meat, it upsets the humors and causes excruciating pains of the stomach and bowels." He grimaced for effect. "I know from personal experience. One thing I regret about this association is the barbarian predilection for undercooked meat, and lots of it."

"It is easy to bring herds on a migration, but impossible to cultivate vegetables and grain." The general joined the conversation, taking a large joint of beef. "Hunger is a constant threat. That is why our king is so anxious to secure a grain supply from the Emperor. If he refuses again, we go to Africa."

"Is that likely?" Placidia speared a small roasted fowl with a knife, its crispy skin redolent of rosemary.

Ataulf gave an expressive shrug and looked disapprovingly on her choice of meat. "You must eat, Princess. You are little more than a bird yourself. All our women eat heartily. They know how hard food is to come by."

"Perhaps." Placidia picked over various rolls, taking a light brown one crusted with sesame seeds. "Is it harder to sow and reap the grain, mill the flour, and bake the bread, or to simply take that bread from another by force of arms?"

She cut a slice of sharp goat cheese to put on her bread, and munched both with satisfaction.

"What we do, we do out of need. We've wandered for two generations, since the Huns drove us from our own land into yours. Instead of settling us where we could be of some use, Rome sought our destruction—you starved us, stole our children, and harried us from place to place."

"The misbegotten actions of Emperor Valens are no part of me or mine. He executed my father's father," Placidia said with heat. "My father sought peace. He was known as 'Friend to the Goths.' "

The general laughed. "Emperor Theodosius was a friend only because being our enemy was too costly. Neither he nor Stilicho could fight us, the Persians, and every military upstart who wanted to be Emperor, so they paid us to fight their wars."

"You should be grateful the Divine Theodosius allowed you to follow your nature." Attalus raised a cup in salute. "The warrior cult is as old as your people. If you do not take up arms, you cannot become a man. What of you, General? Do you plan to conquer this land, settle down, and become a farmer?"

"My clever Attalus." Ataulf's eyes flashed. "You have learned something, living with us these many months. I fight for my people. Do you?"

"He fights in his own way." Placidia smiled sweetly over her wine. "As do I."

ATAULF WAS RELIEVED when Gaatha took the princess back to her quarters and the Roman Prefect excused himself from the revels.

That woman has a tongue sharper than a Spanish blade.

They had done nothing but thrust and parry all evening, and words were not his weapon. The feelings she aroused surprised him, especially in her attention to that wily Roman politician. Ataulf's handsome features had turned women's heads since he was a boy. It had been a blow that Placidia did not immediately fall into the fluttering ways he had come to expect from women, young or old, married or not.

Best not go down that trail. The Emperor will send word soon, and the princess will be on her way.

Ataulf shook his head to clear the wine fumes. He got to his feet; pleased he didn't stagger or sway on his way to the latrine trench. He relieved himself with a sigh and a blessing for fanatical Roman hygiene. There were far fewer deaths from fever and plague since the Goths adopted the Roman habit of burying their waste away from their water sources.

The fresh air revived him, but the cursed mosquitoes drove him back to the tent. He replenished his wine and joined his fellows in a rousing song about a lonely shepherd and his special love for his sheep.

THE NEXT MORNING ATAULF did, indeed, wake with a sore head and a furry tongue. After dousing himself with cold water, he called two of his personal body slaves to attend him, and strode off to the baths, a complex set slightly apart from the villa itself.

He wasn't the only one with that idea; a tunic hung on a peg in the disrobing room. He doffed his own and entered the steamy heat of the *caldarium*, where he spied a familiar form on the marble steps leading into the heated pool.

"Valia." Ataulf clapped his friend on the back. "You're turning red as an apple."

Valia opened bloodshot eyes and grinned. "How do you fare?"

"The worse for wine." Sweat trickled down Ataulf's face. He scratched his short beard with blunt fingernails. "But it is seldom we celebrate such a victory. Rome has not been taken in eight hundred years, and it fell to us." He leaned back in satisfaction. The sack brought enormous wealth to his people and honor to his warriors. Little of the vast Western Empire remained under the Roman Emperor's control. Ataulf dreamed of what it would take to establish Gothica in the place of Rome in the West.

"And is it the same with the Roman princess?" Valia laughed. "From what I saw last night, her walls held. She even sent a few barbs your way."

"It is useful to spar against such a worthy adversary. You learn their strengths and weaknesses."

They sat in companionable silence. Ataulf admired the craftsmanship of the wall mosaic showing Neptune riding the waves, accompanied by dolphins. When suitably steamed, they moved directly to the cold pool, laughing and daring one another to see who could stand the icy water longest.

"I concede!" Valia cried as he left the pool, shivering. "You're more foolish than I."

They followed the dip with a massage.

"I see why the Romans have grown so soft, with these luxuries." Valia groaned as a slave worked on a sore muscle.

Ataulf thought for a moment. "I don't believe it is the bath houses, or the theaters, or the arenas that make these people soft. It is their unwillingness to defend what is theirs. How many generations has it been since the Roman citizens of Italy served in the army? Now they send slaves, or pay others to take their place. The sheep hire the wolf to guard them, and bleat piteously when the wolf follows its nature."

"I see why they would be reluctant to risk their necks, if this is the life they give up."

"They lose this way of life either way. We should learn from their lesson." Ataulf sat up to allow the slave to pat him down with linen towels. "Speaking of the lost, any word from the Senators you sent to Emperor Honorius?"

"No. They should be on their way back by now." Valia frowned. "I hope, for their families' sakes, they return. I've had enough blood of women and children."

"Are you going soft, old man?" Sergeric, a Gothic chieftain, lounged in the doorway to the exercise yard.

Ataulf's lips skinned back from his teeth in a snarl. Something about Sergeric raised his hackles. The man was all swagger and belligerent talk. When it came to actual fighting, Sergeric favored overwhelming odds and the easy kill.

Valia ran a hand through his thick hair and eyed Sergeric. "Not so soft that I couldn't take you. Care to join me for a round or two?"

Valia was a massive man. Even with a few years slowing him down, he was more than a match for the slighter Sergeric in wrestling or boxing.

"Honorius murdered our women and children the moment he got rid of Stilicho." Sergeric spat, as if the very name of the Emperor left a foul taste in his mouth. "We should roast that Roman bitch over a slow fire and send her brother the cooked meat."

Ataulf felt Valia's massive hand on his shoulder, holding him in place as his companion mildly replied. "If you feel so strongly, complain to King Alaric."

"Or join your traitorous brother Sarus." Ataulf could stay quiet no longer.

Sergeric paled, then flushed. "Still throwing that in my teeth, are you? Sarus failed to win the kingship. Should he have stayed and let Alaric mock him for that failure the rest of his days?"

"Better loyalty to his rightful king, than cowardly service to the Emperor who butchered his brethren." Ataulf shrugged off Valia and stood, hands clenching and unclenching. "How *did* your brother survive that bloody plot?"

"Perhaps God saved him for some higher purpose."

"The devil, you mean," Ataulf muttered.

Sergeric smiled, sending a shiver down Ataulf's spine in spite of the heat. "The blood of thousands of innocent women and children cry out to us all. You might not hear it, but I do."

He turned on his heel and left the room.

Ataulf stared after the retreating figure.

"Ataulf, my friend, why do you let that little man anger you?" Valia's deep voice boomed. "You know the king's mind. He won't murder the princess."

"I know." Ataulf's face broke into a rueful smile. "Perhaps it's my hatred for his brother that reflects on him, but something about Sergeric brings out the worst in me."

CHAPTER 5

O N HER SEVENTH DAY OF CAPTIVITY, Placidia paced from one wall of her room to the other. Fourteen steps. A large room by all accounts, but it felt small and bereft. Attalus attended the Gothic King. Gaatha was kind, but busy; her ladies shy. Paulus and Lucilla no longer needed her nursing. Unused to idleness, Placidia realized she was most happy when dealing with ministers and petitioners.

I must leave this villa, if only for a walk in the orchard. They cannot refuse such a simple request.

Placidia strode into the colonnade and into the middle of a ruckus.

"Please, Nana! Father said we could. Please!" General Ataulf's four children besieged their nurse.

"My bones ache today, children. I can't walk all the way to the practice fields."

"Perhaps I could take them." The moment the words left her mouth, Placidia wondered what possessed her. She had never had the care of children. What would she do with them?

Four pairs of wide blue eyes, and one pair of tired brown ones, turned in Placidia's direction. Ataulf's three girls were smaller copies of each other, with thick red-gold hair and rosy cheeks, each with one of those long convoluted names the Goths favored for their girls. Luckily, the children themselves shortened them to something manageable. The oldest, Vada, missing her front teeth, spoke with a faint lisp. Lilla, the middle girl, was the wildest of the bunch, braids in disarray and face smudged. Maltha chattered constantly, driving her nurse mad with questions. Ediulf, the youngest, was a sturdy child with a mop of golden hair, and dimples in his baby cheeks.

The nurse cleared her throat. "But, Princess, it's a long way, and the little ones…"

"I have the service of four strong men." Placidia indicated her ever-present guard. "I am sure they can carry a tired child with little difficulty. Besides, I have heard that exercise makes for a restful sleep." At least, that's what her nurse had told her when she hauled Placidia protesting from the library.

"Please, please, Nana! Can we go? Can we?"

"I will have to speak with Queen Gaatha first." The nurse hushed their shouts and looked up at the bright blue sky. "Put on some proper sandals and take your cloaks. The ache in my bones says the weather is changing."

The children raced each other to their bedrooms, little Ediulf crying for his sisters to wait for him. Vada stooped down and carried him to his room.

Placidia retreated to her own room to slip a pair of tight-fitting trousers on under her *stola* and exchange her house slippers for sturdy sandals—double cowhide soles with softer flaps that laced into a closed shoe. Heeding Nana's advice, Placidia grabbed her woolen cloak. On the way to the atrium she found herself humming a nursery song, and smiled to herself.

She met the nurse and the children by the atrium entrance. The children looked neat—even Lilla's braids were replaited and her face clean. But they seemed subdued compared to their earlier enthusiasm. Gaatha or the nurse must have sharpened her tongue on the young ones.

The old woman handed two large baskets to the guards. "A little something to eat later."

"Did you pack a whole pig in here, grandmother?" One of the men groaned.

"If these old arms can carry both baskets from the kitchen, your young ones can carry one down a hill," the old woman huffed. She made a final inspection of the children. "You'll do. Now behave yourselves. The guards have permission to swat you if you get out of line, and don't think your father won't hear!"

The children looked at one another and nodded.

"We understand, Nana," Vada said.

"No need to fret, grandmother. We'll take good care of 'em," the first guard said.

"It's not them I worry about." She looked the guard up and down. "Who'll take care of you?"

He roared with laughter. His fellows joined in.

"Now go on." The nurse shaded her eyes and looked at the sun. "It's near mid-morning already."

As soon as the door closed behind their backs, the children gave wild whoops and assailed Placidia.

"Thank you, Princess!" Vada said.

"I want to see the horses," Lilla cried.

"You always want to see the horses." Maltha frowned and stamped her foot. "I want to pick flowers."

"Father said we could come to the practice field," Lilla said.

"Children, I'm sure we can…" Placidia looked down as Ediulf tugged on her tunic. He hopped from foot to foot; his little faced screwed into a mask of concern. She hoped he wasn't ill. "What is it, my dear?"

A wet spot appeared on the front of his tunic and continued down his trousers, to puddle in the dust.

"Ediulf!" all three girls cried. The little boy hung his head and put his thumb in his mouth.

"Nana thought this might happen." Vada sighed and looked up at Placidia. "He was too excited to go before we left, and he can't take his trousers down by himself."

Placidia was at a loss. "What should we do? Take him back in to change?"

"No need." Lilla brusquely stripped the damp tunic and trousers off her brother and put them on a rock by the wall to dry.

Vada provided dry clothes from her folded cloak and dressed the little boy. "There, good as new." The girl looked up at Placidia through her lashes. "If we weren't with you, Princess, we would just let him dry on his own, but Nana said you weren't used to vulgar smells."

"Don't worry about my sensibilities. My brother raises chickens. You haven't smelled vulgar until you've smelled wet fowl." Placidia pinched her nose shut and grimaced. The children giggled. "Come. I believe we can gather flowers *and* watch the horses on our outing."

They walked through the orchard to a short, steep hill. The children raced, whooping, to the bottom. Ediulf tripped and rolled the last few feet, screaming in a high pitched voice that sent Placidia pelting to his side.

God's mercy, he's surely broken his neck!

The little boy grinned at her and shrieked, "'Gin, 'gin!"

Placidia grabbed Ediulf by the arms. "Don't ever do that again!"

The boy's face went ashen. His lips trembled with the effort to hold back tears.

Vada came running to her brother. "He didn't mean to do anything wrong, Princess. He's little and doesn't understand."

Placidia released the boy's arms. He scuttled behind Vada's skirts. Placidia wiped the nervous sweat from her face. "I am so sorry. I thought he had hurt himself, and I was frightened."

"I didn't know princesses got scared."

"We just don't show it often." Placidia squatted and held out her hand to Ediulf. "I'm sorry I shouted. Can we be friends?"

He peeped from behind his sister.

"Would you like to ride? I can take you down to the stream on my shoulders."

Ediulf's face split into a smile. He hesitantly stepped from behind Vada.

Placidia swung him up to straddle her neck and firmly held onto his legs. *At least now I can keep him from harm.*

Vada shook a finger at her brother. "Don't wet on the princess."

Ediulf grabbed Placidia's braid with both hands and cried, "Horsie, go!" She strode out in a smooth glide, vowing not to jostle the child's bladder.

The party made it to the stream, where Lilla picked flowers and Maltha wove them into chains.

Placidia stooped and helped Ediulf dismount. The boy immediately ran for the stream. "Keep him out of trouble," she instructed a guard. "If he drowns, you'll have to account to his father."

The guard smiled and quickly caught up with the boy.

Maltha shyly held out a lopsided circle of purple clover. "I wove a diadem for you, Princess."

"Thank you!" Placidia looked it over critically. "It's the most beautiful diadem I've ever seen."

Soon the entire party was decked out in flower necklaces and crowns.

Lilla, with a tear in her tunic and burrs in her hair, came running. "We've picked all the flowers in this meadow. Let's go see the horses!"

They crossed the narrow stream on stepping stones and climbed a short rise to view the practice field. A brisk breeze tugged at their tunics and sent cloud shadows racing across the flat meadow. Placidia observed with grudging approval the orderliness of the units. Three groups of twenty were on horseback. One group practiced shooting arrows at targets, a second threw javelins, and a third hacked at stakes with swords as they galloped by. They all seemed young, practicing blood curdling yells as they attacked their 'enemies.'

"There's Papa!" Lilla spied her father demonstrating to a huddle of beardless boys how to mount from the ground. Ataulf threw himself into the saddle with one swift movement. The new recruits tried the mount with varying degrees of success. Most made it astride with some grace, a few landed belly-down on the saddle, and one unfortunate youngster was bucked off in mid-mount. His horse danced away, trailing its reins. The recruit pursued his horse, but the animal eluded him, to the merriment of his companions. Laughs and taunts followed the unlucky lad until Ataulf took pity on him and captured the errant horse.

The recruits were on their sixth attempt when Placidia and the children drew close. Ataulf left the boys to their practice and trotted up to the party. A smile showed through his dust-streaked beard.

He plucked Ediulf off the shoulders of his guard and tossed him in the air, holding the horse still with his legs. The child gave a shrill shriek. Placidia held her breath and didn't let it out until the boy was safely in his father's arms. She shook her head. Children were evidently less fragile than she thought.

The girls clamored around the horse, but it stood its ground, eyes rolling. With a quick, snake-like move, the horse snatched the clover crown from Lilla's head, taking a few strands of hair with it.

"Ouch! You rock-headed piece of dog meat." Lilla threatened the horse's nose with her fist. Placidia stayed out of range of the big yellow teeth.

"Serves you right, tempting the poor beast with such delicacies." Ataulf dismounted, leaving Ediulf in the saddle clutching one of the four horns that helped keep the riders astride during battle. He tossed Maltha and Lilla up as well.

Vada refused to ride pillion behind the saddle, but did take her father's hand. "We brought delicacies for you, too, Father." She waved toward Placidia and the guards holding the baskets.

"I see." Ataulf's smile grew wider. "The princess is a most welcome delicacy."

"I believe Vada referred to the food her nurse prepared for us," Placidia said.

"Of course." His grin did not diminish. "There's a perfect place for a picnic over by that boulder."

Ataulf led the way to a depression filled with drying fall grass. They spread their cloaks. Placidia took custody of the baskets. "There's plenty here for all." She began passing out trenchers of bread, olives wrapped in grape leaves, whole roast chickens, yellow cheese and sliced cucumbers and onions marinated in a red vinegar. Placidia unstopped a wide-mouthed jar. "These must be for the children."

"Honeycombs!" Vada cried. "My favorite."

"Sweet after savory." Placidia handed the girl a packet of olives. The company fell on the food as if they had subsisted on gruel for days. Even Placidia ate more heartily than usual, but the most nourishing part of the meal was the warm feeling of belonging in some strange way—the lessening of the ache of loneliness.

The girls soon left to explore a nearby spring, followed closely by the guards. Ediulf fell asleep clutching a sticky honeycomb. Ataulf reclined on the cloaks, stroking the child's head. Tenderness smoothed the lines on his handsome face.

"He's a fine boy," Placidia said.

"He looks much like his mother."

"How did she die?"

"She was weakened by Ediulf's birth, and never recovered. She died of a fever last year." Ataulf spoke matter-of-factly, but his gentle caress belied the bluntness of his words.

"I'm sorry." Placidia covered his hand with hers. "It must be difficult for the children."

"I believe Vada misses her most. Lilla has a resilient spirit, and the younger two barely knew her." Ataulf turned her hand over, looked at it carefully, and rubbed the faint calluses she had developed while riding with his more deeply callused thumb. "I did not believe you when you said you were a good rider."

Placidia was surprised at how intimate that small movement of his thumb on her skin seemed. She retrieved her hand. "I learned from the best—my guardian Stilicho."

"Of course." He laughed at her puzzled frown. "You learned from a barbarian like me."

"Stilicho was nothing like you," she said hotly. It was true, physically. Taller than most men and strongly built, Stilicho had carried himself with such presence that people automatically gave way to him on the street. But, she grudgingly admitted to herself, Ataulf had his own presence. His compact body

38

exuded athletic grace, and his confidence stemmed from success.

"Because he was raised Roman?" Ataulf raised an eyebrow. "I, too, was raised in a Roman household—as a hostage in Constantinople after your father's treaty with our people."

"So that is the hurt you hold against Rome?"

"No," he laughed. "Princess, you are as prickly as a hedgehog. I value my experience among the Romans. I know how you think."

"Papa! Catch me!"

Placidia looked up to see Lilla launch herself from the top of the boulder, arms wide as if to fly.

Ataulf surged to his feet, caught his daughter under the arms, and swung her around using her momentum to toss her into the air again and catch her in both arms on the way down. Lilla screamed in delight. Ataulf laughed until he glanced at Placidia's face. "Princess, are you well? You are as pale as the clouds."

Unsticking her tongue from the roof of her mouth, Placidia managed, with only a slight quaver, to ask, "Does Lilla do that often?"

"As often as she can." He nuzzled his bearded face into the child's neck, sending her into a paroxysm of giggles. "Don't you, my little Amazon?"

"I'm going to be a warrior when I grow up, just like Papa."

Placidia frowned. She had lived in an Imperial court. She knew how savage and bloody-minded the female sex could be, but the idea of those who give life taking it in bloody combat seemed fundamentally wrong.

A distant crack of thunder intruded on her thoughts. Nana had been right. A storm approached—fast. Beyond the shelter of the boulder, Placidia saw grass and trees bowing before the wind.

Ataulf mounted his horse. "You'll be caught in the storm if you try to run. I'll bring mounts." He rode off, shouting to the guards to gather the children at the boulder, and soon returned with six horses and riders. The youngsters dismounted and held the horses. Placidia ran to the shortest one—a sturdy gray with black mane and tail.

"Do you want a boost up, Princess?" the boy asked.

"No, but give me your knife." Placidia held out her hand. Her look of command and the authority in her voice cowed the lad into obedience. Once he surrendered the knife, he frowned, looking as if he wanted to ask for it back.

Placidia cut the stitches in her tunic from mid-thigh to hem, then handed the knife back, much to the boy's relief. She leaped on the horse, gathered the reins, and settled the animal with her legs.

"Nicely done, Princess." She turned to see Ataulf grinning at her. "Maybe you should train my troops." He looked up at the clouds rolling in. The grin vanished. "Make a sling of your cloak. You'll take Ediulf. I'll do the same with Maltha. The older girls can ride astride with two of the guards."

"What of your men?"

"Wars aren't fought only in sunshine. They will stay and practice in the storm."

They soon had the children secured. Ediulf, still sleepy from lunch, settled into the sling and turned his small head toward Placidia's breast. His sticky lips made smacking sounds until his thumb found its way into his mouth. Unfamiliar warmth spread from deep in her chest, to throb in her breasts. But Placidia had little time to ruminate on this sensation, as Ataulf took off across the valley.

Placidia kicked her horse into a lumbering lope. Army horses had to carry fully armored men and all their possessions. They were bred for sturdiness, not speed. Placidia felt the beast's lack of grace between her thighs, and regretted the loss of her own easy-gaited horses.

The storm raced across the hills toward the villa. Lightning flashed from cloud to cloud, and occasionally to the ground.

Ataulf kicked his horse into a full gallop down the rise toward the creek. The other horses followed suit. They jumped the creek and headed up the hill into the orchards, ducking under branches. Placidia's gray extended his neck as he pounded up the slope.

She smelled the lightning before it hit—a metallic scent that tickled her nostrils and coated her tongue.

CRACK!

The flash caught in the top of a nearby apple tree. Her horse screamed and reared. Placidia clutched Ediulf with one arm, fought the horse down and urged him, nostrils flaring and eyes rolling, past the blasted tree. They raced through the orchard, ducking low branches as the first fat drops of rain fell.

By the time they reached the gate, all were soaked. The two unburdened guards came in last, shooting admiring glances at Placidia. She supposed there would be wild tales of her ride told around the fires tonight. She shoved straggling wet hair from her face. *By morning I will have the reputation of Queen Hippolyte—she of the stampeding horse.*

The nurse, waiting anxiously in the atrium, immediately took charge of the children. "I knew I shouldn't have let you go out…Lilla, look at your hair… What does the little one have smeared all over his face…You're soaking…You'll all catch your death; then what will become of me…"

Placidia turned to see Ataulf conferring with a massive barbarian. Valia, she remembered from the banquet. She caught the words "senators" and "Honorius" before they noticed her and stopped talking.

Ataulf waved over her sopping guard. "See the princess to her quarters, or to the baths, if she wishes." He and Valia hurried out of the atrium toward Alaric's reception room.

Placidia shivered, but not from the chill brought by the storm.

CHAPTER 6

ATAULF ENTERED THE *TRICLINIUM*, dripping rain water onto the mosaics. His king stood alone, chewing his mustache with fury. Most of the chiefs clustered in small groups talking, a few with frowns but most with cautious grins—the widest on Sergeric' s face.

"So Honorius refuses to negotiate, even for his sister." Sergeric's voice rose over the clamor. "I say we slit the Roman bitch's throat, and that of every other Roman noble we run down between here and Africa. We can feed them to our dogs."

Ataulf opened his mouth. A languid voice from the corner cut him off.

"The princess is much too valuable to waste as dog meat." Attalus, the former Emperor, casually drew a knife and cleaned his nails. "The man who marries the princess will control the next heir to the Roman Empire."

A few scattered voices rose in agreement. Ataulf remained silent.

"What man…" Sergeric spat. "… would want to father the next Emperor on that arrogant bag of bones, when he could take the diadem for himself?"

This drew a more sustained acclamation from the assembled chiefs.

"Fool! How would you cross the marshes of Ravenna?" Attalus drew himself up, pointing his knife at Sergeric. "Even if you could take Ravenna, do you think Emperor Theodosius will sit idly by in Constantinople and allow you to dismantle half of his empire? Your armies fled from the East to the more vulnerable West. You do not want to force the Eastern Emperor to send his troops."

Sergeric crossed the room to confront the Roman. "Do you challenge me?"

"Not in the least." Attalus reversed his knife and slid it into his belt.

"Enough!" The Gothic King pulled Sergeric around to face him. "I pledged the princess my protection and—for now—she lives. Perhaps Honorius will be more accommodating when we control his grain supply. We leave for Africa tomorrow. Go, all of you. Prepare your people for the journey."

Sergeric backed down, scowling. Not a few of the chiefs grumbled as they left the room.

"Your decision is not a popular one," Ataulf said.

The king finally noticed his brother-in-law's state. "God's blood, man! Were you trying to drown yourself?"

"Here." Attalus tossed a woolen cloak to Ataulf, then turned to the king. "Sergeric's influence is growing among the chiefs, particularly those not of your tribe. King Goar of the Alans is unhappy with his portion of the booty, and the pagan Huns grumble about your Christian sensibilities."

"I will take care of the Huns—they follow me." The cloak muffled Ataulf's voice as he dried his hair. "I'll allow them a few sacrifices and have a soothsayer give a favorable fortune." His hair curled about his forehead and ears in an unruly mass of dark red ringlets.

"Sergeric and Goar are easily countered," the king agreed. "I will send some handpicked men to drink around the campfires tonight and talk up the riches of the African province—not just plentiful food, but cities filled with gold. The thought of additional plunder will turn their minds from desertion."

"An excellent strategy, Sire. Lead the men, and the nobles will follow." Attalus' teeth showed brightly. "Now that you have decided on a course, I will take my leave."

Ataulf followed the Roman out, clapping a hand on his shoulder. "You put up a most spirited defense of the princess, considering you are not in the most secure of circumstances."

"I would give my life for Placidia. She is an exceptional woman."

"I see." Ataulf scowled.

"I don't think you do." Attalus gave him a warm smile. "I was married once to a very lovely girl with little on her mind beyond the latest fashions. She died several years ago giving me a son. I much prefer my unmarried life. Placidia is a valued friend and ally, no more."

"Has she bestowed her affections on anyone in particular?"

"Placidia was quite fond of her cousin Eucherius, to whom she was betrothed, but he was executed along with the rest of Stilicho's family three years ago."

"Do others press their suit?"

"General Constantius is quite taken with her. He is a formidable man and much in the Emperor's favor at the moment." Attalus thumped him on the back. "If—at some future time—you wish the key to Placidia's heart, look to the man closest to her in her youth—Stilicho. She measures all men by his standard."

They arrived at a back stairs leading to the private rooms on the second floor. Ataulf scratched his bearded chin. "You give me much to think about."

"Good. Now I must assemble my meager possessions for the coming trek." The Roman put on a rueful face. "I suppose we will be eating journey food again?"

"I AM SICK TO DEATH OF EATING DUST!" Placidia swished a mouthful of water and spat over the side of the lumbering wagon. "When will we reach Naples?"

"Soon enough, Princess. Within a day or two." Paulus, fully recovered from his head wound, seemed to enjoy Alaric's trek down the length of western Italy. The young, sick, and infirm rode in heavy wagons, while the rest of the women, children, slaves, and foot soldiers walked. Placidia had tried the wagons and wondered that any sick person could survive, much less recover, amid the wretched bouncing. She preferred to walk, but occasionally jumped into her wagon to ease her legs or take some water.

Placidia called to the back of the wagon. "Cook, how does Lucilla?"

The battered girl could not walk far without pain.

"About the same. She seems not to mind…oh!" The wagon hit a hole and jarred all their bones.

Placidia let loose a string of curses under her breath. Paulus turned with wide eyes. "You blistered my ears, Mistress. Where did you learn such language?"

"From a crude old soldier, where else?" The coppery taste of blood filled her mouth. "This cursed wagon made me bite my tongue. How bad is it?" She stuck out her tongue and looked down her nose cross-eyed to see for herself.

"My mother once told me that if I made such a face, a cold wind would freeze it forever." A pleasant male voice came from above and to her right.

Placidia glanced up to see Ataulf grinning from the back of his horse. She thanked the angels that her cheeks were already flushed with the heat and Ataulf could not see her blush.

"My nurse told me something similar, but I felt it safe in this heat." She fanned herself with her hand and envied him his mount. The cavalry ranged ahead and to the sides, scouting for food, campsites, and enemies—away from the dust.

"I'm sorry we don't have a litter for you, princess." Ataulf pulled his mount to a slow walk beside the wagon. "But I might be able to procure you something of equal value in avoiding this dust."

"The king will allow me a horse? Does he not fear I will escape?"

"We will find you a slow old nag, and you will be well escorted." He offered a hand. "Come up behind me. We'll find you a suitably decrepit mount."

"Paulus, I'll return before we camp for the evening." She grabbed Ataulf's hand and swung up behind him, one knee around a horn for balance, grateful for the barbarian trousers she wore under her full tunic. Placidia put her arms around Ataulf's waist and felt the solid warmth of him beneath his clothing. She knew she should draw back and cast down her eyes like a virginal maiden, but she had given up such stratagems when she decided not to be a tool in her brother's or others' marital machinations.

Ataulf picked his way through the wagons, baggage carts, and foot soldiers to the rear of the horde, where the cattle and spare horses were herded. One of the wranglers came forward to meet them, leading a trim black mare with a white star on her face, saddled and bridled in fancy leather tack with silver inlay. The saddle was the eastern kind—padded with a high ridge front and back to hold the rider in place—not the four-horned military style.

"Here's your nag—a gift."

"She's beautiful." Placidia slid to the ground and approached the horse. She opened the mare's mouth. The cavalry generally used bridles with a protrusion that cut cruelly into the roof of their horse's mouth and insured instant obedience. She understood the need for control in a battle, but she would not use such a torturous instrument on her mount. Satisfied with the civilian bit, she felt each leg and inspected the hooves for splits, fungus, or stones. Placidia straightened and patted the mare on the neck. "She's in excellent condition. Where did you get her?"

"One of my men brought her in yesterday. The tack is mine, but not suitable for battle. She's too light for cavalry and too pretty to eat."

"You do not really eat horses?"

"Only when we have to."

The mare whickered and lipped her palm, looking for treats. Placidia rubbed the horse's nose. "What's your name, pretty one?"

"Name her what you wish. She's yours."

Placidia traced the star on the mare's forehead with her finger. "I'll call her Night Sky."

"A good name."

She took the reins, held the front ridge, and threw herself into the saddle without waiting for a helping lift from the wrangler. Night Sky held steady until Placidia sat firmly astride, her tunic hitched above her knees. Then the mare arched her neck and pranced sideways for her new mistress. Placidia put her through her paces under Ataulf's watchful eye. The animal was so responsive to leg and heel, she hardly needed the reins.

"She's perfect!"

"She'll do," Ataulf agreed. "You can have one of your escorts bring her back when you are done riding. She should be put with the other horses to graze. Do you have room in your wagon for her tack?"

"I will make room if I have to throw out my clothes chest."

"No need for that. Just tell me and I'll assign you a baggage cart." He grinned, flashing bright teeth. "Come, I promised you a change from the dust. We can get away from it up in those hills."

They headed east toward low foothills. Placidia noticed they did not travel alone. Her personal guard followed at a discreet distance. She didn't mind. Traveling on a well-mannered mount, in companionable silence, with an intriguing man, was a pleasure she hadn't enjoyed in countless months. That pleasure didn't stop her speculating on Ataulf's motives.

When they reached a low rise, she stopped to watch the horde of people and wagons crawl its way down the coast. Ataulf reined in beside her.

Placidia patted the mare's neck as the horse reached for a likely tuft of grass. "Sky is a fine animal. Why so generous a gift?"

"A princess should not ride in the wagons like a child or slave. Gaatha thought you might enjoy being with her and her ladies."

"So this was Gaatha's gift?" Placidia felt disappointment that Ataulf had not done this on his own.

"She suggested you join her, but the horse was mine to give. You performed so well on that jug-headed nag during the storm; I thought you deserved a better mount." He ran his hand through short-cropped hair. "I wish I had thought of it earlier. The first two or three days on the march are usually chaotic, and I'm called upon to sort out many a tangled knot."

"Thank you. It's a most thoughtful—and appreciated—gift." She sat in silence a few moments. "What will you do in Africa?"

"Put your brother between the anvil and the hammer."

"My brother sees only the here and now and what's best for Honorius at the moment."

"I suspected as much. Alaric believes Honorius responds only to direct force and immediate threat. If we can cut off Italy's food supply, your brother may yet be persuaded to treat with us."

She turned away to stare across the valley. "And my fate?"

"My people are of two factions. Some want to continue the fight with Rome, destroy their cities, and take their gold. They seek to persuade Alaric to put you to death. Others see the advantage of allying with Rome, learning new ways, and sharing in the prosperity they see around them. They would renew negotiations to return you to your brother."

"And to which faction do you belong?"

"Both...and neither."

"You would seek my death?"

"Never." He inched his horse closer until his leg lay next to hers. "Alaric and I travel a narrow path between the factions. I find much to admire about the Romans, but also much that I abhor. Most Romans in power live on the graft and perfidy of others, without regard for the good of their people."

"You give favors to your retainers and honors to your relatives. It's the way of the world to take care of your own." Placidia did not rein Sky aside, but left her leg touching his. Heat radiated from the touch, even through the fabric. His? Or hers?

"Yes, but my men are bound by loyalty oaths. They share in the wealth and fate of their tribe. Rich Romans take, but do not give back."

"The sycophants do seem to infest the court. But a strong Emperor can contain and punish such behavior. A few good men resist temptation, even in my brother's court. You know of General Constantius?"

Ataulf gave her a quizzical look. "Yes. He negotiated with us in good faith."

"He is renowned for his honesty and loyalty; first to my father, and now my brother."

"And to you?"

"He has expressed duty, affection, and concern for my safety in letters since I left the court." Placidia raised an eyebrow. "Why do you ask?"

"The General's affection for you complicates matters. On one hand, he might be more open to negotiation, and pressure your brother in our favor. On the other, he might be more implacable in our destruction out of revenge."

"He has no army lapping at your heels." Sky wandered a few steps in search of fresher grass.

"Perhaps." Ataulf asked, "Do you return the General's affection?"

"What an impertinent question! I needn't provide you with the intimate details of my life to further your tribe's ambitions." Placidia pulled the mare's head up and heeled her forward.

Ataulf grabbed the bridle as she passed, this time bringing them knee to knee. "My apologies, Princess. I do not seek this knowledge on behalf of Alaric, but on my own."

"Do you present yourself as a suitor?"

"No." Ataulf released the bridle and swept her a bow from the saddle. "It would be arrogant for one of my station to so presume."

"Then it is still an impertinent question." Placidia glared at him. "I believe it's time we returned to the march."

"Of course, Princess."

Placidia had the distinct impression he laughed at her the entire trip back.

CHAPTER 7

SIX WEEKS LATER, Placidia rode with Gaatha and a few hardy ladies at the head of a reduced and dispirited horde. The Gothic king's attempt to cross the strait to Sicily and onward to the grain fields of Africa had ended in disaster. Storms destroyed the first force sent to sea. Rumors reached them that a miraculous statue of an ancient fertility goddess protected Sicily from the invaders as well as from the fires of Etna. The remaining men refused to set foot off dry land. Now they trekked north up the west coast of Italy to find winter quarters.

Placidia looked up as a brisk breeze stirred her cloak. A hazy gray curtain, moving slowly across the western plain promised a damp evening. Late autumn rains occasionally turned the ubiquitous dust to mud. She was of two minds as to which she preferred.

The women dismounted on top of a ridge to let the horses rest, and gazed behind them at the wagons and people stretching to the horizon. Gaatha stood next to Placidia. "It's an appalling sight. My people cover the land like locusts, strip it bare, and leave hunger and devastation in their wake. If we could have crossed to Africa, we might have avoided this."

Placidia was not surprised at her candor. She had found the Gothic Queen to be honest and without guile. In many ways, Gaatha had become a friend, but Placidia's status as hostage kept them from acknowledging that fact.

"What will you do?"

"My husband wants to go into winter camp near Naples and try the crossing again in the spring."

"It will be a hungry winter." Placidia looked over the bare fields and stripped orchards. "You left little behind on your way south. You might be able to buy food in the markets, but prices will be high."

"I know." Concern crinkled the corners of Gaatha's eyes. "We carry the wealth of Rome in our wagons, yet we will go hungry."

"What advice does your brother give?"

"Ataulf would take ship in Naples to fresh fields in Gaul or Spain, but the nobles will not support him in a sea voyage. We will go by land in the spring."

"So you will leave Italy." Placidia chewed her lower lip.

Gaatha, noticing her agitation, took her hand. "Do not be disturbed, my dear. I know we provide but a poor shadow of the life you led before, but you will come to no harm with us."

"There have been some consolations in my captivity." Gaatha for one, and Ataulf for another.

In spite of his denial, Ataulf acted like a suitor. He had been most attentive during the past weeks, insuring Placidia and her people had the best food and most comfortable lodgings. An Imperial Princess might expect such attention, but not the rides into the country or the gifts of books. When he learned what she liked to read, Ataulf searched among the looted treasures of Rome for her favorite authors. Placidia smiled at the memory of the last one—*Amores*, a book of love poems by Ovid.

Gaatha squeezed her hand, bringing Placidia out of her reverie. The Queen nodded toward the west. "We should repair to our wagons before the coming rains douse us, and I must speak to Machaon." Gaatha hid her concern from her ladies, but Placidia knew from Ataulf that Alaric was seriously ill of the fever that had plagued him since they left Rome.

"I seek his advice as well. I'll accompany you to his wagon."

PLACIDIA RETURNED FROM MACHAON'S WAGON to find Lucilla under a tent lit by a smoky torch. She looked pale, her hazel eyes red-rimmed; her light brown hair hung in ragged wisps. As Placidia entered, the girl lifted her eyes with a gleam of anticipation. Then, seeing the male escort, her gaze fell to the fire and she crossed her arms tightly, clutching her body.

"Lucilla, come with me. I need your services." Placidia indicated the wagon. The girl rose and clambered after her.

Placidia settled herself on a chest and indicated a box for Lucilla to sit, where the flickering light from the torch illuminated her face. The cuts had scabbed and healed, leaving livid scars across the left side of her face. The girl had a habit of reaching up and rubbing them, as if they itched.

"Lucilla, you know I am your friend?"

The girl nodded and grabbed Placidia's hand, bringing it to her good cheek.

"Cook tells me you have been sick lately, most often in the mornings."

Lucilla dropped Placidia's hand and grimaced, pantomiming eating disgusting food.

Placidia chuckled. "I agree, the food is less than appetizing, but I must ask you some questions. How old are you?"

She held up ten, then four fingers.

"You are just fourteen years old?"

Lucilla nodded.

"Have you ever had monthly courses?"

Even in the firelight, Placidia saw a touch of color stain the girl's cheeks. She cast her eyes down and held up two fingers.

"How many weeks between?"

Lucilla shrugged.

"Were you... with child before we left Rome?"

Lucilla looked puzzled and shook her head vehemently.

"No courses in seven weeks and frequent sickness are signs you might be pregnant."

Lucilla plastered her hands on her stomach, stretching the material of her tunic tight. She looked up at Placidia with wild eyes and started rocking back and forth, her mouth stretched in a silent scream, fingers clawing at her stomach.

Placidia took the mute girl's hands in hers. "Stop that! Listen to me, Lucilla. I have something which will bring on your courses." She showed Lucilla a bottle. "Machaon said to take half tonight and half tomorrow night, if you do not bleed during the day. There will be pain, and more blood than usual. Do you wish to do this?"

Lucilla stared at Placidia. Tears welled in her eyes to trickle down her cheeks; the first Placidia had seen since she rescued the girl. Lucilla nodded and reached for the bottle.

"I'll pour it for you." Placidia took a cup from a box and poured half the bottle into it. The potion smelled musty, of earth and mushrooms. Lucilla drank it eagerly, then again captured Placidia's hand and brought it to her cheek in thanks.

"If the blood flows heavily and does not clot, let Cook know at once. Try to sleep now, Lucilla. We'll talk again tomorrow."

Placidia left Lucilla to go to Gaatha's nearby wagon. She pulled her woolen cloak over her head to counter a steady drizzle. She noted that the women busied themselves with cooking, but there was none of the usual banter and song. Even the children were solemn, a rarity in the Goth camp.

She spied Ataulf speaking with a knot of Gothic nobles, and approached. He said a final word to the men. They dispersed with glum faces.

"Is the king worse?" Placidia put her hand on his arm.

"His fever is high. He thrashed about this afternoon, but now he's in an unnatural sleep. Even Gaatha cannot rouse him." Ataulf covered her hand with his. "Machaon is tending him."

"What does he say?"

Ataulf shrugged. "What does any healer say? Alaric might live or he might die. But he is a strong man, not yet forty."

"But if he dies?"

"Then we elect a new leader."

"I thought you were his heir."

"The Gothic King cannot rule without the consent of his people, particularly the other nobles. Most will follow me, but food is growing scarce and some think with their stomachs. I might be challenged." He lifted her hand to his lips for a brief kiss. "No matter the fate of the kingship, I swear to protect you, Princess. Alaric promised no harm would come to you or yours, and his promise is my promise."

"Thank you." She lowered her eyes and reluctantly withdrew her hand. "I should attend your sister. Perhaps I can be of some use."

"THE KING IS DEAD!" The cry spread through the camp late the next morning, followed by shouts and wails.

Placidia hurried to the open center of the circled wagons, seemingly with every able-bodied male in attendance. For once she was grateful for her guard, who made a wedge of their bodies and lanced through the crowd. Ataulf stood on a rude wooden platform, Gaatha at his side. Their children ranged behind them, little Ediulf conspicuous for being the only male child.

Gaatha stepped forward. Grief marred her face; deep shadows bruised her eyes. "My husband, your king, is dead of a fever. We have no son to follow in his footsteps, but we will not go leaderless." Ataulf joined her. Gaatha put her hand on his arm. "It was Alaric's wish—witnessed by his nobles—that Ataulf succeed him as your king. My brother is a brave warrior and skilled leader. He will serve us well." She stepped back, leaving Ataulf to address the crowd.

"Alaric was a great king, beloved by us all. We should take time to mourn our loss and honor his life. I request the nobles join me for a council. The rest of you, go back to your wagons and prepare for the funeral feast."

The crowd milled for several moments. Placidia headed for the platform, arriving in time to see Ataulf's back as he led a number of the Gothic nobles off to a sizeable open space. Gaatha and the children clambered down from the dais. Placidia approached the Queen and took both her hands.

"I am so dreadfully sorry."

Gaatha looked around, distracted. "There are so many things to do. I must arrange the feast, and…the body…it must be prepared."

Tears tracked down her cheeks. Her body shook with suppressed sobs. Her half-grown daughters tried vainly to comfort her with pats and murmurs, but Gaatha seemed inconsolable.

A knot of Gaatha's attendants stood a short distance away. Placidia motioned to one of the older, more levelheaded ladies. "The Queen is in need of sleep and food. Perhaps Machaon has a draught to calm her nerves and allow her sleep. There is much to do, and Lady Gaatha should not have to do it all."

"I will take care of everything, Princess. We have buried many a man, woman, and child these past years. We know what to do." The older woman took Gaatha's arm and clucked soothingly, leading her toward her wagon. The other attendants followed.

Placidia thought to accompany them, but hesitated. The wall of female backs seemed unassailable. At a loss, she returned to her wagon. Her people huddled around a noon fire, looking anxiously about. They were outsiders, as was she. This tragedy put the lie to her fragile feelings of safety and belonging.

She motioned to Paulus, who limped to her side. "Mistress, what will become of us?"

"General Ataulf has pledged protection."

"Can we count on him, or should we use the confusion to try an escape?" His eyes glittered at the possibility. "The wilds of Mount Vesuvius lie just beyond those hills."

"We cannot safely take everyone, and I will not abandon Cook, Lucilla, and the others to revenge or torture. I believe we should trust in the general to protect us." She put her hand to her head. A pain was building at her temples. "Tell the others that we are safe, and to go about their duties."

"As you say, Princess."

Cook stirred some stew at their hearth. "Have some food, Mistress. The bread is fresh baked."

Placidia sat and munched on a roll. "How is Lucilla today?"

"She started her courses. She bleeds heavily and is in pain. I gave her some willow bark tea and it's eased somewhat." Cook poured a minty-smelling brew into a cup and handed it to Placidia. "You look in need of some yourself, Lady."

"A slight head pain." Placidia sipped at the tea. "Thank the heavens; Lucilla is relieved of her trial. She would have hurt herself or the babe, once she knew she was with child."

"Or died in the birthing." Cook shook her head. "My brother gave my niece to wed when she was but thirteen. The poor girl was dead, and her babe with her, within the year. A girl's body needs to grow a bit itself before it can safely grow a child."

"I thought most girls are married after sixteen."

"Our betters have the right of it. But poor girls are just extra mouths to feed. After their first courses, they are frequently given to a man."

Placidia handed the empty cup to Cook. "I'll see if she needs anything."

As evening shadows lengthened, Ataulf came to visit. "May I speak to you in private?"

Placidia nodded. They stepped out of the firelight into the wagon's shadow.

"I've been elected king, but at a price. The feeling against Rome is strong. I cannot negotiate your release at this time."

Placidia stood silent, ashamed of her feelings of relief. She didn't want to return to Rome or her brother's court. Yet what could be gained by staying? The Goths were not her people. She was an Imperial Princess and, although now a king, Ataulf could not aspire to her hand. At no other time did she so bitterly regret the accident of her birth.

"Do you share this anti-Roman feeling?"

"Not for all Romans." He put his hand to her cheek. She trembled. "You're cold. Here, take my cloak." He enveloped her in his woolen cloak, which smelt of horses and his own musk, and held her in the warm circle of his arms, which only increased her trembling. "Romans are a dying people," he murmured into her hair, "corrupt and greedy. The future is with my people. As you saw today, we freely elect our leaders. People can leave, if they choose."

She stiffened. "Is this truly what you believe, that I'm greedy and corrupt?"

"No, Princess. Not you, but your brother and his advisors, they bleed this country, enslave its people. Rome was once great, but now it cannot even field a decent army."

She, better than most, having grown up in the royal household, knew that the rich had their hands on the levers of power. They held all the most powerful and lucrative posts in the government. But it had ever been so.

She stepped away from his embrace, and searched his shadowed face. "It is the nature of things that the rich rule the poor, and that God-anointed emperors rule them all. Without a strong hand to administer the laws, there would be chaos. You speak of your ways as superior, but I've not seen it. Blood feud and right of arms do not make a stable government."

"Placidia, I did not come to you to argue." He held out his hands, empty palms up. "I know you are anxious to return to your own people, but that is not possible at this time."

"It's true, I did not come here of my own will, but," Placidia faltered, "I have developed some affection for…your people, and understanding of their plight."

"Only my people?"

"That is all I can allow myself. I hope, when I do return to court, I can influence my brother on their behalf."

"I see." His eyes searched her face. She hoped she schooled it to some bland demeanor.

They stood in silence. Placidia longed for his touch, but feared it as well. She could not give her heart to a man who despised her people and way of life.

"We should go back," she said at last, taking off his cloak and returning it to his empty hands.

"Yes."

The disappointment in his voice brought a constriction to her throat. Ataulf was a proud man. She hated hurting him.

A thought tugged at her as he escorted her back to the light. Could she soften his heart towards Rome?

Maybe.

If she had time.

CHAPTER 8

Two days later, Ataulf stood beside his sister as nobles and their chief supporters filed past Alaric's elaborate limestone sarcophagus. The pastoral scenes carved on the sides were better suited to the rich villa owner from whom they took it than a warrior king, but they had little choice. The nobles ranged themselves in the front of the crowd, which stretched down a hill and filled the valley. People wailed their grief, women tore at their hair, and men beat their breasts. Gaatha stood tall and dry-eyed, adorned with gold and jewels in honor of her husband's generosity.

Ataulf found it hard to believe the wasted corpse in the red silk tunic and purple cloak was Alaric. With his sunken cheeks and gray complexion, the former king looked old and withered—a victim of a foe he couldn't fight. Ataulf had witnessed and dealt gruesome death, but this sent a wave of cold dread splashing through his bowels. Better to die in battle, looking your foe in the eye, than waste away from disease.

At least the stricken king was honored with appropriate treasure: the body surrounded with jeweled knives, silver plate, gold coins and gems. Alaric wore a golden diadem inlaid with emeralds on his forehead, and a gold torque around his neck. Ataulf had personally placed a long sword's ruby-encrusted hilt in his dead leader's hands.

The nobles and their lieutenants processed past the open sarcophagus. When the last one stepped off the dais, Ataulf addressed the mourning people. "We have come to honor a truly great and worthy man—a king and a warrior.

King Alaric spent his life forging us—Tervingi, Greuthungi, Alan, Alamanni, Hun—into a sword that scythed through the heart of the Roman Empire!"

A sustained roar lifted from the crowd.

When it died down, Ataulf resumed, his voice cracking with passion. "Alaric led us in battle and in peace. He strove to find us—his beloved people—a homeland where we would be safe from hunger and want. He provided us with the riches of Rome and Italy…"

Another clamor from the crowd gave Ataulf a chance to watch the faces before him. Most expressed honest sorrow, a few anger. He had asked Placidia and Attalus to remain at the camp, under heavy guard, so they would not become targets of misplaced grief or the tools of another's political ambitions. When the crowd quieted, Ataulf continued, listing Alaric's military accomplishments and extolling his virtues.

He ended nearly an hour later. Bishop Sigesar said a final prayer as four hefty slaves lifted the stone lid onto the sarcophagus. Two more men brought out the elaborately decorated chair Alaric had used as a throne, and a smaller, but no less ornate, one for Gaatha.

His sister stepped forward. Her strong voice wafted over the crowd. "By the grace of God and the wisdom of our nobles, we have a new king. Long may he reign, King Ataulf!"

The shout rising from the people surpassed any before, and settled into a chant acclaiming Ataulf as King. Gaatha turned to him with a sad smile, placed a gold torque about his neck, a plain circlet of gold on his head, and a massive signet ring on his finger. She kissed him on the cheek, then whispered, "May God bless you with wisdom, health, and happiness, my brother."

"And you," he replied.

Ataulf and Gaatha took their seats for the ritual oath-taking and gift-giving. He leaned back, eyes sharp. Any noble who did not wish to take service with Ataulf could return to the widow the oath-gift from Alaric and half the booty he acquired during his service to her husband.

In strict order of precedence, the nobles approached. Valia bowed on one knee, head down.

"I pledge my honorable service and that of my noble men, My King. We are yours to command. We will serve you bravely and faithfully, until your death or ours. I swear this in the name of God the Father, Christ the Son, and the Holy Ghost."

"I accept your oath. Rise, Valia, my friend, and take this gift from my hands as a symbol of our bond. You may keep this oath-gift in perpetuity, to hand down to your heirs—may they be plentiful."

A murmur ran through the crowd. Ataulf smiled. Oath-gifts were usually for the term of service only and returned to the patron if a noble took service with someone else. Ataulf would give permanent gifts to all his nobles, thus binding them tighter to him and showing his generosity. No King of the Goths remained king long who could not, or did not, spread rewards among his nobles. That, and self-defense, was what held these disparate people together.

Valia rose, grinning through his mustache at the sword Ataulf presented him. It was Spanish Roman, with a reworked hilt showing interlocked rings to symbolize the relationship between king and noble. Valia drew the blade from its gold-worked, red leather scabbard and flashed it in several practice swings. The long heavy sword fit Valia's massive frame.

In addition, Ataulf held out a fine leather baldric to hold the sword on Valia's back, and a heavy bag of gold.

"You are too generous, My King," Valia said, handing the additional gifts to an attendant.

"Use it well, my friend." Ataulf grasped Valia's forearm. His lieutenant would undoubtedly distribute the coin to his own men, thus spreading Ataulf's reputation for generosity.

The afternoon passed as Ataulf accepted oaths and passed out further gifts—less valuable swords, helmets and pieces of armor, jeweled belt knives, decorated drinking horns, and gold—always valued according to the noble's rank and precedence. No one refused to take service with him. No one returned their oath-gift to Alaric's widow. When the last of the treasure had been distributed, Ataulf rose.

"Let the feasting begin!"

The savory smell of roasting meat, mixed with the sharp scent of wood smoke, permeated the camp. Ataulf, Gaatha, the nobles and their ladies retired to the same tent used only a few weeks before to celebrate the fall of Rome. Food grew scarce this time of year, but this was no time for parsimony. Ataulf had ordered cattle, pigs, and sheep slaughtered. Tables groaned under the last of the vegetables, olives, cheese, and bread. People drank their wine unwatered. Singing rose in the camp as the nobles enjoyed the talents of musicians playing lyre, flute, and drums.

"Remember the time Alaric…" Tales of the former king's courage, wit, and strength circled the table, growing more elaborate and outrageous as the drinking continued. Ataulf drank lightly and of well-watered wine. He had a final duty to his king to perform that night.

Gaatha ate and said little. After a suitable time, she and her ladies retired to a quieter tent, leaving the men to their revels. Placidia had asked to join the ladies after the feast and Ataulf had given his permission. Perhaps the princess would bring some comfort to his grieving sister. He had watched with pleasure their growing friendship. He welcomed anything that bound Placidia closer to him. *If only she wasn't so stubborn about her privileges…*

He shook his head. Then she would be little different from all the other women he knew.

Well after the moon had set, Ataulf rose and nodded to Valia. They left the feast and gathered together an escort of Valia's most trusted men, who likewise had partaken lightly of spirits. They advanced toward the women's tent. Ataulf lifted the flap.

"It is time, Gaatha."

She rose. One of her women put a warm wool cloak around her shoulders.

Placidia half rose. Her dark blue gown, edged with silver, looked almost black in the dim light of the oil lamps. It accentuated her pallor and made pools of her large eyes, reflecting her concern and questions.

Ataulf shook his head. "This is for family only." He took his sister's arm and escorted her into the overcast night.

"WHERE ARE THEY GOING?" Placidia asked, after Ataulf and Gaatha left the tent.

"To bury the king," one of the ladies replied.

"In secret?"

"We are in Italy. We don't want Romans despoiling the body or looting the grave."

"But won't the men who prepare the grave…?"

The women looked at each other with knowing glances.

Placidia, remembering her tales of Egyptian Pharaohs, gasped. "Oh! But that's monstrous—the cold-blooded slaughter of innocent men."

"They are but slaves," one of the ladies explained.

"Roman slaves. But the King, Gaatha, Ataulf—they are Christians."

"Romans," another said, with some malice, "do not let their fine Christian sentiments interfere with their slaughters. I lost three sisters and their children to bloody Roman swords. Why should we mourn a few Roman slaves?"

Placidia scanned the faces in the flickering lamplight. Most cast their eyes down; a few returned her glance with a cold stare. Only two seemed to encourage her with shy smiles.

"I see." For the second time in three days she felt cast out of their company. She reflected on Ataulf's attitude toward the Romans. Maybe too much blood ran between both people for there ever to be reconciliation. "Good health to you, ladies. I will retire for the night." Placidia rose and left the tent stiff-backed. How could she have been so naïve as to believe she might find friendship among these women, or love from a barbarian man?

"ALL IS ARRANGED." Valia's massive form loomed black against black.

Ataulf and Gaatha continued to the hill where the sarcophagus was guarded by a contingent of warriors with torches.

"You are dismissed," Valia growled. The guards passed on their torches to the relieving warriors and headed eagerly for the feast. A half-dozen brawny slaves lifted the limestone coffin into a two-wheeled cart, most recently used to haul vegetables to market.

"This way." Valia led the procession down the hill, through a sparse wood, to the bank of an empty river. The bottom was muddy. The stench of rotting fish greeted them long before they reached the edge.

Ataulf put his hand on the coffin and whispered, "Farewell, my king...my brother. May you sit on God's right hand in Heaven."

Gaatha kissed her fingers and lightly touched the lid, tears sparkling on her cheeks in the torchlight.

Ataulf nodded.

The slaves maneuvered the cart down the crumbling bank, accompanied by Valia's curses as the heavy sarcophagus nearly slid out into the mud. At the bottom, Ataulf knew, flat stones placed in the riverbed eased the way to a deep pit in the center of the empty river. Torches flickered as slaves lowered the coffin into the pit with ropes, then filled the hole. They used the nearest paving stones to cap the grave.

Gaatha muffled her sobs with her hands.

The slaves clambered up the bank, legs and arms splashed with mud. Valia followed with about half the warrior escort.

"How far?" Ataulf asked.

"About a mile upstream." Valia wiped the mud off his boots with a rag.

"You, there. Get moving." One of the guards poked several slaves with a spear. Valia, his men, and the slaves loped up the river, leaving Ataulf, Gaatha, and a few trusted guards with torches.

"It'll not be long, Sister." They stood quietly for several moments. "Would you care to rest? I'll spread my cloak."

"No." Gaatha put a restraining hand on his arm. "I would rather stand."

After long moments, they felt a vibration in the air, followed by the booming rush of oncoming water. The river, loosed into its course, threw itself against a far curve, sending a muddy spray to drench the bushes. It came on, rolling rocks, branches, and the tumbling bodies of men.

When the river settled into its bed, there was no trace of the burial. Silt covered the capstones and water erased the gouges in the bank.

"It is done, then." Gaatha turned her back on the scene.

"SO THE BARBARIAN KING IS DEAD. It seems God does grant prayers." Honorius chuckled as he spread chicken feed for his pets.

Constantius watched the great black rooster Rome peck a rival for some choice bit. After a brief spat and a few lost feathers, Rome reigned supreme. The story of Honorius' reaction when Constantius had told the Emperor of Rome's fall had spread like a pernicious fever throughout the court. Constantius had had the wine-serving slave flogged and sold for that. Honorius needed no additional rumors of his eccentricities.

"Now, now, my pretties. No fighting. There is plenty for all." Honorius tossed more feed to a corner. The vanquished rooster raced for it.

"The Goths are in a weakened condition, Sire. They starve in their winter camp outside Naples. Let me negotiate for the release of your sister and their departure from Italy. They will likely give her up for food."

"No." Honorius' jaw set in a stubborn line. "Let them starve. They will be the weaker for it in the spring."

"And Princess Placidia?"

"She chose to leave the safety of Ravenna, and refused to return on my request. Let her stay with the Goths a while longer. It might bend her stiff neck."

Constantius' hopes sank. *Will he never forgive his sister's flight?*

"Besides, I have another commission for you." Honorius turned to the general with a sly smile. "It is time to topple that upstart, Constantine, in Gaul. I know not why the troublesome Britons elevate any army man with the name of Constantine to the purple. Since Constantine the Great, the others have all been failures."

"As will this one." Constantius, himself named after a former Emperor, showed his teeth in a wolfish grin. He had been lobbying for this post for two years, but Honorius had kept him close. Instead, that traitor Goth, Sarus, went north to bungle the campaign against the British usurper. Constantius had little respect for the man who first betrayed his Gothic people and then his master Stilicho.

"I know I can trust you, my friend." Honorius bowed to pet a fluffy yellow hen.

Constantius wondered if the emperor still spoke to him.

Honorius straightened. "I have a special honor for you, General. Before you embark on your campaign, you will be raised to *magister utriusque militia.*"

"Master of Both Branches of the Soldiery!" Constantius' heart beat so hard at achieving this ultimate command; he wondered the emperor didn't hear it. He bowed as low as he could without going to his knees in the chicken shit. "I'm more than honored, Most Generous and Gracious Lord."

"It's time. You've shown yourself most loyal and capable. I'm sure you can return Gaul and Spain to my domain." Honorius made a broad gesture with his arm, as if to indicate his domain reached from horizon to horizon. The effect was diminished by the confines of the chicken yard.

Constantius straightened. "I will send you the usurper's head. It will be a long time before the provinces rise in rebellion again."

And I will bring Placidia home.

Chapter 9

Ravenna, spring 412

Gᴇɴᴇʀᴀʟ Cᴏɴsᴛᴀɴᴛɪᴜs ʟᴇᴀɴᴇᴅ ʙᴀᴄᴋ, ᴇʏᴇs ᴄʟᴏsᴇᴅ. Warm water lapped at his chin. The quiet murmur of two ministers talking in the far corner of the pool echoed off the rare marbles inlaid in intricate patterns on wall and floor. *A long soak and a good massage are exactly what I need.* The luxury soothed his soul after his hard but successful campaign against Constantine in Gaul.

"May I join you?"

Constantius looked up at the patrician features and naked body of Dardanus, the new Praetorian Prefect of Gaul. He had found the man pleasant company as they traveled the war-torn province, restoring the local bureaucracy. The Prefect had come to Ravenna to seek provincial tax relief from Honorius.

"Welcome, my friend." Constantius waved over a slave. "Two goblets of your finest red wine—well mixed." Constantius enjoyed the conviviality of these public baths; contesting with friends in the large exercise yard, arguing philosophy in the library, watching the entertainers.

The Prefect walked down the steps into the pool and settled with a sigh on the underwater ledge next to Constantius. "We have some fine baths in the provinces, but none as lavish as these." He swung his hand in an arc, indicating the mosaics, statues, and plants gracing the halls.

The wine arrived, and they chatted about the prospects of various chariot teams in the upcoming races. Constantius laughed at Dardanus' stories about

Claudian, a particularly unlucky driver of late. Then the Prefect turned glum. "Have you heard the Goths are on the move again?"

"Yes, the dogs finally leave Italy." Constantius sipped his wine.

"With the emperor's sister?" Dardanus raised an eyebrow. "It's been nearly two years. I recall a rumor while we were in Gaul that Ataulf proposed a marriage with the princess."

"Yes." He ground his teeth. Constantius had been nearly mad with worry until the emperor replied that no such proposal had been made and he wouldn't approve if it were. The bitter knowledge of her fear and misery had marred the sweetness of Constantius' military victories. "I had hoped to face Ataulf on the field of battle and win Placidia back by force of arms, but..." He shrugged. The Prefect knew the sad state of the Roman army. They had no men to spare after fighting the usurper; reducing Constantius—again!—to negotiating for her release.

"Did you know another usurper has declared himself Emperor in Gaul, and is offering the Goths terms for their support?"

"God's blood!" Constantius overset his goblet. The dregs of his red wine swirled and dissipated in the clear water. "Emperors sprout like weeds in Gaul. Who aspires to the purple this time?"

"I just received word. A local noble named Jovinus has declared himself Emperor and is backed by the Burgundian and Alan tribes. In return for their support, he is letting the Burgundians establish an independent kingdom on the Roman side of the Rhine. I suspect he will offer something of that sort to the Goths."

"Damn the eyes of the short-sighted idiots who pulled the frontier troops back to Italy. Our border has more holes than a poor man's tunic." Constantius leaned back into the water wearily. Another cup of wine arrived near his elbow without his asking. "What is Jovinus' strength? Where is his army?"

Dardanus shrugged. "The report just came in with the post. The military details will arrive later. However, something else of interest came with the packet. Guess who is negotiating with Jovinus on behalf of the Goths?" The Prefect took a deep drink from his goblet, smacked his lips, and relaxed against the wall.

Constantius, who did not appreciate playing political games, snapped, "Come on, man. Don't make me wait till Claudian wins a race."

Dardanus laughed at the jibe. "Attalus, the former Emperor, negotiates with the new one."

"That perfidious snake!" Constantius sipped his wine, looking blankly over the water. "That he is still alive is a testament to his powers of deception. What is he up to?" He shook himself out of his reverie and smiled. *Out of disaster comes opportunity. Placidia will be home before fall harvest.*

"We must speak to Honorius at once." Constantius heaved himself out of the water. "We need to prevent this alliance."

Southern Gaul

"JOVINUS HAS BETRAYED US," Attalus told Ataulf. "He has raised his brother to co-Emperor without your consent."

"Does no one in this God-forsaken empire keep his word?" Ataulf strode about the campfire, slapping his leg with a thin wooden switch. "I brought my people over the Alps from Italy on the promise that Jovinus would share power and land."

"Something may yet be salvaged. I have an interesting message from Dardanus, the new Praetorian Prefect of Gaul. He relays that the Patrician Constantius will settle your people in Aquitaine with a grain supply and payments to your warriors in return for your help in overthrowing Jovinus."

Ataulf turned to face Attalus. A frown marred his handsome features. The Gothic people were running short of food—again—and, to Ataulf, this sounded like the long-awaited offer from the Emperor.

"So General Constantius is now Patrician?"

"Don't you think the Emperor needs a father and advisor? At least Constantius is an honorable man. He deserves the title, after his successful campaign against Constantine."

"Exactly. Why does the new Patrician need us?"

"There is more pressing news from Ravenna. Encouraged by the uprisings, Count Heraclian of Africa has rebelled and is sailing for Italy with a thousand ships. Constantius goes to meet him. He can't fight two battles at once."

"So Constantius, and therefore Honorius, needs us." Ataulf laughed. "At last."

"Deposing Jovinus is not their only price for food, land, and gold."

"Placidia?"

Attalus nodded watching his companion carefully. He had observed the growing affection between Ataulf and Placidia with a mixture of alarm and pleasure. Alarm that it would come to naught and cause them pain. Pleasure in that he harbored a deeply romantic streak and the love story of an Imperial Princess and a Barbarian King had mythic qualities.

"Of course. They could not in honor leave her with us." Ataulf sat, shoulders slumped, and ran his hands through his hair. "I do not want to give her up. I have known no other woman who affects me so. Placidia is a woman of many parts: haughty princess, fiercely protective of her honor; and Amazon, who cares for nothing but the wild ride. She is kind and gentle with the children, but unbending steel when dealing with me."

"She's a challenge, but one worth taking."

"Yes." A rueful smile lit up Ataulf's face. "But her stubbornness angers me to distraction. Can she not be warm and yielding with me on occasion?"

"Has she been cool and sharp-tongued since you sent me to negotiate with Jovinus?"

"A snake would be warmer. Placidia told me she could not support anyone who supported a usurper; that any threat to her brother's sovereignty was a threat to her. She refused to speak to me further on the topic."

"Do not despair, my friend." Attalus clapped Ataulf on the shoulder. "She treated me the same when the Senate raised me to the purple."

"She's right, you know." Ataulf scratched at his beard. "Placidia can't support any other position without undermining her own legitimacy."

"Placidia was born to the purple and raised among the intrigues of the court. Her instincts for self-preservation are good, but her capacity for happiness and contentment withers for lack of either. Have you spoken to her of your feelings?"

"Only in hints and gestures. I believe she favors me, but these past two years have been like clinging to a log in a rushing river. When we occasionally hit a calm eddy, and I feel I can speak openly, the river pulls us into the next rapid."

"Tell her of your feelings, and be guided by her wishes."

Ataulf started pacing again. "If she were any other woman, I would have taken her to bed months ago and declared us married in the morning. Now, with this offer from Constantius, I am torn between my people and my love."

"A dog with two bones," Attalus mused.

"What?"

"A fable. A dog takes his favorite bone down to the water's edge, where he sees another dog in the water with a bone just like his. The dog wants both bones and reaches for the other in the reflection. In doing so, his own bone slips out of his mouth and disappears into the water."

"I see." Ataulf stood, head bowed in the firelight. "In trying to have it all, the dog was left with nothing."

"DISMISSED." MORE NOISE ERUPTED from the children than such small bodies had any right to make, as they exploded across the garden to scatter through the rooms of the "borrowed" country villa she currently lived in with Gaatha, Ataulf, and their families in southern Gaul. They would be on the move again soon, and it would be back to the wagons. She wondered if she should make room in her wagon for a few of the villa's books—for the children, of course!

Placidia had been appalled when she inquired of Gaatha and Ataulf about the children's education, only to find they had none. With the tribe on the move for many years, there had been no time for tutors or anything but basic living skills. She offered to teach any that wished Latin, history, and mathematics. Rhetoric would be wasted on those not destined for the law courts. Philosophy and religion she would leave to Bishop Sigesar.

She smiled, thinking of her own education in the domestic arts, Greek language and literature, and—her favorites—Roman history and law. None of the other girls she knew studied much beyond the domestic arts and enough math to oversee their households, but they were not the daughters of the Great Theodosius Augustus. *And they all have households to run and children of their own to supervise, while I am twenty-four and little more than a glorified tutor!*

Her pique lasted only until she overheard Vada scold little Ediulf as they sought a snack. She did enjoy being with the children. They were bright and took to their lessons well. It gave purpose to her long days. Placidia avoided the domestic arts, which she had always found tedious. Gaatha had tried to include her with the women of her court who spun and sewed, but her threads were hopelessly lumpy and her stitches uneven. After two years, she still did not find acceptance or comfort in the company of the upper class Gothic women. Gaatha once whispered to her that they were jealous. Most had expected their king to take another wife. Some had ambitions for themselves or their daughters, and were disappointed when Ataulf showed a preference for the Roman princess.

She stooped to pick up the stack of waxed wooden tablets on which the children took notes and did lessons with a sharp stylus. A familiar hand swooped in and gathered them up for her.

"Where would you like these?" Ataulf smiled at her.

Placidia stiffened. He had been avoiding her since their heated row about Jovinus. She wished she could take back the harsh things she had said, but Stilicho had taught her well. Her first duty was to the Empire and that meant to her brother, the legitimate Emperor.

"In here." She indicated the door to the library and followed him to the cabinet where he stowed the tablets. He turned to face her.

"How are the children doing with their lessons?"

"Vada and Maltha are doing exceptionally well. Ediulf is coming along. Lilla is bright enough, but diffident in her application."

"My little wild child. Lilla would rather learn to ride and handle a sword than a stylus."

Placidia frowned. "Is that permitted?"

"There is a tradition of warrior women among our people. Have you heard of the Amazons?"

"Of course. Anyone who's read Herodotus knows of the Amazons. Are you telling me they were Gothic women?"

"We were not known by that name then. A legend among my people says we traveled from Scandia and settled by the Pontus Sea in Scythia. Men of several villages went raiding, leaving their women. When a neighboring tribe attacked the women, they took up arms and successfully defended themselves. Heady with their victory, they went raiding themselves and conquered the whole territory. When their men came back, the women jeered at them and would only allow them to come into the villages once a year, to mate. Thus was born the tribe of Amazons."

Placidia laughed. "And you believe this tale?"

"Why not?"

"Your women seem to have a good deal more freedom than Roman women. Their advice is taken seriously and their wishes consulted when taking a husband. But warrior women?"

"When the men go off to war for long periods of time, they depend on their women to keep the homestead. A brave, smart, industrious woman is greatly valued by our men. They must run the household, manage the trading, oversee the harvest, and protect against raiders."

"Oh, dear!" Placidia clasped her hands in her lap. "Then I must be accounted as next to worthless, for I do none of those things."

Ataulf took her hands in his and turned them palm up. He ran his own callused fingers over the soft contours of hers, then looked into her eyes and said, softly, "You, Princess, are above price. How can someone put a value on the sunshine or joy? For when you smile at me, all is warm and light, and when you frown, my world turns cold and gloomy. Above all, I desire to make myself worthy of you."

Placidia sternly suppressed the exuberant feelings that threatened to crack her resolve. "Can you not set aside this alliance with Jovinus and treat with my brother? Offer him honorable service. You could become another Stilicho... with me at your side."

"I have decided to abandon Jovinus and fight for your brother's cause. The Emperor has promised us grain, gold, and a homeland in return."

"Ataulf!" Placidia let her joy show as she threw herself into his arms. "How I have longed to hear those words."

"That I love you? Or that I will treat with your brother?" Ataulf tightened his embrace.

"Both," she whispered as her lips sought his. She stood in the circle of his arms, feeling a warmth and lightness of spirit she had not known since she was a child. *This is where I belong, in his arms, now and forever. I will never love another as I love Ataulf.*

He gently pulled back from the embrace to look at her face. "I'm afraid our arms against Jovinus are not the only price asked. General Constantius wants you returned."

"No." She felt as if kicked in the stomach by a mule. Her hands grew cold.

He pulled her close again to his chest. His heart beat an irregular rhythm and his breath caught in a near sob.

"Placidia, between us as man and woman, I said you have no price, and that is true. But between us, as King and Imperial Princess, you do have one...that of my people's welfare. We are starving and have been wandering homeless for countless years. I will not force you to return to your brother, but I will ask you to for their sake."

Placidia regained her breath, but the pain remained, twisting her gut. Ataulf knew her well, to appeal to her sense of duty. No other plea would have worked. Bitterness and anger lay like ashes in her mouth. She broke away. "After we declare our love, you ask this of me? You expose my heart, then pierce it with this betrayal?"

His eyes glittered. With anger? Tears?

He put his hand under her chin and tilted her face to his. "I would rather slit my own throat than ask this of you, but I see no other choice. That's the sharp point of the sword. I can only be worthy of you by being a good king. And a good king looks after the welfare of his people before his own."

"I understand." And she did, but it didn't free the band around her heart or stop her tears. She grasped at one slender bough of hope. "You must promise that you will not send me back until Honorius fulfills the terms of the treaty."

"That is one promise I can easily make."

She returned to his arms, and they kissed with the urgency of imminent parting.

CHAPTER 10

Southern Gaul, Spring 413

PLACIDIA RODE PAST THE LUMBERING WAGONS, looking for Ataulf. Despite her fears, they had shared a whole winter together in southern Gaul. Now the horde headed north in search of Jovinus. A light spring rain misted the air, but did nothing to diminish the riotous colors of wild flowers and the trills of mating birds. Placidia took a deep breath and let it out slowly, savoring the smell of new grass and apple blossoms. Even the sight of Sergeric with Ataulf and Valia did not dampen Placidia's mood.

"I say we should move to Spain, where there is food, regardless of the treaty with Ravenna," Sergeric argued. "The Emperor hasn't kept his bargain. Why should we keep ours?"

"Because I gave my word to deliver Jovinus. When we turn him over, we will get our reward."

"Princess." Sergeric's mouth turned into a sour sneer as Placidia rode up. "I'll take my leave." He reined his horse sharply away from them.

Ataulf muttered, "That man will be the death of me. Sometimes I wish he would take service elsewhere. Do you think the Vandals would have him?"

"Perhaps." Valia watched the disgruntled noble go. "Pay him no mind. He'll get above himself one day and someone will cut him down."

Ataulf appraised Placidia with an appreciative eye. She loved how his face lit up at the sight of her, but sadness tinged his smile. The possibility of her leaving darkened their thoughts and lent urgency to their feelings.

Valia's smile was unshadowed by such gloomy possibilities. "Why does the princess join us today?"

"I needed the exercise, and so did Sky. Besides," she grinned, "did not my presence drive off the unwanted attentions of Sergeric?"

"Indeed it did." Ataulf laughed. "I much prefer your company to his. And you brought the sun with you!" Golden rays peeked through thinning clouds. Misty rain left crystal drops on leaves and spider webs.

"Iris must have a message from the gods; there is her rainbow." Valia pointed to a faint colored bow ending in a valley to their right.

"Iris? Messages from the gods? Are you not a good Christian, sir?" Placidia asked in mock seriousness.

"Of course, but are not the many gods all aspects of the One?"

"The priests would have us believe the old gods are false and aspects of the devil," Ataulf said.

"Let the priests natter as they please. I will believe what I believe. If Jesus the man and some unseen Holy Ghost can be part of God, so can Iris, especially on this beautiful day." Valia spread wide his arms as if to embrace the world. His silvering brown hair whipped in the breeze.

They turned their heads at the sound of running hooves. A young scout pulled his lathered horse to a walk beside them, and saluted Ataulf. "We've spotted General Sarus about ten miles from here."

Valia raised his eyebrows. "What's he doing in this region?"

"We captured one of his outriders, Sir. Sarus deserted Honorius over a blood feud. He is headed for Jovinus' camp."

"How many?"

The lad grinned. "Only a few dozen, and they're not in good shape."

Ataulf turned to Valia. "Gather your men and my Huns. We end this today."

The color seemed to leach from the surroundings as Placidia's mood turned dark. The thought that someone connected with Stilicho's death was within her grasp loosed anger and pain she thought long buried. "I want to go with you."

Ataulf looked at her, mouth stern. "No. Battle is no place for a woman."

"What of your Amazon ancestors?"

"They are my ancestors, not yours. You will stay here—safe."

"Sarus ate at our table, telling me stories and swearing his love for Stilicho. He butchered my uncle's Hunnish bodyguard and would have killed Stilicho, except Heraclian—with my brother's blessing—beat him to it. I want to watch him die."

Ataulf put a gentle hand on her arm. "I swear. All his betrayals will be avenged."

"Make sure of it."

The depth of her hatred shook her. Placidia had lectured Ataulf on the value of rule by law—how courts and justice avoided the endless rounds of death and pain engendered by a code of revenge and blood feud. Now she urged him on in his—and her—quest for personal justice.

Her hand crept to her throat. *Perhaps I've lived too long among the barbarians.*

ATAULF WATCHED PLACIDIA RETREAT. She continued to surprise him. He had seen her proud, frightened, stubborn, and loving, but never vengeful. The fury on her face as she spoke of Sarus made him proud. One must never forget the obligation one had to family and retainers. That loyalty was the bedrock of his beliefs. Sarus had betrayed every man he called Master.

The jangle of armor and curses of men stirred Ataulf from his reverie. He spotted the scout on a fresh horse, followed by the Hunnish cavalry. The eastern warriors were silent and grim. They had waited long to exact their revenge for the massacre of their comrades in Stilicho's service. Valia joined them with his men.

"Lead the way," Ataulf directed the scout.

They traveled through empty land—fields left fallow, no herds in the meadows. After an hour of riding, a second scout found them. "Sarus and his men are north. If we follow this line of trees we can head them off before they leave the valley."

"Excellent!" Ataulf gave the signal for silence.

They followed the scout to a broad depression that was cut by a meandering stream. A scattering of trees screened their movements from a small band of lightly armed riders making their way down the center of the valley. Sarus was conspicuous in his red Roman General's tunic and fancy white horse.

Ataulf considered the field. *A thousand to twenty-five. This will be more a massacre than a battle. But Sarus deserves little better.*

Ataulf raised his arm, sword in hand, and dropped it with a blood-curdling yell. The Huns surged forward, screaming their pagan war cries, splashing through the stream to encircle the surprised band. The eastern horsemen brought down their enemies with deadly accurate arrows and lariats—a weapon peculiar to their race. The bodies of men and horses littered the field without a Goth bloodying his sword.

Sarus lay pinned under his dying horse. The animal grunted, writhing in pain, arrows protruding from its flank and chest.

Ataulf rode forward at a trot. His horse snorted, rolling its eyes at the smell of blood and shit.

"For mercy's sake, put the beast out of its misery," Sarus grated between teeth clenched against his own pain.

Ataulf dismounted and sliced the horse's throat. It shuddered a moment, then lay still, eyes glazed.

"Your traitorous career is over, Sarus."

Sarus spat. "Do what you came to do and spare me the speeches."

Ataulf severed his head with one clean blow, to the wild cheers of his Hunnish retainers.

THE VICTORS RETURNED TO THE CAMP AFTER DUSK, tired and dirty. Placidia met Ataulf at his wagon.

"He's dead." Ataulf threw a blood-soaked bag at her feet. "A gift for your brother's collection."

She nudged it with her toe. She didn't know which repulsed her more, the bloody trophy, or the satisfaction that filled her heart at the news of Sarus' death? She sighed. What was done was done. She could not deny her feelings any more than she could bring her family back from the dead.

"Are you hurt, my love?" Placidia looked Ataulf over, searching for signs of injury.

"No." He ran a hand over his face, smearing dust and blood. "It was a long ride, and more slaughter than battle."

"What of Sergeric?"

"Sarus' brother?" Ataulf looked at her in surprise. "He has sworn allegiance to me. He could have joined his brother any time, and chose not to."

"I would be cautious of Sergeric."

"He opposes me in council, but that is his right. Better to have open opposition than secret plots."

"He lost a brother today. Traitor or not, won't he harbor resentments?" *I certainly would!*

"Possibly, but he would need to return his oath gift and declare blood feud before acting on them." He rolled his neck cracking the stiff tendons.

"You know your people better than I." Placidia shrugged. "On to pleasanter things." She motioned to a full-length tin tub. "Come, I have hot water on the fire for a bath."

He gathered her up in a hug. "Ever thoughtful, my love."

She laughed. "Let me down, or I might have to join you in the tub. You're covering me with dust."

"That's a tempting offer." He smeared her face with dirt as he kissed her deeply and thoroughly. She didn't protest further.

As the late summer sun climbed higher in the sky, Ataulf and his men ranged outside the city of Valence. Here Jovinus and his brother had taken refuge, after months of skirmishes and retreats. The heat already had the men sweating and the horses twitchy from flies. By afternoon, they would suffer for lack of water.

But Ataulf did not intend to be here past noon.

He gave the signal. Twenty thousand men surged forward, screaming battle cries and beating their swords on their shields. Archers sent a flight of burning arrows over the walls. Soon smoke billowed from the city. The defenders sent a few flights of arrows back, with little damage.

Within minutes of the show of force, the main gate opened and a delegation holding the green branches of truce exited. A troop of infantry escorted them to Ataulf, who remained mounted with his back to the sun. There were five men, four with the look of merchants and one with a military bearing—a balding man with sharp eyes and a stern mouth. He stepped forward, squinting. "Are you Ataulf, King of the Goths?"

"I am."

"I'm the leader of the Valence city council. I've come to ask you to spare our city."

"I have no interest in your city. I came in the name of our Emperor Honorius to apprehend the persons of Jovinus and his brother. They have illegally usurped the power of the *imperium* and must face trial in Ravenna. If you continue to shelter them, your city will be held accountable."

Several of Ataulf's men shouted and beat on their shields, causing all but the leader of the delegation to huddle closer together.

"I have the authority to negotiate Jovinus' surrender."

"And his brother's?" Ataulf leaned forward in the saddle.

"Yes." He waved impatiently. "What are your terms?"

"Both men will surrender to me within the hour. I will guarantee their safety and deliver them to the hands of the Patrician Constantius, who will convey them to the Emperor's presence."

"They will not go in chains."

"If they give their bond not to escape, I will not hold them in chains. They'll be well treated."

"Then you may expect them within the hour."

"We will hold off our attack for one hour. Not a moment longer."

The delegation let out a collective sigh of relief and retreated.

Ataulf sat his horse and waited to see if Jovinus would keep his word.

CHAPTER 11

Outside Valence, early fall, 413

NORMALLY A PATIENT MAN, Constantius moved from table to window to sideboard, back to table in an ever-increasing round of anxiety. He had come to this county villa outside of Valence to take custody of Jovinus and retrieve Placidia. It had been almost exactly five years since she had fled her brother's court for Rome; three since she was taken hostage. How had she fared? Had her beauty faded? Her spirit broken? *If they have harmed you in any way, my love, the Goths will pay in blood and misery.*

A soldier announced her arrival.

Constantius tugged on his uniform like a raw recruit. He took a calming breath and went to the entrance. A score of Gothic infantry guarded Jovinus and his brother. The red-haired barbarian on horseback must be Ataulf. Four burly slaves lowered a litter.

Placidia stepped out.

He caught his breath. Placidia had matured from the fresh innocence of twenty into a stunning woman of twenty-five. The one flaw, the sadness about her eyes, made them all the more large and appealing. She was dressed for the occasion in blue silk, her small waist cinched with a gold girdle. Blue gems glittered on her wrists, ears, and neck; and a pearl diadem held a nearly transparent silk veil over her cascading hair. She walked toward him with back straight and head proud, every inch a princess.

He dropped to one knee at her feet, bowing his head. "Princess, it is so very good to see you looking well."

"General. Or should I call you Patrician?"

"As you wish, Princess, but I prefer you call me Constantius."

She offered her hand. He rose, noticing the calluses on her palm. Did the barbarians make the princess do manual labor? His anger made his voice harsher than planned as he turned to the red-haired Goth. "You are Ataulf?"

"King Ataulf of the Gothic people. Here are Jovinus and his brother, as we agreed." Ataulf nodded toward the two heavily guarded men.

"Centurion, take the traitors into custody." A troop of Roman soldiers took the captives. The usurpers would spend the night in a locked cell; only their heads would complete the journey to Ravenna.

Constantius turned back to his guests. "Will you join me in the villa? We can better discuss the future in comfortable surroundings."

He offered Placidia his arm, leaving the barbarian king to trail them to a receiving room decorated with harvest scenes painted on the walls, and a mosaic of the goddess Ceres and her daughter Proserpina on the floor. Three chairs ranged around an intricately carved maple wood table. Slaves stood by with beakers of wine and trays laden with rich foodstuffs. Constantius settled Placidia in the largest chair, which was padded with red leather, the arms and back lavishly inlaid with mother-of-pearl and onyx. Not the throne she deserved, but it would do for now. He took the chair on her right, facing Ataulf.

Constantius motioned for the slaves to serve. Placidia waved the food away, in favor of well-watered wine served in delicate blue glass goblets with a silver rim.

"You eat well, General." Ataulf took a bite of a boiled egg, halved and stuffed with mushrooms.

"I have an excellent cook, who accompanies me on campaigns."

"My people should have such delicacies. Alas, they barely have bread. The grain you promised has not arrived."

Constantius frowned at the barbarian's directness. As host, it was his prerogative to bring up business.

Placidia distracted him from his irritation by raising a goblet. "Congratulations on your victory over Count Heraclian. I was surprised to hear he had revolted. He was one of my brother's most fervent supporters."

"The Count was infected with the contagion of rebellion which seems to rage throughout the provinces. It is my charge to put down any who get above themselves." Constantius glanced at Ataulf, who seemed not to take the warning.

"I am not sorry he is dead." Placidia's mouth compressed into an unattractive scowl. "His sword severed my guardian's head, and he deserved the same treatment."

"He executed Stilicho on your brother's orders, Princess. He should not be faulted for loyalty." *Has life among the barbarians coarsened your sensibilities as well as your hands, my love? When you are safe with me, you will have no more need of these cares.*

"I understand you are being rewarded for your victory with the Count's lands, wealth, and the consulship in the coming year."

"As well as his *bucellarii*. I'll put his special troops to good use here in Gaul." He threw another significant look at Ataulf, then returned his attentions to Placidia. "Your brother honors me. I hope you will accompany me to the celebratory games."

"The princess remains our guest until you complete our bargain."

Constantius suppressed his anger at the barbarian's interruption. "The Emperor is pleased you have shown your allegiance by apprehending the usurpers. The grain and gold are forthcoming. In the interim, we can settle your people in Aquitaine."

"Forthcoming is not good enough." Ataulf leaned forward, hands on the table, eyes direct. "When we have the grain and gold, as well as the land, the Emperor will have his sister."

Constantius' calm slipped away at the prospect of losing Placidia when he was so close. He stood, towering over the other man. "You greedy bastard. You carry the riches of Rome in your wagons, and you demand more?"

"I demand what was promised—gold, grain, and land for Jovinus and his brother. I have fulfilled my part. I have shown good faith in my actions. The Emperor has not. Until then, the princess remains with us."

"I have the signed decrees awarding you federate status and spelling out the conditions you require. The princess leaves with me today, or I tear up these documents and we will be at war."

"General." Placidia stood and put a hand to his chest. "There is no need for harsh words or hasty actions. Please sit."

Constantius could deny her nothing. "As you wish, Princess." He sat.

"Constantius, you, above all, are known as an honorable man." His blood warmed at her compliment. "And we will treat with you on that assumption."

We? She hadn't used the royal 'we' in conversation before.

"Surely we can come to some understanding? You do not wish to see the Gallic countryside plundered like Italy's. My people need grain. They cannot eat gold."

"'My people'?" Her words shook him more than her savage reaction to Heraclian's death.

A slight flush colored her cheeks. "My brother erred in not treating fairly with the Goths. They make better friends than enemies."

After three years of captivity, Placidia champions their cause? Constantius had heard of hostages identifying with their captors. The boy Aetius had returned from his hostage exchange little better than a Hun.

Placidia and Ataulf exchanged glances. She seemed afraid.

So that's the right of it! Constantius covered her hand with his. "Placidia, there is no reason you must return to the Goths. Whatever threat this barbarian holds over you, you are safe with me."

Ataulf rose, bloodlust in his eyes. Placidia held up a warning hand, and he subsided back into his chair.

"The Goths have no hold on me, other than affection. I am loved and honored among them."

"Princess, I demand you return with me as your brother wishes."

"When Honorius keeps his promise to these people, I will willingly come back to Ravenna. Not before."

"You cannot prefer traveling in a filthy wagon, starving and hunted, to taking your place at your brother's side?" Constantius dropped to his knees, still holding her hand. It trembled. He said in a low voice, "Placidia, my men outnumber the Goths. At your word, I will take you back to the life you deserve."

"It's not only your honor, but mine you would stain with such betrayal." She withdrew her hand. "I have given my bond to King Ataulf. I do not want to journey from place to place, hungry and hunted. You can ensure that does not happen by making good on the Emperor's promise."

"Because of the rebellion, there will be no African grain until next year. Should I starve Italy to feed these invaders?" Constantius' mouth tasted of dust.

"Our business is concluded." Ataulf's cold tones cut through Constantius' misery. "You have until the end of the year to make good on our treaty." He extended a hand to Placidia.

Constantius rose to face them both with what dignity he could muster. "Farewell, Princess. Know that you would be loved and honored among your own people, as well. That is where you belong. I will do everything in my power to see you returned to us."

"You will do what you must—as will I." Placidia turned her back on him and exited with that execrable barbarian.

Constantius picked up his goblet, finished the wine, and crushed the fragile glass. Blood dripped unnoticed from his hand onto the tiles.

PLACIDIA DESCENDED FROM HER LITTER at the door to her borrowed townhouse in Valence. Although she enjoyed the relative freedom and informality of camp life, she preferred the more settled arrangements of town living. Local nobles vied for the honor of providing shelter and provisions for the sister of the Emperor and the court of the King of the Goths—especially when surrounded by thirty thousand barbarian warriors. In spite of Constantius' fears that she lived in the back of a wagon, eating lentils and laboring around the campfire, she lived a comfortable life.

But she did resent living in other people's homes and among other people's possessions, relying on unfamiliar servants. She longed for a home of her own, surrounded by familiar things and a household she could order as wished. Of the servants she had brought from Rome, Paulus, Cook, and Lucilla remained. The three girls had found love among their Gothic captors, and left her service with gold and her blessings.

"May I have a word with you, Princess?" Ataulf opened the door.

"Of course." She preceded him into the receiving room where the owner normally met with his clients and merchants. A few books graced the shelves on one wall—plays and a history or two—but pride of place went to a bronze statue of a marathon runner, a copy of the famous statue from the Greek master Praxiteles. She indicated one of the two chairs facing a work table and turned to take the other.

"Please, Placidia." She felt his warm hand on her shoulder through her filmy silk garments. "Why are you acting so cold and distant?"

She turned to him with a cry on her lips, but stifled it as servants entered to light the bronze brazier and put a tray of refreshments on the table. He dropped his hand and stepped back.

82

"I'll serve the King." Placidia dismissed the servants and shut the door behind them. She stripped the diadem and veil from her hair. "Wine?"

Blood suffused his cheeks. His mouth set in an angry line. Ataulf nodded curtly.

Placidia poured wine into two gilded brass goblets and handed one to Ataulf. The touch of his fingers sent fire coursing down her arm. She flinched, gulping her own wine for courage. She knew what Ataulf would propose after the meeting with Constantius, and sought to postpone it. Looking into his hurt, questioning eyes, her heart constricted.

"Princess, we must discuss the meeting with Constantius."

"I know." She poured herself a second cup of wine and sat in one of the well-padded leather chairs. "My brother will be unable to send the grain he promised, so you will not need to send me back to Ravenna."

"Doesn't that please you?" He set his untouched wine on the table and knelt in front of her chair. "We can stay together."

She ran a hand over his jaw. "Oh, my love. You have no idea what exquisite torture it's been this past year. To be so close and yet so far. How long can we continue this half-life?"

"Then marry me." He clasped her hand in his own.

"My brother—"

"Can go to the devil!" He stood, raising her with him and enfolding her in his arms.

She buried her face in his chest, glorying in the smell of horse and sweat he exuded. She wanted nothing more than to marry and live her life with this man.

She pushed out of his arms. "It's treason for a princess to marry without the emperor's permission. Honorius would hound us to the ends of the earth. We'd know no peace."

"Hang your brother, Placidia." He grasped her upper arms and shook her. "I'm a king! I've led men in battle for years, while Honorius cowered behind the marshes of Ravenna. I took Rome!"

"I know you took Rome." She shrugged out of his grip. "I know you're a great general and a king. I also know my duty. Honorius may not pursue us personally, but you met Constantius. He has his own ambitions, and my brother's ear."

"I don't fear Constantius."

"You should."

"If Constantius were so powerful, he wouldn't need our help to put down the usurpers who threaten your brother." He held out his arms. "Placidia, I love you, and can protect you. Together, we can convince your brother we are better as allies than enemies. Please, marry me?"

She returned to his arms with a sigh. "I'm tired, my love. Give me time to think."

"As you wish, but don't take too long," he murmured into her hair.

"I won't."

THE NEXT EVENING, Placidia dined with Attalus, while Ataulf inspected the camp outside the walls. She recounted Constantius' conversation, including his offer of freedom.

"What did you expect?" Attalus asked as he inspected the food on the table. "I told you Constantius had feelings for you."

"He is the most influential man in the Empire at the moment. I am little more than another trophy he can parade around to show his power."

"I think you misjudge the man. He is honorable in his dealings—one of the few I've met at court, I might add—and honest in his affection for you."

"Perhaps. It matters little. Honorius will not provide the grain. War makes for famine throughout the provinces."

"Is that why we have such light fare tonight?" He waved at the hard-boiled eggs, rabbit in its own gravy, green salad, diced apples and cheese.

Placidia laughed. "It was the best Cook could do on such short notice. I am used to plain fare myself."

"Tsk, tsk." His face took on a pained expression. "I thought I did a better job of training your palate."

"My dear Attalus, I sometimes believe you live to eat, while I only eat to live."

"It is not the quantity." He patted his flat stomach. "It is the quality. I would rather have a small portion of squab in rosemary wine sauce than a half-roasted side of beef."

She took a bite of the rabbit. "I find this rabbit delicious."

"You would." He sniffed. "Has Cook run out of salt and pepper? She could at least spice the dish."

"You are welcome to tell her where her deficiencies lie."

His eyes grew round in mock terror. "And face her wrath? The woman is never without a knife or a pot in her hand."

They chatted in this vein until Placidia gained the courage to speak her mind. "Ataulf proposes marriage."

Attalus looked over his goblet of sweet wine with narrowed eyes. "Do you want to marry him?"

"If I were not an Imperial Princess, I would have him in an instant."

"But?"

"One thing Constantius did do was remind me of my duty." Unexpected tears leaked from her eyes. A painful band tightened around her heart. Her voice caught in a sob. "I love Ataulf, yet we cannot be together. Our love could bring disaster on both our races. I don't know what to do."

Attalus joined her on her couch and patted her back as her sobs turned into a fit of hiccups. He offered her a goblet. "Take some wine."

As she calmed, the hiccups faded. Attalus offered a napkin to dry her eyes. "Since you told me this, I'm assuming you want my advice?"

She nodded.

"I say marry the man you love and hang the Empire."

"But…"

"Happiness is fleeting in this world, and you've known much duty and sorrow. Take this opportunity for some happiness for yourself. Who knows? It might have advantages."

"What advantages?"

"My poor little fawn, can you not give yourself permission to be happy without some excuse?"

She dropped her head. Why did she deny herself this? Because duty to the Empire was bred in her muscle and bone. She knew no other way to act.

At her silence, Attalus sighed. "If you marry Ataulf, you confer on him the legitimacy he lacks in his own right. If you set up court and prove your 'civilizing' influence on the barbarians, they can take their rightful place as federates and citizens. But the strongest argument is, if you have a child, he will be Honorius' heir, and the Emperor will have to accept Ataulf along with the child."

"Are you sure?" Placidia longed to believe him.

"My dear, I am sure of nothing in this life except the inevitability of death. I say marry Ataulf because you love him. If you need other reasons, I've provided some which will do as well as any other."

She threw her arms about his neck and rested her head on his chest. "Thank you. You have been such a good friend through these years. I will think on your advice."

He caressed her hair. "Don't wait too long for happiness, my dear, or it might pass you by."

PART II

QUEEN

CHAPTER 12

Narbonne, January 414

PLACIDIA STRETCHED, FEELING LIGHT AND JOYFUL, as if all her worries had been washed away by the night's sleep. It was a new year, and today she embarked on a new life—today she married Ataulf.

Placidia giggled, which drew Lucilla's attention. The girl graced her with one of her rare brilliant smiles. *I have to stop thinking of her as a girl. She's eighteen, a full-grown woman, and a pretty one at that, if you saw only the right side of her face.*

"Come, Lucilla, to the baths! It wouldn't do to attend my own wedding celebration smelling like a horse."

Placidia returned to her room after the bath to find Gaatha and several servant girls laying out her clothes and jewels. Placidia ran to give her a hug. "I'm so glad you are here. I thought, since you were so recently remarried, you might not have the time."

"Nonsense. You're to be my sister." Gaatha embraced her, beaming. "I'm happy to stand in for the women of your line. It's an important day. You must be properly prepared."

Several of the women giggled. Placidia blushed.

Gaatha gave the gigglers a sharp glance; they quickly stilled. "How much do you know about what happens between a man and woman?"

"I've seen people couple, and heard the stories. There is little privacy in the camp."

"Pah!" Gaatha snorted. "Quick glances into dark corners and raunchy tales told by drunken men are not enough." She sat on the bed and patted the spot next to her.

Placidia sat.

"First of all, do not be afraid. Contrary to what most men say, I have yet to see a male member as big as a horse's." Another burst of giggles came from the corner. "Although it might seem so when you first see him roused."

"What do I do?"

"Nothing. Just relax and enjoy it. Ataulf has had many women. He will know what to do."

"But I've had no experience satisfying a man."

"Men find pleasure with a hand and a bit of pork fat. His job is to satisfy you. Being with a man the first time usually hurts a bit, and there might be some blood. Don't be tense; that just makes the pain worse. If you relax, you will feel pleasure. I told my brother to be gentle with you. Do you want children?"

"Of course."

"Right away? If you want to put off being pregnant, Machaon has an effective potion."

Placidia considered the idea, then shook her head. "I am nearly twenty-six. Half my life is done. Besides, with a child, my brother is more likely to acknowledge my marriage and welcome Ataulf."

Gaatha nodded. "When are your courses due?"

"I finished just five days ago."

"Good. Couple as often as you wish in the next two weeks and you might catch."

Placidia put her arms around the woman she had come to regard as an older sister. "Thank you, Gaatha. I owe you much."

"It is no more than any woman does for another." She smiled. "Now let's get you ready."

TWO HOURS LATER, Placidia inspected herself in a large silver mirror. Her hair was arranged in an upswept confection of braids and curls. The makeup was subtle, but the kohl around her eyes made them look enormous. Her *tunica interior* was of the finest, thinnest silk; her purple silk *stola* stiff and heavy with seed pearls and gold thread embroidery. She fairly blazed with gold and jewels:

from the diadem that held her filmy veil, to the jewels encrusting her sandals, to the magnificent amber *fibula* that closed her gilt-edged cloak.

"I look like a walking treasure chest."

"As befits your station as Imperial Princess and future Queen of the Goths. Ataulf only gives back what was taken from you." Gaatha smoothed a non-existent wrinkle in the cloak. "You honor your people and ours."

Placidia acknowledged the truth of her words. The Romans expected ostentation, and the Goths were exuberantly fond of gold. They took every opportunity to display their wealth in jewelry, weapons, utensils, even on their horses' tack.

The water clock chimed the fifth hour of daylight. Gaatha gazed over Placidia's shoulder in the mirror. "You look beautiful."

That was what Placidia needed to hear.

"It is time, my dear."

They proceeded to the villa's private chapel, where they met Ataulf, Attalus, and Valia. Ataulf was attired in similar splendor, with a purple *paludamentum* to indicate his royal rank and a simple gold circlet. His hair was trimmed shorter, in the Roman fashion. Their smiles for each other outshone their gold ornaments. They knelt side by side for a blessing from Bishop Sigesar, then rose.

"Now for the celebration," Attalus said. "I hope you approve. I've worked for days on the details."

Placidia put a hand on his arm. "I'm sure it will be perfect." Attalus had even persuaded a friend of his to loan them this magnificent villa for their winter quarters. *Another borrowed home.* She shook her head—no unhappy thoughts today!

They proceeded to the entrance where Attalus organized a procession. A troop of trumpeters led off, followed by a Gothic infantry unit, dressed in their finest armor and draped with gold chains. Next came fifty dancing girls dropping flowers on the path, followed by Ataulf's wedding present to her: fifty handsome youths, each carrying two gold cups, one filled with gold coins and the other with jewels. When she had heard of the extravagant wealth Ataulf planned to bestow on her, she protested, but he reminded her she brought the Roman Empire as dowry.

Attalus helped Placidia ascend into a gilded chariot pulled by four matched white horses and driven by the local champion charioteer. The youth gave her a bold eye as he bowed.

Attalus laughed as he handed her several purses with alms for the crowd. "Watch his hands, Princess. He is not only fast with the horses."

"Attalus, you shame me before the princess?" The charioteer drew a long face. "How can I reclaim my honor?"

"By not racing through the streets like a dog with its tail on fire. This is a solemn occasion."

"Then why ask the champion to drive?" The youth reclaimed his grin. "You should have asked the loser."

Placidia laughed at the banter, tension draining from her shoulders. Ataulf approached on a black stallion, accompanied by his nobles and followed by a full troop of cavalry.

"Are you ready, my love?"

She looked up into his face. "Yes."

The procession wended its way from the villa to the forum of Narbonne and back. The entire population of the city, plus the billeted Goths, turned out to cheer and gape. For most of these people, this would be their only chance to see royalty, and the procession would be talked about for decades. By the time they returned to the villa, Placidia's shoulders ached from the weight of her robes. Her face was stiff from smiling, and the celebration had barely begun.

At the door, the trumpeters were replaced with lyre and flute players. The dancing girls renewed their supply of flower petals and preceded Placidia as she processed through the garden to a slightly raised platform, where she stood before the higher of two silk-cushioned chairs. Ataulf stood on her right as Attalus read the marriage contract aloud. They both put their seals to the document and kissed heartily, to wild cheers.

"I love you," Ataulf whispered as they parted.

Placidia gratefully sat to receive the wedding guests and their gifts. Gold goblets, massive silver plates, jewel encrusted crosses, fur cloaks and other treasure filled tables to her left as Gallic and Gothic nobles paid their respects. Scribes took careful note of who gave what, records needed for when these same people came back with petitions for action or appointments.

Just as Placidia felt she could take no more, Ataulf's children came forward. Vada, who at twelve was just budding into young womanhood, spoke. "Princess and Honored Teacher, we welcome you as our mother and hope you find pleasure in these gifts from our hands." She stepped forward and gave Placidia a silk handkerchief embroidered with her initials intertwined with Ataulf's and surrounded by hearts and flowers.

"It's lovely, and the stitches are so even. You must teach me how to do that."

Vada blushed at the compliment.

Lilla, looking perfectly groomed in her silks, presented her with a wreath of myrtle—the symbol of victory. "I went out this morning to get it so it'd be fresh," she said proudly. "See my skinned knee." She raised her tunic.

"Has Machaon seen to that? I wouldn't want you to have a scar because of me."

"I don't care if I have scars. They're signs of courage."

Maltha came forward and read out a short Latin poem she had written in her best hand on a slip of parchment and tied with a purple ribbon.

Placidia clapped. "Very well done, child. You are a credit to your teacher."

Little Ediulf stood shifting from foot to foot. "Is it my turn now?"

"Yes, dear. You may present your gift."

"Good. 'Cause mine's the best." His sisters rolled their eyes, but held their peace. Ediulf took one hand from behind his back and proudly presented Placidia with a finely carved boat, painted red, complete with sail.

Ataulf inspected it with a raised eyebrow. "You did all the work yourself?"

The six-year old scuffed his sandals briefly, admitting, "Paulus helped a little with the carving, but I did all the painting and put on the sail."

"Good lad." Ataulf mussed his son's hair.

Placidia beamed at the four children. "Thank you all. Your presents are more precious to me than gold, because they come from your hearts. I will try to be a good and loving mother to you. Come." They trooped forward and received her kisses with varying degrees of pleasure, depending on their tolerance for such displays.

Ataulf stood to address his guests. "Thank you all for your blessings, and for coming together to witness this union between Romans and Goths. Once, in the full confidence of valor and victory, I aspired to conquer Rome and erect on its ruins the Empire of Gothia. Like Augustus, I sought the immortal fame of the founder of a new empire. It is now my sincere wish that the gratitude of the future ages should acknowledge the man who employed the sword of the Goths not to subvert, but to restore and maintain the prosperity of the Roman Empire. This is the course urged on me by my beloved wife Galla Placidia and so, in the end, Rome conquered Goth."

The Roman guests received Ataulf's speech with enthusiasm. A few Goths showed somber faces, and some outright anger.

Ataulf dropped to his knees and bowed before Placidia, who raised him to her side again. She, in turn, addressed her guests. "I am the granddaughter, daughter, and sister of Emperors, yet I am most proud to be called Queen of the Goths and wife to this noble man. I have traveled with you for four years and measured your worth. The Goths are a strong and vigorous people. Your blood and arms will only strengthen Rome. I welcome Roman and Goth alike to enjoy our hospitality on this historic day."

Most of the guests were ushered to a tent on the grounds to be served food and drink. A select group of nobles, Roman and Goth, remained in the garden, which slaves quickly turned into a *triclinium* by moving dining couches around the perimeter. Placidia took the opportunity to retire to her bedroom and remove her outermost robes. Lucilla helped her freshen her makeup and tuck in a few stray curls before Placidia returned to her guests.

It was obvious from the purple silk hangings which couch was to be theirs. Ataulf, already holding a goblet, circled the garden, talking with various visitors until he saw her return. He joined her on the couch, placing his hand protectively over her hip. "How are you faring?"

"Well. But I long for us to be alone." She chuckled. "How soon may we slip away from our guests?"

He nibbled her ear, sending thrills surging from groin to breasts. "Soon. We will eat a little, drink a little, listen to Attalus' wedding poem, and then make our escape. I have instructed the servants to keep the wine flowing, so most will not notice our absence."

Ataulf speared a fresh oyster from its shell with the pointed end of his spoon, and popped it into Placidia's mouth. She savored the salty taste and chewy texture. Placidia saw Attalus' hand in the menu and his influence on the cooks as the slaves served the various courses. The pungent smell of garlic and lentils vied with the more subtle spices of ginger, mint, and dill in the polentas and greens. Red meats were boiled in the Roman way, rather than roasted, and served with strongly flavored fish sauce, while the fowl were served in their feathers stuffed with their own eggs. The sweet course consisted not only of honey-sweetened cakes and fruits from the local farms, but an exotic rice dish dusted with cinnamon.

The feast took longer than Ataulf promised. Attalus not only sang the traditional *epithalamia*—wedding poem—but provided several entertainments: dancers, jugglers, and singers.

After the singers, Attalus came by with a full goblet. "I apologize for the poor entertainment. It was the best I could do in this backwater."

"You've surpassed my highest expectations." Placidia clasped his hand. "Thank you, my friend."

"You deserve no less than the best." He bowed low, then raised his goblet. "To My King and Queen. A long life, happy marriage, and many children." He took a long gulp.

"Speaking of children…" Ataulf looked at her with half-lidded eyes.

She blushed and nodded.

Ataulf helped her up from the couch and turned to Attalus. "Good night, my friend. Keep our guests happy."

Placidia clapped her hands together when she saw their bridal bower. The bed was draped with purple silk curtains, which they could close for privacy. Cedar wood burned in a brazier. Wine and food sat on a table by the bed; white roses filled the room with a heady scent.

"Where did you get such lovely blooms at this time of year?"

"You'll have to ask our magician, Attalus. He made all the arrangements." Ataulf put his arms around her, pulling her back to his chest. "Are you happy?" he murmured in her ear.

She sank into his embrace. "The happiest I've ever been."

"I've sent messengers to your brother, informing him of the marriage and pledging my affection and support."

"I don't want to think of my brother tonight. I don't want to think of Rome or Gothia. I don't want to be a princess or a queen. I want to be a woman in love with her husband on their wedding night."

She stepped away and, one by one, dropped her garments to the floor, leaving only her silk *tunica*.

Ataulf swept her into his arms and carried her to their bed. Placidia felt the strength of those arms and melted onto his chest, breathing fast. He bent his head to kiss her, a deep lingering kiss that grew more urgent with each passing moment. He laid her on the bed and doffed his own robes and loincloth. She noted the rippling muscles and numerous scars before she allowed her eyes to travel to his groin. As Gaatha had promised, his member wasn't as big as a horse's, but quite big enough.

He slipped to her side and gently pushed her silk *tunica* from her shoulders, kissing her neck, then her breasts as he gradually exposed her flesh. Her nipples hardened. She arched her back in delight. Ataulf moved back to her face, leaving her wanting more. His hands framed her jaw, then gently pushed through her hair, loosening pins and jewels. Her tresses cascaded freely over her bare shoulders. He picked up a strand and curled it around his finger. "I love your hair. If I had my way you would always wear it long and loose."

"That's not very practical for riding."

He let the strands slip slowly through his fingers. "It's good for the kind of riding we'll do tonight." He gathered her into a tight embrace, and Placidia gave up all thought, to glory in her body.

CHAPTER 13

Ravenna, January 414

"MARRIED?" HONORIUS ROARED. He shot up from his audience chair. His pasty face turned bright red. "That dog shit barbarian forced my sister into marriage against my will?"

Blood drained from Constantius' face, leaving him light-headed.

The Gallic nobles who brought the news prostrated themselves before the Emperor's anger. "She was not forced, Your Supreme Majesty. She willingly entered into the alliance, and asks your blessing on the marriage." One held out a packet of letters with a trembling hand.

"Out! All of you!" Spittle flew from the Emperor's lips. The emissaries, servants, and clients fled the room in haste.

Constantius had taken wounds in battle that hurt less than this stab to his heart. This was his consul year, the pinnacle of his career, and the woman he loved had wed another. He picked up the packet, broke the seal, and handed it to Honorius. The Emperor perused the letter, then silently handed it back to Constantius. The hurt grew bitter as he read:

> *By my hand this fifteenth day of January, in the Year of Our Lord, Four Hundred and Fourteen, in the twenty-first year of the reign of the Great Emperor Honorius*

My Most Gracious and Beloved Brother,

My prayers and best wishes for your health and long life. I offer joyous news of my honorable union with Ataulf, King of the Goths. We are wed in the sight of the Lord and our people. I ask your blessing, for my happiness cannot be complete until we have healed the rift between us. In this time of great joy, let us put our differences aside and again embrace one another as brother and sister.

With this union I bring a powerful ally to your side, a vigorous people to settle in the ravaged lands of Gaul, and a strong and disciplined army to guard your frontiers and fight your battles. My husband and I will defend your interest in all things.

I eagerly await your blessing and our reconciliation.

Your Loving and Loyal Sister,
Galla Placidia, Queen of the Goths

Constantius crushed the paper in his grip. He turned to Honorius. "Let me deal with this, My Emperor. I'll destroy these upstart Goths the way I've destroyed all your enemies. Ataulf must be punished for insulting your person in this manner, and Placidia returned to your protection."

"Do you believe the emissary…that she willingly married this man?" Honorius twisted his robe in his hands. "How could she do this to me? Do she and her husband intend to ride on Ravenna and overthrow me?"

The Emperor's fears, fed by the constant threats to his throne these past five years, forced Constantius to control his rage. If Honorius believed his sister engaged in a plot against his life or threatened his rule, she would be forever outside Constantius' protection.

"I do not believe Placidia is capable of such treachery. She has always supported your rule and worked tirelessly even in her captivity for the legitimists. She repudiated that upstart Attalus and persuaded Ataulf to war against Jovinus.

The emissaries brought her gifts and pledges of friendship and support. I believe Placidia to be honest in her affection for you, but she is under the control of that devious barbarian. Him, I trust even less than the murdering Alaric."

"But why would she marry such a man?"

"Placidia is a woman, and this Ataulf is handsome and clever. We have many tales of captives forming an attachment to their captors. I believe Placidia is a victim of her extended captivity and the wiles of an unscrupulous man. Once under your influence again, she will see the error of her ways."

"Perhaps, but she has always been headstrong." Honorius collapsed into his chair, one hand to his head. "Why does God plague me with such betrayal? It seems, since I took over my own rule, I have had nothing but upstarts, usurpers, and arrogant barbarians to deal with." He extended a limp hand to Constantius, looking at him with tragic eyes. "You are my one loyal friend. I can always count on you to do the right thing. Destroy this barbarian king and bring my sister back."

Constantius gave the Emperor a deep bow. "It will be done, My Emperor."

PLACIDIA, FEELING QUEASY, sat in the council with Ataulf. He was in a bitter mood. She took his hand under the table, but he shook it off. Pain constricted her throat, temporarily replacing her nausea. *How dare Ataulf blame me for my brother's intransigence or the Patrician's adamancy? I warned him of this!* Placidia stiffened her back, swallowing her tears. She would show no weakness to these Gothic nobles.

Sergeric fingered the gold torque around his neck. His angry gaze raked the table. "If war is what the Emperor wants, let us accommodate him. Negotiating with the Roman dog and his pet general will get us nothing. Ravening Gaul and Spain will at least give us food and plunder."

A rumble of agreement rose from the council. Placidia could tell from their grim faces and the bloodlust in their eyes that the cause of peace lay mortally wounded. Even faithful Valia nodded his head. She was about to make a futile argument when Ataulf surprised her.

"I agree. Time and again we have shown our good faith to the Emperor and received nothing in return but betrayal, lies, and abuse." His teeth flashed in a grim smile. "Attalus, it is time you retook your rightful place as Emperor."

Attalus had evidently not anticipated these events. His eyes widened and mouth thinned in consternation as he glanced at Placidia.

"No!" Placidia rose, a protective hand over her stomach. "My husband, you cannot do this. My brother might forgive rebellious subjects, but he cannot ignore a usurper. By setting up Attalus as a rival Emperor, you rob me of my legitimacy and your child of his rightful place as heir to Honorius."

"Sit, Wife." Ataulf's eyes flashed with anger. "Your brother has repudiated our marriage and our child. The only way he will accept either is at the point of a sword."

"I agree with our Queen." Sergeric made an ironic bow to Placidia. "We need no puppet Emperor."

The nausea returned. Placidia swallowed hard. She thought never to see the day when Sergeric agreed with her.

"With Attalus as our Emperor," Ataulf said, "and me as Master General, we can claim allegiance from the provinces. I can demand stores from the Imperial arms factories, collect taxes, and raise additional troops."

"Emperors and Master Generals." Sergeric spat on the floor. "What need have we for Roman titles and trappings? We have always taken what we would."

So, Sergeric did not agree with her. They were allied only in opposition to Attalus' elevation. Her stomach roiled. Placidia decided to make an exit before she disgraced herself, but could not resist one last argument. "Raising Attalus to the purple is foolish as well as useless. It will only prolong war."

"My Queen…" Ataulf gritted between his teeth.

"Without Roman law and a stable government, you will strip this land, and it will take years to recover." She rose. "I have said my piece."

She left the council and sprinted down the colonnade to her room, where she rushed to a basin and retched while Lucilla patted her back.

Exhausted, Placidia sat on her bed. Tears leaked from her eyes. It was a large, lovely room, with light coming in from the courtyard, soothing pastoral murals on the walls and the finest linens and silks on the bed, but it was not hers. Placidia wanted a home of her own, a place to settle and raise her children. She saw little hope of that.

Lucilla, worry lines on her forehead, bustled silently around the room. She brought a cool cloth to wipe Placidia's face, a cup of mint flavored water for her to drink, and anise seeds to chew. Placidia sat, staring vacantly. Lucilla pantomimed combing her hair.

"Yes." Placidia closed her eyes and let the tension flow away as Lucilla loosened her hair from the bun of tight braids and combed out the curls. "Thank you, my friend."

Before Lucilla could complete Placidia's toilette, Ataulf stormed into the room. "Leave us." He held the door open for Lucilla. The girl looked to Placidia. She nodded her assent.

"How dare you embarrass me before my council? Is it not enough that I have to deal with so many fractious steeds, that my own wife takes the bit in her teeth?"

"I embarrassed *you*?" Placidia stood up, anger tearing her former calmness to tatters. "You are the one who wanted me to sit with you in council. Am I another puppet, like Attalus—your trophy Roman princess to bear your children, smile, and keep silent on all things of your choosing?"

"I was foolish to believe you might be silent on any topic." Ataulf's voice took on an edge sharper than his blade. "But I had some hope that, out of respect for me, you might raise your objections in private. You are my wife, and my queen!"

"I am an Imperial Princess!"

Ataulf grabbed her wrists, holding them in a crushing grip. "God's balls, but I am sick of having that thrown in my teeth. Your grandfather was an unknown, upstart Pannonian officer who died of a temper fit. Your father stumbled out of Spain to pick up the pieces and pretend to be our friend while sacrificing us on the front lines of his every battle. And your brother—the lying, lack-wit, chicken lover—you should be proud to claim kinship to him!"

"Are you quite through?"

Her cold tone cut through his rage. Ataulf dropped her wrists. Placidia rubbed at the pain. She would sport twin bruises tomorrow.

"My mother's father and my father did come from the provinces, not Rome; and they did come from the military, not the senate. They fought their way to the throne with bravery and blood. This is the line I come from—men who had the courage to rule the Empire and the brains to hold onto it. I may be a woman, but I know how the Imperial court works and how my brother thinks. With Constantius at his side, he will crush any usurper. Be guided by me in this."

The anger flowed out of Placidia with a suddenness that left her knees weak. She sat on her bed, shivering.

"Are you ill?" Ataulf strode to her side, pulled a cover from the bed and wrapped her in a warm embrace. "My love, I do not wish to quarrel with you, but you weaken me with your opposition. My men mutter that if I cannot control my own wife, how can I lead a nation?"

"I know." She looked into his concerned eyes. Her fingers lightly traced the furrows ploughed in his forehead and the gray threads among the red at his temples. Her voice shook with the passion he inspired in her, even when angry. "We must play our roles, and they pit us against one another, just when we most want to be together. We both know Rome cannot be conquered." She felt his arms stiffen. "Not by a starving army, constantly on the run, stealing food and scavenging arms. I must leave the door open for negotiation. Honorius must believe that I pose no threat to him, if we are to have any future."

"My people do not want a future dominated by Rome."

"Perhaps." Placidia closed her eyes, leaning into his shoulder. "But I am not the only woman who wants to stop wandering. I hear the grumbling in the camp. It is summer now, but winter is coming. Constantius blocks the ports, and food will be scarce—again! As king, you must look to the needs of all your people, not just the warriors."

"My nobles are angry. I cannot reverse their course so quickly."

"That is why we must play our roles a little longer." Placidia's voice grew faint with exhaustion. "I will not attend council. Your men will know of our rift, and I will ensure word comes to Honorius of my support for him."

"I do not like these…lies." Ataulf stroked her hair.

"Not lies. We both believe in our cause." Placidia yawned and leaned into his shoulder. When she was nearly asleep, he laid her on the bed and kissed her forehead.

THE WAGON HIT ANOTHER RUT. Ataulf grunted in pain. The Goths had left a trail of burning cities and empty fields down the coast of Gaul, and now trekked to Spain, after a disastrous assault on Marseilles, where Ataulf took a spear in his thigh. Valia held the nobles in check for now, but if Ataulf did not recover quickly from his wound the horde might disintegrate into squabbling tribes.

How much longer can we go on like this? Placidia washed Ataulf's fevered face with cool water and looked at Machaon. "Can you not do something for him?"

The Greek physician shook his head. "Keep honey on the wound." He patted her arm. "Ataulf is strong. He will recover. Give him watered wine for the pain and meat broth for strength. I will come by again this evening."

"Nothing else for the pain?"

"I've used the last of my pain medicines. If we do not get to Barcelona soon, I will have nothing to work with but my hands."

Machaon jumped down from the wagon and moved on to another transporting wounded.

Ataulf moaned.

Her unborn child stirred. She placed Ataulf's hand on her swollen belly. "Feel our child, my love? He is strong and vigorous, like his father. You must live, for him and for me." *Please, God, we've had so little time together!*

Ataulf turned toward her voice and half opened his eyes. "Placidia?"

Tears started down her cheeks. He had not known her for two days. "Yes, my love, I am here by your side, as I will always be."

"Water," he said with a cracked voice.

She propped up his head so he could take small sips from a leather bottle of well-watered wine.

He looked around the swaying wagon. "Valia?"

"He is leading us to Barcelona, as you wanted." She spooned broth into his mouth. "Do not tire yourself with such worries. Valia is keeping all under control."

After a few swallows, Ataulf fell into a deep, fever-free sleep. Placidia went to the wagon opening and waved over her favorite messenger. Since she had become Queen of the Goths, those troops who swore personal loyalty to Ataulf also pledged to her. They would gladly give their lives for her or her child. A teenaged boy with a wisp of a blond beard approached.

"Sigisvult, go to Valia, Lady Gaatha, and the children. Let them know the King sleeps without a fever. He will be well soon."

The boy rode off at a fast trot. The news would spread like fire in a dry hayfield through the traveling camp, bringing comfort to their friends and disappointment to their rivals. With Ataulf out of danger, she could turn her thoughts to another troubling problem—the disappearance of Attalus.

CHAPTER 14

Marseilles, September 414

Ａ TTALUS PULLED HIS CLOAK CLOSER ABOUT HIS FACE as he sat in the shadowy depths of a portside tavern. In the chaos of the retreat from Gaul, he had found himself abandoned at a villa outside Marseilles without wagon or horses. Attalus had tried to get word to Placidia, but his slaves never returned.

He smiled grimly, running his finger through a spill of wine on the table. It looked like someone had taken advantage of Ataulf's injury to rid himself of the hated Roman. Worse, the local Imperial authorities knew of his presence and were combing the city for him. He hoped the man now coming through the door would be the answer to his predicament.

"Captain." Attalus raised his hand and indicated a stool across from him. "Would you care for some wine or food? I cannot recommend either in this establishment, but many eat here and seem to survive the experience."

"The fare's always been good enough for me." The Captain's dull eyes squinted among abundant wrinkles.

"No offence intended, my good man." Attalus motioned to a slave, who brought a pitcher of the vinegary stuff that passed for wine in this tavern and a second cup. His own stood untouched. "And bring my guest one of your best dinners." A joke, since meals in these taverns were all the same—bread, grain boiled with vegetables, and a few chunks of meat of dubious origin. Attalus abstained.

The Captain showed the marks of his profession: deeply weathered skin, callused hands, knife scars and rope burns. Many shipmasters were stranded in port with cargo and no markets. Some tried to slip through Constantius' blockade. A few made it. Attalus hoped some extra gold would be enough incentive for this man to try a run.

The Captain quenched his thirst, wiped his mouth on the back of his sleeve, and smiled at Attalus with half-rotten teeth. "Now, sir, you talked of a commission."

"I want you to take a passenger to Carthage."

"Who?"

"Me."

The Captain scratched under his chin with dirty nails. "Well, now, sir. That's quite dangerous. The fall storms will be blowin' in soon, not to mention the Patrician's ships we got to avoid. The only ones wantin' to run the blockade are those with perishable cargoes and those what want to avoid the provincial officials. Which are you, sir?"

"Nothing so dramatic." Attalus laughed. "I've a rich widow waiting in Carthage. If I don't get to her by winter, she might bestow her favors on someone else. I need to make good time, or lose a fortune."

"Ah, so I'm to smooth the course o' love, am I?"

"I'm told you're the man for the job. I understand you have, on several occasions, managed to avoid paying taxes on cargo which you unload at your... private harbor."

"Now, sir, who's been spreading such slander about me?" The man scowled. "I'm an honest shipmaster and always pay my dues to the custom man."

"Of course you are, Captain, and, if you help me, you could be a rich man as well."

"How rich?"

"Ten pounds of gold."

The Captain snorted. "That wouldn't cover my expenses. I have to leave without cargo so as to make the boat light and fast. I'll make no profit from that voyage."

"Twenty, then."

"Fifty."

"Twenty." Attalus sweated. "And these jewels are worth at least twenty more."

"That's better." The Captain took the proffered necklace and looked at it closely. "Emeralds, aren't they? Real beauties. My men don't have to know about this." He pocketed the necklace. "But they'll get a share of the gold. I'll have that now."

"You have the jewels." Attalus pulled a heavy purse from beneath his cloak. "You'll get this when I'm on board. When can we leave?"

"Fair enough. In three days, we'll have no moon. Best to launch at night. You know where my private harbor is?"

Attalus shook his head. The Captain gave directions to a small cove outside the city.

The slave arrived with the Captain's dinner. Attalus gave him a small silver coin. "Make sure my friend has all the wine he wants this evening." He rose and gave a short bow. "Enjoy your meal. Unfortunately, I have another engagement and cannot join you."

The Captain grunted as he piled soggy vegetables onto his coarse bread.

THREE DAYS LATER, Attalus shouldered a small pack, with money and jewels sandwiched between clothes, and made his way to the cove. Once there, he settled onto a piece of driftwood, taking in the scent of salt air and rotting seaweed. There was no moon, but the sky was clear and the stars bright. He could make out the horizon and the tops of silvered waves as they journeyed toward the shore to lap at his feet.

For a few moments, he knew peace. He loosed his regrets from the past and fears for the future and let the fitful breeze tease his hair and cleanse his lungs. At that moment, Attalus knew life on earth was good, and he didn't want to give it up for the uncertain bliss of the Christian afterlife. *I guess the baptism is wearing off.* He laughed to himself.

A dark shape rounded the eastern headland and angled toward him. Someone on board raised an oil lamp.

"Captain?" Attalus called across the water.

"Here, sir. You got the gold?"

"Yes."

"You'll have to wade out to us. The water is too shallow for us to come farther."

Attalus took off his sandals and cloak and tucked his tunic into his belt. The water took his breath with its unexpected chill. He muffled a yelp as he stepped on a sharp rock, turned his ankle, and almost lost his grip on his possessions. Cursing under his breath, Attalus waded as quietly as possible to the boat. Hands helped him aboard. One man threw a blanket over his shivering frame.

He found himself on a typical small cargo vessel designed for coastal trade. The narrow ship normally carried amphorae of oil or wine, bales of wool, or livestock. A tattered tent for the occasional passenger covered the deck in front of the central mast, which sported one large square sail, now trimmed. Such vessels required only a small crew to handle the sail and rudder. Attalus sniffed at the reek of unwashed bodies. Could the crew not take a dip over the side on occasion?

Attalus dug among his dry possessions for the bag of clinking coins, and handed it to the captain. "It's all there," he said in a low voice

"I trust such a gentleman as yourself, sir, wouldn't cheat a hardworkin' man." The Captain turned to two men. "Raise sail, and keep it quiet." He made his way to the rudder at the rear of the boat.

The men loosed the ties on the sail, and pulled the ropes that ran through a series of metal rings sewn in regular intervals down the front of the sail, allowing the heavy cloth to fold and unfold in even layers. Attalus smiled. He used a similar arrangement for porch shades in his southern villa. The memory of languorous days and chilled wine amongst his southern vineyards and orchards brought a pang to his heart and a hitch in his breathing. Why had he followed his father's wishes and entered politics? He smiled ruefully. *Because it's my nature. No more use denying myself the pleasure of wielding power than denying myself the pleasure of food.*

The rigging creaked, bringing him out of his reverie. Waves slapped the side of the boat, but a gusting wind carried the sounds away, distorting their origin. Attalus breathed easier as the twinkling lights of the city receded.

"Best you go inside, sir, and let us handle the rest." The Captain indicated the tent.

"Thanks." Attalus, suddenly exhausted from the ordeal of the last few days, crawled into the tent and fell asleep on top of fishy smelling blankets.

"Ship, heave to!"

The shout brought Attalus out of a sound sleep. He felt muddled. The swaying of the ship and smell of the sea momentarily confused him. Then memories from the previous night came rushing back.

Before he could inquire, the captain poked his head in the tent. "We've been spotted, sir, and they're gainin' on us. If you have any extra gold, I might be able to bribe our way out of this."

Attalus gave the man the last of his money, but reserved the jewels. "Tell the other captain you have a man with the plague. Maybe he won't come aboard."

"Aye, sir. That might work."

Attalus gathered his things and wiped the sweat beading on his upper lip. The other ship came alongside and grappled the two boats together.

"Captain, do you have my cargo?" a booming voice, roughened by salt air, shouted.

"Aye, sir, I have your special package, there in the tent."

Attalus understood the words of betrayal but firmly tamped his anger. He needed a clear head. He rose, straightened his tunic, and put on a confident smile. As long as he had his wits and tongue, Attalus had hope.

Two Roman naval officers tossed back the tent flaps and threatened him with spears. "Priscus Attalus?"

"No need for intimidation, my good sirs. I will come peaceably." He started forward. "Would one of you be so good as to porter my pack?"

As he strolled out into the dim light of dawn, he spied the Captain receiving another clinking bag. Attalus sneered. "I see you are indeed a hardworking man, Captain, making profit from two customers."

The captain's eyes shifted to his betrayed passenger. He grinned. "I'm only doing my duty to my Emperor, sir, and he's showing his gratitude."

Attalus turned his back on the man and walked across the boarding plank to the other ship. One of the officers followed with his pack. He surveyed the ship that would be his prison until they reached Ravenna—if he reached Ravenna. He was well aware of the headless state of the other usurpers. He had always known the odds were long against his survival of this adventure to comfortable old age.

He spotted the knotted insignia of rank on a stocky middle-aged man, and approached with a smile. "Captain, thank you for rescuing me from that stinking barge. I'm sure the accommodations on your fine ship will be much more to my taste. Speaking of which, have you and your good crew broken your fast? I'm starved for a good meal."

The man gaped at him in surprise.

Chapter 15

Barcelona, Spain, early 415

PLACIDIA STRAIGHTENED HER BACK TO EASE HER SWOLLEN BODY. Though the council room chair was padded, she could find no comfort. With Attalus gone, Ataulf had reinstated her to the council in Barcelona, but the meetings became increasingly fractious. The babble from this one receded into the background.

Only one more month.

As her baby grew, Placidia was increasingly prey to back pain, nausea and headaches. She had rested little the night before, and today the pains grew stronger. She struggled to bring her mind back to the meeting.

Valia reported on the campaign in Gaul. "Constantius continues to harry us. Our troops are falling back to the Pyrenees and running short of food. The Vandals and Suebi who moved into Spain ahead of us threaten from the west." Valia gave Placidia a regretful glance. "We need you in the field, Ataulf."

Other nobles chimed in, urging Ataulf to return to the fray, not a few sending resentful glances at Placidia. She knew they blamed her for Ataulf's tarrying in Barcelona, and they were not wrong. His wound had healed, but Placidia's frequent illnesses during her pregnancy kept him close.

"I agree with your nobles, Lord Husband. Your place is with your soldiers."

Ataulf caught her gaze. She gave him a trembling smile. He nodded. "Then I will prepare to leave tomorrow. The Queen will stand regent for me during my absence. All petitions, disputes, and judgments not handled by lower councils will come to her. She acts for me in all ways." He slipped his heavy signet ring over her thumb.

Sergeric likely spoke for more than himself when he objected. "You put a Roman woman over us? By what right?"

Ataulf said, in icy tones that brooked no argument, "She is my wife, and your queen."

Sergeric rose. "She is none of ours! She is of our enemy."

Placidia's irritability blossomed into anger. She rose, awkwardly maneuvering her belly from under the table. "How dare you insult me and the wisdom of your king? I would have you flogged or worse for such insolence."

A crafty smile crept across Sergeric's face. He waved his hand and addressed the entire council. "See? From her own mouth she proves her ignorance of our ways and laws. We have no history of infallible kings. Our nobles have the right to disagree with, and even challenge, our leaders."

Several nobles nodded, watching her speculatively. Placidia realized her tactical error—letting exhaustion and anger get the better of her. Before she could respond, Ataulf spoke.

"I will need all of you in the field. The Queen is fully competent, and cognizant of her people's needs. I will not be brooked in this." He stared around the room. No one made another objection, but Placidia knew this was one more tally in the increasing list of slights some nobles put to her account.

A sharp pain, much worse than the dull aches she had experienced all morning, clenched her back and tightened her belly. She retrieved Ataulf's hand and squeezed tightly, struggling not to show her distress. She spoke to him in low tones. "I'm not well. I should retire and let you finish your business."

A worried frown creased his forehead. He turned to the council. "That's all for today. Other business can wait." The nobles left in small groups. Valia and another man approached, but Ataulf waved them on. "Placidia is not well. I'm taking her to our quarters."

She smothered a moan as another contraction gripped her body.

Valia smiled. "Ataulf, you stupid lout. Can't you see the woman's in labor? You're going to be father soon."

"I'm not due for another month," Placidia gasped.

"With seven children, the one thing I've learned is that babes come at their own will, not ours." Valia gave Ataulf a shove. "Take the woman to her bed, man!"

Ataulf lifted her in his arms and strode down the corridors to her room shouting for Machaon. Servants scattered in all directions. "Our child, my love. Soon," he whispered into her hair.

"I know," she grunted as another contraction took her.

MACHAON MET THEM AT PLACIDIA'S ROOM with the two midwives who had attended her throughout her pregnancy, his sister Thecla and her daughter Nikarete. They wore plain dark tunics and covered their hair in the manner of Christian nuns. The family resemblance was unmistakable, with the same curly black hair, hooked nose and intelligent eyes, but their bustling self-confidence marked them as colleagues as well.

Ataulf laid her on the bed and kissed her hands. She held him fast. "I'm frightened, Ataulf."

Dread clamped her bowels. She tried, unsuccessfully, to push gibbering fear from her mind. She had attended the labor of one of her ladies last month. The child was born healthy but, despite Thecla's hard work, the mother died in a gush of blood and pain. That death haunted her dreams.

"Men face death every time they go into battle, and women every time they come to childbed." He kissed her hands. "You are young, healthy and strong, my love. Machaon will not let harm come to you, and you have the prayers of our people."

Placidia feared there would be a few curses among the blessings. "Do not leave me." She clung to Ataulf's hand a moment longer.

Machaon approached. "The birthing room is no place for the father. Go have some wine, my friend. It will be many hours yet. Niece, help the Queen undress so I may examine her."

Ataulf retreated.

The young woman helped Placidia shed her heavy outer robes until she sat on the bed with only a silk tunica stretched across her rippling belly. Thecla took her hands. "Look at me, Lady." Placidia looked into the wise brown eyes. "The first birth is always the hardest, but my daughter and I are skilled. We'll get you through it. Fear will only make the pain worse."

"Drink this." Nikarete brought her a cup of warmed wine pungent with chamomile and cinnamon. "It'll fortify the blood."

Placidia took a sip, trying to push the fear away.

"Deep breaths now."

Placidia took a few deep breaths, letting them out slowly. She felt Thecla's calmness take root in her own soul.

Machaon massaged her stomach, feeling for the baby. "Excellent. Since you are early I thought the child might be out of position, but it is where it needs to be. The baby will be smaller, but that's better for you." Machaon's main concern during her pregnancy had been her slender frame. "Where are the pains, and what do they feel like?"

"They start in my back and move around to the front. They feel like stabbing knives." She breathed rapidly as another convulsed her.

Machaon frowned. "Some women experience labor pains in their back."

Thecla, seeing Placidia's worried grimace, said, "Everything is as it should be for now. We will walk you as much as you can, and massage between the contractions. That should help with the pain."

"My sister will see to you, and call me if you have need." Machaon gave her hand one last pat, then left.

Lucilla appeared with Gaatha in the doorway. Placidia's mood immediately lightened. "Thank the Good Lord you're here, Sister."

Gaatha fairly flew across the room to her side. "I would not leave you to such a trial alone. This is a time when women must come together and give each other comfort. Your ladies gather in the chapel to pray for your safe and speedy delivery." She waved the midwives closer. "You are in the very best of hands. These wise women attended me, and know many practices for making the birth easier."

Placidia gripped Gaatha's hand, bringing it to her cheek. "Thank you." Her dread lessened. Joyful anticipation brought a smile to her face. "Just having you here brings me new strength."

IN THAT DARKEST PART OF NIGHT, when fragile souls are wont to slip peacefully from earthly anchors, Placidia gritted, between teeth clenched on a leather band, "How much longer?" The pains were almost constant, and the midwives had sent for Machaon.

"It won't be long now, Lady," Thecla said. "Remember to pant like a dog during the hard ones."

"They're…all…hard," Placidia said, between pants. She felt as if her hips had been separated by the passage of the baby. She wondered if she would ever ride again. She hadn't realized she had spoken out loud until Gaatha chuckled.

"All women feel that way until they have their babes in their arms."

Placidia frowned, then said weakly. "I...meant...ride...a...horse."

Gaatha smiled at the misunderstanding as she wiped the sweat off her brow. The pain changed, lessened, but became more urgent. "I want to bear down."

"Excellent," Machaon said, entering the room. He washed his hands in a bowl by the bed, but did not touch her. "Put her on the birthing chair."

Placidia squatted, held upright by Nikarete and Gaatha on the open chair. Thecla occupied a low stool, facing her. Placidia pushed until she thought her insides would fall out. Over the course of an hour, she grew weaker. Near exhaustion, she clutched Gaatha's shoulder. "I can't go on. I'm so tired. Please, let me rest."

Thecla took Placidia's face in both her hands. "You're near done, Lady. The baby has crowned. Gather your strength. Count with me. One, two, three. Push!"

Placidia drew on her stubbornness and bore down with the remnants of her strength.

"Again. One, two, three. Push!"

This time she felt a change.

"I have the head. Once more, Lady"

Gathering her breath, Placidia bore down again with a low snarl that escalated into a piercing scream. She felt the small body slither from her womb.

"It's a boy!" Thecla held the child by his heels. He was blue and unmoving.

"Why is he not crying? Let me see him." Placidia held out her arms. The midwife wrapped the child in a woolen towel and gave him to Machaon. He opened his bag and took out a hollow straw.

The midwives gave each other worried glances.

"Now, dearie, let my brother do his business. You need to push again, to rid yourself of the afterbirth."

"But my baby..."

"Push!"

Placidia pushed and, as she felt the gush of blood, she heard a weak cry from the table.

Machaon came back, smiling, with a bundle. "You have a son, My Queen."

He laid the babe in her arms. The pain of the past day receded to a dim memory. Her son still had a bluish cast, but that faded as he cried. He was covered in a white cheesy substance and his head was misshapen from the birth, but he was the most beautiful thing she had ever seen. She put a finger on his mouth. He sucked vigorously.

"That's a good sign." Thecla leaned over her. "Let me take the babe and clean him up. My daughter will tend to you." Placidia reluctantly gave up her child, and gave herself over to the ministrations of the younger midwife, who washed her body and packed her womb with moss to lessen the bleeding. Lucilla helped her change into a clean shift. The servants whisked all evidence of the birth from her room and remade her bed.

She was soon clean, and very tired. They laid the swaddled baby in her arms again and allowed Ataulf in. Pale with worry, he rushed to her side. "Placidia, my love." He pushed sweaty hair back from her forehead and searched her face. Tears welled in his eyes.

"Do I look that close to death?"

"No, my love. You look more beautiful than the morning sky."

Placidia regained some composure. She held out the baby. "We have a son."

He picked up the sleeping babe and held him gingerly. "I had forgotten how small they are at birth. What will we name him?"

"Valentinian, after my grandfather?"

"He was no friend to the Goths." Ataulf frowned. "Why not Theodosius, after your father?"

"Perfect." She smiled. "Theodosius, grandson of Theodosius, will rule the Empire."

"A large burden for one so small."

"He will grow into it." Placidia reached for the child. "But for now we both need our sleep."

He pulled the covers over both and kissed her eyes as they fluttered shut.

CONSTANTIUS STRODE DOWN THE DARK HALLWAY of the prison behind the warden. Ravenna was a wet city, and dank crept into these underground warrens. Attalus had managed to get a message to him, begging an audience. Curious as to what the wily ex-Prefect had to say, Constantius consented.

"Here he is, Patrician."

The warden lifted an oil lamp to shine into a dark cell. Constantius hardly recognized the usually dapper Attalus. His beard and hair were grown out and unkempt, his clothes filthy, and bruises discolored his face and limbs. He blinked at the bright light and rose from his huddle of damp straw. Not until Constantius saw the prisoner's confident stature and bright smile did he finally concede he might be Attalus.

"So you came, Patrician. I would offer you hospitality, but as you see I have little. Even the rats hardly bother with me anymore."

"I did not come to banter."

"Of course not. I ask only that you listen for a brief while and, if my cause seems just, plead my case with the Emperor."

Constantius folded his arms over his chest. "I'm listening."

Attalus took a deep breath. "I accepted the appointment as Emperor from the Senate as a ploy to put off the Goths, and I succeeded. They did not ravish Rome, at that time, and I foiled many of their aims with my obstructions."

"Are you saying you did these things on purpose to serve the Emperor?"

"Not the Emperor, but the Empire. I served the Emperor when it looked like my game was lost and the Goths threatened Ravenna. I did not demand the Emperor's head, but offered to let him retire to an island in exile. I convinced the Goths that letting Honorius live with the knowledge he'd lost his throne would be far more painful and humiliating than quick execution. Were it not for the fortuitous arrival of troops from the Emperor in the East, you might be sitting in this cell while I contemplated your fate."

"True. What is it you want?"

"Make the case with the Emperor for mercy. Unlike the other usurpers, I was forced into my station, and I used it against his enemies."

"You could have refused the acclamation."

"Rome needed a champion. Someone else would have taken the purple in my stead, and no one can play the game as well as I."

"I agree it's unlikely any of the other Senators would have been as 'successful' at their appointment as you." Constantius smiled. "But would you not prefer a swift death to this…life." He waved his hand at the damp cell.

"I ask only for the same mercy I offered Emperor Honorius. The loss of a finger and thumb, and banishment."

"I will give some thought to your request."

Attalus picked a wriggling nit from his hair. "Do you think the Emperor will feel more powerful humiliating a wretched beggar, or a man who somewhat resembles a former Prefect of Rome?"

Constantius laughed. "You amuse me, Attalus, and not much does these days. You have a slippery tongue that explains everything to your advantage."

Attalus shrugged. "It is my gift. I have used it for the good of the Empire and the Emperor."

Constantius turned to the warden. "Put him in a cell with light, give him water to wash, and a barber. I'll send some decent clothes and food."

"I will be forever in your debt, Patrician." Attalus bowed low. "I give you my pledge, I will not attempt to escape."

"One final question."

"Yes?"

"How fares Placidia?"

"She survives among the barbarians, doing much as I have. They treat her well, and Ataulf heeds her advice. She advocates her brother's cause and has moderated the barbarian's course. He would make peace with you if you let him."

"That possibility disappeared when Ataulf forced her into that disgraceful marriage."

"The princess was a good friend during our mutual exile. I only wish her happiness."

"That will be achieved when she is returned safely to Ravenna."

PLACIDIA COOED TO HER BABY, laughing when he reached for her finger. He was two months old and fully recovered from the trauma of his birth. Ataulf had consented to the baby being baptized Catholic instead of Arian, knowing that professing the Arian faith would make his son unacceptable to the vast majority of Romans.

The baby began to fuss. She handed him to his wet nurse for feeding. She needed to prepare for the afternoon audiences. Lucilla helped with her hair and robes—not as formal as her wedding—but more formal than her day clothes. Placidia wore a diadem of pearls and rubies on her forehead, and carried a gold staff of office.

To the disappointment of her detractors on the council, she had proved an able administrator, settling disputes with wit and fairness. Criminal acts were usually resolved in lower councils, but some few sought the ultimate judge. In addition, the citizens of Barcelona had direct access to the Queen. Today would be for petitioners only.

Placidia strode down the hall, leather sandals slapping on the smooth marble. When they occupied Barcelona, Ataulf took the local governor's mansion for their accommodations. Placidia met her petitioners in the audience chamber. The room was high-ceilinged, with air and light filtering in from the garden. The wall murals showed pastoral scenes in soothing greens.

"Queen Placidia," her guard announced as she entered. The waiting petitioners bowed low until she occupied her tall chair on a raised dais.

"I will hear my people's petitions." Placidia opened the session, flanked by her personal guard and her scribe, an ancient man with ink-stained fingers and a wit as dry as his parchment.

The petitioners approached in strict order of rank and precedence. During the first hour, she approved an appointment to a minor office, disbursed funds to repair the leak in the court building, and approved the carters' guild request to raise fixed prices. Now she was confronted with a heavy-set Gothic woman and a local husband and wife.

"What's your complaint?" her scribe asked.

The local man approached and abased himself. "Your Highness, I am Namatius, a baker. I petition you to remove the Gothic family billeted with us."

"On what grounds?" Placidia asked.

"The woman Matasuentha steals food from us and treats my wife like a slave. She has beaten her!" Angry spots rose to the man's cheeks.

"I take only what I'm due!" Matasuentha surged forward. "Oil and wood."

"You will have your say." Placidia looked over the group. "Why has this come to me? It should have been settled by the city magistrate."

"With all respect, Your Most Merciful Majesty, the Gothic officials refused to hear my petition."

"I see." That was a growing pattern—locals coming to her for redress when the Goths refused to even consider their petitions. Abuses of billeting were rapidly becoming the most frequent complaint. "Make your cases."

Namatius produced witnesses who had heard sounds of a violent argument from the couple's home and saw bruises on the wife. They also testified the couple frequently complained about the Goth woman taking their food. One woman testified she saw Matasuentha wearing a necklace that belonged to the wife.

"She gave me that necklace."

"After you beat me!" the wife said bitterly . "You treat our house as if it were yours, and we your slaves."

"Enough!" Placidia raised a hand. "You." She pointed at Matasuentha. "What's your story?"

"My husband was sent to Gaul, and left me little money to buy food in the markets for my children. I took nothing that was not my due—just oil and wood to cook. I implore you, My Queen, do not listen to these people. They hate the Goths and curse us. I found a sign in my room." She handed over a thin lead tablet curled into a cylinder.

The scribe took it, unwound it and squinted at the tiny markings. "It's a death curse." He shuddered, dropping the tablet into a nearby basket as if it burned his fingers.

A cold chill tickled Placidia's spine. She did not believe in the power of curses or amulets, but many did. The local couple looked at Matasuentha with loathing. *Do they hate the Goths as a race, or this woman for her actions?* Placidia suspected both.

"My judgment is to deny the petition."

Namatius opened his mouth to protest, but his wife came down hard on his foot and all that came out was a moan of pain.

Placidia continued. "Billeting soldiers and their families on the local population is a time-honored, but uncomfortable, necessity for all concerned. By law, the host must provide one third of the space available in his home. But he is not obligated to provide food or services. Matasuentha, you will return any possessions you extorted from your hosts, and you are forbidden to threaten or physically harm them in any way. Namatius, you are to retract and destroy all curses you and your wife have made against this woman, her children, or her tribe. A magistrate will visit your home to ensure all takes place. If either party has additional difficulties, go directly to him."

"But, my children!" Matasuentha was close to tears.

"None of my people will want for food in this land of abundance. Here is a small gift, to keep you until your husband returns." Placidia waved over her treasurer, who kept her alms purse.

The petitioners left, stiff-backed, with considerable distance between them. *Another compromise in which both parties go away unhappy. They will not see the necessity in my decision, only their own losses.*

Paulus entered the room, his tunic in disarray, limping more than usual. He approached Placidia without bowing.

"Mistress, the little one is ill with a fever," he said in low tones that did not carry beyond her ears. "Nurse has already sent for Machaon."

"Theo?" The blood drained from her face.

Placidia turned to her scribe. "Dismiss the petitioners." She took Paulus' arm and they hurried from the hall.

When she reached the nursery, Machaon was already examining the infant.

"What's wrong with him? Can you cure it?" She rushed to the doctor's side and put a hand on her baby's fuzzy head. He was hot to the touch. His face screwed up in pain. He cried weakly, and moved sluggishly.

Machaon shook his head. "His fever is very high, and he's weak. I have a powder that might help." He took a bottle from his bag, measured an amount into a goblet, and mixed it with a little wine. "Try this." He poured the concoction into a stemless lead cup with a spout near the bottom.

Placidia cradled Theo upright and put the spout in his mouth, allowing a trickle of the medicine to enter. "Hush, my treasure. Take the medicine, like a good boy." He sucked briefly, choked and threw up what little he had taken. The nurse handed her a wet cloth.

"Infants are difficult to medicate." Machaon took the cup from Placidia. "If he will not take the potion, we must try to lower his fever with cool baths."

The nurse poured a basin of water without Placidia's asking, and they bathed him. Theo soon fell into a fitful sleep. Placidia and the nurse took turns attending the baby throughout afternoon and night, bathing and singing to him. By the next afternoon, only fear for her child kept the exhaustion at bay. Machaon visited often, but he could do little.

Lucilla joined the fray and mimed that she should rest, but Placidia would not leave the nursery. When next she picked up Theo, a red rash covered his body. His skin was not only warm, but rough. He barely responded to her touch with a mewling cry.

"Fetch Machaon. Immediately!" Placidia felt the uncertain flickering of her baby's small spirit. Her throat closed with dread. "And send for Ataulf."

Chapter 16

PLACIDIA STARED DRY-EYED AT THE TINY SILVER COFFIN delicately engraved with Christ as Shepherd holding a lamb. So tiny a space, so short a life for her son. She would never again cradle his soft head against her breast, or see his bright smile. She would never again smell his sweet scent or hear his gurgling coo.

Her arms felt empty; her breasts ached with loss. A wracking sob exploded from her chest. "My son. My beautiful baby boy." She threw her arms around the casket. The cold metal offered no comfort. Fresh tears spilled down her cheeks onto the lid. She thought she had had no more tears to shed. She did not move to wipe them away.

Ataulf put his arms around her shoulders. "It's time to go, Placidia."

She turned in his arms. "Can he not stay with me just a little longer? Another day? An hour?"

He crushed her to his chest. She heard the grief in his voice. "Oh, my love, I too have lost a child. We must be strong for each other."

Ataulf motioned to two servants, who lifted the coffin to their shoulders and carried it out to the waiting cart. Placidia, bolstered by the embrace, followed. The gilded cart was filled with flowers and pulled by a black pony which Valia led. Ataulf and Placidia walked behind the cart. The rest of the mourners followed.

She wore a mourning veil that fell to her knees, to protect her from prying eyes. Ataulf held her elbow, steadying her when she stumbled. They wended their way through the streets to the small Catholic Church, where only family and close friends attended. Placidia knew many wondered and muttered at her grief. Life was perilous. Children died every day. Many felt an early death saved a child from the pain of this world, and should be thought a blessing. *How can it be a blessing that my child will not learn to laugh, to love, to lead?*

She listened to the bishop's voice without hearing the words. Nothing he said made sense. Placidia knelt on a silk cushion, stared up at the mosaic of Mary with the baby Jesus on her lap, and prayed. *Mother of God, help me understand. You lost your son; you know a mother's grief. My baby was taken from me. Please help me understand why.*

She listened with her heart, and heard nothing. There was only a dead space where her love and faith had resided.

At last the bishop finished, and they interred the silver casket in a vault in the floor. Placidia jumped at the crash of the marble slab as it fell into place, covering her baby with a finality she wanted to deny. She started forward. Ataulf caught her arm.

"Let me go. He doesn't like the dark."

"Placidia, my precious love, our baby is gone to heaven, where there is a holy light. He will not be afraid. All we bury are his mortal remains."

"And all our hopes and dreams."

"Not all. We will have other children. Time will dull this grief. With a new baby in your arms, you will soon forget this ill fortune."

"How could you?" She shook off his hands. "I don't want to forget Theo. I want to remember. I want to feel. But I feel only emptiness."

FOR THE NEXT MONTH, Placidia stayed in her room with the windows covered. She ate and slept little, growing more and more haggard. Lucilla, frantic, plied her with enticing tidbits, which she either refused or nibbled at. Ataulf tried to make love to her, but she didn't respond. He finally just lay with her in his arms, stroking her hair, repeating over and over, "You must let this go, my love. I need you. My children need you." She knew, in some far off corner of her heart, that he was worried to distraction about her, but couldn't bring herself to care.

One morning, Ataulf brought Gaatha to visit, then announced, "Placidia, I must go back to Gaul." She turned a vacant face to him. "I would not leave you in your time of need, but I seem to bring you no comfort, and I cannot sit here and watch you fade away."

Something stirred in her breast, a spark that recognized the grief and love in his voice and wanted to respond. She raised her hand to his cheek. "Be well, my love. I'll be here when you return."

"Will you? Do you promise?" He clasped her hand.

"I'll try." She turned her head so she didn't have to see the anguish in his face.

He dropped her hand and kissed her unresponsive lips.

"Take care of her, Gaatha." His voice was hoarse with unshed tears. He fled.

Gaatha went to her dressing stand and retrieved a brush. "Let me brush your hair, Placidia. I always find that comforting."

She sat on the bed, brushing Placidia's hair and humming a child's rhyming song. Placidia remembered her cousin Serena doing that for her when she was a small child and had just lost her mother. Feelings of comfort and safety hovered at the edge of her consciousness. She closed her eyes. She heard Lucilla's soft footsteps and the clink of a silver tray on a marble stand. Mint, she automatically classified the aroma.

"Sister, I have a special tea Thecla recommends for women who feel sad after childbirth. It might ease your mind."

Placidia opened her eyes to a steaming cup. She sipped the brew, tasting bitter herbs through the disguise of mint and honey. She wrinkled her nose.

"It leaves a bitter taste on the tongue, but Thecla says to have four cups a day, one with every meal and one before you sleep. By the end of a month, you will feel much better."

Placidia nodded. She wanted to feel better. She just didn't know how.

GRADUALLY, DURING THE SPRING, when apple blossoms sent their fragrance wafting on gentle breezes, her sadness lightened. There was no sudden rebounding of her spirit, just a slow dawning realization that she wanted to experience life again. One morning she asked Lucilla to help her with her makeup. The next week, she asked after Ataulf's children. Finally, one night, she fell into a deep and dreamless sleep.

Gaatha attended her, telling her the court gossip while she spun an even wool thread on her drop spindle. Placidia watched her sister-in-law's deft hands twist the wool and make the spindle twirl. "Why do you do that?"

Gaatha looked up in surprise. "Do what?"

"Spin. There is no need for thread. We can buy what cloth we want."

"It's a habit." Gaatha laughed. "It's one of the first skills my mother taught me. Whenever my hands idled, she put a spindle in them. On the farm where she grew up, the women spun the wool and wove the cloth. Most of my life has been spent traveling from province to province, but I still spin."

"What do you do with the yarn?"

"Give it to less fortunate women. They knit it, weave it, sell it if they wish."

"I have no talent for spinning, weaving, or preparing food." She laughed at a half-forgotten memory. "When I was a child, my foster mother Serena made me weave a girth for my brother's horse. It was an ugly thing, but Honorius pretended to cherish it anyway. He was a sweet boy and loved me well, in spite of my lack of domestic skills."

Gaatha stopped the twirling spindle and put a comforting hand on Placidia's arm. "I know. Your gifts lie elsewhere. You are an inspiration to your husband, and your people miss you. Valia has been handling the administration, but he has no patience for it. He chafes to return to the field."

"I will hear the petitioners next week." The thought of taking some action, any action, comforted her.

Gaatha smiled.

Taking up her duties helped keep her mind off her grief. Placidia still experienced an aching sadness when she glimpsed a child's toy or saw another woman with an infant, but she no longer needed to smother the wrenching pain with nothingness. The day finally arrived when she went to the nursery to be with Ataulf's children.

Little Ediulf ran to her, threw his arms about her knees, and cried, "I'm so glad you didn't die. I should have been ever so sad if you did."

His sisters exclaimed in dismay. "Ediulf, no! How could you say such a thing?"

The final bit of ice melted in her breast. Placidia smiled. She may have lost a baby, but she had four children that needed her. She took Ediulf's hand. "I knew you would be sad, so I told myself I had to get better and return to my family."

She moved to a bed and held out her arms to the girls. She hugged each, smelling their hair and filling her empty arms. "Vada, you've grown so. Lilla, we must do something about that stain. Maltha, your doll is lovely."

*****

PLACIDIA TOOK THE CHILDREN RIDING one perfect day in May, escorted by her personal guard, including young Sigisvult, who had been promoted from messenger. They picnicked in an apple orchard and raced to the top of a hill. Lilla won. Ediulf complained she should have run on one leg because she was twice as tall as he. They mounted their horses for the return trip and took to the road, the children laughing and squabbling.

A shout pulled them up short. "Off the road. King's messenger." A man on a well-lathered horse bore down on them.

"Sigisvult, stop that man and see who the messages are for."

The young Goth quickly overtook the tiring horse. Both stopped in the road as Placidia's party approached. The dusty messenger bowed from his horse. "Queen Placidia, I bear messages from Lord Ataulf."

"Yes. Unless they are secret, you may speak."

"He wished you to know he approaches, and will be in Barcelona by nightfall."

The children squealed with delight. Placidia's heart beat faster. She hadn't realized how much she missed her husband until he was nearly home. She couldn't wait for him to saunter in, tired and dusty.

"How far away?"

"About an hour."

"Come, children, let's surprise your father."

She reined Sky around and touched her flank with a spur.

"Lady!" She heard Sigisvult cry as she took off. "Don't go alone!"

The little mare broke into a ground-eating lope. Placidia felt exquisitely alive. Wind whipped her hair; her blood pounded, and her breath came in concert with the bunching of the smooth muscles of the horse between her thighs. They raced down the dusty road until Placidia felt Sky begin to tire. She slowed her to a walk and looked over her shoulder at the sound of galloping hooves.

"Please, My Queen." Sigisvult's horse was lathered from the run; the boy's face a mask of concern. "Your husband would have my head if anything happened to you."

Placidia laughed. "No ill wind blows today. Ataulf returns."

They walked their horses until the children and the rest of her escort caught up with them. When she sighted dust on the horizon, Placidia spurred ahead again. Coming over a hill, she spotted a large contingent of warriors, Ataulf in the lead on his black charger. She raced Sky down the slope, Sigisvult and the children pounding behind her. Several warriors grabbed their swords as the screaming horde bore down on them.

"Ataulf!" she shouted.

At the sound of her voice, he put spurs to his own horse and rode out to meet her. Placidia feared they might crash into each other, but Ataulf pulled his horse to a stomping stand and let her approach.

"Placidia?" His teeth showed through his dusty mustache. He pranced his horse close to Sky and swept Placidia out of the saddle, into his arms. "Oh, my love. I didn't dare hope."

"I told you I would be here when you returned." She reached up to his face and drew it down to hers in a deep and hungry kiss.

CHAPTER 17

THAT SUMMER WAS THE HAPPIEST OF HER TWENTY-SEVEN YEARS. She and Ataulf renewed their passion. His children could not replace her lost child, but they closed the open wound in her heart. Placidia gloried in her personal contentment, knowing the outside world would soon intrude. Summer lingered in the September days, but winter would come. Only Attalus' unknown fate marred her happiness. She missed his sage advice.

"What do you think of Africa?" Valia asked as he threw a knife at a well-notched log in the garden.

Ataulf threw his own knife, to stick next to Valia's. "As a homeland for our people?" They retrieved their knives. "Alaric thought to settle there. It's a rich land, but Italy holds it dearer than a moneylender does his coin. It would be a costly fight. Besides, we have neither the ships nor the stomach for a sea voyage."

"We could make the trek across Spain to the Pillars of Hercules. I'm told you can see Africa from there. We wouldn't need a fleet, just some ferry boats."

Placidia looked up from her book. "I've heard the seas are particularly wild at the Pillars. That's why merchants take the longer route. Besides, Constantius will not allow us to emigrate. He will blockade the ports and keep us bottled up in this devastated land until we starve. We should try to talk with him again."

The two men exchanged glances. "Constantius will never negotiate with me, Placidia."

"What's wrong with the man? Is he as thick as my brother when it comes to the Goths? Neither can see the value of having you fight for them rather than against."

"This is not a matter of one people against another." Ataulf pulled her into a hug. "It is between him and me. Constantius blames me for his loss."

"His loss?" Placidia relaxed into his arms. His physical strength and warmth provided a welcome illusion of safety. "The man is as rich as Midas. He runs the Empire in all but name. What more could he want?"

"Your hand in marriage."

Placidia blushed, remembering the awkward letters Constantius had sent to her in Rome, the look on his face in Valence. "He only wants me to consolidate his power."

"I saw how he looked at you when we met in Gaul. Those were the eyes of a man in love, not one who coveted a prize."

"God's bones." She snorted and pushed him away. "He only wants me as the jewel in his crown."

"Constantius seeks to rescue you from your hapless and dishonorable marriage." Ataulf grinned at her discomfort. "It's the only explanation for his implacable pursuit of us."

Placidia rejected the notion that she was personally responsible for their fate. Constantius' passion may influence his actions, but life was too complicated to reduce to one man's wishes. God constantly stirred the pot of human ambition—a charismatic ruler dies of a fever, winter storms disburse an invading army, a child dies. An ache constricted her heart. She laid a protective hand over her empty womb. She had hoped by now…

"We should go to Africa," Valia said.

Placidia took Ataulf's hand. "Your women grow weary of this constant wandering, giving birth beside muddy roads, raising children in other women's homes. We should at least try to talk to Constantius."

"I'll send another message to him, for our women's sake, but I'll prepare for war." Ataulf clapped Valia on the shoulder. "Come, my friend, I have a special mission for you. Tomorrow I want you to journey to the Vandals and Suebi. Perhaps we can arrange an alliance."

THE NEXT NIGHT, AFTER EVENING MEAL, Ataulf and several of his retainers went to the stables to inspect the horses, leaving Placidia to her own company. She decided to visit the children. Vada was growing into quite a beauty. Placidia had caught the sly glances between her and Sigisvult. *I should keep my eyes on those two.*

Lilla had talked old Paulus into giving her sword-fighting lessons—with her father's permission—and now swaggered about with a knife tucked in her belt. She teased little Ediulf so, he wheedled Paulus into carving him a short wooden sword. Maltha, the studious one, was nearly lost among the babble.

Placidia had almost reached their quarters when Lucilla caught up. Tears streamed from her eyes. She opened her mouth as if to speak. Placidia grabbed her by the shoulders. "What is it, Lucilla? What's wrong?"

Placidia heard the slap of running feet. It was one of Ataulf's retainers, face pale, eyes haggard. "My Lady, come quickly. It's the king."

"Ataulf." Fear prickled her spine. "Where?"

"Your quarters."

Placidia raised up her skirts and ran, nearly outstripping the long strides of her escort. She halted in their bedroom doorway. The backs of several men screened the bed. She pushed her way through to find Ataulf, blood seeping through a bandage pressed to his lower abdomen, breathing raggedly.

She froze as if turned to stone. Ataulf turned toward her and raised his hand but an inch, before dropping it again to his side.

"My love." Placidia knelt by the bed. "Who did this to you?" Ataulf gritted his teeth in pain. She pushed the hair back from his face. "Hush. Don't try to talk."

The retainer who came for her spoke up. "One of the grooms, a man named Eberwolf, stabbed my Lord as we inspected the horses."

"But why?" Her cry sounded like a wounded deer. "Why would he do such a thing?"

"Eberwolf cried out, 'For my master!' as he did the deed."

"What master?" Placidia felt the cold nothingness she had fought all winter creeping back into her soul.

"He named Sarus before he died by our swords," the man spat.

Sarus! How could he reach out from the grave to strike down another of my loves?

"Blood feud," Ataulf whispered. "The children."

Placidia trembled. There might be other assassins. "You." Placidia pointed at two of her escorts. "Gather some men. Take Lucilla, Paulus, and the children to the chapel and put them in the care of the Bishop. Claim sanctuary and guard them with your lives. Hurry!"

The men bowed and exited quickly.

Placidia turned back to her wounded husband, stroking the sweaty hair from his brow. "You'll be fine, my love. You've had worse cuts."

"This…my death."

"No, Ataulf, you can't leave me alone. I love you. What will I do without you?"

"Care for…the children." He grunted in pain.

"I won't let you go." She held his hand in a crushing grip. "You have to live for me, the children, your people." Her heart beat so hard, she could barely hear his whisper.

"I will…always…love you."

"Somebody fetch Machaon!" she cried.

"He is on his way, My Lady," her escort said. "But there is little he can do."

Placidia pulled the soaked bandage off Ataulf's stomach and saw for herself the awful truth of the man's words. The ragged wound slashed across his belly, exposing ruptured intestines. The smell of feces wafted from the cut. Men did not recover from such wounds.

She rose to stare at the men until their eyes dropped. Placidia wanted to give into the dark nothingness, but that would have to wait.

"Give me your knife." She held out her hand to the retainer.

"My Lady…" The man's eyes showed fear. "I need to cut a new bandage." He handed over his knife. She cut a strip from the silk bed hangings, folded it, and covered the wound.

Darkness lapped at her soul.

I cannot give in. I must be here for Ataulf. He needs me.

He gripped her hand with little more than a child's strength. "Be strong… my love…You are…Queen."

Tears clouded her eyes. She could barely speak around the knot in her throat. "You are my strength. Without you, I'm an empty shell."

"You…go back…fight…for our people."

"Go back to my brother?" She couldn't believe he would ask it of her. "I will not leave the children."

"Only way."

"We will find another, my love."

"My Lord," the retainer asked, "what of the succession?"

"Valia…beware Sergeric."

"All of you, out!" Placidia spat, and pointed to the door. "I want time alone with my husband."

They trooped out. Placidia climbed into bed with Ataulf and cradled his head on her lap. His voice grew weaker. "I'll…always…be with…you… Do what…you must." He sighed, exhausted by the effort.

He became paler with each moment. His hands grew cold. She spoke in low, soothing tones, reminding him of the day he gave her Night Sky. "I knew then I loved you, but could not let myself have such happiness. The Imperial Princess and the Barbarian King was an impossible match." She recounted as many of their happy moments as she could recall. Even after he stopped breathing, she continued murmuring and stroking his hair.

Machaon, who must have entered the room some time ago, put a hand on her shoulder. "My Lady, he is gone."

"I know. As is my heart."

"You should rest. Let me care for the body."

"I must do this. I do not want to send him to rest mutilated. Will you sew the wound?"

"Of course."

Machaon pulled a needle and thread from his bag. Placidia rose and stripped the bloody clothes from her husband. A servant brought her a basin. She gently washed the cooling flesh, her tears salting the water. When Machaon finished, the servant helped her dress the body in the robes Ataulf wore for their wedding.

She stroked his face one last time, and kissed his unresponsive mouth. "Good-bye, my love. If God has mercy, we will meet again." She stood and walked out of the room, oblivious of the blood staining her clothes.

"What shall we do?" one of her ever-present guard asked.

Placidia waved a vague hand. "Tomorrow. Now I must go to the children."

She headed down the corridor to their private chapel and the suite where the Arian Bishop Sigesar presided. Halfway, she heard sounds of swords clashing.

"Protect the Queen!" Her escort, swords drawn, formed a protective barrier, two in front, two in the rear. "Back! We must get her out."

The clash of swords stopped, but the shouting came closer.

"The children!" Placidia screamed. She ran toward the nursery.

One of the men in front grabbed her and threw her over his shoulder. "Forgive me, My Queen. We are too few."

"This way," another cried. They retreated at a run. Another band of armed men cut them off. The man put her down and handed her a knife. "Use this."

To take another life, or my own? She tucked it into her girdle.

Her guard, trapped in the narrow corridor front and back, bellowed war cries. They mounted a valiant defense, but the invaders used spears to outreach their swords. One by one, her defenders fell. The last, shielding her with his body, sagged into her arms.

Silence, much worse than clanging metal, filled the air.

A tall barbarian with a broken nose and close-set eyes knocked the body of her last defender aside, grabbed Placidia's right arm and twisted it behind her back. The pain dragged her from her state of shock.

"I'm the queen. You have no right to handle me this way."

"You aren't our queen. You're nothing but a Roman whore." He motioned to the rest of the men. "We got her. Let's get back to Sergeric."

Sergeric. He was behind the attack. He took my love from me.

Cold nothingness prowled the corners of her mind, threatening to extinguish all thought. She had to banish it. She reached for a tiny spark, flickering in the dark, and pulled it closer. Anger. Hate. If love was sand, forever escaping between her fingers, anger was a bright sword she could grasp firmly, and hate was the fire that forged its sharp edge.

They dragged Placidia toward the chapel. When they entered, Broken Nose shoved her to her knees at Sergeric's feet. Her hair came loose, tumbling about her face.

She had little time to take in the scene. All she saw was blood. Blood everywhere.

CHAPTER 18

PLACIDIA SWEPT THE HAIR FROM HER FACE and slowly rose to her feet. Her eyes took in the horrific scene while her heart fought to deny its reality. Blood splashed the wall murals of Christ with a flock of lambs, pooling beneath the altar with His cross. Bishop Sigesar, tears streaming down his face, rocked back and forth next to the altar, holding the bloody body of little Ediulf, mumbling, "Sanctuary. Sanctuary." The girls lay before the altar like pagan sacrifices, throats slit from ear to ear. Paulus slumped nearby, a spear through his chest, sword still clutched in his lifeless hand. Lucilla's limp body lay beside the wall.

"God's mercy." Placidia raised her hands to her mouth and swallowed hard to keep from vomiting. The stench of blood and fear clogged her nose, but she had no more tears.

Sergeric laughed. "No mercy here. They put up quite a fight, your little band. One of Ataulf's spawn even scored me with a knife before I slit her throat." He indicated a wound on his left forearm. "The old man died a warrior's death. Not like your gut-stuck husband, sorry excuse for a king."

Placidia gripped the hilt of the knife secreted in her gown. Screaming, she leapt at Sergeric, raked his face with one clawed hand and aimed the knife at his heart. The blade ripped his tunic, twisting in chain mail.

Broken Nose pulled her off the surprised Sergeric before she could redirect the blade. He forced her back with an arm across her throat, choking, wrenching her wrist until the knife fell.

Placidia kicked at his legs and clawed his arms until her sight turned dark.

"So, the Roman bitch is quite a hellcat." Broken Nose put his own knife to her throat, pricking the skin. "Should I end her misery, My Lord?"

"No. She still has value to me. Constantius will pay her weight in gold to get her back." Sergeric looked over her slight form as he tugged on his torn tunic. "Although that won't amount to much. I'll ask for more."

Placidia husked, through a bruised throat, "You Godforsaken bastard. Why the children? They could do you no harm."

"Blood feud." Sergeric sneered. "I will not make the same mistake as Ataulf. I leave none of his spawn to rise against me in the future. Alaric humiliated my brother and drove him from our ranks. Ataulf murdered him in a shameful ambush. I'll be King now, and all that was theirs will be mine." He put a finger under her chin. "All except you. I won't have a Roman whore for a wife."

"Exterminate the rivals, root and branch. What a Roman thing to do."

He punched her jaw. Her head snapped back and her lip split. Her mouth filled with blood as she tongued a loose tooth. She spat the blood in his face. "You'd better kill me now, because, with God and the Mother Mary as my witness, I will have your head."

Sergeric laughed. "Lock her up. We'll see how much fire she has after tomorrow."

Broken Nose hauled her out by the hair. Sergeric turned to the Bishop. "Clean up this mess, old man."

They locked her in a bare storage room behind the kitchens, with neither pallet nor chamber pot. When she could hold her bladder no longer, Placidia squatted in a corner. The stench of her own waste clung to her hair and clothes. Finally, exhausted, she fell into a fitful sleep on the bare floor, near the door.

BROKEN NOSE WOKE HER IN THE MORNING with a sneering laugh. "Some Imperial Princess, sleeping in your own filth." He tossed her a bundle. "Strip. Sergeric wants you to wear this."

She sorted through the rags—a filthy slave's tunic and a broken pair of sandals. She threw them to the floor. "Tell Sergeric I want a bath and my own clothes."

"You'll wear what I give you. Now take off your clothes, or I will." He grinned. "That would be a pleasure."

She turned her back to him and dropped all but her *tunica*. She pulled on the slave's garb. It smelled of its previous owner, who evidently eschewed bathing. A large red wine stain over the left breast reminded Placidia of blood. She exchanged her felt slippers for the broken sandals, then turned. "At least allow me to wash the blood from my face, and comb my hair."

Her tormenter sneered. "Come here." He tied her wrists together before her, with rough twine. "That should keep your claws from my face."

Placidia set her jaw, suppressing a wince from the bruised flesh.

Broken Nose escorted her to the audience chamber, where Sergeric resided in barbarian splendor. He wore a leather tunic and trousers; a wolf's skin hung over his shoulders, the front legs tied over his chest and its head acting as a hood. He wore so much gold on his ears, neck, and arms that Placidia wondered he could stand. He had raided Ataulf's treasure chest and given generously to his followers. Placidia recognized many a *fibula*, knife and torque on their persons. Sergeric rose to inspect her.

"Our Imperial Princess seems suitably attired." He sniffed. "And wearing the latest in scents as well."

"Gold doesn't make you a king, any more than slaves' rags disguise my royal birth. You're a cowardly dog under that wolf's skin. Nothing can clean the stench of innocents' blood from your filthy carcass."

His face reddened. Sergeric punched her in the stomach. Air exploded from her lungs. She fell to her knees, retching. The men laughed as she recovered her breath. Placidia rose up onto one knee and glared through her curtain of hair. "A cowardly dog who can do no better than hit a woman with her hands tied."

Sergeric yanked her up by the hair, holding her face inches from his own. "I may yet decide the pleasure of killing you is worth the price."

She stared back, mouth twisting into a sneer. "Do it." *And spare me the pain of living in this world without my love.*

"Don't tempt me further." He stepped back and handed Broken Nose an iron slave collar. "Put this on her. We'll see how the Queen likes our little triumph."

Broken Nose snapped the collar into place and yanked her toward the door by her shackled wrists. Placidia blinked at the bright sunlight streaming through the streets of Barcelona. Sweet air mocked her bitter mood.

For all his disdain of things Roman, Sergeric had arranged a triumph with himself in the role of victorious Roman general. Wagons heaped with booty looted from the mansion trundled after Sergeric. About two hundred of Ataulf's household—servants and slaves, including two pregnant women and a number of children—preceded Sergeric's mounted troop of warriors. Placidia looked in vain for Gaatha or her daughters. She prayed to an ever-more-distant God that they had escaped the slaughter.

Sergeric mounted Ataulf's favorite black stallion, but it proved restive and hard to handle. He pulled cruelly on the bridle. The animal reared, rolling its eyes. By the time he had it under control, its flank was slick with sweat, and bloody foam dripped from its mouth. The triumph snaked through streets lined with people who cheered half-heartedly and quickly dispersed when the procession passed.

The sun was hot for late September. Placidia soon grew thirsty. A few captives cried for water, receiving blows for their troubles. Placidia cursed under her breath. She walked as upright as she could, encouraging those close by. A girl no more than ten fell to the ground in front. She had blood on her tunic, a dazed look, and lay whimpering, knees to chest. Placidia tried to lift the girl with her bound hands. "Someone help."

"Let me, Mistress. I'm a carter, used to hauling heavy burdens." A large man with black hair and kind eyes picked the girl up and carried her like a baby.

"Thank you, and God's blessings." Others followed his example. The stronger lent their shoulders to the weaker; children rested on the backs of adults until they could walk again. Placidia lost a sandal to a broken strap. Her bare foot left a trail of blood on the ground. Her face throbbed and her gut ached, but she trudged for twelve dusty miles, buoyed by the thought of peeling the skin from Sergeric, inch by bloody inch.

By the end of the trek, she could barely put one foot in front of another. Her tongue was swollen with thirst, seeming to fill her mouth. Sergeric's men herded the captives back onto the mansion grounds, into a hastily erected compound with wooden fences on three sides and a stone wall on the fourth. As each passed through the gate, he or she was handed a cup of stale water and hunk of bread. They greedily drank. Placidia was pleased to see no one tried to rob another of their sustenance.

Sergeric rode into the compound. "You were once Ataulf's. Now you are mine, but I have no need of additional slaves. You will be sold as soon as I can find a buyer."

"But I'm a free man," one captive rose to protest, "from the city."

Sergeric nodded at one of his followers, who strode to the man and struck him across the face. "You are my captives, the spoils of war. Any foolish enough to try to escape will be killed."

A sneer spread across his face. "You may thank your former queen for this. Had she not weakened Ataulf with her Roman wiles, we would have conquered all of Gaul and been marching on Italy as we speak. It is left to me to make the Gothic people great again."

He was greeted with stony silence.

"Spare us your speeches, regicide," Placidia croaked.

"Have a pleasant night, Princess." Sergeric rode from the compound, laughing.

Two guards pointed out the waste pits dug in a corner, then passed out thin blankets. Captives dropped to the ground, huddling in small groups. Placidia sat in a conspicuously empty space, the lump of bread sitting in her stomach like a fiery coal–or maybe it was hate that roiled her stomach. She spied three men approaching, and rose to greet them.

The carter who had carried the girl during the march bowed low and spoke for his fellows. "Mistress, what would you have us do? We have several strong men willing to try the guards on your command."

"I am most grateful for your valor, but would not have you sacrifice yourselves needlessly. The guards are well armed. Let us rest a day, gather what knowledge we might, and make a plan tomorrow."

The men backed away, bowing, "As you wish, Mistress."

Placidia rolled herself in her blanket and fell into an exhausted sleep, frequently interrupted by cries of people in the throes of nightmares. Some of the cries might have been her own.

THE NEXT MORNING, guards rolled in barrels of water. Everyone drank their fill. There was even enough to wash some of the cuts and bruises the captives had received. Placidia limped about the camp, accompanied by the carter and two other free men, to assess the needs of her people. Many had cuts that could turn deadly if they grew infected. One of the pregnant women thrashed in the throes of fever. A thin man cradled a broken arm. The little girl the carter had carried lay curled up, eyes unblinking. A familiar figure held the child in her lap, and looked up at Placidia with unseeing eyes.

"Nikarete?" Placidia squatted, placing a gentle hand on the young midwife's shoulder. She flinched at the touch.

"Yes, Mistress."

"Your mother?"

"Dead." Tears glistened in the girl's eyes as her mouth twisted into a snarl. "A blow to the head when she tried to protect a newly delivered kitchen slave from…rape."

"You were there?"

Nikarete shuddered uncontrollably. Placidia pulled her into an embrace, patting her back. She looked from one man's face to another. "How many?"

Most cast their eyes down, but a few blazed with fury.

"All the women, from grandmothers to children," the carter said. "God rot their cocks."

Thank the Good Lord, Lucilla is dead.

"Are there any other healers?"

"None."

Placidia sighed and held the young midwife until her shuddering stopped. "Nikarete, I would not ask this of you now, but you are our only healer. The pregnant woman, the little girl, the man with the broken arm, they all need you." Placidia held her at arm's length, looking into her eyes. "I need you."

Nikarete nodded.

Placidia rose and looked from face to face. "I need all of you. Organize a place for the sick and injured. Tell me what supplies we need."

PLACIDIA APPROACHED THE GUARDS AT THE GATE. "We need a doctor, medical supplies, and additional blankets."

A rough fellow with long braided mustaches turned. "What for?"

"A number of people are ill or injured."

"What of it?"

"Sergeric will not be happy if his slaves die. A dead body brings him no gold." Placidia put the steel of command in her voice. "Get the captain of the watch."

The guard sauntered off to consult his superior, who in turn left for the mansion. The second man returned with a third. "I'm captain of this watch. You want something?"

"We need a doctor."

"Impossible. The physicians are tending our wounded."

"Then we need wood for a fire, pots to boil water, clean rags for bandages, and herbs to treat fever and infections." Placidia ticked the items off on her fingers.

The captain entered the compound and surveyed the miserable captives, his jaw firming. "I'll see what we can spare."

"Thank you."

After the supplies came—not as many as she had hoped—Placidia moved from group to group, learning their stories. Focusing on others kept her crushing loss at bay. That night, after a supper of thin broth and stale bread, Placidia met with her informal "council."

"The man with the broken arm is still in much pain." Nikarete seemed better for the distraction of work. "The pregnant women's fever is down; she's resting more comfortably. Two of the worst wounds are showing signs of infection, Mistress, and should be cauterized. The child shows no change."

"Do what you can for them. I'll ask for a doctor again tomorrow."

The carter pulled on his ragged beard. "My Lady, we have news."

"What?"

"Some of the boys play near the guard station and listen. The guards are bored. They talk of much they should keep to themselves."

"What did our clever youngsters learn?"

"Sergeric keeps what's left of the King's personal guard in the cellar of your mansion. Others escaped to the surrounding countryside."

Placidia's heart raced. "If they have any sense, they will ride for Valia in the west. Sergeric took the kingship through violence and murder. He does not command the allegiance of all the nobles. Valia will surely contest him."

"When?"

"I don't know." Placidia shook her head. "But we must keep our spirits up until he comes."

THAT WAS HARDER TO DO THE NEXT DAY, as boredom took its toll. Placidia nursed the sick, told stories to the children, and was finally reduced to counting the paces along each fence. With the coming of dark, she willed her tired body to sleep, only to be disturbed by someone shaking her shoulder and whispering.

She started at a dark shadow by her side. "A voice on the other side of the fence is calling your name. I came to fetch you."

"Who is it?" Placidia whispered.

The figure shrugged, turned, and crawled toward the corner where the wooden fence met the stone wall. Placidia followed on hands and knees, glancing back at the gate where two guards stood with torches. They seemed not to notice the scuffling in the shadows.

Placidia approached the fence. She saw where cracks would make it possible to see in or out, but the moon had already set and she saw nothing but blackness. "Who's there?" she whispered.

"Mistress, you're alive! I was so afraid after the ch…children…" The unfamiliar voice choked on a sob. "It's me. Lucilla."

CHAPTER 19

L ucilla?" Placidia hesitated in confusion. "You're alive? How?"

"I was stunned by a blow. The murderers left me for dead. The Bishop hid me until I could come to you."

"You're speaking!"

"I never had the will before. The Bishop said I spoke in my delirium. When I came to, I asked for you and he told me wh-what happened." Lucilla swallowed convulsively. "The poor children…"

"They will be avenged, Lucilla. Do not fear for that." They sat quiet for a moment. "Are you safe here? Where are you staying?"

"The guards get lazy late at night, and don't make their rounds. I stay with the Bishop, but work in the kitchen during the day. There are few friends of Sergeric among the slaves." Lucilla wiggled two fingers through a hole. "Oh, Mistress, we must get you away from here."

Placidia touched the fingers, taking strength from their warmth. "I won't leave without these people, and my revenge on Sergeric. What do you know of Valia?"

"Sergeric's men tell of his approach, but boast he has not the men to take the city."

"They are probably right." Placidia chewed her lower lip. "We must help him. Let me think on it. We will talk again tomorrow night. I will need your help, Lucilla. Can you get word to Valia of our plans?"

"I will move the heavens and earth for you, Mistress."

Placidia chuckled for the first time in days. "Such a heroic feat won't be necessary, Lucilla. Send a message to Valia that we will help him gain access to the city. He should wait to hear from me."

"Yes, Mistress."

"Lucilla, what of Gaatha and her daughters?" Placidia held her breath in fear.

"Safe, My Lady. Her new husband smuggled them out of the city as soon as they had word of trouble."

"Machaon?"

"He cares for Sergeric's wounded, and demands the release of his niece."

"Can you get word to him?"

"Yes."

"Good. We'll include him in our plans." She released Lucilla's fingers. "Now you must go. Return tomorrow night when it is safe. I'll sleep in this spot."

Lucilla slipped away. Placidia lay down to consider her plan.

The next day she circulated among her people, talking to those she trusted. When Lucilla returned, late that night, she had her plans in place, and hastily whispered them through the fence.

Lucilla returned the night after to confirm all was in place.

Placidia slept well, with a grim smile on her face.

As the sun set on the seventh day since her family's slaughter, Placidia sat near the gate, playing a game with the children. She heard Lucilla approach the gate guards.

"Sergeric is feasting tonight and wants you to join in the cheer. He sent me with these cups of wine."

"Only one cup each?" a guard complained.

"He doesn't want you to be negligent in your duties."

"I could drink a barrel and hold these sheep. They haven't tried a thing in days."

"When your shift is done, come to the kitchen. I'll save you some of the feast."

"I hope that's not all you'll save me." The guard slapped Lucilla on her bottom as she scurried away.

"What would you want her for?" the second guard asked. "There are plenty of prettier slaves."

"I don't plan to have the candles lit." The first guard laughed and gulped his wine. "Good stuff. Not that vinegar they usually serve us."

As the guards finished their drinks, Placidia sent the children to gather her helpers. They drifted toward her through the crowd, talking in low tones to those they passed. Placidia was surprised the guards didn't feel the sense of excitement and hope that swept the camp, but when she checked they were barely standing. By the time ten of the strongest men had gathered at her side, the guards were snoring from Machaon's sleeping draught.

Placidia and her cohort broke through the gate and dragged the guards inside. "You two," Placidia pointed at two men, "change into the guards' clothing. We need someone at the gate, in case anyone looks this way."

She and the rest of her escort crept in the shadows of the stone wall until they reached a spot where a tree's branches dangled over the side. Two men formed the base of a human ladder, helping four of their colleagues into the branches.

"Gather what friends you can and attack the South Gate. Lucilla said it is lightly guarded. Valia and his troops will be waiting." Placidia waved the remaining four men to her back. "This way. Lucilla will meet us at the kitchen."

Lucilla met them with a finger to her lips and a lit oil lamp. They followed her through the pantry and into a service corridor.

"I was only able to bring these." Lucilla held out an assortment of kitchen knives. "But they are freshly honed." Her face took on a fiendish quality in the flickering lamplight.

Placidia took a carving knife, testing the edge on her thumb. A drop of blood welled up. "Perfect. How many guards?"

"Only five between here and the cellars, and they have all had a special cup of wine to celebrate the feast."

The journey proved almost as easy as Lucilla claimed. As they passed the unconscious men, some of her escort tried out their kitchen knives and confiscated the guards' weapons. The last guard, however, proved more conscientious.

"Who goes there?"

Two of Placidia's men jumped silently from the shadows. One grunted as the guard ran him through with a spear. He slumped to the wall, panting.

Our first casualty.

Steel rang on steel as another of her escort joined the fray. The guard fended off two men.

"To me!" the guard shouted. "I am attacked!"

"Quickly, before he rouses the house!" Placidia hissed.

Another shout ended in a bloody gurgle.

Cries came from the other side of a sturdy door that was closed with a solid beam. "Who's there? Let us out!"

"Sigisvult?" Placidia recognized the voice. "It's your queen and the good household servants, come to free you. Stand back."

The carter pushed up the beam and pulled the door open. A troop of fifty odd warriors blinked in the light. Sigisvult squinted at her filthy slave rags and the grime on her face, then knelt at her feet. "Forgive us, My Queen, for not coming to your aid when you most needed us." Tears tracked his dirty face.

"Sergeric took us all by surprise, but tonight we turn the wheel. Here are weapons we took from the guards." The servants handed over spears, knives, and swords. "Valia will be here soon. We wait for the sounds of his arrival before we attack Sergeric and the feasters. This way."

Placidia led them back up the staircase and into the service corridor. They waited for a seeming eternity. *Did the men not get through to the gate? Was Valia not there?* She was revising her plans when she heard shouting at the front of the mansion. Her confidence returned. Placidia cried, "For your queen and honor! Kill them all, but I want Sergeric alive."

The warriors streamed through the corridor and into the garden. Lightly armed, they slipped through the flickering torchlight to attack their half-drunk opponents. One by one, Sergeric's supporters fell under the onslaught, and her men took up their arms. The now-familiar stench of blood and shit overpowered the delicate scents of trampled rosemary and lavender. Placidia saw Broken Nose go down with a spear in his neck, and smiled grimly. Within minutes, the garden was hers, and Sergeric in the hands of two of her men. Shouting and sounds of metal on metal came from the entrance. Placidia did a quick count. She had lost only three men.

"I want five of you here as escort. The rest of you, support Valia from the rear."

The men left the garden, shouting war cries. The sounds of battle quickly diminished.

Placidia approached Sergeric, Lucilla at her heels. Her guard forced him to his knees, head bowed.

"No, pull his head up. I want him to look into my eyes. I want him to see his fate."

Sergeric spat at her.

Sigisvult knocked his head aside with a spear butt. Blood ran from the ragged cut into his left eye.

"I know my fate, you Roman witch."

"Placidia!" She turned at the sound of her name. Valia entered the garden with several of his troop, all dusty, many covered in blood. "Are you all right?"

"I'm safe, now that you're here. Have you secured the city and the villa?"

"Yes, My Queen. We have Sergeric's supporters. What do you want done with them?"

"Execute them all."

At his indrawn breath, Placidia turned to her captive. "I told you, you should have killed me. You thought me a weak woman, with thin Roman blood."

She pointed to the men holding Sergeric. "Bring him to his feet."

She moved in close to whisper in his ear, in a parody of intimacy. "You forgot I am a princess, raised in the Imperial court. Treachery and betrayal were my tutors and playfellows. Revenge is not only a Gothic custom."

Placidia shoved her carving knife into Sergeric's gut, and pulled it downward. Blood spurted onto her hands. "For my husband and children." *And my life.*

She stepped away; her lips pulled back, more in a grimace than a grin.

Sergeric stared at the knife protruding from his gut.

Valia shouted, "No, Placidia!" He ran forward, hand outstretched.

"Valia, leave off. I want to watch him die. I want to watch the life leak from him with every drop of blood. I want him to know that I'm the one who brought him to this fate. My face will be the last thing he sees in this life."

Placidia stood, arms crossed, glaring at the man who had stripped all chance of happiness from her life. Sergeric fell to his knees. He did not moan or cry out. As usually happened with gut wounds, he took a long time to die. Placidia savored every moment. She saw the horrified look on Valia's face and heard murmurs among her retinue, but there were more grim smiles than frowns.

When Sergeric's head flopped forward, Sigisvult held it up by the hair. Finally, when he coughed blood and breathed his last, she ordered, "I want his head on a pike and his skin nailed to the gate."

Valia dutifully severed Sergeric's head from his corpse. It took three hacking blows.

"What now, My Lady?" Valia picked up the grisly trophy.

"A bath and bed. I leave the ordering of the people in your capable hands. Will you meet with the nobles for the election tonight, or tomorrow?"

"Tomorrow will be soon enough."

"Good." A wave of darkness overtook Placidia. She swayed, hand to her head.

"My Lady!" Valia dropped the head, which landed with a sodden thump, and rushed to steady her.

"I'll be fine. It's just lack of food and rest." She righted herself. "Lucilla, can you attend me?"

The two women made their way to one of the guest bedrooms. Placidia did not want to sleep in the bed where Ataulf had died and Sergeric took his pleasure. She decided to forgo a bath in favor of a standing wash, and fell into the bed before Lucilla could bring her food. Her initial wave of fierce satisfaction gave way to an aching loneliness.

THE NEXT TWO DAYS, while the nobles wrangled over the leadership, proved more difficult than the previous seven. Then, she had had a goal, a consuming passion to occupy her thoughts and actions. Now she had nothing to stave off the grief but petty routine. Placidia freed all the slaves who had borne captivity with her, and settled money on former free men and slave alike, so they might make their own way in the world. She rewarded Ataulf's retainers. Most of his *bucellarii* swore allegiance to her and her alone.

On the morning of the third day, Bishop Sigesar came to her. "My Lady, I thought you would perhaps seek my counsel in these trying times. God in his mercy can lighten your heart."

"God's mercy?" she nearly spat. "Where was God when my husband was murdered? Where was God when four innocent children and a faithful friend were butchered? Where was God when my women servants were raped and male servants beaten? Do not talk to me of God's mercy."

"Do not confuse man's wickedness with God's neglect." The old man shook his head. "Turn your heart to his love, and be healed of your grief."

Placidia turned her back on the bishop. "My heart is burdened with hate. I did murder with my own hand, and I am glad. I will never repent my actions."

The old man gasped. "You must repent, or condemn your soul to everlasting hellfire."

"Then I am condemned."

The bishop put a hand on her shoulder. "Perhaps it is too soon to talk of these things. Time has a way of healing the soul."

Time. It took me months to recover from Theo's death. Will I ever heal these wounds? Do I want to?

Placidia covered his hand with hers. "Thank you, Bishop, for your kind words and concern. Tell me, what of…of the children? Paulus?"

"I gave them a Christian burial."

"Without father or mother to mourn them." She sighed. "And Ataulf?"

The bishop shook his head. "Sergeric disposed of the body. I know not where."

"Another account settled." She snarled. "I had Sergeric's body fed to the dogs."

Pity replaced the concern in the bishop's eyes. "I can take you to the children's burial place, if you wish."

Her shoulders slumped. "I would like that…to say good-bye."

"Tomorrow then, after the morning meal."

"Yes. Thank you for coming, Bishop."

With the dismissal in her tone, the bishop left Placidia to her own demons.

PART III

EMPRESS

SEPTEMBER 416 - APRIL 437

CHAPTER 20

Ravenna, September 416

"PRINCESS, WE ARE ALMOST THERE."

Placidia pulled aside the curtain of her litter. General Constantius rode next to her. He straightened from his usual posture—bent low over his horse, as if needing to grasp his mount's neck to prevent a fall. *Not like Ataulf.* The memory of her dead husband tugged at her heart, but Placidia swallowed her tears. The year since his death had been filled with continued wandering. Valia led the Goths to the Pillars of Hercules, only to be turned back by another disaster on the turbulent sea. The new Gothic King finally took her advice and negotiated a homeland in Gaul, in return for providing troops to the Roman army and her return to Ravenna.

"All of Ravenna waits to welcome you home," Constantius said.

"Ravenna has never been my home." She pulled shut the curtain on his disappointed face. Rome with Stilicho, Serena, and her cousins had been home. Barcelona with Ataulf and the children had been home. Even the jouncing wagon with Lucilla and Paulus had been more of a home than the marble halls of the Imperial palace at Ravenna.

Lucilla, ever sensitive to Placidia's moods, held her hand in silence, radiating comfort. The raging fires of Placidia's hate for Sergeric had burned to ashes after his death, leaving an empty space in her soul. She did not collapse, as she had after little Theo's death, but neither had she regained a sense of joy or purpose. At twenty-eight, her life lay before her, bleak and formless.

*****

SIGISVULT SWATTED A BITING FLY. The insects had been a constant harassment since the convoy entered the main road through the pestilential swamps surrounding Ravenna. His horse twitched and snorted under the onslaught. "Easy, Hammer. We're nearly there." The young Goth patted the horse's sweating neck. At sixteen, Sigisvult had attained his adult height of just over six feet, but he needed to build some muscle on his promising frame.

"Sigisvult, are your ears stuffed with wool? I've called you twice." The captain of the Queens' Guards scowled. When Valia negotiated the Queen's return to Ravenna, Placidia gave her *bucellarii* the choice of staying in Gaul or accompanying her to Ravenna as her personal guard. Over two hundred Goths took sacred oaths of loyalty and received gifts of gold and weapons from Placidia's hands. They pledged their lives to her until she dismissed them from service or they returned her gifts.

"Yes, sir." Sigisvult's tanned face darkened further with embarrassment. "I mean no, sir, I don't have wool in my ears."

"Then look sharp. Put on your armor. We march through the city and we don't want the people thinking the Queen's Guards are wild barbarians."

"Yes, sir!"

Sigisvult untied his mail shirt from his saddle, donned his tight-fitting helmet, and settled his small round shield. All were new, not dented or worn like his usual armor, which had been scavenged from a battlefield. Best of all, they matched his fellow guardsmen's. The Queen had insisted her guards be outfitted with the best—horses from Spain, armor from the workshops in Gaul, tunics of the finest wool, dyed deep blue and edged with yellow. They would make a fine escort.

He sheathed his sword in a bronze-studded leather baldric over his right shoulder as the column came to a halt. The horses stamped and twitched. Sweat ran down Sigisvult's face and back. Toward the head of the column, the captain and General Constantius shouted at one another, but he couldn't hear their words. The queen left her litter to confront the general. Even on the ground, facing a mounted man, she stood straight, a commanding presence. Her voice sounded calm and firm. The general nodded, and the captain rode back to his troop.

"What's the row?"

"What do the bloody Romans want this time?"

"Why'd we stop?"

The captain spat on the road. "The general wanted to send us back to guard the baggage and the women."

Angry shouts rumbled from the troop. Sigisvult chafed under the humiliation.

Even the cheek guards of his helmet could not conceal the stubborn set of the captain's jaw. "I refused. The Queen insisted we accompany her in the progression. Move up. Flank the litter." He put a hand on Sigisvult's arm. "Wait."

"Yes, sir?"

"The Queen has a special commission for you." The older man grinned. "Report to her at once."

Sigisvult trotted his horse to the litter, his breath ragged with anticipation. "My Queen?"

She pulled the curtain aside. Her smile brightened her face, but didn't quite touch her eyes, where grief pooled. He would give his life to see that sadness banished. Since the day she stuck her knife in Sergeric's gut and twisted, he knew he would serve no other.

"Sigisvult, I want you to carry my standard."

His heart raced. "It will be my honor." He bowed low in the saddle.

She handed him a tube of white silk, longer than a tall man's height, decorated with a running wolf, jaws open, teeth bared.

He fixed it to his lance. An errant breeze whipped it straight, the first wind he had felt since they entered the marshes.

"Precede me. I will follow in a chariot." She stepped out of the litter and leaned in close. "Keep watch. Some at court might not be pleased to see me return."

"Of course, My Queen."

Trumpeters led the procession through the main gate, announcing their entrance with a surprisingly harmonious tune. Sigisvult kept his face forward, but his eyes darted back and forth, taking in this city no army had ever breached. Stables and warehouses gave way to modest apartment buildings with shops on the ground floor. The rich smell of manure mixed with the tang of hot cooking oil and sickly sweet stench of meat hanging in the hot sun.

Ravenna was a city of canals and bridges. People stood in their boats and cheered from the rooftops. All seemed genuinely pleased to have their princess back—or maybe it was the Patrician they cheered as he rode his horse behind

Placidia's chariot. Hammer curved his neck and stepped high, as if the horse thought he was the center of attention. The procession broke through to the forum—the heart of all Roman cities. The law basilica flanked the left, providing shade under roofed columns. A church with open bronze doors sat on the right. At the palace, the sun bounced off the polished armor of a solid wall of *scholae*—Emperor's guards. Sigisvult sat tall, banner flapping, as Placidia dismounted from her chariot.

The captain picked six men to accompany the Queen to her rooms, dismissing the rest to the less than tender regards of the *scholae*. Sigisvult heard some angry mutters as they looked over the Goths. As grooms led the horses to the stables, he smiled at the *scholae's* covetous looks. *Our queen should be proud of us. We put the Emperor's pitiful guard to shame.*

"This way." A servant led the remaining troop to a long barracks, outside the palace proper but connected through a roofed walkway. The servant motioned with his chin. "Pallet. Box for gear. Posts in the wall for your tunics. Baths and toilets that way; kitchen there. Anything else, ask your captain."

"Charming fellow." Sigisvult grinned at the man next to him as they dropped their packs. "Do you think all Romans will be as welcoming?"

CONSTANTIUS ESCORTED PLACIDIA TO HER QUARTERS IN THE ROYAL PALACE.

"I hope you find the rooms to your satisfaction, Princess. I furnished them myself."

"Thank you, Patrician. They are quite…impressive."

Constantius shared one trait with Ataulf—he liked to display his wealth. The rooms were crowded with gilt furniture, reflecting the light from oil lamp chandeliers. He must have spent a fortune on the frescos alone. The pictures of gardens and hunts painted on the walls were so realistic, Placidia could almost smell the flowers and feel the breeze bending the trees. The fine mosaics on the floors were a subtle black and white geometric pattern, which did not detract from the colorful walls or the painted statuary filling the corners.

Constantius seemed to favor a dark red for the fabrics and backgrounds. *A passionate color.* Placidia passed her hand over silky brocade. *And the color of dried blood.* She walked through the rooms, mentally marking the items she would have removed on the morrow. With luck, she wouldn't be here long.

"Put the chests there." She pointed under a bed piled high with feather mattresses and covered in a riot of red and purple cushions.

Her guards shoved several bound and locked chests under the bed. The keys to her personal fortune jangled from a ring on Lucilla's girdle. She would have to buy a chamberlain soon, obtain cooks, serving girls, tiring women, fullers. The list seemed endless. She had forgotten the excessive number of servants it took to run an Imperial household. She should have funds from her own estates on deposit—six years' worth—assuming her brother hadn't appropriated them for himself. *I'll think about it tomorrow.*

Constantius hovered. "Your brother is most anxious to meet with you."

"Should I wear my old sandals?" At his puzzled expression, she clarified, "Will he meet me in his chicken yard, or the audience chamber?"

He smiled, displaying large, even teeth. "His private apartments, actually, which adjoin yours. I'll escort you there." He offered his arm, which she lightly touched with the tips of her fingers. After a few steps, Constantius stopped before a bronze-bound door. "Your brother wanted to meet with you alone. Send for me later…if you wish."

"Thank you, Patrician." Placidia graced him with a fleeting smile. "I will inform my brother of the excellent care you took on my behalf."

She entered the private parlor. Honorius sat in a cushioned chair beside a sideboard covered with delicacies. A brazier burned in the corner. Sweat gathered at Placidia's hairline and trickled down her neck, but she dared not complain of the heat.

"You may go." Honorius waved at the servants. They bowed and backed out with only the slightest hint of disappointment on their faces.

Placidia thought her brother was aging poorly. In only six years, Honorius had lost any firmness of flesh he had as a youth. He looked bloated and pasty—not from lack of sun, but with the gray tinge of illness.

Placidia knelt at his feet, head bowed, and said words that chafed her very being. "Dear brother, I have returned to ask your forgiveness for any grief or pain I have caused you."

"My sweet sister, there is no need for you to abase yourself in this way."

She looked up into his eyes, searching for some understanding of her pain, but saw only brown pools reflecting a vacant soul. "I understand you feel I have disgraced you. With your permission, I will retire to a private life in Rome."

Honorius put his hands on her shoulders and raised her up. "You will do no such thing," he said, voice harsh with tears. He crushed her to his chest.

"Yes, you gave me pain, but only because I could not stand the thought of you suffering at the hands of that barbarian."

The slur against Ataulf was not unexpected, but she stiffened anyway. Placidia broke out of her brother's embrace and moved to the sideboard. "May I pour you some wine?"

"I have some already." He raised a silver goblet. "Try it. It's an excellent white from Campania."

Placidia poured herself a generous portion, unwatered in the barbarian style, and walked around the room, touching the riches of an empire—translucent vases from the far east, an ebony table inlaid with ivory from Africa, marble statues from Greece, furs from the forests of Germania, gold plate, silver goblets, jewels… *I would give it all for a rude wagon and Ataulf.*

Honorius' eyes followed her. "Isn't it good to be home among familiar comforts, safe, protected?"

She settled in a chair opposite her brother. "I know you feel betrayed by my marriage to Ataulf, but I loved him and went with him willingly."

"You had little choice, all alone, no brother to guide you."

Placidia held her tongue.

"Now you are home again, and I can arrange a proper marriage."

A chill settled on Placidia. She suddenly felt grateful for the stifling heat. "Brother, I truly appreciate your care for my welfare, but I have no wish to remarry."

"You feel that way now, but in three months—the first of January—you'll welcome a strong man in your bed."

Placidia's eyes darted around the room, looking for an escape. "I cannot marry then. It is unseemly."

"You've been widowed for a full year." Honorius grinned over the rim of his wine goblet. "Are you not even curious about your bridegroom?"

"I assume you intend me to marry Constantius."

"He told you!" Honorius pouted. "I asked him to let me tell."

"He did not tell me. It was obvious from his attentions during our travels. He gave me no peace." She had ridden in her litter, complaining of headaches, just to avoid the man's constant attendance.

Honorius' face went red. "Did he offer you offense?"

"No, the Patrician was always polite and attentive." *So this is what Constantius has dealt with these past six years. My brother goes through more* phases in a brief conversation than the moon does in a month. Placidia lowered her eyes and sighed dramatically. "The fault was mine. I wished to be alone, and at every stop he had arranged for banquets and entertainment."

From anger, Honorius gave way to laughter. "Constantius is quite entertaining on his own."

"He certainly gives the mimes and players competition." Placidia had found Constantius' conversation quite witty. His understanding of the intricacies of state showed a subtlety and depth she had only encountered with Stilicho and Attalus. But her appreciation of Constantius' gifts was shallow compared to the depths of her grief. "He can expect little happiness in a marriage with me," she murmured. "I had hoped he was over his infatuation."

"Placidia, the Patrician has been my closest advisor and most loyal friend, but this involves more than your feelings or his." Honorius' words rang with the false sincerity of a well-rehearsed speech. "It's a matter of state. I have no heir and am unlikely to have children of my own. If my throne is left empty, there will be civil war. As you well know, the western part of the Empire is already under threat." He scowled at her. "Constantius has accomplished a miracle in putting down usurpers and controlling the barbarians within our borders, but he can't make me an heir without a royal wife."

Placidia swallowed the bitter gall that rose in her throat. If she were an ordinary widow, she could decide if, when and who to marry, but royal women were bartered and bought like cattle. "I understand your dilemma, brother, but we need not rush into this. You are young, only thirty-two, and sure to live many years yet. Perhaps we can find you a suitable wife. There are many who would vie for the honor."

"I have no wish to take another wife. I have married twice, and found no pleasure in either experience."

Nor they in him. Both her cousins had confided in her that they left the marriage bed as virginal as they arrived.

His eyes and mouth screwed up in a pout. "No one can force the Emperor to take a wife if he does not wish it."

Unlike the Emperor's sister. Placidia lowered her eyes, trying to keep the desperation out of her voice. "I wish a period of mourning. Let me retire to Rome for a year. Please grant me this one favor?"

"I cannot." His eyes hardened. "You married against my will before, but you will obey me in this. The nuptials are set for January first and will not be delayed."

So that's to be the way of things. Placidia had defied him, something unthinkable in a Roman woman or Imperial Princess, and her brother needed to bring her to heel. She set aside the wine, which had soured with her mood. "As you wish, Brother. May I retire to my rooms? I am still weary from the journey."

"Of course, my dear." Honorius escorted her to the door and kissed her full on the lips. "Rest as long as you need. I will visit you tomorrow."

Placidia shuddered. She wiped the kiss from her mouth when her brother turned his back. *I have fewer choices in the things that matter in my life than my most humble subjects.* Yet Placidia had chosen once. She had chosen love and lost it. Her shoulders slumped with the burden of her birth.

THE FIRST OF JANUARY DAWNED COLD AND GRAY, with a sharp wind blowing off the Adriatic Sea. The day proceeded to mock the happiness of Placidia's first wedding with pale similarities: servants twittering as they prepared her royal robes, the processions, the ceremonies, even the feast, brought back memories of a happier day.

Placidia and Constantius shared the couch of honor at Honorius' right. She felt the heat from her husband's body through her thin silk gown. She ate little and drank less.

When the dancers bowed away from them, Constantius whispered in her ear, "Let us retire."

Placidia caught her breath. Despite his many good qualities, she could engender no passion for the man. Initially, in some dark corner of her soul, she wanted to blame him for Ataulf's death. If Constantius hadn't hounded them, if he had accepted their marriage… But she always came back to the truth. Constantius had nothing to do with Sergeric and his poisonous hatred. The Patrician was a good man, doing his duty, loyal to the Empire and her brother. She should honor him for that, yet she approached her wedding night with resignation and painful longing for the arms of her dead husband.

"Let us wait a bit. The mimes are next."

He frowned. "I thought you might be tired after the day's activities."

Giving in to the inevitable, Placidia said, "You're right. We should retire." She rose from the couch and they slipped away, but not fast enough to escape the ribald remarks of her brother and their guests.

Upon entering their bridal chamber, Constantius turned Placidia to face him, and pulled her into his arms. "I have waited long for this day, my love. I cannot tell you how happy you've made me." He tipped her face up and kissed her passionately. Placidia stood, not responding. He broke off the kiss and studied her with concerned eyes. "You are tired. I'll call your servants to prepare you for bed. I am eager, but I have waited six years. I can wait one more day."

She pushed free of his grasp. "Constantius, we must speak."

"It can wait till you are rested."

"No. This is important." She sat on a chair by the side of the bed. "You know this marriage is not of my choosing. I have come to respect you and your abilities, but I have no love for you. I still mourn Ataulf." His jaw tightened; lines of pain settled around his eyes. "I'm sorry, but I want always to be honest with you. You deserve more, but this is all I can offer."

"Do you feel you could have some affection for me…in time?"

"Perhaps. But it is too soon. You have every right to demand access to my bed, and, if you wish to assert that right, I will not deny you. But I ask, in the name of the love you claim for me, to give me more time." She despised the pleading in her own voice, and straightened her back.

Constantius took her hands in his and knelt at her feet, head bowed. The sharp lines marking his face softened into sadness. "I had hoped we might celebrate in mutual happiness. I'll leave you to your attendants, and call upon you in the morning."

"Just Lucilla, please. I want no other."

He nodded and left.

Chapter 21

Rome, Summer 417

Home at last.

The prospect of residing in her favorite city—if only for a brief while— invigorated Placidia more than anything else in the six months since her marriage. She peeked from the jolting litter, looking for the walls of Rome. They passed through the suburban cemetery lining the Via Appia, the ceremonial approach into the city. The years had not been kind to the forlorn tombs of generations past. Many sported smashed columns and defaced carvings. But even the evidence of fires and looting didn't dampen Placidia's mood. The horrific memories of that day, long ago, when she was taken from the city, had been replaced with happier ones.

Lucilla, on the other hand, sat mute and shuddering. White showed around her eyes, and she clutched a silver crucifix.

"Oh, Lucilla!" Placidia took her hands. "I've been thoughtless. Do you wish to go back? I can send you with an escort."

"I will not leave you, Mistress." Lucilla squeezed her hands. Her voice trembled. "I will face my demons, with God's help."

"And mine. Whatever you need, ask for it. If the memories become too much, we will leave, I promise you."

Lucilla nodded, taking great breaths of air.

Trumpets blasted. They passed inside the walls. Wildly cheering crowds lined the broad expanse of the Via Imperialia. They passed the Flavian Amphitheater and the massive bronze statue of a long-dead Emperor standing watchfully beside it. Tomorrow there would be games in the venerable structure, and races at the hippodrome to honor her husband and brother. They continued up the side of the Palatine hill to the royal residence.

Constantius escorted her from her litter. Taking her arm, he said, in low tones, "Honorius requests that we attend him in his audience chamber before the triumph tomorrow."

"Of course." Something in her husband's sly manner pricked her curiosity. "Does Honorius have some surprise?"

"Yes." Constantius grinned through his beard.

"Will I like it?"

"Yes."

"Do not vex me so, Husband. If you know something, tell me." She tapped her foot on the marble floor.

"Tomorrow. Consider it a late wedding present from me."

Placidia raised one eyebrow and glared at Constantius, but he had faced more intimidating foes.

"I will see you in the morning, then."

Constantius stopped grinning. Eyes narrowed, he offered a brief bow. "As My Lady Wife wishes." He turned on his heel and left her.

Placidia put out a hand towards his retreating back, regretting her harsh words, but did not call out. Instead, she turned and entered the garden where she had first seen Ataulf. Lucilla would not be the only one wrestling with her demons.

THE NEXT MORNING, Placidia, dressed in full Imperial regalia—ruby and pearl diadem, purple robes embroidered in gold and encrusted with gems—made her way to her brother's audience chamber. Constantius came forward to escort her. They trooped through the vast hall, filled with Senators and other men of importance, all whispering about the mystery of the meeting. He led her to a purple-cushioned chair set lower and on the Emperor's right., which normally would be Constantius' place or that of the Augusta, if Honorius married.

Once Placidia was settled, Honorius turned to her and smiled. "I trust the morning finds you rested and cheerful, Sister."

"How could I be otherwise, on this special day honoring both you and my husband as Consul?"

He nodded, turned to face front, and clapped his hands. A troop of Imperial *scholae* paraded into the room in a hollow square formation, lances held high, armor polished to mirror brightness. In the middle of the square a slim man, dressed in a plain white tunic, stumbled, his hands and feet encumbered by chains.

Attalus come back from the dead a second time—thin, with more gray than black in his hair, but alive.

Placidia let out a breath she was unaware of holding, but her heart beat an uneven rhythm. Had Constantius said she would be happy because he knew of her friendship with Attalus, or because he thought she would welcome the execution of the puppet Emperor?

Attalus caught her gaze and shook his head, warning her not to speak on his behalf. She stiffened and raised her chin. The prisoner shrugged, allowing a flicker of a smile in her direction.

The guards in the front of the square peeled off to both sides, leaving an open pathway from Attalus to Honorius. The captive threw himself prostrate on the floor before the Emperor and cried, "Mercy, my Most Wise and Beneficent Majesty. I beg your forgiveness for the crimes I have committed against you."

"Those crimes have been terrible, indeed. The heads of the other usurpers adorn the walls of Ravenna. Why should your fate be any different?"

"Because, while I pretended to the purple, I worked on My Merciful Emperor's behalf."

"A bold assertion." Honorius looked around the crowed of Senators. "Who speaks for this man, your former colleague and proclaimed Emperor?"

Blood drained from many faces in the audience chamber. Not a few Senators eyed the doors.

Before Placidia could rise, Constantius came forward. "I will speak in his defense."

"Proceed, Patrician."

"My Most Gracious Lord." Constantius gave Honorius a deep bow. "This man, Attalus, has served you well and loyally in the past. He showed great ability during his term as Prefect of Rome, yet was seemingly incompetent as the Emperor promoted by his fellow Senators to treat with the Goths. I can only conjecture that it was by design he counseled the barbarians in such ways as to ensure their failure to invade Africa."

Placidia didn't know the truth, but the argument was clever. Even a few Senators nodded to themselves. Mutters of 'our plan all along' reached her ears.

Constantius took a deep breath. "Add to that the fact that, when the Goths seemed victorious, in spite of all his efforts to the contrary, Attalus offered you most merciful terms."

Honorius scowled. Placidia shook her head. Constantius should not have reminded her brother of that humiliation. Only troops arriving from Constantinople at the last moment had saved his diadem.

Constantius perceived his blunder and quickly moved on. "Finally, I ask mercy for this man out of respect for your esteem for me." He bowed low again.

"And my sister?" Honorius turned to her. "What would you recommend?"

"I concur with my wise husband." Placidia tilted her head in Constantius' direction.

"It seems everyone is of the same mind. But what constitutes mercy in this case? A quick death, or a life of humiliation and isolation?"

Attalus raised his head. "That is for My Most Wise Emperor to determine."

Honorius stared at his fallen rival. A wicked smile lit his face. "This is my pronouncement. Attalus, for your crimes you will precede my chariot in chains, as befitting a conquered enemy. At the end of my triumph you will suffer the fate you proposed for me—mutilation and banishment to a small island." He motioned to the guards. "Take him away and prepare him for the triumph."

Later, as they exited the audience chamber, Placidia turned to Constantius. "Thank you, husband. Attalus' life is, indeed, a great gift."

ATTALUS RAISED HIS HEAD FROM HIS COUCH at the teeth-clenching squeal of the opening door. It hung crooked on its hinges and had scraped a groove in the stone floor. Pain streaked up his arm from his mutilated left hand—missing the thumb and index finger—as he propped himself up on his elbow. The wine they allowed him did little to dull the pain. He looked blearily at a menacing form outlined by an oil lamp held by a blond giant.

"Mercury, have you come to drag my sorry soul to Hades? It will do no good. I don't have the money for the ferryman." He laughed and fell back to the couch.

"Attalus, I thought you were baptized a Christian."

"Just for show." He squinted into the light, trying to focus. "I don't believe you *are* Mercury."

The apparition pushed back the hood of its cloak.

"Placidia." He sat bolt upright. Some of the wine fog cleared from his brain. "I'm sorry I can't receive you in a more appropriate fashion." He tried to kneel but fell forward, smashing his wounded hand on the stone floor. A moan escaped his lips.

"Help him!"

The blond giant picked him up and sat him back on his couch.

"Silly man." Placidia sat beside him. "We are friends. Why did you do that?"

"It seemed appropriate, Princess."

She took his mutilated hand. "Machaon, come look at this."

The little Greek doctor appeared as if by magic out of the dark. He shook his head. "Attalus, what have you done to yourself?"

"This is no slit wrist, you poor excuse for an army doctor. Can't you tell the difference between a self-inflicted wound and one gained in honorable execution?"

Machaon snorted while he unwrapped the bloody bandages. He examined the stumps, then nodded. "Well done. The wounds are clean and cauterized. There should be no infection."

" 'Well done'? I lose my thumb and finger and you say 'Well done'?"

"If poorly done, you lose your life as well as your digits. If the flesh grows red, streaked with yellow, or shows pus, cut off the hand to stop the poison from reaching your body. Cauterize the new wound and cover it with honey."

"Are you mad?" He cradled his hand close to his chest, as if Machaon threatened to cut it off immediately.

"Enough." Placidia ran her hand across the furrows in Attalus' forehead. "Attalus, are you in pain?"

"Not with you here, Princess."

"Don't be gallant. If the wound hurts, tell us. Machaon can give you something."

"I don't know that I would take anything from that butcher. Cut off my hand, indeed."

She gave him a sharp look.

He dropped his eyes. "Yes, I am in considerable pain."

"Take this—five drops—no more!—in some wine." Machaon handed him a vial stoppered with wax. "It's an extract from the poppy seed. It is the strongest remedy for pain I know, but it will make you sleepy. I'll send more tomorrow."

"Thank you."

Machaon packed and left, taking the giant with him, presumably to guard the door.

Attalus turned to Placidia. "I thought never to see you again, Princess."

"Nor I you. How did you wind up in such a state?"

He told her the whole story, including Constantius' role in saving his life. "He is a good man, Placidia. I know you mourn Ataulf, but you could do much worse than Constantius for a husband."

"I know this in my mind, but my heart refuses to listen."

"My little fawn. Still not allowing yourself happiness? If not love, at least allow affection and friendship."

Tears trickled down her cheeks. He brushed them away with his good hand. Placidia continued. "I didn't come here to bring sadness. I came to lighten your burden."

"You've hired a good cook for my exile?"

That brought a smile to her face.

"Yes, and a companion—a saucy boy who can sing and play pipes and the lute. Lipara has a small villa on a hill overlooking the harbor. It's stocked with books, wine, and food. I will send an agent to check on you. Make requests only through him. I doubt my brother would appreciate my providing you comforts."

This time she brushed tears from his cheeks.

"Princess, you are too kind. Do nothing that will bring you grief."

"Without you, I would never have married Ataulf. I would never have known the joy or passion of our love."

"Or the pain?"

She shrugged. "I don't regret my love for Ataulf, or my friendship with you."

He kissed her palm. "You should go now, before you are missed."

"I will write."

"Use Lucilla's name." Attalus saluted her with the vial of poppy extract. "Now go and leave me to a painless sleep. Goodbye, Princess."

"Goodbye, my friend."

The wretched door squealed as she closed it. Attalus didn't mind.

*****

Placidia dropped her cloak to the floor of her bedroom.

"Where have you been?" Constantius' voice, from the shadows, startled her. She turned to face him. "Is this the reason you deny me your bed? You have a lover?"

"I have no lover."

He strode into the lamplight and caught her wrist. "Don't lie to me."

"I don't lie to you, and never will." She twisted her wrist from his grip and rubbed the burning flesh. "I went to see Attalus."

"Attalus?" Constantius stepped back, a puzzled frown on his face. "Why the need for stealth? I would have arranged for you to see him."

"I didn't want my brother to know. Court gossips would have brought the tale to him and put it in the worst possible light. They might have accused me of treason."

"Do you doubt my influence with your brother?"

"You cannot have his ear every moment. And I would do nothing to damage your relationship with him."

A rueful smile crooked his lips. "That is why I am here. Your brother questions me almost daily about our lack of a child. He accuses me of dereliction in my husbandly duties."

Honorius was not the only one who watched her figure closely, looking for signs of pregnancy. The entire palace, from top administrators to lowly slaves, buzzed with rumors. If she ate little or much, if she was afflicted with a headache or stomach complaint, if she was happy or sad, they all attributed it to fecundity, and counted on their fingers the months until the expected birth.

"Placidia, it has been six months, and I have been most patient." He paced the room, hands behind his back. "It has been nearly two years since your… since you were widowed."

"Sit, Constantius. You make me nervous." He settled on a couch. She joined him and took one hand in both of hers, running her thumb over his palm, callused from sword and reins. When she looked up, his eyes shone with unshed tears at this first hint of intimacy. "You are an honorable man and deserve much more than I can give you. You made a bad bargain when you married me."

"I do not believe so." Constantius leaned toward her, pleading. "If you would only give me a chance, I believe I can make you happy. Let go your memories of the past. Look to the future. I love you, Placidia. Let me into your life."

"I told you I would not deny you access to my bed, and I stand by my word."

She stood, dropped her outer robes to the floor, leaving only a sheer silk *tunica*. She reached up to let down her hair, but Constantius rose and imprisoned her hands.

"Let me," he said in a husky voice. Constantius loosened the pins, unknotted the braids, and combed his fingers through the curls until her hair lay glistening down her back, past her waist. He raised several strands to his face and inhaled deeply. "Attar of roses. I've always loved the scent of your hair."

He dropped his own tunic. Placidia felt a cold dread, but did nothing to stop him. She shuddered at his touch. He must have taken that quiver for passion, for he smiled and pulled the final garment from her body. He picked her up and laid her on the bed. "I've waited so long for this."

Placidia lay passively as he kissed her throat and nipples. He did his best to be gentle but, when he thrust himself into her, she grunted in pain. He continued thrusting a few minutes more, then moaned, shuddered, and rolled off her, breathing hard. She lay still, eyes closed, tears leaking, listening to his breath slow as sleep overtook him, wishing he were someone else.

Chapter 22

Ravenna, January 418

SIGISVULT SAT AT PLACIDIA'S WORKTABLE, trying to make sense of the dispatches from Valia and others in Spain. Uncomfortable in such rich surroundings, he chewed on his moustache until the marks on the page resolved into words. "The Alans are pushed to Lusitania, and the Suebi to the north and west." He turned to look at a map, a beautiful creation in blue, red and green on thick parchment. His fingers caressed the smooth surface. Central and South Spain are again under Roman rule.

"How goes your study?"

He twitched at the sound of Placidia's voice and leapt to his feet. His queen was as beautiful as ever, even big with child. "Well, My Queen."

"Show me." She leaned over the table, smoothing the map. "It is not enough to read the words. You must understand what they mean; project what will happen next. To lead men requires that you think ahead, not just react."

"Yes, My Queen." He pointed on the map. "The Alans are here and the Suebi here."

"The Vandals?"

"Valia says they are destroyed. Some seek sanctuary with the Suebi. Small bands gather in Andalusia."

"What do we know about our enemies' numbers, supplies, willingness to fight?"

"The Suebi seek federate status. They must be weak and in need, or they would stand against us."

"What should we do?"

"Attack. Smash them while they are weak, so we take few deaths."

Placidia nodded. "Normally, I would agree with you, but the Goths are weakened as well. Two years of war has devastated the countryside. Food is scarce. It is time for peace."

Sigisvult hung his head. The Goths were reduced to ten thousand men. Soon they would be little more than the scavenging bands they pursued.

"Why do you do this?" He waved his hand over the littered desk.

"It is my husband's policy to keep the tribes at each other's throats, and they readily oblige him. I hope to convince him to finally settle the Goths. Perhaps here?" She pointed at Aquitania, in the southeast of Gaul. "It is good land along the Garonne River."

"No." Sigisvult ran a hand through his hair. "I mean, why do this with me? Why teach me to read and write? Why teach me to think?"

"The answer is complicated." Placidia lowered herself into the chair he had vacated. "Ataulf saw potential in you. So do I. He had planned to train and promote you himself. He would have been proud to have you as a son-in-law." Lines of pain drew her brows together.

"Forgive me, My Queen." Sigisvult dropped to his knees. "I did not mean to open old wounds." He still felt a twinge when he thought of Vada. But that had been the love of a boy for a girl—stolen kisses and sweaty palms. His devotion to Placidia was different—mixed with a man's yearning for a compelling woman was pride of service and loyalty to a worthy queen.

Her forehead smoothed. She smiled sadly. "I can think of the children now without tears." She rested a hand on her rounded stomach. "You remind me of the happy times, Sigisvult."

"Placidia, what are you doing here?" Constantius stood in the doorway, looking concerned.

Placidia's jaw firmed. Color suffused her cheeks. Her eyes narrowed as she levered her body out of the chair to face her husband. "I am reading the dispatches from Spain."

"I banned you from the council meetings to keep you from such labors. You should be quiet in mind and body, to protect the baby."

"Just because I carry a child does not mean I am an invalid, or have lost my power to think. Exercise is good for me and the baby. Ask Machaon or Nikarete. My mind needs exercise as well. I go mad with nothing to do, no decisions to make!" A sly smile crooked the corners of Placidia's mouth; her eyes still contained fire. "In fact, I have made a decision. Sigisvult?"

"Yes, My Queen!" Sigisvult smiled. He served a strong, confident woman, a warrior in her own way.

Constantius winced at the title.

"Tell the captain of the Imperial barge I wish to sail for a week."

"At once." Sigisvult marched toward the door. He stood half a head taller than Constantius, but the older man outweighed him by many pounds. He fervently hoped he would not have to fight his way out. Placidia had often drummed into his thick head that diplomacy could accomplish as much, or more, than a battle. Sigisvult took a deep breath and stood before Constantius. "Please step aside, General. I am loyal to my queen, and will obey her orders with my last breath."

"Placidia, stop this nonsense, before the lad gets hurt."

Blood rose in Sigisvult's cheeks. He carried no sword, but his hand crept toward his knife.

"No, Sigisvult!" Placidia's voice stayed his hand. "Step aside. Let my husband enter."

Constantius bulled past him. "Placidia, I forbid you to sail. The winter storms are on the sea. I will tie you to your bed if I have to, to protect my son."

"Your son, your son!" She stomped her foot, then strode back and forth, swinging her arms. "I am sick to death of playing the brood mare. This is my child, as well. I'm giving it life with my body. I know best how to care for it and myself."

"Be easy, Placidia. Do not upset yourself. You might harm the baby."

Constantius reached for her. She twisted out of his grasp.

"This is what I mean. I can do nothing for myself." As suddenly as the storm blew up, it passed. Placidia's shoulders slumped. Sigisvult saw tears in her eyes. "Do you not understand that I can't sit in idleness? Boredom frets me more than a thousand reports or a hundred petitioners."

"I'm sorry, Placidia." Constantius dropped his hands and bowed his head. "I only want to keep you and the baby safe and healthy."

"I know this is your first child, but it is my second." She spread both hands protectively over her stomach. "Believe me when I say I would never do anything to harm this baby."

"Then cancel your sea voyage."

"I will not go to sea." She sighed. "I do not know where that notion came from."

He put his arm around her. "I'll try to be less fearful."

Placidia leaned into her husband's embrace, then noticed Sigisvult standing awkwardly by the door. "You may go now, Sigisvult. We will continue the lessons tomorrow."

He left, disappointed at being dismissed, but pleased he did not have to brave the winter sea.

April 418

"It's a girl!"

A groan of disappointment echoed round the chamber as the attending noblewomen witnessed the royal birth. The baby cried out. Nikarete cut the cord.

"Let me see." Placidia reached for the child. She had been so sure this baby would be a boy—she needed it to be a boy. Nikarete handed her the baby wrapped in linen cloths. Placidia wiped blood from its face as it looked up with blue, unfocussed eyes. She pulled open the linens. She could not deny the baby's sex.

Crushing disappointment filled her throat. She suffered Constantius' physical advances solely to give her brother an heir. Her daughter could not inherit the Imperial diadem, any more than she could. She would have to try again.

"I'm sorry, little one." She held the baby close to her chest. Like herself, her daughter would be little more than a pawn in Imperial marriage politics. "I will try to spare you my fate, if I can."

Placidia handed the child back to Nikarete. "Give her to the wet nurse."

A YEAR AND A HALF LATER, Constantius hoisted his daughter up to look into the cradle that held his three-month-old son. "Honoria, see your baby brother?" The infant lay swaddled head to foot in linen wraps, and smelled of sour milk. Constantius thought he looked like one of the mummies common in Egypt.

Honoria wriggled in his grasp, babbling. Her noise woke the baby. He began to cry. That caught her attention, and she babbled more.

The nurse shooed them both away. Constantius laughed at his daughter's frown and set her on the tiled floor. Honoria pointed at the cradle and stomped her bare foot with a small slap. This seemed to interest her. She stomped some more, giggling. He picked her up and swung her around until she laughed and screamed. A familiar emotion tugged at his heart. This fragile child was so like her mother: curly brown hair, large brown eyes, and a mind of her own. *She'll be trouble when she's grown.*

He unwrapped a sticky date, filled with almond paste, from a piece of paper, and handed it to Honoria. She stuffed it into her mouth with a glad cry, chewing as best she could with tiny teeth.

"You spoil the child." Placidia's voice came from the door of the nursery.

Constantius picked up his daughter and perched her on his shoulders. It was not unusual for mothers to favor a son over a daughter. But, having suffered Placidia's indifference on more than one occasion himself, he felt keenly for his little girl. "Someone has to."

Placidia's mouth compressed into a thin line. "That is what nurses and tutors are for. And you should not fault me. I come to the nursery daily."

Only since Valentinian was born. Constantius held his tongue. This was an old argument. Noblewomen almost always gave their children to wet nurses and rarely bothered to do more than check regularly on their health and wellbeing until it was time to hire tutors.

He felt a tug at his hair. A sticky hand crept down his forehead. "What are you doing up there?" Honoria giggled and tugged again. Constantius growled like a bear and reached up to tickle the toddler. She screeched.

"If you two must play so loudly, please go to another room." Placidia strode to the crying baby, taking him from the nurse's arms. "How's my baby boy?"

Constantius watched her sway from side to side, like all women did when holding a small child. Despite three pregnancies, Placidia retained her slender form, slightly more rounded at bust and hip. The sight of her sent blood rushing to his groin, then his cheeks. Even with her sharp edges, Placidia still bewitched him.

Honoria squealed. Constantius removed her from his shoulders and growled into her belly.

"Husband, please take her out of here. She's disturbing the baby." Placidia sat with the infant in her lap.

A puzzled frown furrowed Honoria's brow. She stuck a thumb in her mouth. Tight-lipped, Constantius gathered up his daughter. "Come, my precious little princess. We'll go explore the garden." She clapped her hands in delight.

They left Placidia singing a lullaby to baby Valentinian.

Summer 420

"Is this not the perfect domestic scene?"

Placidia looked up to see Honorius in the doorway of her favorite room, a cozy parlor with a table for her work, a sitting area, and warm carpets. Constantius and the children were on the floor. Little Val chased a gilded wooden ball, while Honoria practiced her letters on a waxed slate.

"Look, Unka!" Honoria rushed to her uncle, waving the slate.

He swung her up into his arms. "Let's see." He looked over the scrawled letters. "Are you going to be a scholar when you grow up?"

"No. An Emperor."

"Honoria!" Placidia looked to her husband. Why did he always leave the disciplining to her? Someone had to be firm with the child, or she would grow up wild. "I have told you many times: girls can't be Emperors."

The little girl stuck out her lower lip. "Why?"

"That's enough, young lady. I will not have you argue with me." Placidia waved to the nurses. "Take the children to the nursery."

"No! Stay here!" She clung to her uncle's neck.

"I'll be in to see you later, Princess," said Constantius. "I have things to discuss with your mother and uncle."

"Promise?" Honoria looked at her father with pleading eyes.

"I always keep my promises, don't I?" Constantius took his daughter from Honorius and kissed her on the cheek. "Now go with your nurse." He set her on the floor and, with a gentle swat on the behind, sent her on her way. She ran out, giggling, followed by a nurse carrying Valentinian and his ball.

"Precocious child." Honorius took a seat and motioned a slave to serve him wine.

"Just like her mother." Constantius joined him with his own goblet. "She already knows her letters, and her numbers up to ten."

It chilled Placidia when he pointed out how alike she and Honoria were. She had made peace with her fate, and enjoyed her role in administering the Empire, but Placidia wanted more than a loveless political marriage for her daughter. She put aside her quill and rose from her table to join the men. She declined the wine. "I'm glad you've come, Brother. Honoria, in her childish way, brought up a subject much on my mind. Don't you think it is time to confirm Valentinian as your heir?"

Her brother and her husband exchanged glances. They had obviously discussed this without her. She felt the annoyance rising with the blood in her cheeks. Before she could issue a few sharp words, Honorius said, "Now, Sister, there is plenty of time. Valentinian is still an infant."

He swirled the wine in his cup, not meeting her eyes.

She stared at Constantius, challenging him to take up his son's cause. As the silence stretched, she realized he was as incapable of advocating for his son as he was disciplining his daughter. Placidia pursed her lips. If Constantius shrank from the task, she would not.

"You rushed me into this marriage to assure the Empire an heir of your line. I've fulfilled my part of the arrangement. It is high time you fulfilled yours."

Constantius changed the subject. "Did you hear the news from Constantinople? Your nephew Theodosius took a wife. From all reports Athenais is a beautiful girl, the daughter of a pagan scholar at the Athenian school."

"I hear it was a love match," Honorius said. "Niece Pulcheria heard her petition for redress in the matter of her father's will, and was so impressed with her rhetoric she introduced Athenais to Theodosius. They fell in love, and married as soon as she converted to Christianity."

Placidia flinched. She had heard the story of her nephew and his wife, and had the grace to wish the couple happiness. But the discussion brought up another of her complaints.

"You two gossip more than the servants. We have more important business. Constantius, are you going to tell Honorius what we discussed?"

Her husband colored and took a gulp of wine. She frowned. Both her brother and her husband drank to excess, in her opinion.

"Placidia believes you should do me the honor of making me co-Emperor, and name her Augusta." His eyes darted away from Honorius.

"Really?" Honorius looked at Placidia with a hint of calculation. "Does this have to do with your honor, Patrician, or hers?"

172

"It is an honor we are both long overdue," *and earned a thousand times over*, she thought. "Pulcheria declared herself Augusta and ruled for Theodosius when she was but fifteen. I have over twice that number of years. Constantius has served you loyally, without asking a thing for himself."

"Except land, riches, consulships, and the patriciate, but that is not enough?" Honorius thumped his wine cup down. "So I am to name your husband co-Emperor, your son Caesar and heir, and yourself Augusta—all in a stroke. Should I then go to my quarters and drink hemlock to make matters easier for you?"

"God's bones, Honorius, don't be so dramatic. No one has been more loyal to you than we have. For years, in exile, I opposed every usurper. Constantius put his life on the line to dispose of six men who challenged your right to the diadem. All I ask is a little recognition for our loyalty."

"We speak of honors which are yours and yours alone to confer, my friend." Constantius put a calming hand on the Emperor's arm. "We only ask that you consider the proposition."

Placidia opened her mouth to speak. Constantius sent her a warning glance.

Honorius rose. "I will think on it. Good night, Patrician. Sister."

After her brother left, Constantius said, in a weary tone, "I asked you not to try him about this. He comes to our quarters for a bit of comfort and diversion. Instead, he has you harrying him like a harpy."

"His indecision drives me to distraction. You and I do all the work to ensure this empire survives. Even with the Church! We handled that debacle with two Popes in Rome last year and he didn't even thank us. We should at least have the titles to go with the responsibility."

"Hounding Honorius on the subject just makes him suspicious and more intransigent; giving our enemies an opening. I hear General Castinus has been speaking against us—in subtle ways—pointing out how rich and ambitious we are. Leave this to me."

"But will you pursue it? You've been reluctant ever since you had that silly dream. I think you use that as an excuse."

Her husband paled.

He obviously regretted telling her about the dream he had interpreted as meaning he would rule as Emperor for only seven months. Placidia knew her husband's reluctance to take on the title had more to do with his dread of rampant criticism and speculation about his intentions toward Honorius, not to mention the hated ceremonial burdens.

"Yes, Wife, I will pursue it—in my own time! You need not hound *me* about it, either." He bolted from his chair. "I must check on the children. After all, I did promise Honoria."

"Good night, Husband." She stood, offered her cheek for a kiss, and returned to her worktable satisfied.

CHAPTER 23

Rome, February 421

ARE YOU HAPPY, MY DEAR?" Constantius and Placidia stood in the Imperial box at the hippodrome. The crowd of Senators, Roman officials, and citizens in the stands attending the ceremony looked restive. Constantius studied his wife's face. She was always happier in Rome, and had worked hard for this day. *Hell's blazes, she drove me like a chariot horse.* He smiled at the image.

Placidia's gaze turned inward, as if searching for the answer to his question. She gave a smile that made his heart constrict. "I am. Thank you, Husband."

A harsh February wind chased fluffy clouds from the sky. They had been sheltered from the cold on their way here by the tunnel linking the palace with the hippodrome. Constantius hoped Placidia was warm under her layers of robes and jewels. Snow-white fox trimmed her royal purple cloak, but she could not don that until after the ceremonies. He motioned to an attendant. "Bring a brazier and a hot stone for the princess."

The Master of Offices came forward and, with a trumpet fanfare, read out the proclamations establishing Constantius as co-Emperor with Honorius, and Placidia as Augusta. Valentinian had received the title *nobilissimus puer*—Most Noble Boy—the month before. *It is only be a matter of time until my son is acknowledged Caesar and heir. Placidia had been right to insist on this. Now that I'm an Augustus, my son should succeed me to the diadem.* The crowds cheered, devolving into lengthy acclamations led by key Senators. One-and-a-half-year-old Valentinian was brought out for his acclamation.

Constantius held the child in his arms as he fidgeted. He whispered in the boy's ear. "I don't like this part either."

"Itchy!" Valentinian tugged at his embroidered tunic.

"Smile, dear," Placidia chucked the boy under the chin. "The people should see their future Emperor in good cheer."

"Don't wanna."

"Then you may go back with your nurse." The woman stepped forward to take the boy away.

"Lucky boy," Constantius said under his breath. He erupted into a paroxysm of coughs.

"Are you well?" It was gratifying to see the concern on Placidia's face. She had been much less prickly since Honorius reluctantly agreed to their elevation.

"Just dust. A little wine will cure it."

She motioned for a slave, who immediately brought over a goblet.

His feet were numb by the time the crowd finally quieted and Honorius gave his speech.

Constantius sighed. *And so it begins.*

"I DON'T KNOW WHY HONORIUS PROTESTED my elevation for so long," Constantius said, shedding his stiff Imperial robes. "I meet with all the delegations, attend the ceremonies for everything under the sun, and propose all the laws. He does little these days besides play with his chickens!" He tossed his plain gold diadem onto a lacquered table and slumped into his favorite cushioned chair. "I have no time to do the real work of the Empire, and that leaves the burden to you, my dear."

"I don't mind." Placidia looked up from the stack of personal requests she had brought from her work room, and set them aside. Her furrowed brow smoothed as she rose to pour him a cup of well-watered wine. Oil lamps cast soft shadows on her face and slender form. His chest constricted; he suppressed a cough. *With the weight of the Empire on her shoulders, she's still beautiful.*

She handed him the gilded cup—a gift from her, and one of his favorites. "Surely, Honorius takes on some of the Imperial duties."

He sipped, grimaced, and gave the cup back. "Damn few. Have the slave bring me a cup of unwatered wine. This stuff tastes worse than horse piss."

"Have you tasted it?" She nodded to a nameless servant lurking in a corner, who hurried to attend his wants.

"What?"

"Horse piss. Have you tasted it?"

Constantius blushed. "I apologize for being crude in your presence."

Placidia waved her hand, as if it were of little consequence, and sat opposite him. "I've lived with soldiers my entire life, Husband. I've heard much worse."

"It's just that I hate all the fuss and bother of court. Some men like the scraping and bowing and false flattery, but I do not. I've become the slave of eunuchs and protocol masters." He ran a hand through his graying hair. "However, there was a diversion in court today."

"Yes?"

The servant returned. Constantius took a deep draught of his unwatered wine.

"Are you going to keep me waiting?" Placidia scowled.

"Sorry." He put the cup down.

"A man named Libanius. He claims to be a magician. For a price, he will use black magic against the Vandals in Spain."

"Did you consider his plan?"

"I did not reject it out of hand."

"In the court? In others' presence?" Placidia gasped.

"What is it, love?" He rushed to her side.

"You must execute that…that…man! Our enemies could use this to their benefit. If Castinus hears of this—and he will—it could be your death. He might have even sent this man to you as a trap. He knows well your fondness for entertainers and fools."

"It was more a jape than a plan. Everyone knew I wouldn't—couldn't!—do such a thing."

"The Church executes people for such practices. Not even an Emperor would be exempt; if it were thought you employed someone who used the black arts. Shortly after I returned to Ravenna, I had my land agent in Sicily find the pagan statue that was used to thwart the Gothic invasion of Africa, and destroy it. I wanted no taint attached to my name." She clutched his arm. "Please, Husband, be decisive. Execute this Libanius. Promise me!"

"I don't think Castinus could be so subtle as to plan this, but…" He raised his hand to cut off her protest. "He would take advantage. I promise Libanius will not see another full day." *Always one step ahead, in thought and deed. Placidia would have made a good general.*

Constantius coughed—a deep dry rasp, which had been plaguing him lately. He had trouble drawing breath.

Placidia put a hand to his forehead. "You have no fever, but I want Machaon to tend that cough."

"It's nothing. Just the dry air."

Placidia raised a skeptical eyebrow.

He knew he should call in a physician, but he had enjoyed extraordinarily good health his whole life and disliked doctors, with their poking, noxious potions, and ridiculous talk of humors. "It's nothing a good cup of wine won't cure."

"It would make me happy to know you are healthy."

Her happiness—his one soft spot. He could deny her nothing.

"I'll have Machaon attend me tomorrow."

"Tonight."

"God's mercy, woman, tomorrow!"

"Very well."

They sat in silence. Constantius sipped his unwatered wine, contemplating his now suspiciously compliant wife. "What is it?"

She looked up at him guiltily. "There is also news from Constantinople of a disturbing nature."

"What news?"

"The Master of Offices reports that our agents see no sign that Theodosius and Pulcheria confirm our elevations. They did not put up the statues we sent, and the agents say the eastern court is not pleased by the development. I suspect we will receive something of a formal nature in the near future."

"What possible objection could they have?" His blood warmed. He could feel it throbbing in his temple.

"Officially? I don't know. Possibly because they were not consulted on the matter. A mistake on my part. I failed to take into account the coolness that part of the family had always felt towards my mother and Stilicho's guardianship. I thought the years were enough to soften their attitudes, and they would recognize the service I—we—have rendered to the Empire." She sat quietly, chewing her lower lip in thought. "Perhaps Theodosius sees himself as Honorius' heir. After all, he is the son of a full brother, and Val is the son of a half-sister. Theo has the stronger claim. He might harbor ambitions to unify the

Empire under his sole rule if Honorius were to die.

"Unofficially, the agents say Pulcheria felt I was unworthy of being Augusta, because of my marriage to Ataulf."

"That bloody pious bitch has no right to judge you." He gathered her in his arms. "You had no choice in that sordid affair."

She stiffened and pushed away. "No matter the cause, this affects our son. We must respond to it."

Hurt by her rebuff, he turned his anger in another direction. "Their actions are an insult. I should go there with an army at my back and demand recognition."

"Their actions *are* insulting, but armed confrontation is not the answer. I would not plunge the Empire into civil war over a couple of statues. We need to talk to my niece and nephew. Perhaps a visit to Constantinople is in order."

"I leave the arrangements to you." He slumped back into his chair, suddenly tired and breathless. "Maybe I will call Machaon tonight."

Ravenna, September 421

PLACIDIA SAT BY HER HUSBAND'S BED, watching as Machaon put an ear to Constantius' chest and asked him to breathe deeply. She had had his bed moved to a well-lit room with a view of the garden, and filled it with late summer blooms. A young female slave played a cithara quietly just outside his window. Constantius took a few shallow, panting breaths, and exploded into a paroxysm of dry coughs.

Machaon shook his head. "The Emperor has been getting steadily worse for two months and hasn't responded to any of my medications."

"Can you do nothing?" Placidia's voice stayed steady, but her hands trembled. She had thrown all her energy into caring for her ailing husband these last few weeks.

"We can make His Majesty comfortable. Give him this for the cough as he needs it." Machaon uncorked a large bottle that smelled of cherries, poured a half measure into a cup, and held it to her husband's lips. He swallowed, then settled back onto his pillows. "It also has something for the pain." Machaon handed the nursing slave the bottle and the measure. "Don't give him more than half the measure at a time."

Placidia followed the physician out. "Machaon?" He turned. "How long?"

"Soon." He stroked his beard. "He hardly takes in enough breath to sustain life. I would say, not more than a day or two."

Placidia, choked with sadness, had trouble getting her own breath. She groped her way to a bench.

"Augusta?" Machaon hovered near her, concern in his black eyes.

Unshed tears made her voice harsh. "I did not realize he had so little time. I must prepare the children." Honoria had been asking to see her father since his confinement a week ago. Little Valentinian seemed not to notice his father's absence.

"Thank you." Placidia rose, offering her hand. "You and Nikarete have been such good friends to me and mine for so many years. I don't know what I would do without you."

"It's an honor to serve in your household, Augusta. You know in what esteem we hold you. Your bravery saved our lives."

Lucilla, Sigisvult, Machaon, Nikarete. How few of those I love remain with me from that most glorious and most dark time of my life. She bowed her head. She would like to take the little man in a warm hug, but knew how that would be construed by gossip mongers.

Speaking of…she glanced into the anteroom, which was stuffed with muttering courtiers waiting for the death announcement. She would have to call in the council members soon, or they would think something amiss. Poor Constantius. He hated ceremony, and now his last minutes will be sullied by the presence of those he likes least.

Placidia retrieved her hand and nodded toward the anteroom. "Please say nothing to those vultures. I will call them in when it is time."

Machaon bowed and made his exit.

Placidia returned to the sick room. Constantius turned haggard eyes her way as he struggled for breath. He looked every one of his five and fifty years, plus twenty more. He had always been a vigorous man; it pained her to see him so wasted. *I hope my own death is quick and clean.*

She went to his side and smoothed wiry gray hair back from his forehead. "Hush. Don't try to talk. I think it is time to say good-bye to the children. Should I bring them in?"

He nodded.

The priest Constantius had asked for hovered near the entrance to the room. She waved him over. "Please, the Emperor needs your prayers. Go in and comfort him."

"Of course, Augusta."

Placidia stopped at her own chamber to compose herself.

Lucilla started up from a chair, where she had been embroidering. "Is the Emperor dead?"

"Soon. I must bring the children."

At Lucilla's sorrowful gaze, Placidia threw herself on a couch. "I was such a poor wife to him. He deserved much better." Her chest felt ready to burst, and her throat constricted—with grief or guilt?—whichever, she didn't know it would hurt so to lose the man she had so reluctantly married. With Ataulf, she had had no time to grieve; his death came quickly, and she had to act to save herself and her people. Constantius' slow decline gave her time for reflection. She was not always proud of her actions.

Lucilla put her arms around Placidia's heaving shoulders. "Hush, Mistress. You had no choice in the marriage."

"Oh, but I did." Kohl streaked Placidia's cheeks where she rubbed tears from her eyes. "I could have been a better friend to him. Instead, I made his life harder. He didn't want to be Emperor, and I pushed and pushed…" Her sobs subsided. "I only hope he can forgive me."

"Your husband loves you, Mistress, and he's a generous man. I doubt he feels there is anything to forgive." Lucilla rose. "Let me fetch water so we can repair your makeup. It wouldn't do for the children to see you in such a state. Would like me to come as well?"

"Yes, Lucilla. You're my rock."

AT THE NURSERY, Placidia gathered Val onto her lap and hugged Honoria close to her side. "We are going to see your father. He is very sick, but I don't want you to be frightened by how he looks. He won't be able to talk to you, so don't ask questions."

"Is Father going to die?" Honoria looked up with enormous eyes.

"Yes, and he wants to say good-bye to you."

"What happens when we die?"

Placidia had thought much on that question. The child was not ready for complicated answers. "You stop breathing, your heart stops beating, and your soul goes to heaven to be with God."

Honoria frowned. "What's a soul? Can I touch it?"

"You can't. Your body stays here on earth, and your soul—that part of you that is most pure and good—goes to heaven. God takes your soul and you are happy forever, with no pain and no fear." Placidia's fragile hold on her composure grew shakier with each inquiry. At least Valentinian was too young to ask questions.

"Will Father miss us in heaven?"

"No, dear, but we will miss him very much here on earth. He will watch and care for us from heaven." With a touch of desperation, she added, "Now, let's go see your father."

The girl stuck her thumb in her mouth, as she always did when upset. It couldn't be helped. Placidia carried her son and held her daughter's hand as they entered the sick room. Lucilla joined the priest muttering prayers in the corner.

Constantius turned to look at the children. He lifted his arms a fraction of an inch. Placidia settled Valentinian on the bed, beside his head. Constantius kissed the boy and Placidia took him back into her arms.

"That's not Father." Honoria wrinkled her nose. "He smells funny."

Placidia leaned down to whisper, "I told you your father has been ill. Now come up on the bed and say good-bye."

"No." The little girl stomped her foot.

"Child, this is no time to be obstinate." Placidia barely kept the tears from her voice.

"Honoria?" A breathy voice came from the bed, followed by a cough.

"Father?"

"Yes," he husked.

She climbed on the bed without assistance. "Mother says you are going to die."

"Honoria!" Placidia moved to snatch the girl from the bed. Constantius put up a hand, and nodded yes to his daughter.

"And you will go to heaven, where you will watch me?"

Again he nodded.

"I don't want you to go to heaven. Stay with me."

182

"That's not possible, Honoria." Placidia patted her daughter's back.

"Why not?"

"It just isn't."

"Love...you," Constantius wheezed. "Be...good."

"Stay here with me!" Honoria wailed.

"Take the children back to the nursery, Lucilla" Placidia ordered. "I don't want them disturbing the Emperor."

Lucilla carried Honoria screaming from the room, and engaged one of the ever-present slaves to take Val. Placidia turned back to Constantius. "I'm sorry. I should never have brought her here."

Constantius took her hand with surprising strength. "Be...kind...to...her."

"Of course. I'll take good care of both our children. You rest."

He closed his eyes. His ragged breathing slowed.

Just past midnight, it stopped.

Chapter 24

Ravenna, October 422

WHAT TROUBLES YOU SO, MISTRESS?" Lucilla asked. She uncoiled Placidia's carefully coifed hair, methodically placing the gold pins and jewel encrusted combs in her jewelry box.

"What does not trouble me?" Placidia frowned, ignoring her image in the polished silver mirror. Barely a month had passed since Constantius' death, and already her enemies moved on her. "Reports and complaints come from all quarters, accusing Constantius of having seized possessions of various persons unlawfully. Such slander of a good man! As an added insult, they blame me, saying he was generous before our marriage and became grasping and greedy at my instigation. I must get closer to my brother again; resume sitting in the council meetings and attending court sessions." She sighed. "I do miss my husband—he was such a good friend to Honorius, allowing me to do the planning."

"If this vexes you so, can you not retire to Rome or one of your estates with the children; enjoy life away from the poisons of the court?" Lucilla smoothed olive oil onto Placidia's skin, loosening the dirt and make-up. "If you remove yourself, you'll no longer be a target."

"Sometimes I dream of such a quiet life." A smile quirked the corners of her mouth, then faded. "But that is only a dream. If I do not act, there will be no Empire for my son to inherit. Britain asks for help to repel the Saxons, and we have none to give. The Vandals in Spain move with their allies into Andalusia. Now this." She pointed to a report from the Master of Offices. "A new group, called *Bagaudae*, threaten Gaul. 'Rebels' indeed! They are little more than brigands and bandits, taking advantage of the unrest in the Empire to carve out their own little territories."

"Can we not send troops to wipe out these *Bagaudae*?" Lucilla gently removed the oil and make-up with a soft cotton cloth.

Placidia shook her head. "We have no troops to spare. Constantius was clever in his use of the barbarian federates against one another. It masked the fact that the Roman army in the west is much depleted and ill equipped. The common soldier makes do with a hidebound shield, leather cap, poorly made arms, and little training. The mighty Roman army is little better than the barbarians they face, because they are barbarians—bought with Roman gold."

"Surely, Mistress, the Emperor can remedy that." Lucilla brushed out Placidia's long brown hair. "Rome is the richest land on earth."

"The treasury is bare of taxes. Britain is overrun. Spain is devastated, and Gaul is just now recovering. The great nobles of Italy control the bureaucracy, insuring that they pay little or no taxes, leaving the burden of supporting our troops and the costs of government to the curial class. No wonder city merchants and leaders refuse the 'honor' of the curial rank, or join the church to avoid taxes. Thank the Good Lord for Africa, or we would have no food or coin."

Placidia closed her eyes and sighed, luxuriating in the feel of her hair being brushed. Her shoulders relaxed and hands stilled. Lucilla hummed a familiar tune, which Placidia couldn't quite place. She opened her eyes as Lucilla deftly braided her hair for bed. Placidia touched the frown line developing between her brows. "I begin to look like a wrinkled hag."

Lucilla looked past her into the mirror; the scarred left side of her own face was in shadow. "You are of an age where, to keep your beauty, you must take more care." Lucilla rubbed rose-scented cream onto Placidia's face, neck, and hands. She clucked over the ink-stained fingers.

"I have little time for such indulgences." Placidia fidgeted. "I cannot leave the fate of the Roman Empire in the clumsy hands of my brother and his sycophants. If I do not prevail over my enemies, nothing will be left of my father's legacy for my son."

"You have more friends at court than you know."

"What have you heard?" Placidia raised an eyebrow. Lucilla was often a source of interesting gossip. Her muteness in company led others to talk freely in front of her.

"Lady Padusia, the wife of General Felix, vigorously comes to your defense."

"Felix is out of favor with my brother. She seeks another sponsor for her husband."

Lucilla shrugged. "Can you not use that to your advantage?"

"Yes, but I long for people who give loyalty out of love, like you and Sigisvult." Placidia sighed. "But you are so few. I must look farther afield."

"What of your late husband's men?"

"He recommended Boniface as a loyal and competent man, who has ties to Africa. I need to secure that province, or there will only be Italy and Sicily left."

"What of Aetius?"

"Castinus has his leash. Too bad. Constantius thought him an outstanding soldier and valuable asset, with ties to the Huns from his youth as a hostage."

Her shoulders slumped. She rubbed her face with both hands. "Without Constantius, I am forced to rule from the shadows, through puppets and intrigue. It is a dangerous, thankless task, but I must hold the Empire together for Valentinian." Her face softened at the thought of her lively son.

"Time to rest, Mistress." Lucilla held out her sleeping shift. "Tomorrow will be soon enough to deal with these matters."

Placidia shrugged off her robe and donned a silk shift. "Yes. Have my wardrobe mistress lay my court clothes. It's time I returned to the fray."

PLACIDIA APPLAUDED WITH THE REST OF THE COURTIERS as her brother raised General Castinus to the rank of *magister militum*, just one step away from the supreme command, but her smile felt false. *What's next? The Patriciate? And Constantius dead but a few weeks.*

"I have a special commission for my dear friend, Castinus." Honorius rose from his well-padded throne clasp the general by the shoulders. "We will raise a large force, and he will clear the rebels and barbarians from Spain!"

The crowd erupted in loud cheers: "Praise to Our Esteemed Emperor!" and "The Good Lord protect and guide Rome!"

Placidia, as Augusta, refrained from the acclamations, but continued nodding and smiling from her seat on Honorius' right. The Emperor returned to his throne. Slaves bearing wine and food circulated among the crowd—a large number of whom clustered about Castinus, the newest imperial favorite. Placidia made note of who seemed most enthusiastic, and who kept their distance.

Boniface lingered on the fringes. A handsome man, medium height, whip-thin, topped with a mop of golden curls uncommon among Romans. In contrast to the somewhat corpulent Castinus, whose protuberant eyes and sensuous mouth always made Placidia feel she was being assessed like a horse.

Placidia accepted the goblet of rich red wine a servant offered her, then turned to Honorius. "An excellent reception, Brother."

"You think so? I left the details to Castinus and his chamberlain." He gulped his own wine.

"How do you plan to raise this large force you speak of to clear the rebels and barbarians from Spain? It's my understanding we have few men to spare."

Honorius waved his hand as if dispersing a bad smell. "There are always young men for the army."

"The land owners of Italy loathe letting their workers go to war. Will you collect gold from them instead? Perhaps King Theodoric of the Goths would join your force. I could send word, asking on your behalf?"

"Sister! These are not my problems. Castinus will handle the details. Relax. Enjoy the celebration." He descended the dais and was immediately surrounded by courtiers.

Placidia swirled her wine, studying the crowd. Castinus as *magister militum* was a blow, but Castinus on campaign far from the court was an opportunity. One she shouldn't waste. Yes, she would join the festivities, and put her plans in place.

"Lady Padusa!" she cried as the general's wife passed before her. "A word, if I may?"

"Of course, Augusta." Padusa bowed, eyes glittering with speculation.

THE NEXT DAY, Lucilla escorted Boniface to the private room in Placidia's quarters where she met with her agents and others who carried out her more clandestine activities.

"Augusta, I am most honored by your invitation." He glanced at Lucilla's retreating back as she left to prepare refreshments.

"Lucilla is totally loyal. She will not speak a word of this."

"I understand she is mute—a valuable trait in a servant."

Placidia smiled, looking him over. If not for the golden hair, he would disappear in a crowd, yet Constantius had seen something special in the young soldier. He stood comfortably, arms hanging by his side, waiting for her to speak. She had heard rumors he was the one who wounded Ataulf at Marseilles, and was feted as a hero for his actions.

Seven years since I held Ataulf in my arms. It feels like a different lifetime. She tried to picture his face, but it had blurred with time. She buried her grief anew, and tried to bury her resentment of the young man. *Ataulf wouldn't hold his bravery and skill in honorable battle against him, and neither should I. This is a different time. I need every ally I can find.*

"My husband spoke highly of you." She relaxed into her chair. "Be seated."

"Augusta," he acknowledged, folding himself into a chair facing hers. "General Constantius was a great man. I served with him in many campaigns, and would do anything to serve you and his children. Yesterday you indicated this mission is somewhat delicate?"

"What do you think of my brother's elevation of General Castinus to *magister militum*?"

"It is not my place to judge the Emperor's choices, but there are other, more competent generals to send to Spain."

"You, perhaps?"

He had the decency to blush. "Or General Felix."

"I agree with you. Castinus is a sycophant, intent on furthering his own cause at the expense of my brother's. Honorius has always been susceptible to flattery, something I am not as skilled in as I should be. Castinus blackens my name and plants suspicion in my brother's ear with every breath he takes. If he is successful in Spain, he could cause me much damage; possibly even banishment." She paused to gauge his reaction.

"Your late husband shared similar concerns with me, Augusta. I pledged my life and loyalty to him. How may I serve you? Do you require an oath?" He leaned forward in anticipation.

Something in his manner reminded her of Sigisvult. *If only the boy—no, the young man!—was experienced enough, he could...*She shut down that thought. She had to trust Boniface. Sigisvult could not execute her plan.

"No oath, but action. I wish you to accompany Castinus."

He frowned. "As a spy?"

"No. You will manufacture a quarrel with the General, then take ship from Portus to Africa."

"Africa?" Boniface grinned. "The breadbasket of Rome. You intend to build support in that most important province, to counter Castinus."

He's every bit as clever as Constantius promised. Now, if he is just as competent and loyal... "I have estates in Africa my husband won when he defeated the rebel Heraclian. These are dispatches," she handed him a leather pouch, "to my land agents, who will provide you with whatever funds or material support you need to recruit a personal *bucellarii* and build support among the local nobles on my behalf."

"Will Honorius consider this treason?"

"I have no intentions toward my brother's diadem—those are ugly rumors started by Castinus. With him away from court, I will have my brother's ear again. I promise your efforts will be rewarded. How does Count of Africa sound?"

"That would make me supreme military commander, and the most powerful Roman official in the province—quite an honor, Augusta!"

"I know how to reward my friends and allies, Boniface. Constantius had every confidence in you, as do I." She indicated Lucilla, who had returned with a tray earlier. "Some refreshments are in order. I understand you have a daughter?"

"About your own daughter's age, Augusta. My wife died giving birth..."

They continued chatting about families, taking wine and nibbling cheese and olives. Placidia's confidence grew. *Constantius was right about this one. He'll be a staunch ally.*

Ravenna, Spring 422

PLACIDIA TOOK IN THE ROWDY CROWD from her elevated height on the Emperor's couch. The usual court officials, rich hangers-on, a few Senators visiting from Rome, and minor nobility from the provinces reclining on the dining couches. She preferred the more modern habit of eating at a table, but the court eunuchs insisted on the old style for formal occasions.

She recognized a major trader from Britain, and took care to avoid his gaze. Many Britons fled before the raiding Saxons onto the shores of Gaul—yet another dislocated population to drain the fragile resources of the Empire in the west. Only Africa, under Count Boniface, remained untouched. Those lands, and the grain that fed most of the west, must be protected at all costs. Boniface—so far—had been a good choice.

There was other good news. She accepted another goblet of wine, and turned to her brother, "I heard General Castinus is doing poorly against the remnants of the Vandals in Spain."

Honorius frowned. "King Theodoric abandoned the General; left him exposed. He was almost captured!"

She shrugged. "Castinus abused the Goths and refused to pay them. The land is so devastated they could not live off it."

"You mean they couldn't loot and pillage." Honorius shook his head. "Sister, you will always be blind when it comes to the Goths. They are no better than any other barbarians."

"And no worse, though you would have them so." The wine loosened her tongue. "I have friends among them. They saved my life, and I theirs. We are bound by mutual pledges of loyalty and ties of blood. King Theodoric is Gaatha's son-in-law, and therefore my nephew by marriage."

"That marriage…"

She realized her error as soon as the words were spoken, and reached up to put her fingers over his mouth. "…was against your wishes and I humbly ask your pardon—as I have on several occasions. Let's not quarrel, brother."

He kissed her fingers and let them go. "I agree, Dearest Sister. We shouldn't quarrel. I am never so relaxed as in your company—when you aren't nagging me for something."

"I promise. No nagging tonight." Placidia laughed.

"It's nice to see a smile on those pretty lips." He leaned over and kissed her fully on the mouth.

Placidia pushed him away with some violence. A circle of silence spread about their couch, as those who had noticed the impropriety watched to see how both would react. She checked her rising anger and said, in a mild voice, "Brother, I believe you have had too much wine, to act with so little restraint."

His flushed face looked puzzled. "I only show my affection for you. Is that not allowed?"

"I always welcome your tokens of esteem, but would it not be more seemly to kiss your sister on the cheek? You do not want to give the court gossips grist for their mill." She smiled at Honorius and pointedly set her wine aside. Her brother seemed unpredictable lately, at times cool and suspicious, at others overly familiar. His skin was pasty under the flush, and his breath smelled sour. Perhaps some illness or physical ailment was at the root of his moods.

Appeased by her words, Honorius turned his attention back to a troupe of dancers in the middle of the banquet hall. Placidia suppressed a sigh as she picked at her food.

Sigisvult was drunk.

The greasy owner of this tumbledown excuse for a tavern didn't serve beer, and the wine tasted like vinegar laced with pine pitch, but he served lots of it for little coin, so the place was popular with troops of all kind.

Sigisvult stared at the portrait of Placidia on a brass coin in his hand. It blurred, split into duplicates, then re-formed. "Don't look anything like her," he mumbled.

"What?" A fellow guardsman punched Sigisvult in the arm. "Put away your money, Sig. This round comes from my purse."

The two other men at the table cheered their generous companion and launched into a rowdy song lauding the prowess, in both battle and bed, of one of their legendary kings. Sigisvult joined in, singing the chorus with more gusto than skill.

As they paused for another round, a voice arose from across the room. "Thank Mithras and his bloody bull, that clamor has stopped. I thought we were beset by harpies."

"Some demon seized their bodies and made them caw like crows," a second man said.

"You have some issue with our singing?" Sigisvult shouted. He could just make out a dim form in the shadows.

"Not me, good man. My ears take issue." This garnered a round of laughter from others in the crowd.

Sigisvult stood, slightly swaying.

The second man said, "Careful, Marcus, he's one of the Augusta's pet Goths."

"What need to take care?" The first speaker—Marcus?—stepped into the light of an overhead oil lamp. "These sniveling slaves will run back to their whoring mistress when faced with real soldiers." He was a stocky man, with the shoulders and arms of a blacksmith straining the scarlet tunic of a *scholae*.

The room stilled. Blood roared in Sigisvult's ears.

"Ignorant pile of shit from a scurvy dog, you dare call our queen a whore?" Wooden benches scraped on stone as his companions rose to join him.

"Everyone knows the Augusta—I'm sorry," Marcus gave a mock bow, "your queen—whores with her brother to keep him under her thumb."

Seven or eight forms materialized at Marcus' back. Sigisvult grinned, clenching his fists. Any one Goth could take on four or five of these foul-mouthed, out-of-shape, ceremonial soldiers.

"Out, all of you!" The tavern owner and another man, who had the look of an ex-gladiator, brandished clubs thick with knurls and bumps. "I'll have no brawling in my tavern."

Sigisvult leaped at Marcus with a piercing cry. He landed a blow on the man's nose with a satisfying crunch while taking what felt like a mule's kick to the stomach. Sigisvult sagged back, air whooshing from his lungs, to be caught by his brethren. They stood him up, then entered the fray with howls of their own.

The tavern owner and the gladiator rained blows with their clubs, pushing the melee toward the door. Two of Marcus' supporters already lay sprawled on the floor.

The odds were getting better.

Sigisvult pushed into the brawl. He ducked a blow to his head, delivering a punch to one opponent's ribs. While the man clutched his side, Sigisvult kicked his knee. He could feel the joint separating under his hobnailed sandal. The man fell to the floor, cursing.

Then Sigisvult slipped in spilled wine. He was caught from behind in a bear-like hug, constricting his arms above the elbows and lifting him off the floor.

Sigisvult clawed at the arms crushing the breath from his body. He butted his head backward and heard a moan as the back of his head met rock-hard jaw. Just as his ribs started to cave, he heard a grunt. The arms loosened.

He gasped and turned in time to receive a club across the temple. He crumpled to the floor on top of Marcus.

*****

PLACIDIA WRINKLED HER NOSE at the musty stench of chicken shit. The poultry keeper hovered in the background as Honorius examined a fancy rooster with white fluffy feathers and an elegant tail. No one else attended except the ubiquitous slaves, ready to provide food, drink, or shade at the Emperor's request.

"A fine looking bird." Placidia extended a finger to caress the silky down on the rooster's neck. The bird turned its head and pecked at her hand. She pulled back, suppressing the urge to put the wound to her mouth. "Damn the creature! It drew blood."

The poultry keeper rushed forward with a cloth and profuse apologies.

"You have much to learn about chickens." Honorius laughed as she cradled her bandaged scratch. "I could have him executed and served as your supper for his audacity, but he is a particularly fine breeder. Aren't you, my Achilles?"

"Put the bird down and walk with me a bit." Placidia took her brother's arm under hers and led him out of the servants' earshot. "Let's talk."

"Not about court business." Honorius frowned. "I come here to get away from that boring drivel."

"This has to do with you and me."

His face brightened. He pulled her closer. She removed his hand from her hip and held it between both her own. "It is this behavior we must discuss. Kisses on the mouth and familiar touches are not appropriate. We are brother and sister—"

"Half-brother and sister."

"We had the same sire, yet these kisses and touches are the acts of lovers. Rumors impugning my honor and yours travel the land. This familiarity must stop."

"Why are you so cold to me?" Honorius withdrew his hand, his eyes shadowed. "Castinus warned me that your affection waned, and your ambition waxed."

"Castinus seeks to poison your affection for me." Placidia steeled herself in the face of his paranoia. "I love you as a sister should love a brother, and a subject should love her Emperor. I have served you loyally, even to giving you a possible heir."

"An heir whom you will control, if I die."

"I want nothing to happen to you, Brother." She placed a calming hand on his crossed arms. "You will live many years. Let us be friends and put this suspicion behind us."

"I don't like to quarrel with you, Placidia. Why do you insist on these restrictions to my affection?"

"Bishop John came to me with concerns. He believes we are indiscreet."

"Pesky priest," Honorius muttered. "I am the Emperor, and will do as I choose."

"Your *scholae* slander my name in taverns, and engage in brawls with my men."

"Whose fault is that? You insist on keeping those uncivilized barbarians around you. It's a disgrace. You should send them back to Gaul."

His words chilled Placidia. *So that is Castinus' game.* Without her Goths, Honorius could put her away, or she might meet with some 'accident.' Castinus would then control both Honorius and Valentinian.

"I'll think on it, brother." She bowed. "Enjoy your pets."

"Are you sure you would not like to remain? I have a beautiful red and gold hen I think you would fancy."

"Another time, perhaps."

Chapter 25

Ravenna, Fall 422

SIGISVULT SPRAWLED IN A CHAIR at the side of Placidia's worktable, an informal pose seven years of lessons and service had earned him. He watched Placidia review a letter while unconsciously curling a strand of hair around her finger. These were the moments he lived for, when he could see the woman behind the public mask of the Augusta.

She folded the message, sealed it with wax, and turned to Sigisvult. "I have a most delicate task for you."

At last! Sigisvult rose, wincing as he reached for the packet.

She frowned. "Are you sure you're well enough?"

He felt the heat rising in his cheeks and covered it with what he hoped was a roguish smile. "Never better, My Queen. The barracks doctor bound my ribs and poulticed my head."

"Good. I can trust no other with this mission."

For the first time Sigisvult noticed the worry lines tracing her forehead did not quite fade when she relaxed her brows. He yearned to reach out and smooth those lines away.

"These letters are no more than casual correspondence to Gaatha and King Theodoric. The real message you must deliver from your own lips." Placidia held out a signet ring—not the one she used as Augusta, but the carved ruby she had used as Queen of the Goths. "Take this. It will prove the message comes from me."

"You do me much honor." He bowed over her hand. "What do you want me to convey to the Gothic court?"

"Tell Theodoric that I and my children are in danger. Castinus and others plot against me. I must know if he will provide us shelter in case of need and…"

Sigisvult waited quietly. Placidia took a deep breath. "What I say next could cost my life."

He knelt at her feet, head bowed. "My life is yours to command, My Queen. I would sooner strike off my own head than endanger yours."

"I know."

She drew a shaky breath. "I must know if Theodoric will rally to me, if I need to oppose my brother or General Castinus on my son's behalf."

SIGISVULT STUMBLED WITH EXHAUSTION as he entered the Gothic King's court at Toulouse. *Thank the Good Lord for straight Roman roads!* He had traveled the distance in five days; changing post horses every ten or twelve miles and snatching brief naps at the overnight stations. He could have made better time, but the posts became irregular in areas controlled by the Bagaudae.

After the splendors of Ravenna, Theodoric's court looked provincial and gaudy; the furniture, mosaics, and clothing spoke of the apprentice, rather than the master. The only superior aspect was the relative informality of the court. Sigisvult straightened his tunic and slapped off some road dust before approaching Theodoric's elevated gilt chair.

There's not much I can do about the smell, but the King is a warrior; he shouldn't be offended by the odor of horse and honest sweat.

"I bring greetings from Galla Placidia Augusta to her kinsman, King Theodoric." Sigisvult knelt on one knee, presenting the package to the King.

"How does our kinswoman?" Theodoric nodded to a courtier, who took the leather packet.

"She is well, and wishes me to present her personal compliments to both you and her sister, Lady Gaatha." Sigisvult tendered the signet ring.

"I see." Theodoric examined the ring. His face stiffened. "My wife's mother is quite ill."

Sigisvult's gut twisted. He had always liked Gaatha for her kindness, especially to Placidia. "I am sorry. Is she well enough for me to pay my respects?"

"Yes, but I suggest you clean up first." Theodoric motioned for a slave. "He will show you to the baths and Lady Gaatha. I wish to speak to you in private afterwards."

"Of course."

After a hasty plunge and a change of clothes, Sigisvult entered Gaatha's chambers. The pungent smell of incense vied, and lost, to the sour odor of illness. Lady Gaatha reclined on a couch covered with sky-blue silk spreads and pillows. A skein of brown wool and a drop spindle lay at her side.

Even by the light of the dim oil lamp set on a table at the end of her couch, Sigisvult could see Gaatha was much wasted. The older woman's hair had faded to the color of a ginger cat's fur, shot with gray. Pain stamped her face with grooves from nose to mouth, and darkened her green eyes to the shade of a shadowed pond.

"Young Sigisvult?" She stretched out a skeletal hand. "I barely recognized you."

"Yes, Lady." He shuffled his feet. Fatigue dulled his senses, and the incense made him sleepy. He stifled a yawn.

"Sit down, boy." Gaatha patted the couch by her side.

"King Theodoric told me of your illness. I hope you are not in pain."

"Constantly. I have a tumor." Her hand moved to her breast. "The army surgeon wanted to cut it out, but I wouldn't let that butcher touch me with a knife. The best he can do is provide me this vile potion that makes me sleep all the time." Gaatha indicated a nearly full bottle on the stand. "I've little time left. I don't want to spend it sleeping."

Sigisvult sat with head bowed.

"But I'm an old fool. You didn't come to hear the complaints of a dying woman." She looked into his eyes. "What news from Placidia?"

Sigisvult told Gaatha about Castinus, Placidia's fears, and her requests.

Gaatha sat up, tapping a fingernail on the spindle. "It's a tangled skein. There is still a faction here that supports Placidia out of past loyalty and for procuring us this land. But a smaller group will counsel Theodoric to eschew the problems of the Ravenna court."

"Where will King Theodoric stand on this?"

"As long as I live, Placidia and her children will have shelter with the Goths."

As long as I live. The phrase lay between them like a dead dog neither wanted to touch.

"What do you advise?"

197

Gaatha leaned back on her pillows and closed her eyes. For a moment, fear that she had passed jolted the fatigue from Sigisvult's body. Then he noticed tears tracking her cheeks.

"Tell my sister I pray for God's blessings on her and her children, but she should not trust her fate to Theodoric."

"TREASON!" HONORIUS SHOUTED. He burst into Placidia's study, General Castinus hard on his heels. "Treason and murder!"

Castinus moved quickly. Placidia rose, her voice steady despite her racing heart and knotted stomach. "Strong words, Brother. How do you come to use them?"

In the face of her calmness, Honorius pulled up short, his complexion alternately flushing and blanching.

"You know very well, Placidia. Your Goths attacked and killed two of my guards. They riot in the streets, and speak against me in the market. You must send them back to Gaul."

"My men were provoked. Your *scholae* called me a whore and worse. My guards have sworn their lives to me, and will protect my honor and my life as long as they are bound by oath. Even so, anticipating your objection, I have dismissed my captain." *And given him a tidy sum and land for his retirement.*

Balked, Honorius spluttered, "You have been corresponding with the Gothic King. Do you plot my downfall with those barbarians at your back?"

"Attack the Great General Castinus and his mighty army with a handful of ragged barbarians?" She nodded at Castinus. "What foolishness. I sent my felicitations to Theodoric and asked for his continued good will to the Empire, as you well know, because the letters were opened and read while my messenger slept at a way station." She had no proof of this, but it was extremely likely that Castinus now controlled the imperial agents.

"We can interrogate the messenger," Castinus said with a triumphant smile. "I'm sure he will corroborate your claims."

"I will not give a free young man over to torture because of Castinus' base suspicions. Brother," Placidia took both Honorius' hands and spoke softly, "when have I ever betrayed you? Disobeyed, yes, but never betrayed. Castinus feeds you lies and tries to drive a wedge between us. Why believe him over me?"

"The Goths must go. I cannot have your private troop of barbarians warring with my men." Honorius took on the lock-jawed, mulish cast that signaled he would not be moved. "Besides, it is not right that my heir be surrounded by such execrable influences. Maybe I should take over his education."

Placidia felt the blood leave her face. *Castinus has been most thorough in alienating my brother from me.*

"I will not give up my men. They are sworn not only to me, but to my children. I trust no others to see to our safety."

"You defy me again over these accursed Goths." Honorius turned nearly purple. Spittle foamed at the corners of his mouth. He ripped his hands from hers. "You dishonored me with your marriage to that barbarian dog—"

"I was happy with Ataulf. Our union was not a disgrace or a threat to the Empire." Betraying tears glittered in her eyes as she stretched her hands again toward her brother. "I loved him."

"But you don't love me enough to obey." Honorius' mouth twisted, as if he tasted something foul.

Placidia looked from her brother to the smirking Castinus. Cold settled in her stomach; frustration resonated in her voice. She had lost the game, but maybe truth would win. "That 'barbarian dog,' as you call him, was a *successful* general." Castinus' smile disappeared. "If you had not listened to jealous courtiers, he could have made you as great an Emperor as our father. Instead, you listen to lickspittles like Castinus, who seek to destroy all those who might thwart their greedy plans. Think for yourself, Brother. I am of your blood, and command the loyalty of the Goths."

"So you do plot against me!"

"No, no, no! I have lived among the tribes and can help you, if you let me."

"The barbarians have no loyalty except to gold, my Most Wise Emperor. If I pay well, they serve me. If the Augusta pays better, they serve her. That is why you must cleanse them from your court." Castinus took a parchment scroll from behind his back and handed it to Placidia. "For you, Augusta."

She opened it with trembling fingers and rapidly read through the flowery script, with her brother's seal at the bottom. Placidia locked her knees to keep from falling to the floor.

Banishment.

*****

Spring 423

CASTINUS, YOU SLIMY TOAD, I'll see your head adorning Ravenna's walls. You will not steal my son's birthright, Placidia vowed as the ships left the docks at Ravenna.

She had persuaded Honorius to let her retire to the Constantinople court, where she could reside in her own palace under the watchful eye of her nephew, Emperor Theodosius II. Honorius allowed Placidia her household and Goths—which he couldn't separate from her if he wanted to—but forced her to leave her considerable personal fortune because, as Castinus put it, "the barbarians will soon abandon her with no gold to hold their loyalty."

I will arrive on my nephew's doorstep little more than a beggar. A better, if more dangerous, fate than poor Attalus. She blinked away tears. Her friend had died two months earlier. She had had his ashes brought back to Rome. *I could use his wits in the coming months.*

Placidia faced into the wind as her ship sped into the Adriatic Sea, accompanied by a small flotilla of six. The Roman navy, like its army, had dwindled over the years. She sailed on a merchant vessel. Most of her household and Gothic guards travelled by land to Constantinople.

Lucilla joined her by the rail. "The children wish to come out."

Placidia glanced at the sturdy wooden cabin built on the deck, small but waterproofed with pitch. "I suppose they will have to, sooner or later." She sighed. "Keep them close to the cabin. I don't want them going below or bothering the sailors at their work. And for the Good Lord's sake, don't let them near the rails. They could be swept overboard."

Lucilla surveyed the tiny patch of deck allowed to the children. "Perhaps, if I tied a rope about each, they could venture a bit farther?"

Placidia nodded.

THREE DAYS LATER, they passed into the Mediterranean Sea and heavy weather. The ship pitched and rolled in the oily waves. Placidia missed the raucous call of the seagulls and the high whistle of the dolphins that normally dogged their passage. The sailors took down the sail and unstepped the mast. Placidia's guards, Sigisvult among them, went below. Only the captain at the rudder, and a few sailors, stayed on deck.

Placidia, Lucilla, and the children huddled in their dark cabin. No lamp or brazier was allowed due to the risk of fire. Of them all, Placidia proved the poorest sailor. Her head pounded. She retched with dry heaves, having emptied her stomach earlier. The stench of her vomit didn't help. She longed for fresh air, but dared not leave the cabin, even if she had the strength.

"Is Mommy going to die?" she heard Honoria whisper to Lucilla.

"No, Sweetling. The motion of the sea makes her stomach hurt. She will be well when we reach land."

"Good, 'cause I don't want Mommy to go to heaven like Daddy."

Placidia felt warmth spread through her misery.

The door opened, letting in a burst of fresh air and a shower of rain. The captain stepped inside. "My apologies, Augusta, but we have a real blow coming from the west. You and the children should prepare for rough seas."

Placidia sat up on her cushions. "These aren't rough?"

The man smiled through his wet beard. "No, Augusta. This is but a mild spring squall."

"Can you not put to shore until it's over?"

"We lost sight of the shore, and dare not make a run for the coast. We would likely run aground and wreck the ship. It's best to brave this storm at sea."

"The other ships?"

"We've signals from all."

"Very well, Captain."

Within the hour, Placidia and Lucilla were clutching the children to keep them from rolling from side to side. The ship moaned as it wallowed through the waves. Placidia felt it shudder and twitch like a horse under her. She could just make out the shouts of the captain over the screeching wind.

In a sudden lull, the captain shouted, "Beware!"

The ship listed to the left, throwing them against the wall. A box of her toiletries broke open, smashing several small bottles and adding roses to the scent of vomit, urine and the seawater streaming under the door.

Placidia landed painfully on her shoulder. A wooden stool crashed into her shin.

The children screamed and cried. Placidia crushed Val to her breast. "Lucilla?"

"Honoria's unhurt."

Another wave hit. Water crashed down on the cabin. The ship shuddered and groaned. Val's heart beat like a captive bird's. He sobbed in her arms.

"Good Lord Jesus, help us!" Placidia prayed, whether silently or shouting, she didn't know. "Mother Mary, have pity on us. Spare the children. Saint John the Evangelist, I vow a church in your name, if you save us!"

The cabin tilted again, and the wall became a floor.

CHAPTER 26

Constantinople, 423

PALE AND SHAKEN FROM THE ROUGH VOYAGE, Placidia and the children moved through the palace at Constantinople. Although she had lived here as a small child, she remembered little beyond the feel of her father's arms carrying her through the marble halls and the sound of his leather sandals slapping the floor. Yet she was sure it had been much more lavish. The rooms she glimpsed felt spartan. As they approached the royal audience chamber, the scent of incense tickled her nose. Droning chants filled her ears.

Placidia ran a critical eye over her children. She used her fingers to comb Valentinian's wind-swept hair. Honoria tugged her robes into place, and patted back in place a strand of hair that had escaped its gold and pearl net. They were dressed in royal purple. Placidia wore the diadem and signet ring of an Augusta. Having arrived storm-tossed and travel-stained, Placidia was pleased they were able to turn out so well.

The herald announced her and the children. Placidia swept into the room, head held high. She was at once struck by the presence of numerous priests and women in religious habits. They seemed to outnumber the courtiers and petitioners. Placidia had heard Theodosius and Pulcheria were devout, to the consternation of those who remembered the free-living court of their father and mother, but she had not expected this. The place felt more like a church than a palace.

She approached a raised dais where Theodosius sat with his older sister on his right hand and wife on the left, both in chairs of equal height, but set lower than his. The herald made lengthy introductions, naming each and their titles. He omitted the title Augusta for Placidia, and did not acknowledge Valentinian as prince. *So that's the way the wind blows in Constantinople. This might be harder to weather than that god-forsaken storm.*

"Welcome to our court, Aunt." Theodosius was a handsome man of nearly twenty-three, with intelligent eyes and a soft mouth pursed in a neutral smile.

Pulcheria seemed much older than her twenty-five years, dressed in the severe robes of a holy woman, her hair covered with a snowy headdress and her face devoid of artifice. She didn't even bother to smile. "I trust you had a felicitous journey?"

"We had one violent storm, but God saw us safely to your shore. Thank you for your concern."

Pulcheria nodded. "I have found that, when God is gracious, it is appropriate that we honor Him in some way."

"I vowed to build a church when I return to Ravenna," Placidia answered dryly. "And I intend never to tempt His good will with another sea voyage."

"A church is an appropriate recompense."

Athenais was the first to rise. Placidia saw why Theodosius was so taken with his bride. She possessed naturally golden curls, the envy of the court. Many women sported the popular hair color, but relied on wigs or a noxious brew that bleached their own dark tresses. Athenais also had unusual violet-colored eyes, a creamy complexion, and a red bow of a mouth. But her beauty was nothing compared to her warmth. "I am so pleased you and the children landed safely. I'm looking forward to your company." She took Placidia's arm with a genuine smile. "Why don't we retire to a less public place, and have some refreshment? I'm sure you are fatigued after your journey."

"I'll join you, when I've finished my audience." Theodosius nodded to Placidia, but did not rise. "My sister and wife will take good care of you, Aunt."

Obviously dismissed, the three women and two children retired to a room as austere as, but smaller than, the audience chamber. The marble walls were bare of paintings; no statues adorned the corners. Pulcheria positioned herself at the head of the room, on a plain wooden chair. Athenais seated herself on a cushioned bench and patted the space beside her. "Join me, Aunt. You will allow me to call you that, won't you?"

The younger woman's voice and manner exuded the feeling that Placidia's needs and interests were close to her heart. A valuable trait in the swamps of a royal court.

Pulcheria waved over the children. "Come, let me look at you."

The children approached, but did not bow. Placidia was proud of the way they stood up under the scrutiny of their older cousin. Valentinian shuffled his feet, but stopped when his sister pinched him.

"Very good. You may go to the nursery."

A servant came forward to take their hands. They looked back at Placidia. At her nod, they went quietly. Other servants provided food and drink—a hearty red wine and honey cakes.

"What of my other nieces, Arcadia and Marina? Are they not to join us?" Placidia looked around.

"My sisters are out doing works of charity. It is our fervent hope you will join us in these missions of mercy, once you have settled into your palace." Pulcheria maintained a neutral expression—not welcoming, but not judging. "Aunt, what brings you so precipitously to our shores?"

Placidia sipped her watered wine, weighing her words. She was certain Pulcheria knew about the breach between her and Honorius. Her niece undoubtedly had agents in Ravenna who used the post horses and good Roman roads to deliver their reports quickly. She didn't doubt Honorius had sent his own account—likely written by Castinus.

"My brother is increasingly prey to suspicions inflamed by those ministers closest to him. Given his current state of mind, I felt it best to remove my children and myself."

Pulcheria's face puckered. "Who then rules in the west? Do we need to send troops?"

Placidia did not want Theodosius invading Italy and supplanting her brother. If her nephew extended control over the entire empire and later had a son, he could reasonably deny Valentinian any portion of rule.

"My brother still rules. His vacillations are of a personal nature. General Castinus manufactured a plot and lured my retainers into an unwise action in order to discredit me. He convinced Honorius that I did not have my brother's interests at heart."

"This breach between brother and sister disturbs me. You are orphans, as were Theodosius and I. You have no family but each other. It is not seemly to have this disharmony."

From her own agents, Placidia knew that all was not as harmonious in the eastern court as her niece would have her believe. Pulcheria had quarreled with her brother over elevating Athenais to Augusta, giving her sister-in-law an equal rank just because she had given birth to a daughter.

Placidia set aside her wine to address Pulcheria with all the authority she could muster. "Our circumstances are different, Niece. You are older than your brother. You shared many experiences, guided him in his youth, and built trust between you. Honorius is my elder by several years, and we lived in different households most of our lives. Over the last years we worked together closely, but rumors and falsehoods easily lead him astray. It is my understanding that my oldest brother suffered a similar...temperament."

Pulcheria gave her a sharp look. "The males of our line do seem to benefit from the gentle guidance of the females." Pulcheria's father, the Emperor Arcadius, had been even duller than his younger brother Honorius, and easily influenced by those close to him—including his infamous wife, Eudoxia. There were even some hard-to-root-out rumors about Theo's parentage.

"Pulcheria is modest." Athenais set down a goblet she had barely touched. "She is Theodosius' wisest and closest advisor. Everyone knows, if they wish something done by the Augustus, they must come to the Augusta."

Placidia understood Athenais' message. *Pulcheria first, then Theodosius.*

"It is well known how ably Pulcheria ruled during her brother's minority." *And to take on that burden at the tender age of fifteen guarantees a formidable personality.* "Your fairness and devotion to God and your brother are admired throughout the Empire."

Pulcheria looked towards the heavens—in this case, a ceiling painted dark blue with gold trim. "God put us on earth as His emissaries. It is through His will that we rule, and we show our devotion through good works and fair governance."

"A most admirable mission, which I would like to duplicate in the west, but, sadly, must bide my time until my brother can be persuaded to the right course." Placidia suppressed a yawn. "I am fatigued after our journey. My residence is hardly fit to live in, and I slept poorly last night on the boat."

"How thoughtless of me." Athenais raised a soft hand to her mouth. "You must stay with us until your residence is properly restored and staffed." She waved over a servant. "Tell my chamberlain to prepare the west suite." She turned back to Placidia. "The rooms will be ready shortly. Let's go to the nursery so you can reassure your children."

Given Pulcheria's stern face, it was hard to gauge her reaction to Athenais' burst of generosity. Placidia rose. "God's grace on you, Pulcheria."

"And you, Aunt."

She followed the younger woman out the door.

"Pulcheria is not a bad sort." Athenais smiled as she took Placidia's arm. "Just a bit stuffy, and very protective of Theo. She will be watching closely, to see if you try to influence him unduly."

"I do not wish to become a power in this court." Placidia sighed. "I just want some rest, and safety for my children." *Time enough later to discuss the best course of action with Pulcheria and Theodosius.* Placidia patted Athenais' arm. "I am most grateful for your warm welcome and any advice you can give me for succeeding in my quest."

"Perhaps we can be of benefit to one another. I have been at court only two years, and yearn for a friend of equal rank." A shadow passed over her face. "Pulcheria's nature does not turn to friendship and, as you are probably aware, the women at court have considerably more than the Augusta's friendship at heart. I am constantly bombarded with requests for appointments and favors."

"I understand your loneliness. Is your husband affectionate?"

"Theo is my dearest friend and perfect love. If not for him, I would have wasted away. Theo and Pulcheria keep such a dull court. I am used to a more lively intellectual set. I studied philosophy and natural history at the Athens University."

"I heard. Why do you not entertain on your own? You could have a salon and invite the leading thinkers and artists."

"I will, but I must move slowly. Pulcheria and Theo still suffer much from the unsavory reputation of their mother. Pulcheria in particular wants no hint of scandal. Here is the nursery." Athenais' face lit up as she entered. She moved to an ornate bed guarded by an elderly heavyset woman. "Nana, how is my angel today?"

The woman continued knitting, showing a gap-toothed smile. "She's been as good a child as I've ever known." She winked at Placidia, a familiarity allowed by only the oldest of retainers. "I heard you were coming. Do you remember me, princess? I used to give you sweets to fatten you up. Always such a little bird."

The warm memory of a soft lap and sticky fingers brought a smile to Placidia's lips. "Of course, Nana. I have children of my own now."

The nurse nodded. "I looked in on them. Your daughter reminds me of you at that age. You were five when Serena took you away to Rome. A sad day for me." The knitting needles continued clicking as the old woman's voice subsided into a murmur.

Athenais picked up the baby and turned to Placidia. "My daughter, Eudoxia."

Placidia studied the sleeping infant. She saw the promise of great beauty in the soft blond curls, long dark lashes, and full lips. Many infants, including her own, were pretty only to their parents, but this child would be accounted beautiful by anyone. "She's precious, Athenais. She will rival Helen of Troy."

"She has already surpassed me. She barely cries and everyone in the nursery comes running to relieve her least discomfort. Theo is so entranced he named me Augusta upon her baptism." Athenais blushed. "Pulcheria was not pleased."

"I heard," Placidia said. "Where are my children?"

"In the next room." Athenais put the sleeping baby back on her bed and escorted Placidia.

"Mother, where were you?" Honoria leaped from a chair, where she had been perusing a codex, and came to hug her mother's knees.

A pang shot through Placidia's heart as she disentangled the little girl. "You know perfectly well I was with your cousins. We will stay here for a while. What do you think of that, Val?"

"I want to live on the boat!"

Placidia shuddered. "We will never set foot on a ship again."

He burst into tears. Placidia picked him up to soothe him. Athenais took Honoria's hand and led her into the next room to see her baby cousin, while Placidia crooned a lullaby to her son. He hiccupped and soon subsided into sleep.

She studied his innocent face. If only she could sleep that peacefully! She leaned back in the chair. Her eyes drooped. Maybe she could find peace here, at least for a few hours.

PLACIDIA GROANED AND STRETCHED her arms over her head. Her temporary work table sagged under piles of paper: financial accounts, invitations to dinners and fetes, and reports on the Ravenna court. She needed to get her household in order and shift the load from her shoulders to theirs, so she could attend to more important matters—convincing Theo and Pulcheria to accept her son as

Honorius' heir and successor in the West.

Within a week of her arrival, her own palace residence was habitable, and Placidia moved in with her children, household staff, and token guards. Most of her personal Gothic *bucellarii* were billeted with Theo's palace *scholae*—a temporary solution until she could pay for their keep elsewhere. She set up her work room in a bright solar. She had the walls painted pale lavender, and would add frescoes or art when she had the time and money to attend to such details.

"Princess, Leontius to see you." A young page stood at the door.

Placidia winced at the demotion from Augusta to Princess. She had briefly considered asking her personal staff to continue using her title, but decided against it. The practice would surely get back to her nephew and niece and cause coolness, if not a breach.

"Show him in." She shifted a stack of accounts to the front of the table. Leontius, her *curator*, administered her business and legal affairs. His advancing age—Stilicho had appointed him to oversee her inheritance when her father died, twenty-eight years ago—did not slow his thinking or his enviable work habits. Placidia wished she could maintain such energy.

"Princess." Leontius bowed low. His scalp gleamed through thinning hair. "I heard your sea journey was perilous. I'm pleased to see you in good health."

"And you, my friend, weathered the land route well?" She indicated a chair in front of her table. He lowered his body onto the padded leather with a small sigh.

"As well as can be expected at my age. The seats on mule wagons are not the most comfortable."

He shifted his rump. Placidia hid a smile behind her hand. "I remember. Why did you not ride a horse or take a litter?"

He smiled, deepening the wrinkles at the corners of his eyes. "I had treasure under the seat that no one knew of. I sat on that board and slept in the wagon the entire trip."

"Treasure?" Placidia's heart rate increased.

"Your brother confiscated your Italian lands, personal cash, and jewels, but he didn't know of the chest at my residence to receive and disburse funds on your behalf. The rents had just come in from your Sicilian estates." He steepled his hands. His gaze turned inward as if he were calculating in his head. "It's enough to take care of your expenses here for a month. That will give me time to set up loans on your behalf."

"Good! I am not entirely destitute. My father left me a small inheritance here in the East. I have this palace, a country villa near Hebdomon, and the income from three estates." She shook her head. "Not enough to cover my household expenses, now that I'm in residence."

"Do you trust your estate agents?" Leontius frowned.

She shrugged. "I've never met them, but I'm sure you will take them in hand."

"Of course." He nodded. "Do you have any other immediate source of funds? Your nephew, perhaps?"

"If necessary, they will feed and house me and the children—it's the Christian thing to do—but, for now, I can count on no more. There was some bad blood between my oldest brother and my mother. He was only ten when my parents married, but resented her presence and my birth. That's why Father established this palace for us, to keep the households separate." She leaned back in her chair, smiling. "I have a vague memory of a great celebration when I was a small child. I wore a stiff robe of gold and a headdress with gold rays, like the sun, that kept tilting. It must have been when Father elevated Honorius to Augustus and gave me the title Princess. I remember Arcadius pinching my arm until I cried, at the reception afterwards." She rubbed her arm as if reliving the pain of that pinch. "It was long ago, but the enmity seems to echo in a coolness in Theo's court."

Placidia turned her attention back to her *curator*. "As to the present, I have a letter from Count Boniface in Africa. He promises funds, if needed. My brother has diverted the rents from the African estates, but Boniface has his own resources, which he puts at my disposal." She handed Boniface's letter to Leontius, and indicated the stack of accounts. "These are for you."

His smile brightened. "Excellent! I assume I'll have quarters here?"

"The chamberlain has prepared your suite and stocked your workroom. Keep the cash chest, and disburse funds to the chamberlain for the household, as needed."

Leontius rose, gathered the accounts, gave a brief bow and left.

Placidia eyed the remaining stacks with a sigh. *Tomorrow, or the next day, this will all be cleared and I can get down to the real work—winning my nephew's favor.*

CHAPTER 27

Ravenna, August 423

CASTINUS THUMPED ACROSS THE CARPETED FLOOR of his workroom, hands clasped behind his back. His blue silk tunic stretched across his slumping shoulders.

Aetius contemplated the fruit on a side table, and chose a pear. "How is the Emperor?"

Castinus glared. "Not well. There's little the doctors can do for dropsy except to make him more comfortable."

"How long before he dies?"

"Less than a month." Castinus stopped by his littered worktable and bowed his head.

Aetius put a hand on his shoulder. "Hard luck, my friend."

"God's balls, why did the fool have to get ill now? It has been only a few months since I sent that meddling bitch of a sister packing, and I have yet to consolidate my power. Count Boniface in Africa remains stubbornly loyal to Placidia. He corresponds with her in Constantinople, even sends her money! The Goths won't speak to my envoys, and have begun to raid again."

"Italy is still yours to command."

"Italy can't supply my armies with men! Without the barbarian recruits, the army dwindles to nothing."

"I can recruit among the Huns. They grow restless in the East, and would glory in the action."

Castinus turned a speculative eye on Aetius. Of middle height and in his early thirties, his well-muscled frame showed the easy grace of an athlete. As a boy, Aetius had been among the Roman hostages given to the Huns, and he'd won their respect in horsemanship and other arts of war. He benefited from his tenure by becoming great friends with their leader. That might come in handy, but not yet.

"I don't want to give the Huns a foothold on Roman soil. Stilicho and Honorius made that mistake with the Goths and the Burgundians. They have been a boil on the Empire's ass ever since." He reached for parchment and quill. "However, I will send my felicitations to their king, along with a suitable gift, and ask his support if I need it." He scrawled briefly on the parchment and rolled it up. "Come, let us wait on the Emperor."

Few people walked the corridors, and fewer still tended to Honorius. Castinus entered the sickroom. Musk-scented steam supposedly made it easier for the Emperor to breathe. Castinus took shallow breaths to keep from choking. Aetius seemed unaffected. They approached the bed where Honorius lay, swollen to nearly twice-normal size with fluids, his breath coming in swift pants.

They bowed low. "My Most Esteemed Emperor, the physician brought me distressing news. Tell me it is not true!"

"Castinus, my loyal friend." Honorius waved for him to take a seat near his head. "I fear I will die. The physicians give me little time to put my affairs in order."

"I will do everything in my power to help, my friend. Make your requests. I will see they are carried out."

"I knew I could count on you, Castinus." Honorius patted the general's hand. "My will tells how I wish to be buried, and distributes my personal wealth. You have been generously provided for." He paused to catch his breath. "Send for Placidia. I want her by my side before I die."

Castinus and Aetius exchanged startled glances. "Is that wise, My Lord?"

"What is she going to do? Kill me?" Honorius wheezed. "I have no one I care for attending me. I want my sister."

"I will prepare the correspondence immediately for your seal. It will be in the morning post." Castinus rose, motioning Aetius to join him.

"The Emperor's request is…uh…most awkward," Aetius said in the corridor.

"What request?" Castinus gave a wolfish grin. "My dear boy, you are too straightforward. Of course a message will go to Theodosius. In it, Honorius will recommend me as Theodosius' agent to administer the West in his name. Holding the entire empire should appeal to the young Emperor. Like Constantius before me, I prefer the role of chief advisor while another is the figurehead."

Aetius seemed unconvinced. "And Placidia? She could influence Theodosius in favor of her son. She has his ear directly."

"The dispatches will make the case for her untrustworthiness and the need to have a strong man in charge." He waved the rolled parchment. "Having a boy don the diadem with Placidia as advisor is akin to giving up the West to the barbarians. Emperor Theodosius will see the merit in those arguments. His self-interest will be in our favor."

PLACIDIA AND ATHENAIS WATCHED LITTLE EUDOXIA lurch around the room. The child enjoyed the new experience of walking, while her older cousins studied with a priest. Placidia and her children had joined the religious regimen of the palace with little effort. She preferred Athenais' more easy-going Christianity to Pulcheria's rigid doctrine, but Placidia's attendance at daily prayers, adherence to fast days, and modest behavior gradually won Pulcheria over. Under the sunny influence of Athenais, Theodosius thawed quickly. He regularly asked Placidia to join him riding and hunting in the countryside, a most pleasant diversion.

"Come to Momma," Athenais coaxed. Eudoxia toddled over to her outstretched arms. Athenais pulled the little girl onto her lap with a grunt and laughed when the child patted her pregnant belly.

"She grows more beautiful every day." Placidia put aside her embroidery, which had not improved since her Gothic days, even under Pulcheria's tutelage. "You have been so good to me and the children, Athenais. I want to propose a match to tie our families closer. Do you think Theo would consent to a betrothal between Valentinian and Eudoxia?"

"Oh, what a marvelous idea!" Athenais clapped her baby's hands together and laid her cheek on the girl's silky hair. "Since she was born I've dreaded the day she would be sent off to some foreign land and a strange prince's bed. I pray this second child is a boy so I will not lose him." Athenais smiled. "And of course Eudoxia will have the best mother-in-law. I can count on you to love her as much as you do your son."

Placidia reached for the child. "Would you like to marry Val, my precious?" Eudoxia bared her baby teeth and laughed. "I think that means 'yes'." Placidia sobered. "We still have to convince Theo and Pulcheria."

"Leave them to me. Theo no more wishes to lose Eudoxia than I do. This is a perfect solution. Pulcheria vowed never to marry, not only because of her religious convictions, but to avoid the very entanglements we fear for my little one. She did not want to be bartered off to some stranger, Roman or not, as part of a political settlement."

Placidia, who well knew the vagaries of Imperial marriages, applauded Pulcheria's strategy. Perhaps Honoria could follow that path. "I leave you to argue the merits of the case, then."

"We will make this marriage happen." Athenais' voice resounded with resolve.

Placidia was pleased at Athenais' enthusiasm, not only for familial reasons, but because marriage ties would make Valentinian a more favorable successor to Honorius in Theo's eyes. She had made little headway attaining his backing on that goal.

"Speaking of my love…" Athenais rose to greet her husband with a robust kiss as he came through the nursery door.

A vivid memory of Ataulf sweeping her up in a passionate embrace brought unexpected tears to Placidia's eyes. She blinked them away before Theo or Athenais could notice, and picked up Eudoxia to bring her to her parents.

"What brings you to the nursery at this time of day, Nephew?"

He lifted Eudoxia and chucked her under the chin before handing her to Athenais. "I'm afraid I bring distressing news."

"What?" Placidia put her hand to her heart.

"Honorius is dead. We just received the dispatches."

"Oh! God rest his soul." Placidia searched her heart. She found no joy in her brother's passing, but no sadness either; just pity for a life lived in fear and to no great purpose. "What did he die of?"

"Dropsy."

"My poor brother." Placidia shook her head. "His health has been fragile for some time."

"Honorius knew he was dying and sent several documents. Among them is a strong recommendation that General Castinus administer the West in my name."

Placidia suppressed a cry of outrage, but could not keep the anger from her voice. "I've known some with dropsy who were not quite right in their minds at the end. It would not surprise me if Castinus persuaded Honorius to this course, or even substituted his own wishes for those of my brother. By rights, Valentinian should be Emperor. Honorius confirmed my son as heir three years ago."

"Without my consent. It is my right to make that choice."

Behind her husband but in view of Placidia, Athenais put a finger to her lips. Placidia moderated her tone. "Of course it is your decision, Nephew. You are now the sole Emperor of the Roman Empire, and will choose the colleague you feel best. Now is not the time to discuss this important matter; after the mourning period will be soon enough."

His hesitation sent warning flags to Placidia. Could Theo want to rule singly, as his grandfather did? If this next child were a boy, would he want to name him to the Western throne?

She bowed. "I should tell the children. Honoria in particular was fond of her uncle."

Two MONTHS LATER, Lucilla burst into her room, breathless from running. "Mistress, astonishing news!"

"What?"

"A man named John calls himself Emperor in the West, and sends envoys to Theodosius to confirm his elevation. Emperor Theodosius and the two Augustas request your presence in the consistory at once."

With hope and alarm, Placidia hurried to the council chamber. There she immediately sensed outrage and confusion. Only the top administrators and advisors were present, including Helion, Master of Offices, and General Ardaburius, whose father was of the Alan tribe.

Theo brooded on his elevated chair. Athenais offered Placidia an encouraging smile. Pulcheria paced, red staining her sallow cheeks. When Pulcheria spied Placidia, she came over and took her hand. "Dearest Aunt, we have had a serious development in the West."

"I heard a man named John has declared himself Emperor. If I remember, he was but a clerk—*primicerius notariorum*—with no military background, and certainly no blood claim to the diadem."

"The upstart has the nerve to demand—demand!—I acknowledge his claim over your son's." Theo's mouth twisted with rage. "I imprisoned his envoys and asked General Ardaburius to join us."

"You then favor our claim?" Placidia's heart thumped faster. Castinus' impatience did what her own lobbying could not. John was surely Castinus' creature, and held his offices by his grace. Theo might have looked favorably on sole rule with Castinus as his agent, but a usurper not of his choosing—never. The question remained: would Theo invade in his own name or Valentinian's?

Pulcheria waved her hand, as if dismissing an insignificant problem. "Of course we favor your claim. The empire is too big to rule alone. Theo and I have all we can handle here in the East, with the Huns threatening our borders. We leave the rest of the barbarians to you."

A scribe brought several parchment pages to the Emperor. Theo grinned as he signed each with a flourish and put his seal to the wax. He handed three to Placidia. The first posthumously proclaimed Constantius Augustus. The second proclaimed Placidia Augusta and *tutela* or guardian for the minor Valentinian, allowing her to rule for her son during his minority. The third proclaimed Valentinian legitimate heir to Honorius.

"This one," Theo waved the last sheet, "is an order to General Ardaburius to prepare an army to invade Italy and take back the *imperium* for Valentinian. I will accompany you myself, and crown my young cousin in Rome."

At last! No more cajoling, no more influencing from the shadows. I have it all now—legitimacy, power, and an army to back it up. Placidia stood, energy coursing through her. *I will take back the West for my son.*

She bowed low. "My sincere thanks to you, dearest Nieces and Nephew. God sent me to you for succor in my darkest hour, and you gave freely of your love and wisdom. I and my children have lived with you in amity. We will not forget to whom we owe our future good fortune."

Both Theo and Pulcheria offered smiles of genuine warmth, but Athenais' was tinged with sadness. She stood to embrace Placidia. "I will miss you, dearest Aunt, and so will little Eudoxia. You are my closest friend. I will count the days until we are reunited. God keep you safe."

Theo joined them, putting a hand on his wife's shoulder. "Fear not, my love. It will take many months to complete our plans and gather the army. Placidia and the children will be with us through the winter. Leave us now. You need your rest."

Placidia watched Athenais retire with a mixture of sadness and anticipation. She enjoyed the young woman's warmth and intelligence. She was unlikely to have such a friendship again, yet she was eager to be off. As magnificent as Constantinople was, it was not home.

CHAPTER 28

Greece, early spring 425

A YEAR AND HALF! Placidia fumed, watching from her horse, as the army
formed ranks to board the ships at Thessalonica. In the distance, slaves
and women, who served the army as cooks, laundresses, and nurses,
packed supplies.

By all that's holy, Theo took his time. She had chafed through the winter in
Constantinople and a second winter in Thessalonica as General Ardaburius and
his son Aspar recruited and drilled the troops. She thought the death of his
baby son Arcadius, shortly after his birth, blunted her nephew's will to action.
Remembering the loss of her own first child, she was most sympathetic.

She shook off her gloom. They were ready now.

Her horse stirred at the sound of hooves coming up behind her. She glanced
over her shoulder. Ardaburius, riding up with his sun-bleached brown hair and
deeply weathered face, was no arm-chair general. "The men look in fine shape,
General."

"The armories worked all winter to outfit them with new spears, shields,
and swords, Augusta." Ardaburius scanned the horizon. "It seems a fair day
for sailing. Are you sure you would not prefer to travel to Ravenna by ship? It
would be far more comfortable than horseback or wagon."

"I spent most of five years on horseback and in wagons. By the grace of God,
we barely survived a storm coming over. I vowed never to sail again." Placidia

shuddered. "Are you sure you wish to chance the spring storms?"

"It is the most efficient way to transport troops and supplies, but horses do not take well to sailing." General Ardaburius shrugged. "Aspar will see to your safety. His cavalry is second to none."

"I am most impressed with your son. I have considerable experience with cavalry units. His are well ordered and maintained, his men loyal, and horses sound." She placed a hand over Ardaburius' capable one. "We are not joining in this enterprise unsupported. The senate in Rome refused to recognize John, and issued coins in Valentinian's name. Count Boniface has cut off the grain supply to Ravenna. John has weakened himself by sending troops to Africa, leaving a token force to defend Italy. I still have many supporters in Ravenna among my late husband's friends and retainers. This usurper will not stand against us."

"Too bad the Emperor's health doesn't permit him to join us. It will be a triumph."

Placidia was just as glad Theo's stomach troubled him. She preferred to enter Italy on her own terms. Sending Master of Offices Helion would be recognition enough. Helion had brought additional good news: Theo finally elevated Val to Caesar. They held a simple ceremony, and the troops acclaimed him. *We'll do it right in Rome, when he's made Augustus.*

The General's horse stamped and snorted. He patted its neck. "I should join my troops, Augusta."

"I am well attended, General." Placidia indicated her ever-present Gothic retinue. "I'll join Aspar at his camp outside the city. Fair weather and Godspeed to you. We will meet on the plain of the Po."

NEARLY A WEEK LATER, Aspar accompanied Placidia through the cavalry camp— neat rows of tents, a latrine trench, and temporary wooden walls a half-day's ride from the marshes of Ravenna. She had traveled to the camp from her base in Aquileia when her agents brought word that storms had scattered Ardaburius' fleet and the usurper John held the General prisoner. She rode on horseback, with a minimal escort and no trappings of her rank, to keep her presence secret. It wouldn't do to be captured so close to her goal.

Her agents had combed the countryside for the boy who helped her flee Ravenna seventeen years ago. His knowledge of the secret ways through the marshes was key to her plan, but she needed to see for herself if the young rogue had grown into a trustworthy man. *I pray to God he still lives.*

"The Augusta should have stayed in Aquileia. It is not safe in this troubled countryside." A frown marred Aspar's face. Placidia was drawn to his honest blue eyes, but she most liked his hands—square, strong, and callused in the same way as Ataulf's. She shook herself. *Don't be a fool, mooning after a man that young.*

"The loss of the army is a terrible blow, but we can use your father's presence in Ravenna to our advantage." Aspar looked skeptical. She continued. "Keep your men sharp. We will do all in our power to free your father. Trust in God... and me."

The next day, one of her agents ushered into her tent a short man sporting dark curly hair under his woolen shepherd's cap. Dirt stained his knees and fingernails, but his teeth showed white and strong. The man's sharp brown eyes took note of the sparse furnishings of her tent and the armed guards. He took a deep breath when he saw the signet ring on her finger.

"Angelus, do you remember me?"

A smile dawned over his tanned face. "The Lady who was not a Princess." He looked her over, from the plain blue veil covering her hair to her muddy boots. "From your dress, I take it today you are the Lady who is not the Augusta?"

Her attendant cuffed Angelus' ear. "Here, now. Be respectful."

Placidia struck the attendant a solid blow across the shoulders. "You may leave. This man is my guest and will be afforded all courtesy."

The cowed man scurried from her presence.

"You." She indicated a slave. "Bring food and wine for my guest."

He scrambled to attend her wants.

She turned back to Angelus. "You are right. As far as the countryside is concerned, the Augusta is safe behind the walls of Aquileia. I'm sorry for the blow."

He rubbed his reddening ear. "I've had worse. Mostly from my wife when I come home late."

"She sounds like a good wife." Placidia chuckled. "How is your granddam?"

"Dead these last nine years, but she died with a smile on her face and a great-grandchild to spoil."

"You have a child?"

"Three now. Two strapping boys and a little girl who is the very image of her mother."

"Are your boys as much trouble as you were?"

He rubbed the back of his neck, and gave a crooked smile. "Much worse than I ever was, always running into the marshes when there's work to be done."

The slave arrived with wine, cold roast duck, cheese and sweet cakes. Angelus sipped his wine and made a face. "This here's too fine for me. Better water it down a good bit."

Placidia nodded. The slave poured the wine into a mixing bowl, added water, and offered Angelus the altered drink. "Is this more to your satisfaction, sir?"

"Much better." He smacked his lips. "I'm used to wine that tastes of vinegar and swamp water." He piled a plate high with food and ate standing up.

"If I remember right, my gold was too fine for you as well. You insisted on silver, so as not to be accused of stealing."

"Your silver let me buy a good ram and two new ewes for breedin'. We have a prosperous farm now." His eyes narrowed. "But, Lady, I sense you didn't send for me just to stuff me with duck and talk about times past."

"No, I didn't." She sat opposite him on a folding campstool and sipped her own goblet of watered wine. "I hear from your neighbors that you speak against the false Emperor. That is a dangerous course to take."

"Only if he survives." He gave her a speculative glance. "I'm not alone. Those selfsame neighbors don't want war in their fields either, and that's what's likely with such as them tramping back and forth." He indicated the camp with his chin. "Forgive me for saying so, Lady, but no matter which general wins the war, the people always lose."

"A wise observation." Placidia nodded. "With your help, we can avoid war. The fields will remain untouched and the flocks peaceful in the meadows—no babies slaughtered, women raped, or men sold into captivity."

"What do you need me for?" Angelus gnawed on a plump duck leg; crumbs of crispy skin flaking his beard.

"Do you still sell fish to the palace?"

"Mostly meat now." His eyebrows crooked in puzzlement. "Although the boys still catch fish and snare ducks, if that's what you need."

"It matters not what you sell, as long as you can get into the palace. We need to get word to and from a General named Ardaburius, who is held captive by the usurper. I have trustworthy friends among the palace staff. I will tell you who to contact."

"It's my duty, Lady." His eyes twinkled. "As well as my pleasure."

Placidia smiled back, confident in his loyalty. He would enjoy the intrigue and adventure as much as the reward he was sure to get.

CASTINUS GROUND HIS TEETH to keep from snapping at Emperor John. "Tell me why, Most Esteemed Emperor, you let General Ardaburius have the freedom of the city."

John blinked near-sighted eyes at his sponsor and chief advisor. "He gave his word he would not try to escape."

"You fool! Ardaburius has no allegiance to you, and will keep no oath except to Theodosius and, through him, Placidia."

"The man is honorable." John straightened to his full height, but could not achieve an imposing stance because of his sloping shoulders and soft belly. The fight seemed to go out of him. "But, to please you, I will restrict his freedom to the palace."

"I hope the damage is not already done."

"Will not your able Aetius relieve us with his friends, the Huns? Ardaburius' army is scattered by storm, and Placidia sits isolated with a small cavalry force in Aquileia." John patted Castinus' back. "My friend, we have nothing to worry about."

Castinus left the Emperor's presence, knowing he had made a major mistake. He never should have put forward his own Emperor. The news that Theodosius had consented to a marriage between Placidia's brat and the Emperor's daughter had panicked Castinus into unwise action. He slept poorly and was troubled by gas.

His only consolation was that John was right about Ravenna's invulnerability. Placidia had no force to match the horde of Huns Aetius would bring into Italy. Castinus laughed to himself, startling several slaves in the corridor. He had Ravenna. Placidia could sit in Aquileia until she rotted, or the Huns spit her on their spears.

PLACIDIA LOOKED OVER HER SMALL GATHERING AND SMILED. *My best and most loyal men.* Aspar sat straight in his wooden chair. Sigisvult lounged in the corner, eyeing Angelus with some calculation. Angelus, as was his custom, stayed near the sideboard, eating as if the slaves would snatch away the food the moment he stopped.

Placidia cleared her throat. "We have received word from General Ardaburius that all is ready. The guards at the gates and officers of the watch will side with us when we approach."

"The main road is heavily guarded, Augusta," Aspar said. "We will face resistance there."

"Aspar, Sigisvult, I want you to meet an old friend of mine. Angelus, quit stuffing your face and come here."

He wiped his mouth on his sleeve and moved to stand next to Placidia. She placed a hand on his shoulder. His muscles twitched under rough wool. "This is my Angel of the Marshes. He knows every inch of the swamps, and can lead your men safely through a back way to the gates of Ravenna."

Aspar raised an eyebrow. "He hardly seems a messenger from God."

Angelus grinned. "God has sent stranger messengers. The Augusta here knows what she's talking about. I led her out of Ravenna, safe and sound, near seventeen years ago. I can lead you in just as easily."

"I trust Angelus implicitly. He will not let us down." Placidia turned to Aspar. "Can your men be ready to leave by noon?"

"Yes, Augusta."

"You travel to the marshes by day, rest through the evening, and follow Angelus through the swamps to the gates of Ravenna during the dark of the night. Do not use lamps or torches; they may be seen from the walls."

Sigisvult frowned. "How will we see, if we can't use torches? Those swamps could swallow us whole, and no one would know."

Angelus pointed toward the sky. "Full moon tonight. If you follow my footsteps, the marshes won't get you."

"Time is important," Placidia said. "Angelus heard that General Aetius recruits reinforcements from among the Huns. We must take Ravenna and block the Alpine passes before he can return."

"What of the usurper and Castinus?" Aspar asked.

"If possible, take them alive."

Sigisvult's frown deepened.

Placidia stated, in a flat tone, visions of blood-spattered walls and small still bodies springing to her mind, "I know what to do with those who threaten my family. Fear not that the usurper will be treated softly."

Silence blanketed the room.

*****

Outside Ravenna, June 425

SIGISVULT SCRATCHED AT THE INSECT BITES ON HIS ARM. *Did the Good God create such pests to torment humans? They drive the righteous mad, as well as the damned.* He slapped another on his neck as he stood in knee-deep mud on the side of the main road leading to Ravenna. They had left the horses at the marshes' edge and trudged all night through the twisted paths in the swamps. Aspar led five men to the closed gate.

"Halloo, the gate," Aspar called softly.

"Who goes there?" came a muffled voice on the other side.

"Open, in the name of Galla Placidia Augusta."

Sigisvult held his breath, half-expecting shouts of alarm and a rain of arrows from the walls.

The gate opened outward on well-oiled hinges. Aspar gave the signal. The force entered as quietly as a thousand men in armor could. They split in two. The larger party secured the gate and spread out along the walls to take any on the watch who might give the alarm.

The smaller group headed for the palace along narrow streets and over bridges. A few curious faces peered out of windows, but most of the inhabitants doused their lamps the moment they recognized soldiers in the streets.

The stealthiness grated on Sigisvult's nerves. He preferred an honest face to face battle to this sneaking in the dark, but he realized the need for it. They could take Ravenna no other way.

As they approached the palace, he heard a shout.

Sigisvult grinned and rushed forward, sword drawn. A squad of ten scholae skirmished with Aspar's advance troops. Sigisvult crossed swords with a young man whose scraggly beginnings of a beard darkened his face. After receiving two cuts, the frightened soldier tossed down his sword. Sigisvult looked to his right. Three scholae lay still on the steps. The rest were herded in a tight knot, weapons on the ground and hands in the air to signal surrender.

"This way!" Sigisvult dashed toward the open door, Aspar hard on his heels. Having lived in the palace, Sigisvult easily led the troop through the public rooms and into the private wing. The building seemed deserted. The slaves must be cowering in the kitchen.

At the crash of stone on stone, Sigisvult turned to see a number of soldiers tipping over painted statues. The arm of the statue of a previous empress stretched toward him, as if in supplication. He strode back, grabbed the first man by the neck of his tunic, and shook him. The man's sword clattered on the floor.

"Do you louts have shit-for-brains?" Sigisvult stared at the other offenders. "Our Augusta will not be pleased to come home to a looted palace. If anyone so much as scratches the wall, I will spit him personally."

Their eyes shifted over Sigisvult's shoulder.

He turned to see Aspar nodding. "Right. We're here to take the usurper, not despoil the palace. Now follow Sigisvult."

Another band of scholae guarded the door to the Emperor's rooms, but surrendered without a fight when they saw the colonnade filled with soldiers.

Aspar and Sigisvult burst into the Emperor's chamber and slashed at the bed curtains. John huddled at the head of his bed, a cushion clutched to his chest, his hand outstretched.

"Please! Don't kill me!" The terrified man looked from one face to another. "It was Castinus. He forced me."

Sigisvult grinned through his blond beard and put his sword against John's neck. "Where is the general?"

"I d-d-don't know! I swear to God, I don't know!" John gibbered.

Sigisvult turned to the waiting soldiers. "No one leaves the city until we find him."

CHAPTER 29

Aquileia, July 425

THE CROWD ROARED WITH APPROVAL as the hunter cleanly severed the head of the last ostrich with a keen-edged arrow. Placidia, having seen enough blood, had little use for the games, but understood the needs of her subjects. The people of Aquileia, like most Romans, loved their blood sports. Gladiator contests had been banned for several years, but that did not stop rich Romans from importing exotic animals for mock hunts, or magistrates from sending criminals into the ring with lions or dogs.

After the nearly effortless taking of Ravenna, the people wanted blood, and Placidia provided it in games dedicated to her son. Valentinian and Honoria sat in the Imperial box with their mother, fascinated, as the huge bird continued running without its head. The creature almost reached the far end of the arena when it collapsed in a heap of bloody feathers, long legs twitching in death throes.

Val turned to her. "I want to learn archery, Mother. I want to be as good as that hunter, and kill lots of animals." He pulled an imaginary arrow back from an invisible bow and let it fly.

"You can learn anything you want, my darling." She refrained from ruffling his well-coifed curls, with some effort. "I'm sure you will be good at it."

"Hunting." Honoria sniffed. "I want to learn to fight on horseback. Then I can lead armies, like Father. Rome needs good generals, not hunters."

Placidia felt a chill. The memory of Sergeric's face as she plunged in the knife and twisted invaded her mind's eye. *My daughter will never know such violence—to body or soul.* "Honoria, I have said you may continue to ride, but you will not learn swordplay or practice with spears."

Honoria's face took on that concentrated frown Placidia had come to dread. "Why, Mother?"

"Because Imperial Princesses do not lead armies."

"You did."

"I did not fight."

Honoria rolled her eyes. "Sigisvult said…"

"Enough, Honoria! Or I will have Lucilla take you back to the palace."

The girl subsided with a pout.

Trumpets, pipes, and drums played a lively tune to entertain the crowd as attendants dragged the carcasses from the ring and raked sand over the blood.

With a final trumpet fanfare, Aspar entered the arena in a gilded chariot, pulled by two matching grays with black manes and tails. His gold-chased armor gleamed in the sun. He raced around the ring to the wild cheers of the crowd. Stopping in front of the Imperial box, he bowed low.

When Placidia rose from her seat, everyone in the amphitheater did as well. The noise thundered over her, then gradually changed to a chant. "Galla Placidia Augusta. God grant you wisdom and long life." The acclamation continued for over ten minutes. Placidia's heart swelled. She nodded to the herald, who signaled a trumpet blast.

When the crowd quieted, the herald announced, "Galla Placidia Augusta presents these games in the name of her son and your next Emperor: Flavius Placidus Valentinian Caesar, son of Flavius Constantius Augustus, grandson of Flavius Theodosius Augustus, great-grandson of Flavius Valentinian Augustus!"

The six-year-old boy stood beside his mother as the crowd took up a new chant. "Hail Caesar! Hail Valentinian! God grant you a long and prosperous reign!"

After several minutes, Placidia and her son sat. The acclamations gave way to a sustained roar as Aspar made one more circuit of the ring.

A slave led a shambling figure, weighed down in chains, from the south entrance. Aspar took the lead chain and fastened it to his chariot. He turned to the Imperial box, saluted with his sword, and shouted, "Death to tyrants!" He then led the defeated John around the ring to the jeers of the crowd.

The people roared again when a man with the well-muscled body of a Greek athlete carried a heavy wooden block to the center of the ring and unsheathed a bright sword. Another slave led in an old donkey. The animal flared its nostrils at the smell of blood. It dug in its feet, laid back its ears, and brayed. The executioner had to help pull the animal to the middle of the ring, accompanied by loud laughs.

Placidia took no pleasure in the display. She had met and spoken with the usurper. He was a self-important little man with no idea how he became a pawn in a game of power. Except for his legislation limiting the Church, he had ruled fairly and wisely during his brief tenure. She would have spared him, but leniency would only encourage others to challenge her authority.

Aspar led John to the wooden block, then retreated to the exit. The donkey slave held John's right hand in a firm grip. The bright sword flashed. Blood spurted from the former Emperor's arm. His scream was drowned by the exultant cheers of the crowd. The donkey bucked and brayed.

The slave bound the truncated arm with a tourniquet and placed John backward on the reluctant donkey. He then paraded the mutilated John around the ring for further derision and chants of "Death to tyrants."

Placidia, knowing what came next, signaled to Lucilla. She didn't want the children to witness John's execution.

"But I don't want to go," Val wailed, digging in his heels like the donkey.

"You'll see enough blood in your life, my son. God willing, you will never wield the sword yourself. Now go. I'll join you shortly."

The slave leading the donkey lifted the half-dead man from its back and placed him kneeling at the block. John rested his head on the block, face away from the executioner, lips moving without speech, eyes closed. Silence filled the arena. The executioner raised the sword and swung it down with the distinctive 'thunk' of a blade meeting wood.

John's head rolled to the ground. His body slumped, blood soaking the sand. The crowd let out such a roar that Placidia feared temporary deafness.

It is done.

She had expected to feel exultation or, at the very least, relief that she had the power to protect herself and her family. Never again would another dictate her fate. Those feelings eluded her. Tension knotted her shoulders; blood roared in her ears.

Perhaps when it is Castinus in the ring.

*****

THE NEXT DAY she convened her temporary council: Helion, Ardaburius, Aspar, and Leontius, who she had reviewing the imperial treasury. Sigisvult accompanied her as her 'guard.' At twenty-five, he should learn the inner workings of the council.

Placidia took a cushioned chair at the head of an ebony table, its ivory and mother-of-pearl inlay obscured by two maps and several papers. "Our first order of business is to schedule General Castinus' execution."

Helion exchanged glances with Leontius. "Augusta, I would counsel against such a move. General Castinus was quite clever. He never usurped the Imperial powers directly, but acted first under the orders of your brother, then Theodosius, then John."

"He engineered my banishment and put John on the throne." Placidia's blood rose at the thought that the cowardly snake who had fed her brother's delusions might escape her wrath. "For supporting the usurper alone, he should be executed."

"Then you would have to put over half of the population of Ravenna to death." Helion rubbed at his mustache. "I have been through his records. He left nothing incriminating. He was just obeying orders, to avoid prosecution by John."

"Are you saying I must let the man go?" Placidia balled her hands into fists, but resisted the urge to pound them on the table.

"No, Augusta. You may do with him as you wish, but I advise you not execute the man. These are troubled times. The people look to you for signs of what is to come. Be firm, yet merciful. Banishment is a more appropriate punishment for Castinus."

She looked around the group. Heads nodded. She let her fists relax. "My brother once asked which was more merciful—a quick death or a life lived in misery and defeat. We will find our rebellious general a very small and isolated island. He may have no servants, books, or means of entertaining himself—just shelter and food. Castinus will soon wish he were dead. Notary," she indicated one of the ubiquitous scribes who accompanied her, "write up the appropriate orders."

Placidia turned back to her advisors. "Of a more urgent nature, what do we know of Aetius and the Huns?"

Aspar cleared his throat. "The news is not good, Augusta. My cavalry scouts report that Aetius and sixty thousand Huns are crossing the Alps. They have no baggage train, and move quickly. We expect them at the gates of Aquileia within three days."

"*Sixty thousand*? That's twice the number Alaric had under arms. Can he truly have such a large force?"

Aspar shrugged. "The scouts could have exaggerated, but it still must be a huge force, to inspire such a number."

"Ardaburius, do you have enough troops to counter this threat?"

"Regretfully, no, Augusta." Ardaburius shifted in his seat. "I collected what is left of my scattered army, but they could not hold against twenty thousand Huns, much less sixty thousand. A battle would destroy my legions, to no avail."

"Even with the support of Aspar and his cavalry?"

"Yes." Ardaburius looked up. "It grieves me to come before you so unprepared to do battle."

She leaned back, raking each man with her glance. "Options?"

Aspar spoke first. "Retreat to Ravenna to keep you and Valentinian safe. General Felix approaches from the west. We can merge our forces and harry the invaders."

"No." Placidia shook her head. "That would leave the Hunnish horde free to ravage Italy and the western provinces. They must be stopped here."

"My Most Wise Emperor Theodosius gave the Huns gifts this year," Helion said. "In return, they do not raid the eastern provinces."

Ardaburius turned red. "Pay tribute to the filthy Huns who stole my fathers' lands? A hundred years ago, we would have smashed their armies, sent their women and children to the slave markets, and demanded tribute from them."

"A hundred years ago the Great Constantine had a fully functioning and well equipped army," Placidia pointed out. "We do not have the means or luxury to fight. Gold might give us time to rally our forces and protect the West from future incursions."

Placidia turned back to Helion. "How much gold does my nephew give the Huns as 'gifts'?"

"Three hundred and fifty pounds a year."

"Do you think an equal amount will satisfy this horde?"

"It should, Augusta."

"Do we have that much on hand?" She pinned Leontius with her gaze.

He did a quick mental calculation. "Yes, Augusta, but it will drain the treasury. We still have to pay the troops. Three out of every four *solidus* collected goes to maintaining the army."

Placidia steepled her hands, fingertips to lips. "What about the privy purse?"

"The income from the estates owned by the royal family would more than cover the loss."

"Then it is decided." Placidia put her hands palm down on the table. "I will pay the Huns from my own funds to turn aside and go home. Aspar, send one of your most trusted men with Helion under a sign of truce, to negotiate the terms."

"Of course, Augusta." He bowed his head. "I would be honored to go myself."

"Good. Go immediately. Take Sigisvult with you." She nodded to her guard. "I will provide papers and authorizations. Stop them as far away as you can. I do not want the Huns advancing on Italian soil."

Placidia rose, as did her council. She exited to her quarters, anxious to bring these negotiations to a close and go to Rome to crown her son.

Sigisvult hesitated in the entrance to Placidia's audience chamber. The room was full of court lackeys, petitioners, and the ever-present notaries, who took down every word she said.

The Augusta handed a scroll to a middle-aged man in bishop's robes. "I am happy that one of my first acts on behalf of my son is to restore the ecclesiastical privileges stripped from the church under John."

"Thank you, Augusta." The bishop knelt on one knee, clasping the parchment to his chest. "May God grant you long life. I would also wish wisdom for you, but it is evident you already possess that virtue."

Placidia's lips turned up, but the smile didn't reach her eyes.

How she hates false flattery!

Sigisvult strode into the room. He had the satisfaction of seeing a genuine smile light up the Augusta's face.

She murmured to her secretary, who nodded and announced, "The Augusta will hold audience again tomorrow."

The notaries herded the crowd out the door, then exited themselves, leaving Placidia alone with Sigisvult. He approached and bowed.

"What news, my friend?"

"The Huns will accept the gold and withdraw, on condition that Aetius be pardoned and receive a command in the army."

"Aetius is as clever as his mentor. He holds Italy hostage." She looked up at Sigisvult. "My brother faced a similar situation. I will not make the same mistake as he. I will pardon Aetius and give him a command in Gaul, away from the court."

"But, Augusta, he betrayed you!" Sigisvult's blood rose. "You cannot reward such treachery."

"For now, I have no choice. In the future…" Placidia shrugged. "I forgive no one who threatens the Empire or my son's birthright."

"He will forever be a danger to you, Augusta, particularly with an army at his back."

"I know," she said softly. "That's why I am sending you with him."

The import of her words sent him crashing to his knees. "Augusta, ask anything of me. Strike off my right hand, but do not send me away from you."

"I must." Placidia touched his cheek. "I know what I ask of you, but I trust no one else. Aetius will know you are my man. Your presence should moderate his course." She leaned back, withdrawing her hand. "Also, while he focuses his attention on you, my unknown agents will have more freedom."

"So I am to be little more than a decoy." Bitterness colored his words.

"You are so much more to me than that."

He raised his eyes.

"You are my loyal right hand, the sword standing between my children and treachery. Learn from Aetius. By all accounts he is a good soldier, but I must know his mind and his character. Learn his strengths and his weaknesses. For me."

"Yes, Augusta."

Sigisvult rose and squared his shoulders. Placidia needed him.

Rome, October 425

"MOTHER, HE'S DOING IT AGAIN!" Honoria burst into her workroom.

"Who is doing what again?" Placidia asked, rubbing her tired eyes—although she knew exactly who the culprit was. Val's tutors and nurses gave her constant reports of his abusive nature since he had been elevated to Augustus a week earlier. She needed to talk to the boy—emperor or not, his behavior was unconscionable.

"Val! Ever since he became Emperor, he lords it over me, ordering me around. 'Stand in my presence.' 'Plumb my pillows.' 'Fetch my ball,' " Honoria mimicked her brother's high-pitched voice. "I'm not a slave!"

"No, you're not, and Val goes too far. I will talk to him." She held out her arms. "Come. I want to show you something."

Honoria climbed onto Placidia's lap and dropped her head onto her mother's breast. The scent of lilacs wafting from the child's hair reminded Placidia of a spring garden in southern Gaul, when she was happy…

"I miss Father." Honoria's tears soaked through Placidia's silk *stola*.

She kissed the top of her daughter's head. "I know, dearest. I miss him, too." *It's been four years. Two husbands dead and I'm not yet forty.* The weight of her child and the trusting embrace brought a mist to Placidia's eyes. How long had it been since she held either of her children in such an intimate fashion? Since before Honorius' death? She had spent the last two years working furiously for Val's elevation and succeeded, but at what cost? She shook her head. She had had no choice.

Honoria sniffed and shifted on her lap. The girl was tall for her eight years, and much too heavy to hold this way for long.

"What did you want to show me?" Honoria raised her head, tears bright in her eyes but no longer overflowing.

"This." She set her daughter down and pulled a document forward.

Honoria read the flowery script. "I, Flavius Valentinian Augustus," she skipped over the many titles and honorifics, "do confer the rank of Augusta, with all its attendant privileges, upon my beloved sister," she snorted and rolled her eyes, "Justa Grata Honoria, on this day of October 30, the Year of Our Lord 425, in the first year of my reign, witnessed by…" She set the document down and turned to Placidia. "I'm to be equal in rank?"

"Your brother is still Augustus." Honoria's smile froze. "But this guarantees certain privileges and protocol. We'll hold the ceremony tomorrow at the court. Your brother will invest you with the imperial robe of state and diadem. Would you prefer pearls or rubies?"

"Can I have both?"

"I'll talk to the jeweler."

Honoria looked over the proclamation again and frowned. "I don't understand why Val has to sign this and invest me. Aren't you an Augusta? Don't you rule Rome? Why can't you sign the paper?"

Placidia sighed. Honoria had hit on a complicated and subtle part of Roman law, dating back to the first emperor, who declared himself 'first among equals' to placate those nobles who longed for the utopian Republic. She tried to simplify. "After my brother died, your cousin Theodosius was sole emperor of Rome for a time. He elevated Val to his rank of Augustus, made him co-emperor, and gave him the legal right to rule over the western provinces of Rome when he reaches his majority. At the same time, he gave me personal guardianship over Val, with the right to govern in Val's name with a council of advisors. I make the decisions, but Val has to sign all the legislation for it to be legal. My father gave similar powers to Stilicho, who was guardian over Honorius and me until Honorius reached his majority."

"Why do you need Cousin Theo's permission? You're older, and his aunt."

"Under Roman law, women are always accountable to men—their fathers until they marry, then their husbands. If a girl's father dies before she marries, and she has a brother who has reached his majority, the brother makes all the decisions. If she has no father or brother, control of the girl and her inheritance passes to her nearest male relative."

"So Val does have control over me?"

"Not until he's fourteen, and then only until you marry."

Honoria shuddered. "Can he force me to marry? Can I not choose for myself?"

"We are both imperial princesses. Our brothers have to give permission for us to marry. Honorius arranged my marriage to your father. Val will arrange your marriage in the future." At the girl's stricken look, she gathered Honoria in her arms again. "That is many years away, my sweet. In the meantime, I am in charge of both of you. Val will do nothing without my approval, and tomorrow you will be Augusta and of equal rank."

"What if he doesn't want to sign?" Honoria pointed to the proclamation. "He might not want to make me an Augusta."

"Then I send him to bed with no supper, or take away his archery lessons until he complies."

"But only until he's fourteen."

Clever girl. "I'll always be his mother, and you will always be his sister. Women usually have more success getting their way using affection rather than force. Val does as I say because he loves and trusts me. I expect to influence him throughout my life. You would do well to build a loving relationship with your brother rather than an adversarial one. Someday he may seek you out as an advisor."

Honoria chewed her lower lip; a habit Placidia recognized in herself.

Placidia rose, set her daughter down, and gathered up the paper. "Come. Let's talk to your brother and get this signed. Tomorrow you become an Empress!"

CHAPTER 30

Arles, Gaul, 427

SIGISVULT TOOK A SWIG OF WATER, swished it in his mouth, and spat it out in the dust at his horse's feet. Hammer stood rock still, ears flicked forward. Other cavalry horses stamped and snorted. They all twitched from the multitude of flies. At least they were concealed in a sheltering copse of alders. Winter came late in the south of Gaul, and he and his small band of cavalry suffered from heat and thirst. He peered at the scene between the tree branches.

Aetius and the bulk of the army had routed the Goths besieging the walled city of Arles. Sigisvult's duty was to round up any stray Goths. Keeping him from the main action spoke of Aetius' lack of trust in Sigisvult's allegiance.

As if I'd side with the Goths. That's how little he knows me, even after two years. My loyalty lies with Placidia and no other. Certainly not Theodoric. The Gothic King had broken his treaty with Rome years ago, before Gaatha's body was cold.

Sigisvult frowned, clasping and unclasping his sword hilt. King Theodoric, surrounded by his best fighters, broke free of the melee and fled.

"There!" Sigisvult pointed to seven Goths straggling up the slope toward them. He kicked Hammer into a lope and whooped as he and his soldiers rushed down on the hapless men.

Their clothes were ragged and armor battered, but the escaping Goths fought as a unit. They stood shield to shield, while two pelted the oncoming cavalry with rocks from slings. The rest held spears low, to thrust at the horses' legs and bellies. Sigisvult heard one horse scream and his rider shout as they went down. He angled to the left of the entrenched men, slashing with his sword as he passed. The shock of iron meeting bone echoed up his arm.

Sigisvult reared Hammer and turned back. One of the seven lay still on the ground; three more had wounds. The one Sigisvult had struck stood with his arm limp at his side, blood dripping from his fingers. When the cavalry turned to attack again, the Goths threw their swords and shields to the ground, surrendering.

After rounding up a few more strays, Sigisvult rejoined Aetius and his troops. They paraded through the jubilant town of Arles to the city forum. A typical Roman provincial city, Arles boasted an arena, theater, hippodrome, and baths. The people cheered their rescuers, but Sigisvult noted the pinched look about their mouths. Food had run low during the siege, and Theodoric destroyed their crops before the harvest. More mouths to feed this winter. Another drain on the imperial treasury.

Sigisvult sent his troop off with the prisoners and approached a group of men—likely the town notables—fawning over Aetius.

"God sent you to deliver us from those heretic devils!" exclaimed a man in bishop's robes. "The Good Lord surely looks after His own."

Sigisvult choked down a laugh. Most of Aetius' soldiers, recruited from various tribes, were 'heretic' Arians—not to mention the pagan Huns!—but the general never made much of that fact when dealing with Catholic Christians.

"As He wills." Aetius gave the bishop a chilly smile and turned to another man, whose face was pocked with scars. "Where may I and my officers rest for the night?"

"This way." The scarred man indicated a large house just off the public square.

Sigisvult scratched under his mail. He longed for a bath. Shouts rang in his ears. He turned, pulling his sword. A royal courier whipped an exhausted horse the final distance to the soldiers. Sweat covered the beast's neck; blood-flecked foam dripped from its mouth.

"General Aetius!" the courier shouted.

"Yes?" Aetius stepped forward.

"General, I have important dispatches from the Augusta." He handed over a leather-bound packet.

The General's eyes took on a calculating glint. "Sigisvult, with me."

Sigisvult winced. Aetius made a great show of opening all of Placidia's mail in front of him, as well as showing his outgoing dispatches, 'to prove his loyalty.'

They entered the house and followed the scarred man to the audience chamber—a modest room, in keeping with the owner's merchant status. After ordering wine for them both, Aetius sat and opened the packet. He inspected the seal on the dispatch, broke it with a knife and started to read. A smile spread across his face.

"It seems you are to be free of your nursemaid duty, my friend. The Augusta requests your urgent return to the court."

At last!

Carthage, Africa

"PELAGIA," BONIFACE MOANED IN HIS WIFE'S EAR. She arched her back and groaned. Exquisite pleasure suffused his body, then ebbed as he collapsed onto her chest. Her heart beat a strong rhythm under his ear. "My love…my life," he panted. *Maybe I'm a fool for taking such a young wife, but she pleases me like no other.*

Boniface started to chuckle.

Pelagia pushed him off and sat up, clutching the fine linen sheet to her breasts. "You find me funny?"

"No, my love." His hand crept up her side to stroke her hair. Sweat streaks darkened the gold strands, bleached almost silver by the African sun. "I was thinking of Augustine."

"Oh!" She slapped his hand away and poked him in the ribs. "Making love to me reminds you of the Bishop of Hippo. That's a fine compliment, especially since he opposed our marriage." She turned her back to him.

The bishop had objected, but Boniface's Gothic soldiers approved his choice of one of their own. They had hailed him heartily when he had his baby daughter baptized in the Arian faith.

Boniface's laugh turned to a low growl. He grabbed Pelagia in a hug, her back to his chest, and cupped her full breasts. Motherhood had filled out her already sensuous form. "The good bishop thought he had me in his snares. Once, I thought I might give up soldiering and become a desert monk."

Pelagia laughed, a high, bell-like sound, incongruous with her normally husky voice. "My lusty stallion? A monk? How could you think such a thing?"

"That was before I met you, my love."

She leaned back into his shoulder. "But I have brought you nothing but disgrace."

"You have done no such thing. Your race and religion are important only to those who wish to drive a wedge between the Augusta and me. She herself married an Arian Goth. What objection could she have? Rumors of her dissatisfaction are just that—rumors."

A discreet cough and knock on the door provided a distraction. "Count, you have an urgent message from the Augusta."

Boniface rose, sweat drying on his naked body. "Come."

His top aide entered, keeping his eyes averted from the tousled bed, and handed Boniface a packet sealed with the Augusta's mark.

Boniface cracked the seal with his thumbnail and scanned the contents. Blood drained from his face. "Placidia orders me to quit Africa and return to Ravenna upon receiving this letter. She gives no reason."

"Aetius warned you of this, sir," the aide said. "If you go back to court, you will be accused of treason."

Pelagia stood, her warrior heritage evident in every tense muscle. "Husband, do not go. The warnings…I fear for you. Stay here with men who are loyal to you alone." Tears sparkled in her eyes, but did not spill onto her cheeks.

"I have no intention of going where my enemies can reach me with their long knives. Be of good cheer, my love. Nothing will take me from you or our child."

Ravenna, Italy

"DOES YOUR MOST GRACIOUS AUGUSTA APPROVE?" Placidia's makeup slave stepped to one side and started rearranging vials and pots on a marble table beneath a great silver mirror.

Placidia critically inspected the result of her slave's cosmetic attentions. She frowned, emphasizing the worry lines in her forehead. Other than a few strands of silver and the faint lines, she did not look her forty years; why did she fret so? *I'm too skinny and worn to be beautiful.* She sighed. She had never had the little rolls of fat on her neck known as Venus rings, or the extra flesh most men liked to hold and caress when making love.

The thought of a man's hands on her body sent blood to her cheeks, a thrill to her groin, and a soft smile to her lips. She felt restless.

"You may go." She dismissed her horde of makeup artists, hairdressers, and wardrobe servants—all but Lucilla.

"So you entertain young Sigisvult tonight." Lucilla looked past Placidia's shoulder into the mirror.

Placidia winced at the mention of 'young' Sigisvult. "Twelve years is not such a great difference."

"No, Mistress." Lucilla cast her eyes down.

Placidia rose and paced the room. Lucilla sat, hands folded, a pool of calm.

"I know what you think—I'm the Augusta. I cannot marry. I dare not take a lover. But I am not Pulcheria, a pledged virgin. My body betrays me and…and I am not so old as to have forgotten the pleasures of a man."

Lucilla rose, took her hands and held her gaze. "Forty years is more than most are blessed with, but no, you are not old." She smiled. "Sigisvult will always see you as beautiful."

"No." Placidia shook her head. "He sees me as a warrior queen with bloody hands, a leader worthy of his loyalty. I *want* him to see me as a woman, but that is foolishness."

Placidia sank onto a padded bench, shoulders slumped. "I'm not sure I can do…*this*…without someone. Powerful factions wait for me to stumble and fail—not only wait—they plot, plan, push me into stumbling."

"You will not fail, Mistress."

"You mean I dare not."

"I mean you will not. You are not alone. You have your children, Sigisvult, and your nephew. The weight of the eastern Emperor is no light feather on the scales."

"And you, my friend?" Placidia leaned onto Lucilla's comforting shoulder.

"Always, until my last breath."

SIGISVULT SUPPRESSED A BELCH and sat back in his padded chair. He was grateful Placidia had adopted the modern habit of sitting at a table to eat, rather than reclining on a couch. There was something sensual and decadent about lolling on silken cushions with another's body an arm length—or less—away. They took this meal in the anteroom to Placidia's personal quarters—a room made more intimate by thick green hangings on the marble walls and the soft light of oil lamps hanging above. The gilt table gave them a respectable sense of distance without making conversation difficult.

Placidia smiled at him as servants whisked away the last evidence of their meal. He felt a blush creep up his neck. *God's balls! I've been a warrior half my life, and the woman still makes me feel like an unblooded boy.*

She raised a cup in a salute. "To my strong right arm."

"It's my pleasure and life's duty to serve you, Augusta." He raised his own cup.

She waved a hand. The ubiquitous servants disappeared. She leaned back, sipping her wine. Two small lines pinched together over her nose. "Now, my friend, tell me what you couldn't in the audience chamber. What of Aetius?"

Sigisvult twisted the end of his blond mustache and frowned. "His men are fanatically loyal to him."

Placidia raised an eyebrow.

"I can't fault his soldiering. He eats the same food and sleeps in the same conditions as his men. He rides like a Hun and can spend days in the saddle. He's brave and cunning; doing more with two thousand men than most generals could do with twice or thrice that number."

"And his ambition?"

"He kept that carefully from me, but there were hints. He does not believe you are strong enough to hold the West. He resents that you have named General Felix *magister militum* and keep him close to you in Italy. Perhaps if you played to his side that craves recognition?"

"A mere two years of exemplary service hardly demands recognition. Aetius supported a usurper and rode against me with his Hunnish friends, while Felix came to my aid. Honoring disloyalty sticks in my throat." She slammed the goblet onto the table, spattering ruby drops of wine. "Will he march against me, now that Boniface is in rebellion? Will they make common cause?"

Sigisvult took a deep breath. The Count of Africa's refusal to return to court had come as a great shock to him. Boniface had always been loyal to Placidia. "Aetius is in winter camp. His troops are few, compared to those of Felix here in Italy. As to Boniface, he has no love for Aetius."

"And now little love for me." Placidia rose and paced, hands clasped behind

FaithL.Justice

her back. "I handled Boniface poorly. Several senators approached me with whispers that he plotted against me. As proof, they urged me to request his presence here at court. They claimed Boniface would fear his plot uncovered, and refuse."

Sigisvult frowned. He was missing something important. "Why poorly? They were right in their suspicions."

"I recently discovered correspondence has taken place between Aetius and those particular senators. I don't know the nature of their discussions, but fear I have been outflanked by our wily general."

Placidia stopped by his chair and put her hands on his shoulders. Sigisvult thrilled at her touch. He ducked his head, to conceal the naked need in his eyes—the need to please her in any way she deemed fit.

"Sigisvult, you know my heart better than any man. You must go to Africa and bring Boniface back to my standard. I cannot, dare not, lose my few loyal friends. If I lose Boniface in Africa, that leaves only Felix to counter Aetius' ambition."

Sigisvult stood. Her hands slipped to his waist. Her touch seemed to burn through his silk tunic.

He saw close up what he had missed in the dim light—dark smudges under her luminous eyes, threads of silver in her curls. He wished he could spare her the pain of treachery, take on some of her burden, but her mind was subtler than his.

"Help me…" she whispered.

"How may I serve, My Queen?"

At the title, Placidia straightened her shoulders and pulled her hands away. "Help me stay strong."

CHAPTER 31

Africa, 428

S IGISVULT, CLOAKED FROM HEAD TO FOOT, waited in a grove of olive trees on a low hill outside Carthage. Stars shone bright in the moonless sky, but cast little light under the trees. Sweat trickled down his neck, dampening his tunic, but he stood still as stone.

A rustling at the edge of the grove caught his attention. Someone blundered through the trees, cursing root and branch. Sigisvult waited until the man passed his position, then stepped out of the deeper shadows and laid a hand on the other's shoulder.

"God's good grace!" the man yelped, flinging himself away.

"Easy, Maximinus. How went your mission?"

"Count!" Placidia had promoted Sigisvult to equal rank with Boniface, and given him command over troops in Carthage. "Thank God, it is you. I thought a wild Berber about to murder me." Maximinus bent, clutching his chest.

Sigisvult smiled at the man, an Arian bishop to his army. It was easy to see how his theatrics appealed to the barbarian need for drama. Word had reached Sigisvult of how Maximinus had debated the celebrated Augustine, Catholic Bishop of Hippo, leaving him literally speechless by taking up all the time allotted to both and exiting before the good bishop could make his argument. He was a wily adversary and, as a bishop and Arian, an acceptable envoy to Boniface.

"When you have recovered your breath, perhaps you could answer my question?"

"Of course. As you requested, I approached Count Boniface privately, in my capacity as spiritual shepherd to the troops..." Maximinus took a couple more deep breaths.

"And...?"

"Your suspicions were correct! Boniface had in his possession a letter claiming the Augusta plotted against him, and the proof would be that she would soon recall him to Ravenna with no reason given."

"That black-hearted scorpion! Aetius did plot against the Augusta, and I saw nothing." Sigisvult tugged on his moustache. That Aetius had nearly succeeded galled him. "Did Boniface agree to meet with me?"

White teeth gleamed in the shadows. "He waits now, on the edge of the grove."

"Why didn't you say so, man?" Sigisvult strode back the way Maximinus had come, deftly avoiding the roots and branches that had tripped the less agile bishop. He paused at the edge. A cloaked figure stood beside a horse on the other side of a stone wall bordering the orchard. Sigisvult stared long and hard, but saw no others lurking in the shadows.

"Count?"

Boniface whirled to face him, dagger drawn, but held defensively. "Sigisvult?"

"Yes. I come alone." Sigisvult heard Maximinus stumbling through the grove. "Except for my envoy."

Boniface chuckled low. "What he lacks in woodcraft, the good bishop makes up for with wordcraft." He sheathed his knife. "I understand you bring word from the Augusta."

"She suspects you were duped by a plot to drive a wedge between you and her, and thus weaken her hold in the West."

"So Maximinus told me. A cunning plot that worked as planned. I am now branded an 'Enemy of the Roman People' and in rebellion." Boniface spat in the dust of the road. "How could I have been such a fool?"

"The Augusta is willing to pardon you, but she must have proof of your loyalty to show your supporters and silence your enemies."

Boniface pulled a parchment packet from a pouch at his side. "Here are the letters I received warning me of the plot. What now?"

"Withdraw your troops from the field. I'll confine mine to Carthage. I'll

244

send these proofs to the Augusta and we'll await her word. Take no more military actions, or all might fail."

"Understood." Boniface mounted his horse and leaned down to clasp Sigisvult's shoulder. "Enjoy your stay in Africa, my friend. It is a most glorious place."

Ravenna, 429

"LADY PADUSA, WOULD YOU CARE TO ACCOMPANY ME?" Placidia approached the general's wife during an afternoon assembly. The receiving room boiled over with senators from Rome, nobles from across the empire, and churchmen seeking favors in business or redress in the courts. She began to hate these social obligations almost as much as her late husband did, but circulating with the courtiers was important, and she found Padusa pleasant company. The woman was a few years older than she, rounded and matronly, but Placidia found her insights compelling and company amusing.

"I would be honored, Augusta." Padusa bowed slightly.

Placidia took her arm in hers as they processed through the marble corridors, nodding to knots of people. "The nobles seem more agitated than normal. Is it the situation in Africa?" She noticed the saintly Bishop Martinus of Milan, and steered them in his direction. The musky scent of church incense tickled her nose from several feet away.

Padusa murmured, "No one expected the Vandals to successfully cross from Spain. The waters between the Pillars of Hercules are treacherous."

"I know. The Goths tried and turned back in 416." *Thirteen years ago. Honorius would be pleased. My ties with the Goths are all but broken, my personal Gothic guards fewer and fewer in number. Sigisvult, my strong right arm, battling the Vandals in Africa with Boniface, God have mercy on them and give strength to their men.* Placidia listened closely to the conversations as they passed. The undercurrent of alarm was palpable.

She squeezed her companion's arm. "I will make an announcement soon which should allay everyone's fears."

"You're not giving in to General Aetius? I know several powerful senators are agitating on his behalf for the supreme command." Padusa turned a worried face to her. "He is an able general, but I distrust his motives. He is ambitious, and your son still a boy."

"Not the supreme command, but a promotion." Placidia reassured her friend, knowing her concern was as much for Felix's status as for Placidia's. "I think you will like my compromise."

They chatted with the bishop, then wended their way back to the head of the receiving room, where Placidia took her seat. She nodded to the herald, who loosed a trumpet blast to call everyone to attention. People crowded from the adjacent corridors to hear the announcement.

When all were assembled and quiet, Placidia announced, "I have good news! My nephew, Theodosius Augustus, is sending an army under the able General Aspar to Africa. The combined armies of Count Boniface and Count Sigisvult, bolstered by General Aspar, will push the Vandals into the sea!"

Acclamations echoed off the marble walls. The Vandal King Gaiseric could muster only fifteen or twenty thousand fighting men. Surely the combined might of the Eastern and Western Empire would destroy him. Placidia let the joyous reaction carry on several minutes, then signaled for silence.

"Closer to home, I have two happy announcements. For his continuing service in policing Gaul, I'm elevating our excellent General Aetius to *magister militum*." This drew significant applause and acclaim from the senatorial contingent.

"And, for his personal service and advice, I'm naming General Felix Patrician." This announcement resulted in more applause from the Ravenna court, but frowns among the senators who supported Aetius. Both Aetius and Felix now held the rank of *magister militum*, but with the Patriciate, Felix still outranked the younger general. All Placidia had done was move both men up one rank, maintaining their relative status.

Padusa beamed.

Ravenna, 430

Placidia rode in her litter, alternately shaking with rage and fear. *At least the children are safe.* Lucilla and a company of her most trustworthy Gothic guards were ready to spirit them both out of Ravenna, if the rioting spread.

"Augusta, we're here." The captain of her *scholae* pulled the curtain back from her litter and bowed low. "I advise against this. You might be in danger."

She looked at him with cold eyes. "You made your case earlier, Captain, and I made my decision. Do not question me again."

He paled, then handed her down to the steps of the Basilica Ursiana. The rest of her guard made a solid wall of shields and spears around the steps.

The canals at low tide blasted her nostrils with the stench of fetid water and rotting fish, but it was the smell of blood congealing on the steps that brought a scented cloth to her nose. Flies gathered above the clotting pools. She marched up the steps, suppressing the pain from a twinge in her knee, and into the cool marble passages of the basilica.

"Where are they?"

A soldier with the dark cast of an Illyrian removed a cloak, exposing three bodies: General Felix, Padusa, and a deacon who happened to be accompanying them up the stairs. Their clothes were rent and blood-soaked; their bodies hacked almost beyond recognition. Their faces reflected the horror of their deaths, not the peace due their souls.

Her gorge rose. She swallowed it back. *It's not like I haven't seen such sights before in a church. Poor Padusa. I'm sorry, my friend. You will be revenged.*

She turned to her captain. "The situation now?"

He motioned a young soldier forward. "Augusta, all the rioters are apprehended. The General's own soldiers murdered him."

"Examine them under torture, Captain. I want to know who was behind this treachery." *As if I don't already know.* "Then decimate the ranks of the rebellious units."

Aetius, you scheming traitor! You tried and failed with Boniface, so you came up with a more permanent solution for Felix. This will not stand!

LUCILLA AND THE CHILDREN MET PLACIDIA on her return. Her arms ached to hug them both, but that would be unacceptable, weak. Both children had impeccable manners, and neither tried to embrace their mother. Nor did they wish to. Val didn't want her fussing over him, and Honoria had been moody and distant for a year.

Honoria, at twelve, had that coltish awkwardness girls get just before they grow into their womanhood. She already surpassed her mother in beauty. Her father's long, incongruous neck gave her a graceful, delicate look. Valentinian, at ten, promised to match his father in height. He did inherit one trait from his mother—he never put on flesh, no matter how much he ate.

"There is nothing for you to worry about, children. Lucilla, you may take them back to their rooms."

Honoria met her eyes. Placidia was startled to realize they were level with her own. "Will you recall Sigisvult from Africa, Mother?"

Placidia settled onto a padded couch with a sigh. "What makes you think I will do that?"

"With Felix dead and Boniface repelling the Vandal invasion in Africa, you need a trustworthy general here in Italy to counter Aetius. You should have brought Sigisvult back long before now. You always said Felix was a dim lamp."

"A most astute analysis, Honoria." The girl often startled her with her understanding of politics. Placidia had so wanted to protect her daughter from the snake pit that was the court. She frowned, sadness settling around her heart. "But when did I ever disparage the good Felix?"

Honoria snorted, a most unladylike action. "I have ears, Mother, and a mind, even if you rarely acknowledge it. Felix was only an adequate general; his chief virtue his loyalty to you."

"General Felix sent the Huns packing from Pannonia three years ago, and kept the alpine passes well-guarded. Italy is safe and prosperous." She turned to her son. "Val, what do you think of your sister's observations?"

He shrugged, pursing his lips in a pout. "I don't know, Mother. All this fuss made me miss my archery today. Now it's getting dark. When are you coming to watch me?"

Honoria gave her brother a withering look. "When will you grow up? You spend your days shooting pigeons and watching the entertainers at the baths."

Placidia smiled at her son. "Archery and mimes are suitable for a boy. He will be a man soon enough."

Val stuck his tongue out at his sister.

"Mother! See what he did."

"Enough!" Her head throbbed with the start of the pain that usually blurred her vision and sent her reeling to a chamber pot to rid herself of her last meal. "Both of you go. I'm tired and feel a headache coming on."

Lucilla ushered the children out of her room. Their bickering echoed off the marble walls.

What am I to do with the girl? I don't want to force her into a marriage, and there is little for a royal woman of talent to do besides charitable works. Maybe I should send her to Pulcheria.

A sharp pain behind her eyes interrupted her reveries. She moaned, hands to her temples.

"Mistress?" Her head bedroom slave approached. "May I bring you cold compresses?"

"Yes," she gasped, "and Machaon's powder." *I will deal with Honoria another day. But she is right. I need Sigisvult.*

Ravenna, 431

"HOW COULD THIS HAVE HAPPENED? Hippo taken. Bishop Augustine dead. The might of both the East and West; my three best generals defeated." Placidia groped for a chair, her face pale with shock. She pulled her night robe closer and tucked a curl that escaped her braid behind her ear. Sigisvult, travel-stained and exhausted, stood before her in her private quarters. At this late hour, a mere handful of servants slept outside her rooms in case she needed anything. Only Lucilla hovered in the shadows.

Sigisvult's shoulders slumped. "I'm so sorry, Augusta. We failed you. I failed you. Gaiseric out-generaled us and his men out-fought us. Others will use more honeyed words, but that is the plain truth." He ducked his head, closed his eyes, and fell to his knees. "Do with me as you wish. I deserve punishment."

Her heart felt near to bursting at the sight of this young man brought so low by shame and despair. She rose to take his stubbled face in her smooths hands, turning it towards her own. He opened his eyes.

"Sigisvult, my strong right arm, all generals lose at some time or another. My father, Stilicho, Ataulf, Constantius—they all lost battles. The object is to win the war." She sniffed. He smelled of horse and sweat. The scent dredged up memories—long denied—of Ataulf. Her breath caught and heart raced. Her head cautioned no, but her body and heart rebelled. She longed for the arms of a strong man, passionate kisses, and tender touches to breast and…pleasure bordering on pain throbbed in her groin. She turned to Lucilla. "Leave us. Let no one in my chambers." Her friend widened her eyes, but nodded and left.

"No, Augusta. I cannot stay here." He blushed to the roots of his silver blond hair. "The servants…"

"Will know nothing. Lucilla is discrete. It is late. The courtiers are in bed or about their own distractions. Tomorrow will be soon enough to break the bad news." She closed her eyes and rested her forehead on his. "Sigisvult, you once said you would do anything for me. I need this. I need you."

He stood and raised her to her feet. The joy on his face was mixed with confusion. "Are you sure? You're the Augusta, and my queen."

"Please," she leaned onto his chest, "don't make me beg."

"Never." He swept her into his arms and carried her to her bed.

In the brightening light of dawn, Placidia smoothed strands of sweaty blond hair back from Sigisvult's forehead and studied his face. The only evidence of sun and soldiering was the healthy bronze of his skin and the cluster of wrinkles at the corners of his eyes; his body was remarkably free of scars.

A slight noise caught her attention.

"Augusta, I've brought you a tray." Lucilla's voice whispered at the door.

"Come in." Sigisvult stirred next to her. She put a finger to his lips. His eyes snapped open, instantly alert. "Breakfast, then you must go. Lucilla will show you a back way to the kitchen."

Lucilla put the tray of boiled eggs, cheese, cucumbers, fresh bread and honey on a side table; poured two goblets of water; and left.

"Augusta, I…"

"Last night it was 'Placidia, my love'." She raised an eyebrow.

His teeth flashed in his brown face. He reached for her. "Placidia, my love?"

She laughed, left the bed, and stood looking at the shadows of her private garden. The sound of water tinkled from a *nymphaeum*.

She heard him approach and leaned back on his chest when he put his arms around her. He took in a deep breath. "Is that lavender I smell in the garden?"

"It reminds me of Southern Gaul." *The happiest time of my life.* Her body shook with suppressed sobs.

"Are you cold, my love? Let me get you a wrap."

"No." She held his arms around her. "Your warmth is enough." The moment passed. Placidia reluctantly broke from his embrace. With the dawn came responsibility. "You should eat, and then you must leave."

"I'm not hungry." Hurt tinged his voice. "Do you care for me at all?"

She turned to him. "Sigisvult, I care for you more than you could ever know. That's why you must leave. It's treason to sleep with me." Her body thrummed with need, but she denied it. "You were right the first time. It's dawn, and I'm the Augusta. I don't regret what we did, but we cannot do it again. We can never be more than the Augusta and her loyal general."

Despair rippled across his face. He firmed his jaw. "Of course, Augusta." He turned to leave.

She put a restraining hand on his arm. "Sigisvult, it's time you married. It's time you moved on."

"Is that a command from my queen?" he said through clenched teeth.

"No. It's advice from a friend who loves you."

"A friend?" He grabbed her in a crushing embrace, his mouth searching out hers with bruising force. After several moments, he released her, gasping. "Remember, My Queen, you can command my body whenever and wherever you wish, but you cannot command my heart."

He gathered his things and left.

CHAPTER 32

Rome, early 432

S EE THE LIGHTHOUSE, SWEETHEART? It's the tallest in the world." Boniface
held his six-year-old daughter tightly around the waist as they approached
Portus by sea. He took no chances on the heaving ship pitching her over
the side, though she could barely see over the railing.

"It's beautiful, Papa." She pointed at the top. "What's that?"

"A statue of one of Rome's ancient Emperors, Claudius. He built the harbor
for Rome's grain fleet." When was the last time any emperor took on such
a monumental project? Two hundred years ago? Three? For the past century,
imperial families mostly built churches, if anything.

The ship sailed between the lighthouse and a shuttered pagan temple at
the end of a vast mole that artificially enclosed the outer harbor. The Claudian
portico running the length of the mole showed signs of neglect: cracked marble
and crumbling facades. At least the columns looked sound.

Pelagia joined them at the bow, looking haggard and a bit green from the
seven-day voyage from Carthage. "I'm so glad to see land."

"We're nearly there, my love." In the calm waters of the harbor, he freed an
arm to twine about his wife's waist. She was much thinner than when they'd left.
Pelagia proved a poor sailor, spending most of the time moaning in the small
cabin reserved for their use on deck, or throwing up in a slop bucket.

A harbor official greeted them from a pilot boat. The captain went through the bureaucratic requirements, declaring his manifest and paying the fees. This ship, and the several accompanying it, carried a precious cargo: his personal *bucellarii* and additional troops returning from Africa, plus their equipment and provisions, including the cavalry horses. The Augusta finally called him home to become the *magister utriusque militia*, the supreme commander of her forces in Italy and the Empire. To think, just three years earlier he had been labeled an enemy of Rome, in rebellion. *Thank God in Heaven, Placidia saw past the trap Aetius set.*

They disembarked in the smaller six-sided Trajanic basin with its multitude of piers—mostly empty—and he sent his second-in-command to see to the men while he ushered his family onto a waiting barge, which would take them the final leg along a canal and up the Tiber to Rome.

"What's that, Papa?" His daughter pointed to builders pouring concrete and raising columns on plinths on the north side of the canal.

"It might be a portico. It looks new." He was used to most construction being either repair or demolition.

"That's the Porticus Placidiana," the owner of the barge said. "Our Augusta commissioned it last year and provides the funds for it herself. It will be over two-hundred yards long when finished. My nephew and many neighbors work on it. There's little work in Rome in the building trades at the moment, so everyone is grateful to the Augusta."

Boniface settled onto his bench with a sigh. It might not be a harbor or grand arena or monumental baths, but it was more than any emperor had built for the people of Rome in several generations.

Ravenna

"THE MASTER GENERAL OF ROME AND PATRICIAN, BONIFACE," the herald announced in the audience chamber.

Placidia eyed the courtiers, looking for dissent. A powerful faction of the nobles backed Aetius. They had forced her to name him consul—again!—for this year, and had been most unhappy with her choice to bring the loyal Boniface back to Italy as Master General and Patrician. All greeted Boniface with enthusiasm, both feigned and real. They would be even less happy with her next move.

Boniface approached the dais where she sat itching under her uncomfortable court robes. He bowed low. "Augusta. It is a privilege and honor to serve you and Valentinian Augustus."

"Welcome to court, Patrician!" Placidia greeted Boniface. She made a mental note to have Val attend more court sessions. He would soon be fourteen, officially in his majority, and should be prepared to take over his imperial duties; although she planned to guide him through the morass of government until he was older and more capable.

She rose, offering her hand. "Join me. I wish to hear your report in private."

They retreated to a small, sumptuous receiving room already laid out with food and drink. He poured himself a goblet of wine, admiring the clear garnet colored glass and silver chasing. He sipped and put the goblet aside with a sigh. "Do you wish to hear of the Vandals? It was a bloody mess. Aspar refused to coordinate with us. Our armies worked at cross purposes. I…"

She held up her hand. "Sigisvult told me all. I'll hear your side another time. I actually want your advice."

Relief lightened his features. "As you wish, Augusta."

"We are old friends and allies, Boniface. Call me Placidia in private." She settled into a padded chair. "Could you pour me a draught?"

"Of course, Aug—Placidia." He poured her a goblet and took a chair opposite.

She sipped the chilled white vintage. The floral scent reminded her of a summer garden. A little strong for her taste. She usually took hers well-watered. She watched Boniface over the lip of her goblet. He seemed ill at ease. Perhaps he still felt responsible for the fiasco in Africa. "Have you heard about the Huns?"

He raised his brows, surprised at this turn in the conversation.

"The Huns, under King Uptar, attacked the Burgundians in the German province. Just before the battle, Uptar died, and the Huns were in disarray. The Burgundians slaughtered over ten thousand of them. There will be a power struggle for who knows how long. This is our opportunity to strike at Aetius."

Boniface frowned. "I don't see how the Huns' defeat helps us with Aetius."

She leaned forward. "Aetius has always had a power base among the Huns. Uptar was his friend and ally. He recruits their cavalry and uses their existence as a threat to get his way. Without the Huns, he would have been executed or, at least, exiled for supporting that usurper John. They are now too weakened to come to his defense. I intend to strip him of his command and recall him to Rome."

"Are the Huns that weak?" He sipped his wine thoughtfully. "If they elect a new king quickly, the loss of ten thousand men will not hurt them. It seems a great deal to us, with our legions half manned and scantily armed, but the Huns conquered many peoples on their trek west. We do not truly know their might."

"All the more reason to strike at Aetius now. The Huns will be focused inward until they elect a king. They may even fall apart as squabbling tribes." She could almost taste the satisfaction of finally ridding herself of the traitor. "Aetius will be on his own, with only his scant troops from Gaul. They cannot match the troops you can raise here in Italy."

"It's not just the Huns. Aetius has many supporters among the nobles and the senate. They will object."

Placidia glowered. Why did he not see this was the perfect time to get rid of a dangerous rival? Maybe she let his loyalty her color her opinion on his abilities. After all, he did lose several provinces in Africa to the Vandals. She shook her head. If she couldn't persuade, she would have to order. "I understand your objections, but I believe this is the best course. Aetius seeks supreme power in the West. He is a threat to my son's rule. I can't abide that. I have supporters of my own among the nobles and the senate. You are well-liked in the army, as well. Now is the time."

He put down his drink. "Of course, Augusta. I will do as you say, and protect you and your family with my life."

"Good." She set aside her own wine. "I'll send out the orders tomorrow, relieving Aetius of his command. If he comes home quietly, I'll allow him to retire to his estates." She extended her hand and graced him with a smile. "It's good to have you home, my friend. I'm sure my son will benefit from your advice for many years to come."

Rimini, Italy, 432

AETIUS SURVEYED HIS TROOPS as they spread across the Via Flamina, outside the Italian town of Rimini. His infantry held the middle, and his Hunnish cavalry reinforced the right and left, but they were outnumbered two to one by Boniface's troops. Sunlight glinted off the waves of the Adriatic Sea and the armor of the opposing army. His own troops were seasoned and willing fighters, fanatically loyal to him. They had followed him over the dangerous alpine passes, and supported him in his rebellion.

Civil war.

She brought us to this, when I need every man to hold Gaul and Spain. Why does that bloody bitch persist in promoting inferiors? If she only acknowledged my worth, I wouldn't have to plot.

A rider in the humble garments of a holy man separated from Boniface's standard to approach Aetius' forward commanders. He carried a green branch of truce.

A last plea for peace, no doubt.

"General Aetius?" The holy man stopped before him.

Aetius nodded.

"I'm Bishop Maximinus. The Patrician sent me to persuade you to reason. This civil war is not necessary."

"Tell the Patrician, I will gladly accept his surrender of troops and title." At the thought of Boniface, in the coveted post of *magister utriusque militia*, Aetius' hands grew cold.

The bishop shook his head. "This war is madness! The Vandals spread like locusts across Africa, destroying all in their path. The Saxons invade Britain. You brought your troops from Gaul, where they are needed to contain the Franks and Burgundians. The Augusta needs all her generals to hold the West."

"The Augusta made the choice to strip me of my command." A grim smile spread over his face. "Today she will pay."

Sadness settled over the bishop's face like a cloud blotting out the sun. "Not just the Augusta, but all the Empire will suffer for this day."

"The Empire will be the stronger with me in supreme command. Boniface sat in Africa for too long, growing soft and rotten in the sun. Even with help from the East, he couldn't stop a paltry army of barbarians. I know these tribes, lived among them, commanded them. I can hold this empire together. The Augusta refuses to see that." Aetius shifted on his horse, waving a dismissive hand at the bishop. "Be gone. I have no more time to waste on talk."

Maximinus spurred his horse away, dropping the green branch between the two armies.

*****

256

BONIFACE WATCHED THE PEACE TOKEN FALL TO EARTH. His stomach lurched at the certainty of combat. He looked at his men. Many would not survive the day.

"Ready the troops. We push on Aetius' left, and roll his line back into the sea."

The men pounded their sword hilts against their shields and chanted, building their courage. When the bishop reached safety on a neighboring hill, archers on both sides let loose volleys of arrows. The missiles darkened the sky, whistling death. The thunk of arrows meeting wooden shields, and the screams of men, turned the chanting into a chaotic roar.

"Infantry forward!" Boniface unsheathed his sword and motioned to the front. His men moved out in formation. Cohorts jogged to fill gaps and make a solid front, three soldiers deep. From his spot on a slight rise to the rear and center, he saw Aetius' troops approach in a thinner, more ragged formation. The front lines clashed. Boniface felt a shout leave his throat, but couldn't hear it in the clamor that washed over him.

Slowly Aetius' left wing gave way, but it exacted a terrible toll for every foot of ground ceded. Writhing, broken bodies and blood-soaked armor hindered the pursuing troops.

"Reserves to the right. Roll 'em up!"

A runner carried his orders. Fresh troops poured down the hill, pushing Aetius' forces toward the sea.

A shout went up from the retreating soldiers. They stiffened their line.

"Aetius joins the battle, General!"

"I've got eyes!" Boniface ground his teeth. Outnumbered, Aetius' troops rallied and pushed back over the blood-soaked ground. Aetius fought from his horse like a savage Hun. Boniface's own horse grew restive, pulling at the bit, snuffling at the smell of blood. His center and left were holding, but not for long if Aetius' troops pushed through on the right and surrounded his forces.

"Cavalry forward!" Boniface raced down the shallow rise, followed by thundering hooves and the shouts of his men. The roar of battle receded, replaced with the sounds of his breath in ragged gasps and his heartbeat pounding in his ears. His vision both sharpened and tunneled as he looked for the weakness in his own lines.

"There!" He pointed his sword to where men engaged in small knots of combat, allowing enemy soldiers to race through the holes and attack from the rear.

He and his cavalry descended like a pack of furies. Boniface slashed one man across the face, stabbed another in the neck. His horse whirled and stamped to avoid spears and swords. For a timeless moment he knew only the shock of metal slicing through leather, muscle and bone. Blood ran down his arm, splattering his face as he hacked his way to the front.

The enemy soldiers moved back, splintered their line, and began to run. He smelled victory in the blood and panic of his enemy.

His horse screamed and pitched forward, a spear in its side. Boniface leapt from its back, crumpling to the ground as his right leg gave out beneath him.

The face of a boy with the beginnings of a moustache stared vacantly at Boniface from a foot away, eyes wide, mouth twisted from his last scream or prayer. The fighting moved beyond both living and dead.

Pain seared Boniface from ankle to thigh. He looked down to see a gash, bone deep, across his right calf. Blood spurted from the wound. He tore the kerchief from his neck and tied it above the wound to slow the blood. When had he got that cut? Where were his bodyguards?

Dazed, he used his shield to lever himself to his knees, then collapsed again, light-headed.

"General!" One of his aides jumped from his horse. "How bad…" He stared at the gash, and the blood pooling by the leg. His face paled.

Boniface saw his own death in the man's face. "God's balls, man. Get me off the field."

"Of course, General." With a grunt, the man lifted Boniface to his feet, then heaved him onto the horse like a sack of grain.

"Tell Pelagia…" Boniface slumped toward the horse's neck. He remembered his wife's arms about his shoulders, and her lips against his. Then all went dark.

PLACIDIA LEFT HER GUARDS at the door of the lavish villa overlooking the Adriatic Sea—one of dozens that dotted the coast north of Ravenna. The sound of waves on the beach and the salt smell might be soothing to some, but they reminded her of that perilous voyage to Constantinople. *Thank you again, gracious Lord, for listening to our prayers that day.*

"This way, Augusta." The villa's chamberlain led her to the *triclinium*. The dining room had been turned into a sick room with a sumptuous bed, tables to hold oil lamps and dressings, and chairs for visitors. It was a pleasant place to recover: colorful frescoes of sea life graced the walls, light and air came through broad doors opening onto the interior courtyard. Although it was late fall, rosemary and other hardy herbs lent color to the eyes and scents to the nose. She had always liked the smell of rosemary.

Pelagia rose from a chair beside her husband's bed. "Augusta." She bowed and ducked in a brief curtsy. Dried tears marred her cheeks; untidy hair escaped from a braid. Her gown was wrinkled and blood-stained. The woman looked as if she hadn't slept in days.

"Please sit, Pelagia." She approached the bed. Boniface lay pale, sleeping under a woolen blanket. His right leg was missing below the knee. She knew he was wounded in the battle with Aetius, but had been told he was recovering. God's bones, she was tired of sycophants telling her only what they thought she wanted to hear. How could she rule if everyone kept bad news from her? "How is he?"

Pelagia ran her fingers over his palm. "Not good. The wound festered and the surgeon had to remove his leg, but too late. The poison travels through his body. The surgeon can do more."

"Is he aware?"

"Sometimes. Less often, lately. He has a fever and delirium."

"I'm so sorry, Pelagia. I too have lost my husband, and know your pain."

"King Ataulf." Pelagia nodded. "A brave man. My mother spoke of him often."

Placidia started. Most people acted as if her first marriage hadn't happened—an embarrassing, unfortunate event that should never be spoken of. She had forgotten Pelagia was a Goth. The tribe had scattered to the far corners of the Empire through the army and trade.

"Augusta?" Boniface whispered from the bed, eyes half opened. "Forgive me."

"For not rising? I don't expect sick people to get out of their beds for me."

He shook his head. "For failing you."

She took his hand from Pelagia. "My brave general and most loyal friend. You have never failed me."

"Aetius?"

"Fled with the remnants of his army. You won, Boniface. You defeated Aetius and saved my son from his evil influence."

"Good." He squeezed her hand. "But my time is done. Who will be your champion now?"

"General Sigisvult will take up the challenge."

"A good man." He closed his eyes and sighed, tucking his chin in the barest semblance of a nod.

"As are you, my friend."

He muttered something she couldn't quite hear, and fell asleep.

She rose and held out her hand. "Come, Pelagia. You need food and sleep." She spied the chamberlain hovering by the door. "You! Call your mistress' servants and see to her."

"But my husband…"

"I will sit with the general until you have rested. He will not be alone."

Pelagia kissed her husband on the forehead and turned back to Placidia. "Thank you, Augusta. My mother spoke of you often, but she was wrong."

"Many among the Goths hated me." Placidia shrugged. "That was long ago. Go, take a bath, have some food, spend some time with your daughter."

Honoria had only been a year or two younger when she'd lost her father. *Be kind to her.*

I tried, Constantius.

Pannonia, 433

AETIUS INSPECTED HIS MEN before they rode into the Hun village. Only a few hundred souls survived that disastrous battle with Boniface. Today they wore their finest, and bore presents for their hosts. "Good. We march into this village like conquerors—heads high—no trace of defeat on our faces. The Huns value warriors above all."

He leapt onto his own horse and motioned forward. When all were formed up behind him, he led the column into the village—a cluster of round wooden houses and a profusion of tents sprawling in a wide valley between a mountain and a shallow river. They headed toward the largest house, set on a hill and surrounded by a wooden wall. Two smaller walled enclosures flanked the King's residence.

Men of various tribes—not only the squat forms of Huns, but the tall fair men of the eastern Goths and the dark countenances of Greeks, lounged outside the houses and tents. Some halted their dice games, or stopped mending their weapons. All stared at the passing Romans.

When they reached the King's walled abode, Aetius called a halt. "My guard with me. The rest of you, find a spot by the river for camp."

Aetius and an escort of five rode through the opening gate. The guard let them pass without comment. Several smaller buildings dotted the area inside the wall. A woman in the rich colors of the Scythians stepped out of one, followed by servants bearing goblets of wine. Aetius smiled—Ruga's wife bore the traditional greeting. Evidently his gifts to Ruga and his lieutenants were sufficient for honored treatment.

"King Ruga welcomes his guest and great friend, General Aetius." The Hunnish Queen met his gaze with intelligent dark eyes.

"Many thanks for your hospitality, My Lady." Aetius drained his goblet, never leaving his horse's back. "My friends the Huns are the most gracious of people. Please accept these gifts as a token of my esteem for the king's royal lady." He and each of his men handed the Queen a gift for her hospitality: Indian pepper, palm fruit, and other delicacies that could not be produced in their territory.

Aetius and his men entered the banquet hall. Woolen mats muffled their footsteps. Light from brass oil lamps chased shadows from the corners. An elaborate dining couch, covered with orange and red silks, stood on a dais at the narrow end. Ordinary wooden chairs lined the long walls, occupied by Hunnish warriors and a few obvious traders. Small tables were set so that three or four men could share meat.

A slave handed Aetius a goblet of wine and escorted him to his place, one chair away from the couch on the left side. Aetius smiled. This place of precedence augured well for his petition for help from the Hunnish King.

Ruga entered with his nephews, Attila and Bleda. He took his place on the couch. The younger men took their seats on his honored right; eyes cast down in respect. The King looked poorly—dark bruises surrounding his eyes made them look like burnt holes in his gray face.

It's past time I cemented my acquaintance with the heirs. Both men shared the Hunnish short stature, barrel chest, and bowed legs, but Bleda had a touch of the dissolute in his sparse, unkempt beard and glazed eyes. Attila dressed impeccably, if modestly, and drank from a wooden cup. *Silver plate as a gift for Bleda, but Attila looks more complicated. A fine horse or shield, perhaps? I must think on it.*

"Friends and guests, welcome." Ruga spoke from the couch. "A salute to my nephew Bleda!" He raised his cup. Bleda rose and did not resume his seat until his uncle had tasted his wine. This ceremony continued as each guest was honored; then Bleda stood again to toast the King. When all had drained their cups in honor of the host, the banquet began.

A feeling of completeness settled on Aetius. His shoulders relaxed at the familiar ceremony and scents. This was the language and company of his youth. All would be well. He speared a slice of roasted meat with his knife.

Outside Aquileia, 434

PLACIDIA STRODE FROM ONE END of the lavish leather traveling tent to the other. She kicked at the edge of a carpet that nearly tripped her. "Where, in God's Good Name, is that traitor?"

Her servants flinched from her.

The tent flap moved back, showing bright sunshine to contrast with the dim light in the tent. Sigisvult entered. "Augusta, Aetius awaits your pleasure."

She halted in front of him. "My pleasure would be to peel his skin off one inch at a time and feed it to the ravens! This is the second time he has brought his Hunnish horde onto Italian soil, and the second time I must give in to his demands." She put a hand to her temple; her sight blurred and contracted.

"Placidia!" Sigisvult rushed up to support her shoulders, settling her in a camp chair. "Where's Lucilla?"

"With the children, in Ravenna."

"Get your mistress a cup of wine, you fools." He glared at the servants in attendance. "You shouldn't have made this trip. It's too dangerous."

Placidia sipped from the cup he held to her lips, feeling the full weight of her forty-six years. "Because I am an old woman, prone to fits and vapors?"

He frowned at her half-jest. "Because Aetius might go further in his betrayal and take you captive."

"I am of scant importance now." The wine soured on her tongue. "Aetius has all he wanted—supreme command and the Patriciate. Taking me prisoner would be more than folly—with my seal on these papers today, my power is ended. Thank the Good Lord, Val has reached his majority."

"Your son is still too young to dispute with Aetius."

"But soon my boy can take on the burdens of government. I will be glad to lay them down." She put a hand to Sigisvult's cheek. "If not for those cursed Huns, you would be *magister utriusque militum* and Patrician. You would be the one to guide and protect the Empire."

"You honor me above all others with your trust. I may not be able to protect the Empire, but will do all within my power to protect you and your children."

"I know." She stood. "I have one honor I can still bestow—the consulship." It was a small jab at Aetius, who also wanted the consulship that year. Primarily, it was a reward for all that Sigisvult had done for her—a nearly meaningless reward, compared to the supreme command and Patriciate, but a reward nonetheless.

She straightened her shoulders and lifted her chin. "Let's get this over with. I want that man gone to Gaul as soon as possible."

Chapter 33

Ravenna, Spring 437

SWATHED IN THICK VEILS, Honoria made her way toward Sigisvult's private rooms, her steps a sibilant whisper of silk slippers on marble floors. This was the time of day he returned from the baths and prepared for the evening meal. At the bronze-bound door, she looked both ways, but saw no one. The same, inside his reception room. Since turning seventeen two years earlier, Honoria had full control of the income her father had left her. For this tryst, she used her gold to pay off Sigisvult's slaves and servants.

She lifted the first veil and let it fall to the floor. Honoria approved of the reception room. Sigisvult showed his power and influence through its luxurious, if slightly barbaric, appointments. A black bearskin covered the mosaic floor; a set of African elephant tusks hung on the far wall with sword and shield; wolf pelts overlaid his receiving chair.

Honoria ran her fingers over the polished marble stand where he displayed the official sign of his consulship—a bundle of carved honorary batons. At the threshold of his workroom, she dropped another veil. A clutter of maps and haphazard piles of books and correspondence littered his worktable—not at all like her mother's fanatical neatness.

Honoria paused at his bedroom and took a deep breath. This was her Rubicon. If she crossed into this forbidden territory, she could never turn back. Her skin prickled with anticipation. She stepped inside. Releasing her breath with a rush, she whirled in a giddy dance of joy. Honoria slowed her feet and calmed her heart. It would not do to have Sigisvult find a silly girl in his bedroom.

She dropped the last of her veils over a chair and reclined on Sigisvult's bed, wearing only a shift of sheerest linen.

"WHAT'S THIS?" Bishop Maximinus picked up the veil and handed it to Sigisvult. "You have a visitor, General. I will leave you to your pleasures."

Sigisvult blushed to the roots of his silver blond hair. "God's blood, I wish the ladies at court would leave me in peace!"

"No chance of that, my friend." Maximinus eyed Sigisvult's tall, battle-hardened figure with a rueful grin. "Unless you take a public vow of chastity, the ladies will pursue you like hounds on the hunt. Likely they would persist even then."

"Fools." Sigisvult chewed on the end of his moustache. He was wary of court sexual politics. Senators offered their wives and daughters for favors. Some women sought trophies among powerful men the way others bedded famous charioteers. For bedmates, Sigisvult occasionally visited one of the high-class brothels, but he much preferred a Greek slave he had purchased in Africa, a plump dim little thing he could satisfy with a few baubles and invest little thought to.

"Good day, General," Maximinus said. "Don't be too hard on the lady. Yours is a predicament most men would envy."

Sigisvult followed the trail of veils to its predictable end. One lamp lit his bedroom, leaving it in flickering shadows. The lack of slaves told of the lady's discretion—not a thrill-seeker who paraded her conquests like a general in a triumph. This lady wanted favors or... Sigisvult's heart leapt as he glimpsed dark curly hair and luminous eyes, then quieted when the lady slipped off the bed. The lamp glowed through the woman's sheer garment, outlining her tall, voluptuous body.

He struggled with relief and regret. She put a hand to his cheek, whispering, "Aren't you going to speak?"

"Honoria?" He grabbed her wrist in a crushing grip. "What are you doing here?"

She chuckled low in her throat. "Isn't it obvious?" Honoria leaned forward to put her head on his chest.

"Why?" He swung her about, so the light from the workroom illuminated her face. "What game do you play?"

She jerked her hand free. Pain pinched the corners of her mouth. "No game. I've wanted you ever since I was a little girl." She rubbed his thigh with her hip. "I just needed to grow up."

His voice came out harsher than intended. "This is impossible, Augusta. What about your mother?"

"She needn't know, if we are discreet." Honoria shrugged. "And if we are not, I doubt it would matter. All Mother cares for is power."

His hand moved without thought. Sigisvult heard the resounding crack of flesh on flesh. "Never talk about your mother like that."

Honoria stumbled back against the wall. The print of his hand on her cheek showed white in a face burning red. Tears sparkled in her eyes.

"I'm sorry. I shouldn't have hit you." Sigisvult cradled his offending hand as if the blow had burned it. "Your mother is a great lady, who has borne more pain than you could ever imagine. She has sacrificed so much…" His voice trailed off as Honoria's face blanched. She looked about to faint. Then the blood came rushing back.

"You love her!"

"Yes."

Honoria threw herself against Sigisvult's chest, pounding it with her fists. "You…love…*her*."

He stood under her blows until she collapsed, sobbing. He held her close, stroking her hair. "Be easy. Placidia will never learn of your…indiscretion."

Honoria stepped out of his embrace, her face a stony mask. "Tell her. I am my own woman and can make my own decisions. I am Augusta, just as she is."

"You misunderstand." Sigisvult shook his head. "I'm not protecting you. I'm saving your mother further pain."

Honoria lowered her brows. "What is it about my mother that bewitches men? My father, my brother, you—you all let her drive you like sheep. Does she keep a clay likeness of you, with spells to bind you to her will?"

"No!" Sigisvult made the two-fingered warding sign against the evil eye. "Placidia would never engage in the black arts."

"She must." A sly smile crossed Honoria's face. "Why else would a healthy man at the height of his powers stay bound here in the palace, close to her?"

It was Sigisvult's turn to flush red with anger. Her barb hit close to home, cutting short his retort.

"Or is she that good in bed? She's so old and boney. I'd think she wouldn't be much fun. Maybe she knows some secret bedcraft that holds you hostage?"

"Out." He pointed to the doorway. "I will not have you spreading your filth in my rooms."

Honoria laughed as she left.

After he heard the door slam, Sigisvult dropped into a leather camp chair, head in hands. "What in God's name am I doing here?" he muttered. "It's been six years—*six years!*—since that night we spent together." And three since Aetius took over the supreme command. Placidia had heaped wealth on him in lieu of the public honors she couldn't. He had estates in the country, a townhouse in Rome, horse farms in Spain, a villa on the sea; yet he cooled his heels here in the palace, waiting for what? The scent of roses in the hall after she passed? A smile from the dais? There would never be another midnight tryst. Placidia made that clear. He sighed, unused to introspection.

So? His love for Placidia was deeply rooted in loyalty and respect. He stayed in the palace to be of service to his queen, her strong right arm.

He raised his head and looked around his quarters. He'd grown soft. It was time to get back out in the field, where his strong right arm could do some good. Tomorrow he would ask Placidia for a field assignment.

PART IV

DOWAGER EMPRESS

OCTOBER 437 - NOVEMBER 450

CHAPTER 34

Constantinople, October 437

PLACIDIA ENTERED THE EASTERN EMPEROR'S AUDIENCE CHAMBER with a lighter step than she had enjoyed in several years.

"Placidia!" Athenais enveloped her in a warm embrace. "Welcome."

"My dear." Placidia held Athenais at arm's length. "You are as beautiful as your patron goddess." Athenais looked little older than she had at twenty-three, but the sadness in her eyes told of loss. Six years had passed since her third child, Flacilla, succumbed to a fever, but Placidia knew the loss of a child leaves at best a scar, at worst an open wound.

Athenais didn't blush as readily as in her youth, but did dimple with a smile. "You will think me a kitchen drudge when you see Eudoxia."

"My wife a kitchen drudge? Hardly!" Theodosius greeted her warmly, but did not touch his wife in the familiar way of spouses. There seemed a coldness between the two.

Pulcheria, thin and severe in her holy woman's robes, nodded a greeting. "Aunt, I am glad to see the Lord brought you safely to our shores."

"The Lord, and my best horses." Placidia smiled at her formidable niece.

Before Pulcheria could retort, Val stepped forward. "Mother, may I present my bride, Lucinia Eudoxia?"

A young woman stepped from the shadows. Athenais' daughter lived up to her promise. At fifteen, the girl was luminous, with porcelain skin, golden curls, and her mother's startling violet eyes. She cast them modestly down as she approached, extending her hand. "Welcome, Mother."

Placidia clasped her hand in both of hers. "Thank you, my child."

"Is she not exquisite?" Val's eyes gleamed. "I shall have the most beautiful woman in the Empire for a bride."

"Maybe then you won't dip your stick in other men's honey pots," Honoria muttered, just loud enough for Placidia to catch. Her irritation with the girl had as much to do with the truth of her jibe as the fact that she said it. Many irate husbands were richer or held higher office because of her son's predilections. She suspected some threw their wives and daughters at Val for that very reason.

Pulcheria clapped. A young female, clad in equally severe robes, approached. "Show the Emperor and the Augusta to their reception, and accompany Princess Eudoxia to her quarters when finished." Placidia hid a smile behind her hand at Val's disappointed look. He would have a lifetime with his bride; he could wait a few more hours.

Theo said, "Let's retire. We have much to discuss, Aunt."

"May I join you, Mother?" Honoria asked.

"No, dear. Go with your brother and enjoy the reception. I will join you shortly." At her daughter's disappointed look, Placidia's smile disappeared. The lines marking her forehead deepened. Honoria stalked off, her face stormy.

"Honoria has grown into a handsome woman." Athenais took Placidia's arm. "But I sense some tension between you two."

"She has always been a difficult child. Willful and argumentative."

"You mean she shows spirit and intelligence?" Theo laughed. "I have much experience with that."

"Lately she has been asking to sit in council meetings."

"The urge to rule runs strong in Theodosius' female line." Pulcheria looked down the corridor at Honoria's retreating back. "She sees you ruling for her brother, and my—our..." Pulcheria nodded at Athenais, "...influence with Theo. Why should she not want a similar role for herself?"

"I hear the truth of your words, but I have experience Honoria does not. Soon Val will rule for himself."

Athenais patted Placidia's arm. "Maybe it is time to think of a husband for her. Give her a domain of her own to rule, if only a household or estate."

"I could never see Honoria's future as clearly as I could Val's." Placidia's expression softened. "I only knew what I didn't want for her—a forced marriage for the sole purpose of producing heirs. Let's pray Eudoxia will have many healthy children and make that fate unnecessary."

"The palace will seem empty without my only child." Athenais' lips trembled. "But she will be well loved with you. Perhaps, after you all leave, I will go on a pilgrimage to Jerusalem to ease my soul."

"An admirable ambition, Sister," Pulcheria said. "Time in the Holy Land may have a moderating effect on you."

Placidia felt Athenais' arm tense and saw her mouth tighten. There was unhappiness in the younger Augusta's life beyond the loss of her children.

They came to a sitting room, much more lavishly appointed than the last time Placidia visited. Slaves provided a repast of shellfish, cheese, black olives, cold fowl with a pungent fish sauce, and a selection of fruit tarts. Athenais had made her presence felt—at least in the palace. Could that be the source of the tension between her and Pulcheria?

Pulcheria removed a cushion from a chair and sat on the bare wood. When all had settled down with wine and food, she said, "I've had the opportunity to speak on several occasions with young Valentinian over the past weeks. Your son seems to know little of the state of his empire, for one who is to rule."

Placidia colored at the bald criticism. "Val is an active young man, and grows impatient with administration. Age and marriage will settle him into his duties." She gave Pulcheria a level stare. "And I will be there to guide him."

Pulcheria started to speak again, but Theo interrupted. "How fare your borders? The Huns have been raiding our provinces again."

"The Patrician Aetius assures me the Huns are under his control. He recently used them to put down the Burgundian rebellion in Gaul." Placidia pursed her mouth in distaste. "As much as I detest the man, he is a cunning general. Aetius guards the western provinces with the fierceness of a mother lion protecting her cubs."

"But he leaves your African provinces orphaned and prey for the Vandals." Theo frowned.

"Will Aetius stay in Gaul during your absence?" Pulcheria asked, getting to the heart of Placidia's own fear at leaving Ravenna.

"General Sigisvult holds the passes to Italy. I will return to Ravenna after the wedding and represent my son until Val escorts his lovely bride back to our home."

"To our children." Athenais raised her cup high. "May God grant they live long and happily."

Placidia sipped her wine, silently beseeching Her Maker to grant Athenais' wish.

THEY SENT THE BRIDAL COUPLE OFF TO THE MARRIAGE BED with fanfare, flowers, and good wishes. The entire empire celebrated the Imperial nuptials with feasts and games. Statues were sent to every major city, and new coins minted with Valentinian and Eudoxia's profiles. In Constantinople, the festivities would continue for a full week.

Pulcheria had other plans. "Aunt, I and my sisters will celebrate the next week by doing good works. I hope you and Honoria Augusta will join us."

Surprised by the offer, Placidia stammered, "Why, yes. We will be honored."

"We leave right after morning prayers." She took note of Placidia's regal attire. "I recommend you wear something plain that you do not mind getting stained."

Placidia offered a crooked smile. "I'll see what I can find among the servants."

THE NEXT MORNING, PULCHERIA took them to a hospital run by the Church of Hagia Sophia. A plump woman with pox-scarred cheeks bobbed her head in greeting. "Welcome, Augusta."

"Sister Helena." Pulcheria greeted. "This is my aunt, Placidia Augusta, and her daughter, Honoria Augusta. They will be helping in the hospital today."

"We are grateful for your kindness, Most Gracious Ladies." Sister Helena glanced past them, as if looking for someone. "May I enquire as to the health of your honored sisters?"

"Arcadia and Marina are well, and overseeing the distribution of food to the poor at the Church of the Holy Apostles. They will be ministering here later in the week."

Placidia had wondered where her two younger nieces labored. The girls seemed to have no personalities of their own, but lived perpetually in Pulcheria's shadow, aping her actions and doing her bidding.

Helena smiled, bobbing her head in acknowledgement. "God's blessings on you all for your holy service."

"What should we do?" Honoria asked.

"Whatever needs doing." Pulcheria shrugged. "Feed the patients, bathe them, clean their beds, pray with them."

"Bathe them and clean their beds!" Honoria's mouth became a grim line. "I'm Augusta. Why should I dirty my hands on the poor and destitute? I can buy slaves or pay others to work here in my stead."

"Because God chose your brother for high office, and Christ instructs us to care for the poor and downtrodden. I understand you wish to advise your brother, help him to rule wisely and justly?" Pulcheria gave Honoria a chilly smile. "How will you know what is right and good for the people, if you do not go among them? That has worked for my brother and me. You could do worse than follow our example."

Honoria took on a calculating look. Placidia hid a smile. She was sure the lesson in humility was meant for her as well as her daughter.

"Come, Honoria, I nursed many among the Goths. I will show you what to do."

"There is no need, Mother. I am sure I can master a spoon and wash cloth."

Pulcheria raised an eyebrow. "Do not neglect their souls. Our prayers do as much good as our hands."

"This way." Sister Helena led them into a long hall filled almost to bursting with women, some with infants, lying on straw pallets. "We had a bad fever outbreak last week. These are the survivors, but they are weak. Soup and hot water are through there." She pointed to a door that led to a courtyard.

They spent the rest of the day tending sick women. Placidia was pleased to see Honoria did not shirk her duties. Placidia addressed the women in low, soothing tones, tending their physical needs, listening to their stories. Most were poor and desperate, but a few were prosperous women abandoned by their families out of fear of the fever.

One woman in a fine robe held a baby to her chest, mumbling in delirium. She convulsed, clutching the child in a bone-crushing grip.

Placidia rushed to save the child.

A rough hand took her elbow. "The babe's been dead since midnight." She turned to meet Sister Helena's pocked face. "Poor soul wouldn't let me take him. She'll be gone soon herself."

"No! You can't have him!" the sick woman shrieked. She turned away, hiding the child from Placidia's gaze.

Tears burned Placidia's throat. She had clutched a dead son in grief and madness. It had been a long time since she thought of that tiny silver coffin in Barcelona. *I will bring my son home. At least I will have that part of Ataulf with me when the Good Lord sees fit to relieve me of my burdens.*

Placidia stayed with the woman, stroking her hair and bathing her forehead with cool water, until she lapsed into the coma that preceded death. Placidia prayed for her soul, then moved on to someone who could use her services in this life. By the end of the day, she was tired, but it was physical exhaustion, not the weariness of spirit that had plagued her the past few years.

The week was filled with such activities: they delivered food and clothing to the poor, visited the sick and abandoned, prayed with the holy sisters, and donated altar cloths and plate to churches. Everywhere they went, people crowded around Pulcheria, touching her robe, talking to her in hushed, reverent tones. The poor of the city truly loved her, and Pulcheria showed genuine, humble compassion for them.

By the time Placidia was ready to return to Ravenna, she had developed a better appreciation of her formidable niece. Honoria could do worse than follow in her cousin's footsteps...as could she. The religious life was not a bad choice for an aging widow, and she had many sins to atone for. It would be a relief to hand over the Empire to her son. She would see how Val got on with his duties.

Ravenna, 439

"WE'LL NAME HER PLACIDIA, AFTER YOU, MOTHER." Val beamed at his second daughter, who lay in the arms of his exhausted wife. They had named their first child Eudocia, Athenais' baptismal name. Two babies in two years had drained some of Eudoxia's beauty, but her youth would help her recover. Placidia, on the other hand, felt betrayed by a body increasingly prone to aches and twinges.

"She's a beautiful baby, Eudoxia." Placidia kissed her daughter-in-law's cheek. "Rest now. We'll talk of the baptism later." She took her son by the arm and steered him from the bedroom to his private sitting room "We must talk, Val."

"Of course, Mother, but my friends await me."

"They will wait a little longer. Sit." He took refuge in his favorite leather chair. She pulled up a padded stool to sit opposite him. "This is serious. I have more reports of your dalliances with other men's wives. This must stop."

Val rose to tower over her. "I am twenty years old, and the Emperor. I will do as I like."

"I am your mother, and the Augusta. Sit down and accord me the respect I deserve."

Val sat again, looking more like a sulky boy than the ruler of a great empire.

"Have you learned nothing from me?" Placidia grabbed both his hands in hers, forcing him to look into her face. "Yes, you are the Emperor, yet you cannot do as you like. You hold your power at the sufferance of the people and the army. Either could go into rebellion if they think you do not rule wisely and fairly. Roman history is filled with failed emperors who ignored that fact. Seducing other men's wives makes enemies you cannot afford—enemies who might plot against you. Is not Eudoxia enough for you?"

"Eudoxia spent too much time with her pious aunt to enjoy the pleasures of the marriage bed." Val withdrew his hands with a sigh.

Placidia had to admit she found her daughter-in-law disappointing. She resembled her mother only in outward beauty. Eudoxia had only sparks of Athenais' blazing spirit and intelligence.

Val hung a leg over the arm of his chair, swinging his foot. "Besides, she has spent most of our marriage pregnant. What do you propose I do, take a vow of abstinence?"

"Take a slave to bed. Acquire a concubine. Visit the brothels!" Placidia waved her arms in frustration. "But leave other men's wives alone!"

Val laughed. "Yes, Mother. Is that all?"

"No." Placidia sat again. "You made a point. You are twenty, and the Emperor. It is time you took over more duties. I grow old and tired."

"You are not old, Mother." Val approached her and kissed the top of her head. "The gray in your hair makes you look regal. You are still counted among the most beautiful women in the Empire."

"Posh!" She snorted. "I am too old to be taken in by court flattery, from you or anyone else. I have many sins to atone for, and little time."

"You're not ill?" Val knelt, clasping her hands.

The genuine concern tinged with fear that passed over his face warmed her heart. "No more than anyone my age."

"Then retire to Rome!" With a relieved smile, Val repaired to a sideboard to pour himself a goblet of wine. He raised the vessel in a salute. "The ambassadors, court duties, hippodrome appearances—you can leave all to me."

"Those are ceremonial duties. You need to propose laws, guide the ministers, hear petitions in person." She rose, set his goblet aside, and said, "My dear, you must act, not react, or others will rule through you. As it is, Aetius and those he favors govern more than you."

"Aetius slaves away in Gaul on my behalf. As to the rest…" He shrugged. "That is why I have ministers and slaves, to take over the drudgery and leave me my pleasures. Speaking of…" Val glanced at the door, "I have a birth to celebrate."

A chill stole over Placidia at the indolence on her son's handsome face.

"Go," she croaked.

When he'd gone, Placidia poured herself a goblet and sat brooding. Had she failed her son? He was a bright lad, affable; he could be a great leader if he applied himself. She sat back and sighed. There would be no retirement to Rome, no full-time dedication to good works. Her son needed his mother—for the near future, anyway.

CHAPTER 35

Ravenna, 439

PLACIDIA ENTERED VAL'S NEW PALACE, *ad Laureta*—by the Laurel Groves—and strode to the audience room, trailed by the Master of Offices, a handsome young man who shared her son's love of archery and aversion to work. She heard workmen in the back halls and smelled fresh plaster and paint. The public rooms were lavishly decorated, with multi-colored tiles on the floor and marble and bronze statues in every niche and corner. Gold glinted in the mosaics on the vaulted ceiling. Placidia particularly admired the wall frescoes of gardens, forests, and harvest scenes so realistic you might think you looked out a peristyle into open country.

She shook off her reverie. She was not here to admire art. Servants clustered in the halls, buzzing with excitement and dismay. Entering the audience chamber, she sensed panic in the pale looks and hastily sketched bows of the courtiers. Several people clustered in the center of the room. Three men, their formerly fine clothes torn and stained with soot, stood seemingly oblivious to their surroundings. One woman held a filthy linen shawl over hair that hadn't seen a comb in days. Tears tracked through the dirt on her cheeks.

Placidia approached the woman. She reeked of smoke and a sour body. When the woman saw the Augusta she dropped to the floor. "All dead," she wailed.

"Carthage?" Placidia looked at her son, pale under his sun-darkened skin.

"Gone."

Placidia knelt with a grunt and took the woman by the shoulders. She ignored sounds of disapproval. "What happened, my dear?"

The woman lifted her dazed face, eyes ringed with white. "Bodies. The children!" She clasped Placidia' hand with a bruising grip. "Blood. In the streets. Splashed my robes." She released Placidia rubbing with both hands the dark stains crusting the hem of her garments.

"How did you survive?"

"Survive?" She looked around at the richly dressed court. "I don't kn… My husband. Hid me in a boat. I'm with child." The woman spread her hands over her slightly rounded stomach. "He went back for his mother and…" Her voice drowned in moaning sobs.

"You're safe here." Placidia held the woman to her breast. Another of the survivors turned gray and swayed, hand outstretched. She looked sharply at her son, who frowned at her from the dais. "How long have these people been standing in your august presence?"

Val reddened. "Tend them!" Several slaves came forward to usher the group away. "Deacon, repeat for the Augusta what you told me."

Placidia stood and handed the moaning woman over to a servant.

A fourth man, a veteran from the scars on his arms and the experience stamped on his face, stepped forward. "The bloody Vandal dogs do not limit their pillage to rape and murder. They commit sacrilege! They steal the plate and candlesticks from the churches, then burn them down about the ears of the congregations. Men, women, children; none are spared if they are Catholic. The Arians are merely taken as slaves."

The old man, passion spent, closed his eyes. "God have mercy."

Placidia's fingers curled into tight fists. Burning churches, murdering congregates in sanctuary. She turned to her son. "What does the Emperor intend to do about this…this violation?"

"I will take counsel." Val nodded to several of his most trusted associates. "Join me in the consistory."

He did not explicitly invite Placidia, but all knew she would come. She took her accustomed chair at the foot of the table while her son occupied the head.

Val cleared his throat. "The loss of Carthage is most unexpected."

Placidia suppressed a snort of disbelief. She had told Val that King Gaiseric would not be content with rocky Mauretania, when Carthage and its rich hinterlands beckoned just beyond his borders.

"It is…was a walled city with the best soldiers protecting its citizens."

Another lie. Aetius had siphoned the best units north to protect Gaul. "How should we respond?"

"Do nothing, Your Excellency," the Master of Offices said. "Gaiseric will be sated with Carthage. His warriors grow fewer with each engagement. Soon he will be spread too thin. Then we can attack."

Heads nodded. Murmurs of, "Yes, do nothing," echoed down the table.

"Cowards. Lackwits," Placidia mumbled.

"Augusta?"

"I said you are all cowards and lackwits. With every engagement the Vandal King grows stronger, not weaker, as warriors flock to his victorious banner. With the Carthage fleet, he now commands the sea and can reach any shore. The Emperor's agents report Gaiseric is preparing to invade Sicily. If he takes it, we no longer have an independent source of grain and the people will riot for food."

"What do you propose, Augusta?" asked a man who had not even been born when Alaric took Rome.

"The Emperor of Rome cannot leave this challenge unanswered." Placidia steepled her fingers under her chin.

"Recall Aetius from Gaul to handle this crisis," the Master of Offices said.

"No!" Placidia curled her fingers into fists. "There is no need to bring Aetius and his troops into Italy. Send to Constantinople for help, arm the populace, and set General Sigisvult to guard the coasts."

"Excellent points, Mother, but I will also bring Aetius home. The people have faith in his abilities."

Val's firmness made her pause. Had her hatred for Aetius blinded her to the best interests of Rome? But if he rode to the rescue while Val lazed behind impregnable marshes, the people, and—more importantly—the army might wonder why they bothered with an Emperor.

"Of course, the Emperor will do as he wishes. Might I make another suggestion?"

Val nodded.

"Move the court to Rome."

Mutters of dismay rose from the rest of the council. "The Emperor shouldn't risk himself. It's safer here in Ravenna."

Placidia sneered. "The Emperor needs to show the people he is with them. He needs to put some backbone in the senate, rally the populace to his cause, and show Gaiseric that Italy is not a rotten fruit he can smash under his heel."

Val turned to his personal scribe. "Send orders as the Augusta directs. We leave for Rome within the week."

He stood. His council scrambled to rise as well. Placidia saw sparks in her son's eyes. *Good! The boy is not stupid. Maybe his father's blood will show at last.*

SIGISVULT SPURRED HIS HORSE to a ground-eating lope outside the walls of Naples. His retinue kept up the brisk pace. Their mounts came from his own horse farm in Spain, a lucrative contract and particular interest of his. He missed Hammer, Placidia's first gift to him, but this gelding shared his grandsire's blood bay color and markings. He touched the animal with his heel and gave only the slightest pressure on the reins. Well-trained, it immediately slowed to a trot. Sigisvult grinned. It felt good to be in the field again, even under such dire circumstances.

Sigisvult and his retinue approached the first training camp and entered the walls without being challenged. Patched tents and lean-tos dotted the inside. A cloud of flies and the stench of offal hovered over the combination latrine and garbage pit. "Where's the commandant of this camp?" he roared.

"Sir?" A balding man, his paunch straining wine-stained leather armor, stepped out of the only wooden building. Seeing Sigisvult and his heavily armed retinue, the man blanched and bobbed his head. "I didn't expect you until tomorrow, General."

"Obviously." Sigisvult pranced his horse closer. He glared at the man. "No one stopped or challenged me. Gaiseric himself could ride in here and slit your throats before you realized he was among you. Who is watching the coast? Why are no troops training in the field?"

Blood suffused the commandant's face, turning his cheeks the same ruddy hue as his nose and eyes. "With all respect, General, you don't know with what weak reeds I have to build a stout wall. I have a handful of veterans—most brought out of retirement—to watch the coasts, and a herd of farmers who don't know a sword from their own asses."

"You have no more or less than any commandant on the coast. A good commander makes the most of his men. Set some sharp-eyed boys to watch the coasts and light the signal fires. Bring your veterans back to train the farmers." Sigisvult dismounted. "Call your troops to order for inspection."

A horn summoned the men to the parade ground beyond the walls. Barely two hundred recruits shuffled into ragged lines. Sigisvult felt some sympathy for the commandant. These soldiers still had dirt under their fingernails and straw in their hair. A few wore metal helmets or brandished swords that looked as if they had been in the family for generations. Some carried bows or slings. Most had no kit beyond patched red tunics and leather helmets.

Such as these will not save us from Gaiseric's hordes. Our only hope is reinforcements from Theodosius. Until then…

"Men, by order of our most Gracious Emperor Valentinian, you will be armed and trained to defend your homes and farms. Gaiseric and his Vandals are in Sicily. They have swift ships and can land anywhere on our coast. You are our first defense."

Frightened murmurs rose. Many turned pale. The stench of fear soured the air. A lean man, skin darkened and creased by a lifetime in the sun, spoke up. "What can we do? We know nothing but farming and herding."

"Can you pitch hay with a fork, or wield a knife to butcher meat?" Several heads nodded. "Then you can learn the spear and the sword. Can you hunt with sling or bow?" More nodded. "Then you can attack from a distance. Can you run or ride?"

"That's what I want—to run or ride from here!" someone shouted. Several chuckled.

Sigisvult smiled. "I know you are not professional soldiers. You'd sooner be home, but," his face turned grim, "if Gaiseric lands, he will show no mercy. In Carthage, on Sicily, his men kill all they find—men, women, and children. They torture their captives: rape the women and little girls before their father's eyes. Is this what you want for your mothers, daughters, and sisters?"

"No," came the shocked response.

"The Vandals cut off men's cocks and make them eat them before cutting open their bellies and pulling out their entrails. Is this what you want for your fathers, brothers, and sons?"

"No!" Some rattled their meager weapons.

"The Vandals burn fields, slaughter animals, and carve unborn children from their mother's wombs. Is this what you want for your farms and wives?" Sigisvult roared.

"NO!" The recruits raised their fists in the air, chanting. "NO! NO! NO!"

"Then you must learn to fight!"

And may God and Constantinople help us.

Sicily, 441

"THE ROMANS HAVE LANDED, GREAT KING."

Gaiseric, King of the Vandals, scowled at the messenger; a mere boy but already scarred across the face from battle. His troops were few, but effective. "Where? How many?"

"In the east. Over twenty thousand."

"Four times our number." Gaiseric rubbed his stubbled jaw. "So Theodosius pulls his cousin's balls out of the vise—again." His eyes flicked over the villa he occupied, a rustic place compared to his estate outside Carthage. Stone walls, an overgrown herb garden, broken fountain; it would be no great loss. "I had hoped to take the Augusta's farms, but the old bitch still has some bite in her. It's time to negotiate again, eh, son?"

Huneric eyed his father. "What do you have in mind this time? Corsica? Sardinia? Rome itself?"

"In time, my son. The Empire is a toothless wolf, whining and licking its wounds, but a wounded animal can still be dangerous." Gaiseric levered himself out of his chair, favoring the leg that had been injured by a horse fall. He put his arm about his boy's shoulders. "For now, we will have our freedom. No more 'Allies of the Empire' forced to send grain and tribute."

"An independent kingdom? But all pay tribute to Rome."

"Not the Huns. Theodosius pays Bleda and Attila seven hundred pounds of gold a year to stay clear of his borders. I will be King, under no man's yoke, and you will have an Imperial marriage." He eyed his son with calculation, then clapped him on the back. "The Theodosian blood grows thin. They produce only daughters. My grandson will wear the diadem and command the legions of Rome."

Huneric stepped back. "How do you propose ridding me of my current wife without angering her father?"

"Theodoric is a poor excuse for a king—squatting on the tiny patch of Gaul the Romans gave him. We have nothing to fear from his anger. You are not fond of that Gothic whore, are you?"

"Amaltha is of little consequence to me. I wed her only at your orders, Father."

"Good. I have a plan that will rid us of our unwanted baggage and strike at Theodoric, as well." Gaiseric bared his teeth in a grin that showed more cunning than mirth. "Now let's send to the Roman commander and sue for peace."

Carthage, 441

AMALTHA MET HER HUSBAND AND FATHER-IN-LAW in the atrium of their villa outside Carthage. Her father's Gothic court in Toulouse had nothing so lavish. White marble colonnades sheltered the rooms from the southern sun. Fountains splashed in the atrium and garden, cooling the air. Mosaics and murals festooned the walls and floors with brilliant colors: red, turquoise, gold—gold paint, gold tiles, gold plate, gold drinking cups. The Vandal court was an exile of sorts, but it had its compensations.

She held out a cup encrusted with lapis lazuli and filled with rich red wine. "Welcome home, Great King."

Gaiseric took the goblet, drained the wine, and wiped his mouth on the sleeve of his tunic.

"Husband." Amaltha bowed to Huneric. "I've prepared a feast for this evening, to celebrate your victories." Huneric refused to meet her eyes.

"Excellent, Daughter." Gaiseric's cool gaze chilled her blood.

THAT EVENING, Amaltha shared a couch and plate with Gaiseric. He gorged on one of his favorite dishes—pigs' testicles lightly fried in olive oil and seasoned with fish sauce. He held a bloody morsel up to her mouth.

She turned away.

"Eat, woman. Is there something wrong with the meat?"

"I have no appetite for that dish, Great King."

"I thought all women ate balls when they got the chance," one of the Vandal chiefs cried. His companions acclaimed his wit by pounding their fists on the table. She ignored the jibe, inured to their coarse humor.

Gaiseric frowned. "You never turn away from food." He pinched a roll of fat on her upper arm until she gasped in pain. He roared with laughter. The rest of the men joined in. Amaltha, uneasy, reached for her wine.

Gaiseric popped the morsel into his mouth and chewed, smacking his lips in mock ecstasy. He reached for another piece, then shivered, moaned, and clutched his belly.

"What?" Amaltha sat up. "Are you ill, Great King?"

Foam flecked Gaiseric's lips.

Great God in Heaven, what's amiss? Amaltha recoiled from her father-in-law.

Huneric leaned across to sniff at the plate. "This sauce smells of almonds, Father. She wouldn't eat because it is poisoned!"

"Poison?" Gaiseric gaped at Amaltha. "You murdering Gothic bitch. You poisoned me! Did your father send you here for my death?"

"No!" Amaltha's blue eyes widened. "I would never harm you, Great King." She turned to Huneric, clutching his arm. "Help me, Husband. I am a faithful daughter to your father. I could never take part in such a vile undertaking."

"Murderess! Poisoner! Kill the witch!" echoed around the room. Warriors drew their knives.

Huneric firmly removed her hand from his arm. "I renounce you, Amaltha, daughter of Theodoric. You are a murderess."

Amaltha took a deep breath, looking around the table at the agitated men. She saw her fate looming. "I am falsely accused. Is no man here my friend?"

"She has killed me!" Gaiseric pointed a shaking finger at Amaltha. "I must be revenged."

"So that is how the wind blows." Amaltha folded her arms tightly over her breasts. "I am to die. My father will take revenge on all your diseased hides!" She spat her anger.

"No, you will not die. We will pack you off to your father with a message never to cross the Vandals." Huneric yanked her before the others. "Hold her."

Two burly Vandals grabbed Amaltha's arms, pulling them tight behind her back. Huneric drew a knife and tested its edge on his thumb. "I always liked your pretty nose."

"My...no," she moaned. Amaltha backed into her captors' stalwart bodies. One man twisted his hand in her hair to hold her head still. "Huneric, have mercy. Kill me, please, but don't do this." Mutilated, disgraced. Death would be kinder.

In an instant, Huneric sliced off his wife's nose. Pain shocked her brain into stupefaction. Two more cuts, and her ears decorated the tile floor. Blood ran down her arms, and her screams echoed off marble walls.

Ravenna, 442

PLACIDIA RESTED HER FOREHEAD IN HER HAND as she read the proposed treaty with the Vandals. She dropped it on her worktable. "Val, you cannot go through with this."

"Mother, this is my decision."

"And it's the wrong one!" She slapped the table with the flat of her hand. Why did he have to be willful at all the wrong times? When he needed backbone, he bent like a reed; when he needed flexibility, he was stubborn as a mule, just like his uncle Honorius.

"You are a fool if you think giving Gaiseric more land, and pledging your oldest daughter to his son, will keep him from our shores. Let Sigisvult raise an army and attack with Aspar from Constantinople."

"Aspar failed once." Val shook his head. "My councilors agree, this is the best course of action."

"Your other councilors are plotters or pawns, with less than the best interest of the Empire in their hearts. There is a time to delay, and a time to take action. Now is the time to strike the head off the Vandal snake."

"Do you have the best interest of the Empire at heart, Mother, or are you blinded by your loyalty to the Goths? Amaltha tried to poison Gaiseric."

"He survived, didn't he? I know these people. The Goths hunted the Vandals in Spain at Rome's behest. This mutilation was a deliberate insult to Theodoric, and cleared the way to propose an imperial marriage." Placidia grabbed her son's arm. "Would you truly send your daughter to that savage Huneric? Eudocia's only four."

"What would you have me do, Mother? That's what daughters are for—to cement relations with foes as well as allies." Val shook off his mother's hands and paced the marble floor. "I could send him Honoria, and bag two birds with one arrow."

"No!" Her heart rose to her throat. "You can't give your sister over to such a fate."

"She's become quarrelsome lately, but no, I will not send Honoria. I have no sons—yet—and don't want Gaiseric claiming the diadem for Honoria's child, as you did for me."

"He will anyway, if you give him Eudocia." Placidia folded her hands in her lap, as if in prayer.

"They will have to wait for her. Much can happen in ten years. Gaiseric or Huneric might die."

"Better Eudocia die than go to those...butchers!"

"Mother, you were happy with your barbarian marriage. Why curse this one?"

"Ataulf was more Roman than Goth and...I loved him. These Vandals are savages, little more than pirates." Placidia lowered her voice to a whisper. "I beg of you, don't sign this treaty."

"I have no choice, if we want peace." He applied the royal seal with solemn deliberation.

Placidia turned away, shoulders stiff, tears of frustration welling in her eyes. She had wanted Val to be more decisive. Now she must live with the emperor she molded, and hope he would be good enough.

CHAPTER 36

Ravenna, 449

PLACIDIA PRAYED FOR PEACE—not for the Empire, which, in spite of her fears, had had seven years of relative peace—but for her soul. On this brisk fall day, Placidia sat in her private chapel, reflecting on her sixty-one years.

Would it have been different if I had never met Ataulf? Yes. I never would have known love—nor had my heart broken. That is the price of love and long life, bearing the losses. So many losses, so much blood, and what have I to show for it?

She looked up at the mural of Mary holding baby Jesus. *Mother of God, forgive my sins. What I did, I did for the children—both living and dead.*

She rose from the floor with aching knees. Lucilla, growing a little stiff in the joints herself, helped Placidia to her feet. "Do you go to the hospital today, Mistress?"

Placidia had taken up charitable works out of boredom, as Aetius and his minions took over more of the government. "No. Today I visit one of my own who is sick." At Lucilla's puzzled look, she explained, "I hear Honoria has been unwell of late."

They made their way to the wing of the Imperial palace that Honoria had claimed for her own. Placidia had few occasions to visit Honoria in her quarters, and looked with disapproval on the subtly erotic tone of the murals, mosaics, and statues decorating them. They were all classic scenes—nymphs bathing,

Pan coupling with a goat, Venus rising from the sea—but seemed more suitable to a brothel than a maiden's rooms. Placidia and Lucilla entered Honoria's antechamber and made for her bedroom. A delicate boy, probably a eunuch, made a feeble attempt to block their way.

"Move, boy. Do you not know who I am?"

"Yes, Augusta, but my mistress asked not to be disturbed. She is ill."

"And who better to see to her health than her mother?"

Placidia pushed the boy aside and strode into the bedroom. Lamps shed some dim light, but Placidia stumbled over a pair of sandals. As her eyes adjusted, she took in the disarray of the room: clothes left in piles, food spilled on a table, wine staining the carpet. Whimpers and moans came from behind the bed curtains.

Placidia's anger towered. *I'll have her chamberlain whipped. Where are her slaves? Why is there no one to care for my daughter?*

She moved quickly to the bed and pulled the curtains apart. "Honoria, my child…"

She did not see the pale, ill daughter she expected, but one flushed in the throes of pleasure with a man. The three froze for a moment. Then Honoria smiled.

"Mother. What brings you to my quarters?"

"Who is that?" Placidia pointed a shaking finger at the sensuously handsome man rolling off her daughter.

"Eugenius, my chamberlain." Honoria reached for his hand and kissed the palm. "You may leave, darling. I have things to discuss with my mother."

Eugenius clutched a tunic over his genitals and retreated backwards, bobbing his head. At the exit, he turned and ran. Honoria climbed out of bed, carelessly draping a silk sheet about her body. It did nothing to conceal the telltale thickness of her waist or the bulge of her stomach.

"What is the meaning of this?" Placidia flushed red, veins throbbing in her forehead; fury made her voice hoarse.

"I should think that is obvious, Mother. We made the beast with two backs and, as sometimes happens when a man and woman engage in such activities, I am with child."

Honoria poured a goblet of wine and handed it to her mother. Placidia took a gulp.

"Who is the father?"

"Eugenius, of course."

"Honoria, how could you disgrace us so?"

"Disgrace? I found love where I could." Honoria filled a second goblet and smiled at Placidia over the lip. "You bore a child to a barbarian. At least Eugenius is of Roman stock."

Placidia struck her daughter's hand with all her strength, sending the goblet flying. She shouted, "Lucilla, bring Val!" then turned back to her errant daughter. "I bore a child conceived in wedlock to a king, not a bastard gotten by a servant."

Honoria wiped the wine from her face and neck. Her mouth thinned. "What of Sigisvult? He is not royalty, although you treat him so."

Placidia stood, choking on a retort that would not come out. She said, between clenched teeth, "I do not commit treason with Sigisvult."

"Do not or did not? Do you think me a fool?" Honoria raised a brow. "I've seen the way you two look at one another." Her shoulders slumped. She held her hands out to her mother, palm up. "I'm thirty-one, Mother. What would you have me do? Become an avowed virgin, like Pulcheria?"

"Better virginity and holy works than this abomination!"

"I know your plans for me. I'm a pawn in your game of power. If Val and Eudoxia had had no children, I could step in as the dutiful breeder to continue the line. But they do have children, and might have more, so any child of mine would be a threat—a rival—to your beloved son. Therefore, you keep me barren."

The blood drained from Placidia's face. "You did this to gain power over your brother, to plot treason?"

"No!" Tears came to Honoria's eyes. "Mother, do you not see the way your mind leaps? You cannot even conceive that I did this for no other reason than to be happy. Eugenius is kind; he makes me feel loved."

Placidia put her hands to her mouth, eyes wide. The whispery voice of Constantius on his deathbed echoed, "Be kind to her." She thought freeing Honoria from responsibilities and the specter of a forced marriage would make her happy. How could she have been so wrong?

Before she could reply, Val burst into the room, face suffused with blood, eyes bulging like his father's.

"What's this I hear?" He strode to his sister and grabbed her arm, dislodging her sheet and exposing her pregnancy. "So it's true. My whore of a sister brings disgrace on my name." Holding Honoria firmly, he turned to Placidia. "Did you know about this, Mother?"

Placidia covered Honoria again. "I just found out. Let me handle this, Son."

"No. I am the *pater familias* of this family, and this is my business." He shook Honoria, the flesh under his fingers turning white. "Who is the dog that rutted with you, bitch?"

"You call me a bitch, when you hop into more beds than a flea?"

Val slapped Honoria. Blood gushed from her nose. She clamped her mouth shut and jutted her jaw. Placidia knew that look. She also saw the murderous rage in Val's face. For the first time in her life, Placidia feared her son, but not for herself. Imperial princesses had been executed for fornication.

"Eugenius," Placidia said.

"No, Mother!" Honoria turned a horror-stricken face to her. Placidia dreaded what she had to do.

"His name is Eugenius. He's her chamberlain."

"Guards!"

Two uniformed officers stepped into the room.

"Arrest the Augusta's chamberlain, a man named Eugenius."

The soldiers saluted and exited.

Honoria struggled in Val's grasp. "Eugenius did nothing wrong. I seduced him."

Placidia grabbed Val's free arm. "Let your sister go, before you harm her or the babe."

Val released her. "Better the babe dies now than after it's born."

"You would murder an innocent child?" Honoria's hands hovered protectively over her stomach. Meeting his determined eyes, she curled her hands into claws and snarled like a wolf defending her cub. "If anything happens to my baby, I'll see you dead!"

"Enough!" Placidia wedged herself between them. "Both of you. The slaves have enough to tattle through the palace. I will not have you giving them more. Honoria, you are confined to your room. I will post a guard." She escorted her daughter back to the bed and murmured, "I will do what I can to moderate your brother's rage."

"Don't let him hurt Eugenius," Honoria pleaded.

"Val, come with me. We will discuss this calmly." Placidia took her son by the arm and escorted him from the room. She nodded to Lucilla to stay with Honoria.

Val muttered imprecations all the way to Placidia's sitting room. She dismissed all her servants and served them both a strong red wine. He downed two goblets before his brow unfurrowed.

"You should leave this to me," Placidia said.

"No. I will not have people sniggering behind my back that I am not a man in my own home."

"What do you wish to do?"

"That treasonous chamberlain will be executed as soon as I sign the order. I will have the palace doctor abort the child and send Honoria to Constantinople for safekeeping. A few years living with Pulcheria and her nuns should drive the lust out of the slut." He took another gulp of wine. "It drove it out of my wife."

"Son, I know this is a shock, but we should not make decisions in haste. Especially ones that cannot be undone." Eugenius' fate had been sealed the moment he entered an Imperial Princess' bed—a treasonous offense. She only hoped to save her daughter more grief. "An abortion at this late date would be dangerous for Honoria. She is at least five months gone. I recommend we keep her in close confinement, and expose the child once it is born."

"You know best about these women's things. I just want the bastard gone."

"I understand completely, and will ensure it happens. As to Honoria," Placidia stared into her wine. "Sending her to Pulcheria will not solve the problem."

"Pulcheria can handle anything, including my wayward sister."

"Pulcheria could keep her under her thumb, but at what price? Honoria is bitter and unhappy. If you two have an obvious break, she will draw dissidents like sweets draw stinging wasps."

"You propose we reconcile?" Val snorted. "I doubt Honoria would agree."

"Honoria has no role, no importance, other than as your sister. Since you have children, even that role has diminished. She has no husband or children of her own, no household to run or care for. Boredom and loneliness have brought more than one woman low."

Val sipped a third goblet of wine, frowning. "I will consider another solution for Honoria, but the chamberlain and the child must die."

"Of course."

PLACIDIA GRIPPED HONORIA'S HAND as she grunted and pushed.

"Almost there, dearie. Push again." The midwife Nikarete, Placidia, and

Lucilla were the only ones in attendance. Unlike a normal Imperial birth, where nearly every woman of the court cluttered the room, this birth took place in dark and secret. Nikarete was skilled and discreet; the only one Placidia trusted with this task, since Machaon had died of a fever five years earlier. Luckily, it was an easy birth for a first time mother.

Honoria groaned and pushed the baby from her womb. The child gave a lusty cry.

Honoria sat up on the birthing chair and reached for her baby. "Let me see."

But Nikarete had her instructions. After cutting the cord, she bundled the baby in a receiving blanket and handed it to Lucilla, who left the room.

Honoria cried, "Mother, no. Let me hold my baby."

"It's for the best, dear." Placidia smoothed the damp hair away from her daughter's forehead. "The baby is dead to you."

Tears spilled down Honoria's cheeks, mingling with the sweat.

Nikarete said, "Push once more, princess. We have to get the afterbirth out, or you could die."

"I would rather die than marry that prig Val found for me." Her body betrayed her with an involuntary push.

"Bassus Herculanus is a rich senator of excellent character. He will take good care of you."

"Keep me hidden away from court, you mean." Honoria turned such a pitiful look on Placidia that her heart nearly broke. "I want my baby, please, Mother."

"That won't happen, my child. Marry Herculanus and have more children."

Tears streamed down her daughter's face. She turned her head away.

PLACIDIA LEFT HONORIA SLEEPING, and made her weary way to her quarters. She found Lucilla cooing to the fretful baby. Lucilla raised her scarred face to her mistress. "It's a boy."

"Of course. That makes things more complicated. The first son of this generation—a bastard who can only be the pawn of treason and center of dissent. A daughter we might have been able to keep close." Placidia dropped into a chair. "Bring him to me."

Lucilla placed the bundle in her arms. She had cleaned the blood from his body, but the baby still had the misshapen head, squashed features, and vague blue eyes of all infants. His helplessness tugged at Placidia's heart. She should have followed her own advice to Honoria and not seen or held the child. She handed him back to Lucilla.

"You know what to do."

The faithful servant wrapped the baby in a plain wool blanket, nodding.

HONORIA SOBBED INTO HER PILLOWS. A week had passed since the birth, and the pain hadn't gone away. Her breasts ached, leaking milk. That wretched midwife had prescribed poultices, but they did little good. She cramped and bled, and yet that was nothing compared to the turmoil of her mind. She stared around her dark, confining rooms. Guards were posted outside her door. Mute slaves cared for her daily needs.

She started pummeling her pillows. The softness absorbed her blows and fed her rage.

Just like Mother. Nothing stops her. Nothing hurts her.

Fire burned in her belly. Her heart hurt and her head throbbed. Dark shadows shimmered with the shapes of her demons. She clawed at the cushions, succeeding only in breaking two of her nails. The new pain drove her to more frenzy. She smashed a glass vase and used the shards to rip open the pillows.

Feathers exploded in the air, drifting like snow.

Blood dripped on the whiteness.

Honoria looked at her hand, sliced with cuts from the glass. She laughed.

It would be so easy.

She held a shard over her left wrist, then caught her reflection in a mirror.

Who is that madwoman covered in feathers and blood? Surely not Justa Grata Honoria Augusta. She would never let herself be so used.

The fire subsided, replaced by an icy calm. Honoria let the shard drop, brushed off the feathers, and bound her hand in a silk scarf.

No. They will not be rid of me so easily.

CHAPTER 37

Rome, 450

PLACIDIA WATCHED THE SUN SET over the city of Rome. Val, seated across from her, put his seal to the orders bringing Sigisvult home from his command in Spain.

"Is this all, Mother? I'm late for a dinner with Herculanus. We are settling the marriage contract. Then Honoria will be another man's problem."

Placidia sighed. She had hoped to mend the breach between her children over the three months since Honoria gave birth, but all her efforts went to naught. Honoria was silent and truculent, blaming her for the death of Eugenius and the loss of her baby. Val was noisy and truculent; blaming Placidia for Honoria's continued defiance.

"That's all for now." She rose from her chair with the help of a cane, which she had started to use to ease her swollen knees and painful hips. Before she could reach the door, the Master of Offices entered and prostrated himself, face white, hands shaking.

"What dire news do you bring?" Val asked, recognizing a new barrier to his pleasurable evening.

"My Emperor, my fastest post rider brought this from the court in Constantinople, with greetings from your co-Emperor Theodosius and his most urgent desire that you read his message immediately upon receipt." The man rose and handed Val a flat leather-bound package.

Val took out several folded parchment pages. He broke the seal and scanned the first page. His face went white, then red. His mouth twisted in an ugly snarl. He tossed the pages at Placidia. "That treacherous whore! Sister or not, this time she dies." He rose and strode purposefully toward the door.

Placidia grabbed his arm as he passed, holding on tight. Her heart thumped painfully. She had trouble getting the words past her fear. "What did the message say? Surely it can't warrant such a drastic response."

He ground his teeth. "Attila, King of the Huns, demands Honoria's hand in marriage, and half the western empire as her dowry."

"Great and Merciful Lord Jesus! Why would he make such an outrageous demand?"

"Because your daughter sent him a ring and money, asking for his assistance. He chose to interpret the gesture as an offer of marriage. Theo says I should send her packing to the Hun and hope that satisfies him." He tore his arm from her grasp and bolted out the door, shouting for his guards.

Placidia grabbed her cane and hobbled after him as fast as her swollen joints allowed. She heard the shouts and screams coming from Honoria's rooms. Bursting in, she found Val holding Honoria by her hair, pummeling her. From the scratches on his face and arms, she had put up some resistance. Now she hung limply in his grip.

Placidia rushed to her son to hold back his arm with both hands. Her feeble strength could not deter him. Bone crunched as he smashed his fist into Honoria's face. Placidia put all the authority of over thirty years of rule into her voice. "Stop this instant! Valentinian, you are making a spectacle of yourself."

He lowered his hand and stood there, panting. He let go of Honoria's hair. She slid to the floor.

Val turned to his guards. "Arrest all her household. I want them tortured. Find out who helped her in this treachery. Bring their statements to me, then execute any and all involved."

"No," Honoria protested from the floor. "Spare my people and I will tell you everything."

Placidia's heart steadied. Her daughter retained some sensibility.

"Yes, you will tell me, Sister, and so will your people." Val motioned to the guards. "Arrest the younger Augusta as well."

"Val, is this wise? Why not set a guard on her door and let me get a doctor?"

"A guard did not keep her from sending a ring to Attila. I take no chances that she plots further treachery. She goes to prison until I decide in what manner she should die."

"Son, you must promise me, on the soul of your father, not to make any rash decisions. If Attila hears that you executed Honoria, he might use that as an excuse to invade."

Val shook his head, eyes clouded with rage at being balked yet again.

"You must promise this!" Placidia demanded. "It could mean your empire."

"I will wait, but not long." Val turned his back and stalked from the room.

Placidia rushed to her daughter's side. "My child, why? Why did you do this terrible thing?"

"You of all people should understand, Mother." Honoria smiled through split lips. Two teeth were missing. "You taught me everything I know."

One of the guards nearby shuffled, clearing his throat. "I'm sorry, Augusta, but I have my orders."

Placidia stood. "The Emperor ordered her imprisonment, but not the manner of the accommodations. She is to be housed in a cell with light, air, and a clean bed. I will send a doctor to attend her."

The guard bowed low. "As you wish, Augusta. I will see to it myself."

Placidia left, back bowed, retiring to her rooms. It was best to let Val calm down before approaching him. She also needed to calm herself. Honoria's actions necessitated a death sentence—conspiring with the enemies of the Roman Empire.

My own daughter!

After all the years Placidia spent countering invasions, her daughter had invited the barbarians in.

A sudden pain shot through Placidia's head, behind her eyes. She clutched her temples and sat, dizzy and moaning.

Lucilla entered immediately, kneeling to examine her face. "The head pain?"

Placidia nodded, gripping Lucilla's hand.. "Have you heard?"

Lucilla shook her head. Placidia recounted the events of the afternoon. "Will you see that the doctor attends her?"

"Of course, Mistress. Should I ask him to attend you first?"

"No. The pain is subsiding. I fear for Honoria. She is quite battered."

"I will see to it at once. I will also have your maid prepare you a warm bath."

"Thank you, my one true friend. I do not know how I could have survived without you all these years."

*****

THE NEXT MORNING, Placidia visited her daughter. The cell was better than most, with light and air from barred windows high up on two walls. The room was dry, and the bed of feathers rather than straw. A three-legged stool sat in one corner. The other had a stand with a wash bowl, pitcher, and chamber pot.

Placidia carried a lamp, to chase the shadows from the corners. Honoria lay on her bed, eyes closed. Her left eye was so swollen it could not open. A bandage on her right cheek attested to a wound that would scar. Purpling bruises covered her face, arms and legs.

At the sound of the door opening, Honoria opened her good eye. "Mother. Did you come to take me to the executioner?"

"Of course not." Placidia rummaged in a bag and pulled out a brush. "I came to brush your hair."

"Go away." Honoria rolled onto her side, her back to Placidia.

Placidia sat on the bed, picked up a strand of her daughter's dark brown hair, and began brushing. She caught the delicate scent of lavender. Honoria didn't move.

"One of my few memories of my own mother was of her brushing my hair as she sang a lullaby. She died when I was very young."

"Is that your excuse? You didn't know how to be a mother, because you never had one?"

"I make no excuses. I am what God made me—an Augusta, and a ruler of the most powerful empire on earth. You never truly understood what that meant." Placidia put down the brush and extended her hands. "I have killed with these hands, ordered men executed, sent others to their death in battle. It scars the soul and hardens the heart. I had hoped to spare you such a life."

"Spare me?" Honoria rolled over and sat up. "Look what your mother love condemned me to—a useless life."

"I made a terrible mistake." Placidia picked up another lock of her daughter's hair, felt its silkiness against her fingers. "You and I are very alike. Had you been a son, your ambition and ability would have stood the Empire in good stead."

"But you have a son."

"He is unfit to rule in these troubled times." At Honoria's surprised look, Placidia continued. "I never wanted to admit it. He is not a bad emperor, but I fear his lack of greatness will hasten the dismantling of the Empire. We have already lost half of Africa to the Vandals. Aetius is the only bulwark we have against the Huns, and I have poisoned Val against him."

"I am surprised to hear my infallible mother admitting to mistakes." Honoria tossed her hair over her shoulder, wincing.

"I have made many mistakes, but only in hindsight. At the time they seemed the right things to do. A ruler learns not to regret past mistakes, but to minimize the consequences." Placidia looked hard at her daughter. "Are you willing to live with the consequences of your actions? Attila stands ready to invade in your name."

"It seemed the right thing to do at the time," Honoria echoed. "I only followed in your footsteps. The Goths were always yours to command. You used them as a threat against your brother on several occasions."

"Never a threat, only a refuge. I never would have chosen the Goths over Rome."

Honoria snorted. "If you choose to believe so."

"What if Val sends you to Attila? Will you be for or against Rome?"

"Val is lazy, but he's not stupid. He can't afford the chance Attila would use a son of mine as an excuse to claim the whole of the Roman Empire. Val also learned from your example. That is why he wanted me barren, or married to a nice safe man he could control."

"You leave him few choices. Death will likely be your fate."

"You left *me* few choices, Mother. If you had not jealously kept me from my brother and the government, I could have taken your place. Val and I might have ruled as do Theo and Pulcheria." Honoria set her jaw. "Better death than this barren life. You must live with the consequences of your actions. I suspect my death will cause you little grief."

Placidia gasped. "You truly believe that?"

Honoria remained silent.

"Oh, my child! I did what I did out of love for you. I thought I was giving you freedom."

"And your love for me left you free to rule, with no interference from Val or me. It is convenient when love lets you do as you wish."

Honoria's words struck Placidia to the heart. Had she stunted her children to satisfy her own needs? She grasped the edge of the bed to keep from falling as another blinding headache struck.

As the pain subsided, she rose, leaning heavily on her cane. "May God forgive both of us for our thoughtless actions. I will not ask your forgiveness, because you have hardened your heart against me. I only hope you can look back on your own decisions with more compassion than you give me. Good-bye, Daughter."

Placidia was met with stony silence. She dropped the bag of toiletries on the bed and left.

"No, MOTHER. SHE MUST DIE." Val paced the floor of his little-used library. His mother sat, frail and tired-looking, in a gilt chair. When had she grown so old? It seemed only a short while ago she had raced him across the countryside on a hunt, or just for the pleasure of the ride. She had laughed when her hair came loose and whipped in the wind. His wife was far more beautiful, but bloodless. She never had the sense of life his mother had. He understood why Placidia had inspired love and devotion all her life.

She rose and hobbled over to her son. He stopped his frenetic movement and took her arm. "Sit, Mother."

"No." She lowered herself to her knees. Pain flitted across her face. She bowed her head. "I ask this not as an empress to an emperor, advising against angering a dangerous foe. I ask this as a mother who loves both her children. Do not blame your sister for my mistakes."

"Mother, please get up." Val lifted his mother to her feet and helped her to a chair. "How can I forgive her? She conspired with barbarians against the Empire."

"As did I, in my youth. As did General Aetius, in his. Attila has been consolidating the tribes and rattling his sword for years. Constantinople is too well defended; it was only a matter of time before he set his sights on Rome. Honoria's foolish action gave him an excuse for something he would have done anyway."

His mother closed her eyes and raised her hands to rub her temples.

"Are your headaches back?"

"It is nothing; it goes quickly." She grasped his hand. "Please, my dear son, forgive me and your sister. Promise me you will not be the instrument of her death."

"You ask much of me, Mother."

"And you have always given me much. Please grant me this last wish. I feel my age, and fear I will not be long with you."

Val had given no thought to life without his mother. He did not want to think of it now. "You are fatigued from all the commotion. We will go to our villa on the coast. The sea air will revive you."

"Honoria?"

"I will see."

His mother rose unsteadily, groaned, and fell back into the chair.

"Mother!"

The right side of her face drooped like melted wax. He rushed to her side.

"Mother, you cannot leave me. I need you!" Blood raced in Val's veins, but his hands were cold. "Guards!"

His captain raced into the room, sword drawn against a possible enemy.

"Get the doctor! The Augusta is unwell."

The man dashed out, Val's curses speeding him on his way.

Rome, November 27, 450

SIGISVULT CARRIED PLACIDIA'S FRAIL FORM into the garden. Under the weak November sun, bees furiously gathered the last of the nectar. Wood smoke scented the air.

He settled, with her in his arms, on a bench beneath a barren grape arbor. The dappled sunshine did little to disguise the ruin that was once his beautiful queen. Placidia weighed little more than a child, her once lustrous hair more white than brown, the right side of her face and body drooping and useless. Tears stood in his eyes. He looked away.

She raised her left hand to his cheek and said, in a slurred voice, "My strong right arm. I need you for one more task."

"As you command."

"You must free Honoria. Hide her. Lucilla knows my plans. When I die, Val will take his revenge."

"You will recover, with Lucilla's care and a little rest." An icy fist grabbed his heart. He had seen rivers of blood and dealt gory death without flinching, but the thought of a world without Placidia numbed his mind. He held her as if she were made of the thinnest glass.

"Six months like this." She noticed a spider struggling in the grasp of a wasp.

"I grow weary of this half-life. If only I could have stayed Queen and not been Empress. If only…" She smiled with the left side of her mouth. Some of the old life came back to her eyes. "Don't mourn me when I'm gone, my friend… my love."

Her breathing didn't slow. It simply stopped, between one breath and the next.

Sigisvult couldn't get enough air into his lungs—he could only gasp. Tears streamed down his face as he clasped Placidia's body to his and kissed his queen good-bye.

Epilog

Rome, 461

HONORIA SLIPPED FROM THE PORTICO of St. Peter's into the adjoining plaza, past Caligula's obelisk, and through the door of the round building that served as a mausoleum for her family. Dressed in plain brown robes, her lumpy nose, scarred cheek, and graying hair effectively disguised her from anyone in her past.

This was her first visit to the recovering city of Rome since her mother's death. The Vandals had leisurely and thoroughly looted the city six years earlier, carrying off anything and anyone of value, including her sister-in-law and nieces. She heard recently that Emperor Leo of the East had negotiated a release for Eudoxia and Placidia the Younger. They would soon escape to his court in Constantinople. She shuddered. Poor Eudocia was stuck as the wife of that odious Huneric.

Better you than me, niece, Thank you again, Sigisvult, for saving me from such a fate.

Sigisvult had secreted her away shortly after her mother's death, saving her from her brother's wrath with a story she had died of fever. He settled her and Lucilla outside Milan, where she lived quietly, posing as a widow with her companion. Her neighbors believed the pension she received from the former Augusta was for her service in some capacity.

Poor Sigisvult. He never fully recovered from her mother's death. When

Honoria heard he had died in the great battle against the Huns, ten years ago, she thought it just as well. He died a hero's death. Mother would have been proud. Her Goths fought bravely that day, but many died, including the Gothic King Theodoric.

Honoria entered the dimly lit building. She had planned never to set foot in the mausoleum, but an urgent need brought her to Rome. Curiosity and nostalgia guided her feet. The building was unique in design and sumptuous in decoration. Where most modern mausoleums were in the shape of a Latin cross, this one was a throwback to pagan imperial days—two round buildings attached by a covered walkway. The cupola was covered with a magnificent mosaic of a night sky glittering with golden stars, surrounding a large gold cross. A mosaic of St. Lawrence graced the entrance, but the mosaic facing the door made Honoria smile. How typical of royalty. There sat Jesus as a shepherd with his sheep, but not a humble Jesus. This Good Shepherd wore robes of gold and a royal purple cloak, and around his head glowed a halo of gold.

Placidia's alabaster sarcophagus stood upright behind the altar, with Constantius' and Valentinian's marble ones in front of the altar to Placidia's left. Honorius' lay to her right.

So you still rule over the family, Mother. All except me. I understand you even had a small silver casket taken from Barcelona and placed beneath the altar.

She glided to her brother's sarcophagus and ran her hand over the dusty edge. *When Mother said your lack of greatness would doom the West, I told her you were lazy, not stupid. But you proved her right again, my foolish brother. Why did you murder Aetius after he defeated the Huns? Did jealous courtiers whisper in your ears, or mother's ghost come back to bid you send Aetius to the next world where they could continue their rivalry?* She shook her head. *It matters little. You did the deed with your own hand, and his followers murdered you but a year later. If only…*

Small rustling sounds and a stifled giggle from behind the alabaster sarcophagus interrupted her thoughts. A momentary thrill of fear shot through Honoria's body. *Are you haunting me, Mother, or perhaps you have rats?* She skirted the altar to look behind Placidia's stone casket.

"Not rats, but mice." Honoria grabbed two boys by the necks of their patched tunics. They looked about six and eight—brothers or close kin, judging by the similarity of their smudged features. The elder held a lit rush light, dropping ashes on the floor. She gave them a shake, making their shadows waver on the wall. "Did you come here to steal? The gold from the altar, perhaps?"

"N-No, Mistress!" The older one's eyes went wide in a look of innocence Honoria did not believe.

"If not to steal, why do you skulk around my mo—my mistress's final resting place?"

"Tell 'er, Jules." The younger one twisted loose and hid behind his brother.

"It's on a dare."

"A dare?" Honoria's laugh echoed around the mausoleum. "Do you expect ghosts?"

The older boy shuffled his feet. "No, Ma'am. We come to see the Augusta. The older boys say if you shine a light into her coffin, she'll turn her face to you. But you hafta get away before she looks at you or you'll turn to stone."

"Like Medusa?" An apt image for her mother.

"Who?" Jules pulled his brows together.

"Never mind. How do you see into the coffin?"

"Here." The youngest boy pointed to a small crack in a seam at the back. "You won't call the guards on us, will you, lady?"

"I don't like guards any more than you do. Here." Honoria dug into a purse. "There's a copper piece for each of you. Give me the light and don't come here again."

"No, Mistress. Thank you, Mistress." The boys scampered away.

Honoria held the light to the hole. She saw how the flickering light might give the impression of movement to the embalmed body in royal robes seated on a throne-like cypress wood chair. But her mother kept her face turned resolutely away.

Mother, would you be happy to know that Valia's grandson is now kingmaker in Ravenna? The Goth Ricimer decides who wears the diadem. You and Aetius held the rotten body of the Empire together, but now it's breaking up: civil war and chaos, Rome stripped and burned by the Vandals, little more than a ruin.

Honoria sighed.

If I had not been so foolish with Eugenius, I might have taken your place... Would another woman of the Theodosius line have kept back the dark a few more years, as you and Pulcheria did? She shrugged her shoulders. *Maybe...but we will never know.*

Honoria leaned her forehead against the cool stone. Tears trickled down her face.

"I found my son, Mother," she whispered to the cold stone. "Lucilla told me your secret a month ago, just before she died. He's happy running wild in the swamps, fishing and snaring ducks. Happy...an emotion foreign to us. They named him Angelus, after the man he calls grandfather. I thought to take him away and put him on the throne with me, to rule as you once did, but it would mean his life. I have had to live with the consequences of so many of my actions; I will not have that death on my soul."

Honoria pushed away from the smooth alabaster.

"Good-bye, Mother. God rest your soul." Honoria wiped her eyes and put both palms on the sarcophagus. "I forgive you."

Author's Note

I FELL IN LOVE WITH THE THEODOSIAN WOMEN: Placidia, Pulcheria, and Athenais many years ago when I was writing my first book *Selene of Alexandria* which featured a fictional student of the historical Hypatia, Lady Philosopher of Alexandria. As I researched the life and times of Hypatia, I kept running across these great women who ruled the failing Western Empire and set the stage for the rise of the Byzantine Empire in the East.

And it wasn't just the dry fact of their power; they each had compelling human stories. Placidia was held hostage for five years by the Goths and married their king for love. Pulcheria outwitted the Constantinople court worthies and claimed sole regency over her brother and the Empire at the tender age of fifteen. Athenais, a beautiful, but poor daughter of a pagan Athenian scholar captured the heart of a Most Christian Emperor. Why hadn't I heard of these women before?

I originally planned a single book with each telling their intertwining stories, but soon found I had way too much material. Each woman deserved her own story, so this is the first in a set of three books about the Theodosian women. I hope to have *Dawn Empress* about Pulcheria out in 2018 and the book on Athenais out the year after.

Throughout the series I attempt to stay as close to known historical facts as I can. However, the fifth century is a notoriously chaotic time as Western Rome disintegrated under repeated attacks by barbarians and failed leadership over the course of several decades. In many cases records were destroyed, damaged, or altered to reflect better on the ruling parties. Primary sources are scant and sometimes contradictory, so modern scholars occasionally interpret them differently. Where there is disagreement, I chose the interpretation that best suited my story.

Many of the incidents used to color the story are attested to such as Honorius' love for his birds and his reaction to being told "Rome is taken" by thinking the speaker referred to a favorite pet. Placidia's bloodless coup in taking the "invulnerable" Ravenna was ascribed to an "angel of the Lord" who led her troops through the swamps. I came up with my own less divine intervention and if you want to read Angelus' origin story check out "Angel of the Marshes" in *The Reluctant Groom and Other Historical Stories*. Honoria really did send Attila the Hun a ring and ask for his help in freeing her from a proposed marriage.

In others places I took literary license to fill in the unknown. We have a couple of extant letters from Placidia to her nephew Theodosius II late in their lives concerning religious matters, but nothing that indicates her personality or those of other characters. That's where the author's craft takes over. I tried to create real motives for historical actions. How close I came to truth is unknowable.

Placidia is not always treated kindly by older scholars from less enlightened times. Gibbon in his *The Decline and Fall of the Roman Empire* felt she "corrupted the noble Constantius" leading him to avarice he hadn't shown before their marriage and forcing her brother to give her honors he was reluctant to bestow. Others felt she deliberately stifled her son to keep her hands on the reins of power. Some, comparing her political skills and piety to Pulcheria's, felt Placidia a pale imitation of her niece. Those that count General Aetius a hero and savior, fault her for their feud and his assassination at the hands of her son. Aetius' death and Valentinian's assassination two years later, opened the gates for invading barbarians and "The Fall."

Modern scholars such as Stewart Irvin Oost in *Galla Placidia Augusta: a Biographical Essay* take a more nuanced view of her life. He concludes his work by saying: "Galla Placidia was proud, a thoroughgoing Roman; she loved power—this last hardly a sin unless we are to condemn all politicians. She managed fairly well to play a role in politics and government despite the disadvantages of her sex. She was a chaste wife, devoted mother to her children…and unlike her half-brothers Arcadius and Honorius, she was a worthy child of the most

Christian and Roman Emperor Theodosius the Great." There is no doubt that as empress in the twilight years of Western Rome, Placidia's decisions and actions set the stage for the development of early medieval Europe.

Every story has more than one side. I doubt Placidia was either the sinner of Gibbon's tale or the saint of Oost's. She was a complicated, powerful woman—subject to the beliefs and prejudices of her times and position. I tried to tell my version of Placidia's life while staying close to the facts and giving her very human motivations. Placidia's love of, and marriage to, the Gothic King Ataulf is a matter of record. There were even some primary sources that said the match was prophesied in the Bible. They did have a son named Theodosius who died shortly after birth and was buried in Barcelona. In an elaborate ceremony, late in her life, Placidia reinterred his body in the family mausoleum in Rome. After Ataulf's death, she was captured and paraded as a slave in a brutal twelve-mile march. We know Sergeric was overthrown after only seven days and Valia took the kingship. The rest is from my imagination, including Placidia's bloody revenge on Sergeric.

I felt most sorry for Constantius, a competent general, able negotiator, and honorable man. Historians agree that he was witty at parties and generous to his friends. His tragic flaw? He loved a woman who didn't love him back. Every source said that Placidia resisted the marriage, although she did give him two children. Supposedly, he hated being an Augustus because of the rigid rules and restrictions forced on him by court protocol. He had a premonition that he would live only seven months after he became Augustus. I hope Placidia did appreciate his good points—even if belatedly.

Both Honorius and Valentinian III were disparaged by older historians for being weak emperors. Many felt the former suffered from many physical ailments as well as mental deficits and the latter suffered from being deliberately stunted by his mother. Both are being re-evaluated by modern historians, especially Honorius, who is now credited with a level of native cunning which allowed him to successfully navigate the treacherous waters of his court for decades. It's unlikely he consummated either of his marriages and the rumors of his incestuous feelings for Placidia might have stemmed from feeling "safe" with her—he wouldn't be expected to act on any sexual feelings, so he could more freely express affection.

Valentinian is faulted primarily for not being up to the (probably) impossible task of saving the Empire. Also Aetius had significant influence over events during Valentinian's later years, so he must also share some of the blame. The fact that Valentinian killed his most successful general—up close with a knife—indicates there was personal animosity between the two. Valentinian may have felt he left his mother's shadow only to enter Aetius'. Or not. That's the fun part of writing fiction; the author gets to choose.

I combined some characters to keep the numbers manageable. Ataulf had six children (I felt four were enough to keep track of) from a previous marriage. We don't know their names, ages, or sex. They were "torn from a venerable bishop's arms" and killed by Sergeric's forces along with Ataulf's brother, his designated heir. I dropped the unnamed brother and used the historical Valia as a confident to Ataulf for continuity's sake. Likewise, the fictional Lucilla and historical Attalus fill in for several attested servants and confidents over Placidia's long life. Placidia's younger nieces in the Constantinople court don't appear, but will have much bigger roles in Pulcheria's story. It is unknown whether Placidia traveled to Constantinople for her son's wedding. She most likely stayed in Ravenna to administer the Empire, but I wanted her to have a last meeting with her Eastern relatives and a glimpse of what her "retirement" might be like if she followed Pulcheria's path.

Placidia did intervene to save her daughter's life after Honoria's affair with her chamberlain and her treasonous offer to Attila the Hun. Scholars disagree about Honoria's age at the time of her affair and nothing is said about the fate of the child (some dispute whether there was a pregnancy). Several believe Honoria was a teenager and Placidia shuffled her off to Pulcheria's less than tender mercies in the Eastern court. When she finally became fed up several years later, Honoria wrote her infamous letter to Attila, and Theodosius sent her back to her brother who arranged a hasty marriage.

J. D. Bury, in a footnote in *History of the Later Roman Empire*, disputes the earlier date as a misunderstanding of a primary source and inconsistent with other evidence. He dates the affair to 449, believes Honoria stayed in Ravenna, and takes no stand on the pregnancy. Valentinian gave in to his mother's pleas to spare Honoria after the Attila debacle—at least temporarily—but we don't know under what circumstances. Honoria might have died in prison shortly after Placidia's death or been hastily married to Bassus Herculanus. In any case Valentinian stripped her of her title of Augusta and she disappears from the historical record. I used the unknown fate of the child and Honoria's lack of a verified death date to knit up several loose ends in my Epilog.

Speaking of the Epilog, my apologies to the city of Ravenna for placing Placidia's final resting place in Rome. Logically that is the most likely place. We know that Honorius, Constantius, and—most compelling of all—her first child with Ataulf—were buried in a mausoleum on Vatican Hill adjacent to the old St. Peter's Basilica. The structure was turned into a church in the eighth century and demolished when the present St. Peter's was started in 1506. Placidia died in Rome and it is unlikely she would have preferred to be buried in Ravenna away from her family.

So how to account for "Placidia's Mausoleum," a jewel-like fifth century building in Ravenna currently containing three empty sarcophagi? I visited the place and it is truly beautiful. So lovely, I borrowed the mosaics and decorations for the lost Roman mausoleum. Some historians believe the building was commissioned by her son Valentinian III in honor of Saint Lawrence, a favorite of his. Placidia might have commissioned it for her own tomb and changed her mind. It's more likely that the current title comes from the Renaissance when Ravenna touted its collection of fifth century churches and mosaics as a tourist destination and possibly upgraded the building from chapel to royal tomb to attract more visitors.

The weird tale of people looking at the seated embalmed body of Placidia from a crack in the sarcophagus also originates from this time period. Supposedly, some boys set the body on fire with a lit taper and it disappeared into a pile of ash—which accounts for the empty coffin in the tomb. Obviously apocryphal, but too wonderful to ignore, I incorporated the tales in my story, but moved them to the more likely mausoleum.

Of the major historical characters, Sigisvult is the one I most fictionalized. The titles he earned are attested to. He is cited for negotiating with Boniface in Africa and fortifying the Italian coast against the threatened Vandal invasion, but otherwise little is known of him. Ralph W. Mathisen in "Sigisvult the Patrician, Maximinus the Arian, and Political Stratagems in the Western Roman Empire c. 425-50" says:

> *"Sigisvult was a Visigoth who had attracted Placidia's attention in the past…Sigisvult's career suggests that when it came to finding solutions to political and military problems in the late Roman west, barbarians could do more than just fight… Throughout his career, therefore, Sigisvult was an important player in Galla Placidia's delicate balancing act of matching one*

general against another. In the game of odd-man-out, first Felix and then Boniface were eliminated. But Sigisvult survived and apparently prospered. In the end only Sigisvult and Aetius remained. What became of Sigisvult is unknown. In 446 he still held the office of Master of Soldiers…To speculate, he may have been forced into retirement in late 450, after the death of his imperial patroness."

Or he could have rescued his beloved queen's errant daughter and died with his fellow Goths fighting the Huns at the Battle of the Catalaunian Plains in 451.

I obviously have a lot of affection for Sigisvult and Placidia. I hope they really did provide some comfort to one another during their long relationship. Since we don't know what happened to Sigisvult, I gave him a warrior's death; my tribute to someone who seemed to be an honorable man in a difficult time. We also don't know how Placidia died, so I gave her time to make amends. Oost says:

"At Rome on 27 November AD 450, Galla Placidia Augusta fell asleep in Our Lord Jesus Christ…Perhaps only after the interval of forty days was she herself buried in the Mausoleum by Saint Peter's. We may be sure that in the presence of her imperial son as well as of the assembled dignitaries of the Roman state and church her interment was celebrated with the full solemnities of holy religion, commending her body to the earth and her soul to God. Thus like David she slept with her fathers."

Faith L. Justice
Brooklyn, NY
May 2017

P.S. I hope you enjoyed *Twilight Empress*. As I mentioned, I fell in love with the Theodosian women: Placidia, Pulcheria, and Athenais many years ago. It took over ten years to get *Twilight Empress* in print, pixels and audio. Pulcheria's story will be out in *Dawn Empress* in all formats in 2020. Athenais' story will follow shortly—"God willing and the creeks don't rise!"—as my mom used to say.

314

I would love to hear from you about your reactions to the story and characters. You can write me at faith@faithljustice.com. Although my daughter had to drag me into the social media scene, you can also find me on Twitter (@ faithljustice) and Facebook.

Finally, I need to ask a favor. I'd love a review of *Twilight Empress*. Loved it, hated it—please give me your feedback at your favorite book review sharing site. No need for a literary critique—just a couple of sentences on what you liked/didn't like and why. Reviews can be tough to come by these days and having them (or not) can make or break a book. So, I hope you share your opinion with others.

Thank you for reading *Twilight Empress*.

GLOSSARY

ad Laureta—"by the Laurel groves" imperial palace built by Valentinian III in Ravenna

agentes in rebus—imperial spy and messenger network controlled by the Master of Offices

Alamanni—a group of Germanic tribes settled in Alsace and nearby areas during the fourth century; some joined the Gothic migration/invasion during the early fifth century.

Alans—an Iranian nomadic pastoral people; when the Huns invaded their ancestral lands north of the Black Sea, many of the Alans migrated westwards along with various Germanic tribes; settled in the Iberian Peninsula and helped the Vandals invade North Africa in 428.

Amores—Ovid's first completed book of poetry; written in elegiac couplets (first used by the Greeks for funeral epigrams); set the standard for erotic poetry; first published in 16 BC.

Aquileia—an ancient Roman city in Italy at the head of the Adriatic about 10 kilometers (6 mi) from the sea on the modern river Natisone; Ausonius (4C) placed Aquileia as ninth among the great cities of the world with an imperial palace and important religious seat; Attila destroyed the city in 452, but it remains in a much reduced state

Arian Heresy—a non-trinitarian Christian sect that believed Jesus Christ to be the Son of God, created by God the Father, distinct from the Father and therefore subordinate to the Father; named after Arius (c. 250–336), a Christian presbyter in Alexandria, Egypt; many of the barbarian tribes

316

converted to Christianity by Arian missionaries under the Arian Emperors Constantius II (337–361) and Valens (364–378); the Council of Nicaea of 325 declared Arius a heretic, but he was exonerated, then again denounced at the Ecumenical First Council of Constantinople of 381

bagaudae—probably means "fighters"; impoverished local free peasants, brigands, runaway slaves, and deserters from the legions, who tried to resist the ruthless labor exploitation, punitive laws, and levies of the late Roman period

bucellarii—private army of the great generals of the 5th Century and later (related to the German comitatus).

Burgundians—most likely of Scandinavian origin; part of a large group of Germanic and Vandal tribes that lived in the area of modern Poland and migrated west under pressure from the Huns; in 411, the Burgundian king Gundahar set up a puppet emperor, Jovinus, in cooperation with Goar, king of the Alans; General Aetius brought Burgundian raids to an end in 436, when he called in Hun mercenaries who overwhelmed the Rhineland kingdom in 437

caldarium—a hot and steamy room heated by a hypocaust, an underfloor heating system; the hottest room in the regular sequence of Roman bathing rooms

comitatus—group of warriors which a successful German war chief gathered about himself

curator—business and legal advisor.

diadem—"band" or "fillet"; originally in Greece, an embroidered white silk ribbon, ending in a knot and two fringed strips often draped over the shoulders, that surrounded the head of the king to denote his authority; later made of precious metals and decorated with gems; evolved into the modern crown

dropsy—an abnormal accumulation of fluid beneath the skin and in the cavities of the body which causes severe pain, heart and liver failure

epithalamia—traditional Roman wedding song

fibula (singular), *fibulae* (plural)—an ornamental clasp designed to hold clothing together; usually made of silver or gold but sometimes bronze or some other material; used by Greeks, Romans, and Celts

forum (singular), **fora** (plural)—a rectangular plaza surrounded by important government buildings at the center of the city; the site of triumphal processions and elections; the venue for public speeches, criminal trials, and gladiatorial matches; the nucleus of commercial affairs

Frigidus, Battle of—fought in 394, between Eastern Emperor Theodosius I and Western ruler Eugenius; Theodosius' win made him the last sole Roman emperor until the collapse of the Western Roman Empire.

Gaul—a region of Western Europe inhabited by Celtic tribes, encompassing present day France, Luxembourg, Belgium, most of Switzerland, parts of Northern Italy, as well as the parts of the Netherlands and Germany on the west bank of the Rhine; Rome divided it into three parts: Gallia Celtica, Belgica and Aquitania

Greuthungi—a Gothic people from the Black Sea steppes with close contacts with the Thervingi, another Gothic people from west of the river Dnestr

Hagia Sophia, Church of—the second church on that site next to the imperial palace; ordered by Theodosius II, who inaugurated it in 415; a basilica with a wooden roof built by architect Rufinus; a fire burned it to the ground in 532

Hebdomon—a seaside retreat outside Constantinople where emperors built palaces and two churches. Several Emperors (including Valens, Arcadius, Honorius, and Theodosius II) were acclaimed by the army on the Field of Mars there

Hippolyte— "Of the Stampeding Horse"; Amazon Queen; Daughter of Otrera and Ares, God of War

Huns—a nomadic group of people who lived in Eastern Europe, the Caucasus, and Central Asia between the 1st Century and the 7th Century; may have stimulated the Great Migration, a contributing factor in the collapse of the Western Roman Empire; formed a unified empire under Attila the Hun, who died in 453; their empire broke up the next year

imperium—"power to command"; a man with imperium, in principle, had absolute authority to apply the law within the scope of his magistracy; he could be vetoed or overruled by a colleague with equal power (e.g., a fellow consul) or by one whose imperium outranked his

magister militum—"Master of the Soldiers"; a top-level military command used in the late Roman Empire, referring to a senior military officer equivalent to a modern war theatre commander

magister utriusque militia—"Master of both branches of the soldiery"; the highest rank a general can achieve

mole—a massive structure usually of stone, used as a pier, breakwater, or causeway between places separated by water, but, unike a true pier, water cannot freely flow underneath it

nobilissima puella, nobilissimus puer—"Most Noble Girl/Boy", title conferred on imperial children by a sitting Augustus before given a higher title

Noricum—a province of the Roman Empire that included most of modern Austria and part of Slovenia

Narbonne—Roman port city established in Gaul in 118 BC, located on the Via Domitia connecting Italy to Spain; its rosemary-flower honey was famous among Romans

nymphaeum (singular), **nymphaea** (plural)—originally Greek grottos dedicated to worship of water nymphs; Romans extended the name to private and public fountains; also applied to the fountains in the atrium of a Christian basilica

palla—outermost rectangular woman's mantle/shawl worn over the shoulders and hair; could be as complicated as a toga or as slight as a scarf

paludamentum—originally a cloak or cape fastened at one shoulder, worn by military commanders. After Augustus, it was restricted to the Emperors, who as supreme commanders of the Roman army, were often portrayed wearing it in their statues and on their coinage

pater familias (singular), *patres familias* (plural)—"father of the family" or the "owner of the family estate"; traditionally the oldest living male in a family; he held legal rights over family property, and varying levels of authority over his dependents: wife, children, certain other relatives through blood or adoption, clients, freedmen, and slaves; in theory, he held powers of life and death over every member of his extended family, but in practice, this right was limited by law

Porticus Placidiana—a 200 meter colonnade along the right bank of the Fossa Traiana, to the south of the Claudian basin; built about 425 in honor of Placidia, the mother of Emperor Valentinian III

Portus—Rome's primary sea port, built by Emperor Claudius to handle large merchant ships including the grain fleet.

primicerius notariorum—first on the list of the corps of notaries.

Rimini, the city—the Roman colony of Ariminum, founded in 268 BC at the terminus of the Via Flaminia, which ended in the Arch of Augustus (erected 27 BC), connected central Italy and northern Italy by the Via Aemilia and the Via Popilia that extended northwards; opened up trade by sea and river; later, Placida built the church of San Stefano there

Rimini, the Battle of (also known as the Battle of Ravenna)—fought in 432 between General Aetius and General Boniface; Boniface won, but was gravely injured and died shortly after

scholae—an elite troop of soldiers in the Roman army created by the Emperor Constantine the Great to provide personal protection of the Emperor and his immediate family

solidus (singular), *solidi* (plural)—a gold coin introduced by Emperor Diocletian in 301 as a replacement for the *aureus*; entered widespread circulation under Constantine I after 312; remained essentially unaltered in weight, dimensions and purity until the 10th Century

stola—long, pleated dress, worn over a tunica interior, generally sleeveless, fastened by clasps at the shoulder called fibulae, usually made of fabrics like silk, linen or wool, worn as a symbol representing a Roman woman's marital status.

Suevi—a large group of related peoples who occupied more than half of Germania, and were divided into a number of distinct tribes under distinct names; classical ethnography applied the name "Suevi" to so many Germanic tribes that it appeared as though in the first centuries AD this native name would replace the foreign name "Germans"; In 259/60, a group appears to have been the main element in the formation of a new tribal alliance known as the Alamanni east of the Rhine and south of the Main; later joined the Vandals and Alans invading Gaul and Spain

Tervingi—a Gothic people of the Danubian plains west of the Dnestr River; remained in western Scythia until 376, when the Huns invaded their lands and one of their leaders, Fritigern, appealed to the Roman emperor Valens to be allowed to settle with his people on the south bank of the Danube; Valens permitted this but a famine broke out and Rome was unwilling to supply them with the food or land they were promised; open revolt led to six years of plundering and destruction throughout the Balkans; during the Battle of Adrianople in 378 the Tervingi slaughtered the Roman forces and killed the Emperor Valens, shocking the Roman world and eventually forcing the Romans to negotiate with and settle the Tervingi on Roman land

triclinium—a formal dining room in a Roman building used for entertaining guests; could hold multiple couches arranged in a hollow 'U' shape; each couch was wide enough to accommodate three diners who reclined on their left side on cushions while household slaves served and others entertained guests with music, song, or dance.

tunica interior—woman's tunic (usually with sleeves) worn under a stola, frequently longer, so the layers of fabric showed.

tutela—"guardian" or "tutor", mainly for people such as minors and women who ordinarily in Roman society would be under the legal protection and control of the pater familias, but who were legally emancipated; legal basis of ones who performed functions of "regent" for underaged Augusti

Vandals—an East Germanic tribe, or group of tribes, believed to have migrated from southern Scandinavia to the area between the lower Oder and Vistula rivers during the 2nd Century BC. They were pushed westwards by the Huns, crossing the Rhine into Gaul along with other tribes in AD 406. In 409, the Vandals crossed the Pyrenees into the Iberian Peninsula. In 429, under King Gaiseric, the Vandals entered North Africa. By 439 they established a kingdom which included the Roman province of Africa as well as Sicily, Corsica, Sardinia, Malta and the Balearic Islands. They fended off several Roman attempts to recapture the African province, and sacked the city of Rome in 455.

ACKNOWLEDGMENTS

It has been my pleasure to write this story and bring these characters and this time to life. Among the many people who helped and encouraged me, I want to particularly thank the members of my writers' group *Circles in the Hair*. For over twenty-five years, they have been there for me; reading drafts of my stories and novels, providing insightful feedback, and encouraging my dreams. Special and loving thanks go to my husband Gordon Rothman for supporting me in countless ways; and to my daughter Hannah, who grew up sharing me with my writing career and showing no sibling rivalry whatsoever.

No historical fiction acknowledgment would be complete without thanks to the many librarians and collections that tirelessly answer questions and find obscure documents. My special thanks go to the New York City Research Library—a world class institution. I consulted dozens of books and hundreds of articles, but relied most heavily on the research of Stewart Irvin Oost from his *Galla Placidia Augusta: A Biographical Essay* and Kenneth G. Holum from his *Theodosian Empresses: Women and Imperial Dominion in Late Antiquity*. A bibliography of the most useful works can be found on my website (faithljustice. com).

Although I tried to get it right, no one is perfect. If the reader should find some errors in the book, please know they are my own and not those of my sources.

Again, thanks to all who helped make this book possible with special thanks to those of you who read it and share it.

About the Author

Faith L. Justice writes award-winning fiction and articles in Brooklyn, New York. Her work appears in such publications as *Salon.com, Writer's Digest,* and *The Copperfield Review.* She is Chair of the New York City Chapter of the Historical Novel Society and an Associate Editor for *Space & Time Magazine.* Her previous novels, collections of short stories, and non-fiction are available online at all the usual places or through your local bookstore. For fun, Faith likes to dig in the dirt—both her garden and various archaeological sites. Sample her work, check out her blog, or ask her a question at her website. She loves to hear from readers.

Connect with Faith online:

Website/Blog: www.faithljustice.com
Twitter: https://twitter.com/faithljustice
Facebook: https://www.facebook.com/faithljusticeauthor/

DAWN EMPRESS (Theodosian Women #2)

After the Emperor's unexpected death, ambitious men eye the Eastern Roman throne occupied by seven-year-old Theodosius II. His older sister Princess Pulcheria faces a stark choice: she must find allies and take control of the Eastern court or doom the imperial children to a life of obscurity—or worse! Beloved by the people and respected by the Church, Pulcheria forges her own path to power. Can her piety and steely will protect her brother from military assassins, heretic bishops, scheming eunuchs and—most insidious of all—a beautiful, intelligent bride? Or will she lose all in the trying? *Dawn Empress* tells Pulcheria's little-known and fascinating story. Her accomplishments rival those of Elizabeth I and Catherine the Great as she sets the stage for the dawn of the Byzantine Empire.

SWORD OF THE GLADIATRIX (Gladiatrix #1)

An action-packed romance that exposes the brutal underside of Imperial Rome, *Sword of the Gladiatrix* brings to life unforgettable characters and exotic settings. From the far edges of the Empire, two women come to battle on the hot sands of the arena in Nero's Rome: Afra, scout and beast master to the Queen of Kush; and Cinnia, warrior-bard and companion to Queen Boudica of the British Iceni. Enslaved, forced to fight for their lives and the Romans' pleasure; they seek to replace lost friendship, love, and family in each other's arms. But the Roman arena offers only two futures: the Gate of Life for the victors or the Gate of Death for the losers.

SELENE OF ALEXANDRIA

This story of ambition, love, and political intrigue brings to life colorful characters and an exotic time and place. In AD 412 Alexandria, against the backdrop of a city torn by religious and political strife, Selene struggles to achieve her dream of becoming a physician—an unlikely goal for an upper class Christian girl. Hypatia, the famed Lady Philosopher of Alexandria and the Augustal Prefect Orestes offer their patronage and protection. But will it be enough to save Selene from murderous riots, the machinations of a charismatic Bishop and—most dangerous of all—her own impulsive nature?

THE RELUCTANT GROOM AND OTHER HISTORICAL STORIES

Dive into this collection of historical shorts by an award-winning author. You'll find stories of heroism, love, and adventure such as a panicked bachelor faced with an arranged marriage, a man battling a blizzard to get home for his child's birth, a Viking shield maiden exploring a New World, and a young boy torn between love for his ailing grandmother and duty to an empress. Whether set in imperial Rome, colonial America, or the ancient African Kingdom of Kush, these stories bring to life men and women struggling to survive and thrive—the eternal human condition.

TOKOYO, THE SAMURAI'S DAUGHTER

(Adventurous Girls #1)

Most noble-born girls of Tokoyo's age learn to sing, paint, and write poetry. Not Tokoyo. She's an adventurous girl, the daughter of a samurai in fourteenth century Japan. Her father trains her in the martial arts. When he is away, she escapes to the sea where she works with the Ama—a society of women and girls who dive in the deep waters for food and treasure. But disaster strikes her family. Can Tokoyo save her father using the lessons she learned and the skills she mastered to overcome corrupt officials, her own doubts, and a nasty sea demon? (Middle grade, illustrated fiction)

HYPATIA: HER LIFE AND TIMES

Who was Hypatia of Alexandria?
A brilliant young mathematician murdered by a religious mob? An aging academic eliminated by a rival political party? A sorceress who enthralled the Prefect of Alexandria through satanic wiles? Did she discover the earth circled the sun a thousand years before Copernicus or was she merely a gifted geometry teacher? Discover the answers to these questions and more in this collection of essays on Hypatia's life and times.

DISCOVER THESE AND OTHER BOOKS BY FAITH L. JUSTICE.
AVAILABLE IN PRINT, eBOOKS, AND AUDIO IN ALL THE USUAL PLACES.

RAGGEDY MOON BOOKS

raggedymoonbooks.com

Printed in Great Britain
by Amazon

20719041R00200